'I loved *The Vacationers*; funny and poignant and beautifully observed' Jojo Moyes, author of *Me Before You*

'Intimate, epic, beautifully observed' Jennifer Egan

'Emma Straub is a magician, full of brilliance and surprise' Lorrie Moore, author of *Bark*

'A gorgeous and witty storyteller' Elizabeth Gilbert, author of *Eat, Pray, Love*

'Witty and big-hearted . . . leaves you smiling for days' Maria Semple, author of *Where'd You Go, Bernadette*

'Charming and absorbing, this is a novel that demands to be read in long, satisfying gulps' Maggie Shipstead, author of *Seating Arrangements*

'Now this is what I call good holiday reading. Straub writes beautifully and amusingly . . . hard to beat for sheer charm and gentle wit' *Daily Mail*

'Straub's novel is cast from the same mould as the likes of Liza Klaussmann's *Tigers in Red Weather* and Maggie Shipstead's *Seating Arrangements* . . . *The Vacationers* is a holiday read in every way with a gently witty narrative that slips down as easily as a beachside cocktail' *Independent*

'Emma Straub puts the fun back in dysfunction' *San Francisco Chronicle*

'For those unable to jet off to a Spanish island this summer, reading *The Vacationers* may be the next-best thing . . . [A] gorgeously written novel . . . When I turned the last page, I felt as I often do when a vacation is over: grateful for the trip and mourning its end' *New York Times Book Review*

'Delicious . . . richly riveting . . . *The Vacationers* offers all the delights of a fluffy, read-it-with-sunglasses-on-the-beach read, made substantial by the exceptional wit, insight, intelligence and talents of its author' *People*

Modern Lovers

Modern Lovers

Emma Straub

PENGUIN BOOKS

PENGUIN BOOKS

UK I USA I Canada I Ireland I Australia
India I New Zealand I South Africa

Penguin Books is part of the Penguin Random House group of companies
whose addresses can be found at global.penguinrandomhouse.com

First published in the USA by Riverhead Books, an imprint of PRH LLC 2016
First published in Great Britain by Michael Joseph 2016
Published in Penguin Books 2017
001

Set in 9.11/14.30 pt Sabon LT Std
Typeset in India by Thomson Digital Pvt Ltd, Noida, Delhi
Printed in Great Britain by Clays Ltd, St Ives plc

A CIP catalogue record for this book is available from the British Library

B FORMAT ISBN: 978–1–405–92156–5
TPB ISBN: 978–1–405–92157–2

www.greenpenguin.co.uk

For Nina,
who made moving to Ohio sound like fun,
and for the Rutland Readers,
with gratitude for seven years of neighborly affection

If I could settle down
Then I would settle down.

– Pavement

You can't help yourself, but neither can we.
Together, mighty past, we dominate things.

– Kenneth Koch

PART ONE

Ruby Tuesday

MARY ANN O'CONNELL REAL ESTATE

New Listing

Gorgeous 5-Bedroom Victorian Showstopper in Prime Ditmas Park. Many original details including pocket doors, moldings, intricately carved grand staircase. Kitchen updated, new roof. WBFP. Two-car garage. Gracious living in the heart of the neighborhood, close to shopping and fine dining on Cortelyou Road, close to trains. A Must See!

One

In June, the book club was at Zoe's house, which meant that Elizabeth had to carry her heavy ceramic bowl of spinach salad with walnuts and bits of crumbled goat cheese a grand total of half a block. She didn't even have to cross a street. None of the dozen women in the group had to travel far, that was the point. It was hard enough to coordinate schedules and read a novel (though only half the group ever finished anything) without asking people to get on the subway. Make plans with your real friends on your own time, drive your car across the borough to have dinner if you want to, but this was the neighborhood. This was easy. It was the last meeting before the annual summer hiatus. Elizabeth had sold houses to six of the twelve. She had a vested interest in keeping them happy, though, in truth, it was also good when people gave up on Brooklyn and decided to move to the suburbs or back to wherever they came from, because then she got a double commission. Elizabeth liked her job.

Of course, even if the rest of the book club was composed of neighbors who might not otherwise have crossed paths, she and Zoe were different. They were old friends – best friends, really, though Elizabeth might not say that in front of Zoe for fear that she would laugh at the phrase for being juvenile. They'd lived together after college way back in the Stone Age in this very same house, sharing the rambling Victorian with Elizabeth's boyfriend (now husband) and two guys who had lived in their co-op at Oberlin. It was always nice to carry a big bowl of something homemade over to Zoe's house, because it felt like being back in that potluck-rich, money-poor twilight zone known as one's twenties. Ditmas Park was a hundred miles from Manhattan (in reality, seven), a tiny little cluster of Victorian houses that could have existed anywhere in the United States, with Prospect Park's parade grounds to the north and Brooklyn College to the south. Their other friends from school were moving into walk-up apartments in the East Village or into beautiful brownstones in Park Slope, on the other side of the vast green park, but the three of them had fallen in love with the idea of a *house* house, and so there they were, sandwiched between old Italian ladies and the projects.

When their lease was up, Zoe's parents – an African-American couple who'd made their tidy fortune as a disco duo – bought the place for her. Seven bedrooms, three baths, center hall, driveway, garage – it cost a hundred and fifty grand. The moldy carpet and the layers of lead paint were free. Elizabeth and Andrew weren't married yet, let alone sharing a bank account, and so they sent their separate rent checks to Zoe's parents back in Los Angeles. Zoe had borrowed more money to fix it up over the years, but the mortgage was paid. Elizabeth and Andrew moved a few blocks over for a while, all the way to Stratford, and then, when their son Harry was four, a dozen years ago, bought a house three doors down. Zoe's house was now worth $2 million, maybe more. Elizabeth felt a little zip up her spine thinking about it. Neither Elizabeth nor Zoe thought they'd still be in the neighborhood so many years later, but it had never been the right time to leave.

Elizabeth walked up the steps to the wide porch and peered in the window. She was the first to arrive, as usual. The dining room was ready, the table set. Zoe pushed through the swinging door from the kitchen, a bottle of wine in each hand. She exhaled upward, trying in vain to blow a lone curl out of her eye. Zoe was wearing tight blue jeans and a threadbare camisole, with a complicated pile of necklaces clacking against her chest. It didn't matter if Elizabeth went shopping with Zoe, to the consignment shops she frequented and to the small, precious boutiques she liked, nothing ever fit Elizabeth the way it fit Zoe; she was as preternaturally cool at forty-five as she'd been at eighteen. Elizabeth knocked on the window and then waved when Zoe looked up and smiled. Zoe gestured for her to come in, her thin fingers waggling in the air. 'Door's open!'

The house smelled like basil and fresh tomatoes. Elizabeth let the door shut heavily behind her, and set her salad down on the table. She shook out her wrists, which crackled like fireworks. Zoe walked around the table and kissed her on the cheek.

'How was your day, sweets?'

Elizabeth rolled her head sideways, from one side to the other. Something clicked. 'You know,' she said. 'Like that. What can I do?' She looked around the room. 'Do you need me to go home and get anything?' Even in Ditmas Park, a twelve-person dinner party was a lot for a host. Usually only a small quorum of the book club was able to come, and so the hosts could scrape by and cram everyone around their normal dining-room table, but every so often (especially just before the summer) all the women would happily RSVP and, depending on who was hosting, the group would have to carry extra folding chairs down the street in order to avoid sitting on the floor like pouting children on Thanksgiving.

Overhead, there was the sound of something heavy falling to the floor – *thump* – and then twice more – *thump, thump*.

'Ruby!' Zoe yelled, craning her chin skyward. 'Come say hello to Elizabeth!'

There was a muffled reply.

'It's fine,' Elizabeth said. 'Where's Jane, at the restaurant?' She opened her mouth to say more – she had actual news, news not fit for their neighbors' ears, and wanted to get to it before the doorbell rang.

'We have a new sous, and I'm sure Jane is standing over his shoulder like a goddamn drill sergeant. You know how it is in the beginning, always drama. Ruby! Come down here and say hello before everyone you don't like shows up!' Zoe rubbed her eyebrows with her fingertips. 'I just signed her up for that SAT prep course you told me about, and she's pissed.' She made a noise like a torpedo.

A door slammed upstairs, and then there were feet on the stairs, the nimble herd of elephants contained by a single teenage body. Ruby stopped abruptly on the bottom step. In the weeks since Elizabeth had seen her last, Ruby's hair had gone from a sea-glass green to a purplish black, and was wound up in a round bun on the very top of her head.

'Hey, Rube,' Elizabeth said. 'What's shaking?'

Ruby picked off some nail polish. 'Nothing.' Unlike Zoe's, Ruby's face was round and soft, but they had the same eyes, slightly narrow, the sort of eyes that were made to look askance. Ruby's skin was three shades lighter than Zoe's, with Jane's pale green eyes, and she would have been intimidating even without the purple hair and the surly expression.

'Graduation is Thursday, right? What are you going to wear?'

Ruby made a little noise like a kazoo, her mother's torpedo in reverse. It was funny, what parents did to their children. Even when they weren't trying, everything got reproduced. She looked toward her mother, who nodded. 'I really want to wear one of Mum's dresses. The white one, you know?'

Elizabeth did know. Zoe was not only good at buying clothes, she was good at keeping them. It was lucky that she'd married a woman who wore the same blue jeans every day and a small rotation of button-down shirts, because there was no room in their giant walk-in closet for anything else. The white dress was a relic from their youth: a crocheted bodice that was more negative space than material, with a skirt made of dangling strings that started just below decent. It was the kind of dress one wore over a bathing suit while on vacation in Mexico in 1973. It had originally belonged to Zoe's mother, which meant it probably had Quaalude dust ground deep into the seams. Before she met the Bennetts, Elizabeth had never met parents who had the kind of life that made their children both proud and embarrassed simultaneously. Cool was good, but only up to a point.

'Wow,' Elizabeth said.

'It's still under debate,' Zoe said.

Ruby rolled her eyes, and jumped down the final step just as the doorbell rang. Before their neighbors began to pour in, each one holding a dish covered with tinfoil, Ruby had streaked in and out of the kitchen and was running back upstairs with a plateful of food.

'Hiiiiiiiiiii,' three women trilled in union.

'Hiiiiiiiiiii,' Elizabeth and Zoe trilled back, their voices performing the song of their day, the enthusiastic cry of the all-female dinner party.

Two

When Elizabeth was out at night, it was up to Andrew to feed Harry. Unlike most teenage boys, who would eat cardboard if it was topped with pepperoni, Harry had a delicate appetite. He ate around things like a toddler, piling up the rejects on one side of his plate: no olives, no avocado unless it was in guacamole, no cream cheese, no kale, no sesame seeds, no tomatoes except in tomato sauce. The list was long and evolved regularly – it seemed to Andrew that whenever he cooked, something new had been added. He pulled open the fridge and stared inside. Iggy Pop, their skinny calico, rubbed his body against Andrew's shoe.

'Harry,' he said, turning his head toward the living room. He could hear the repetitive beeps and bloops of Harry's favorite video game, *Secret Agent*. The game starred a frog in a trench coat and deerstalker cap and, as far as Andrew could tell, was made for eight-year-olds. Harry had zero interest in *Call of Duty*, or *Grand Theft Auto*, or any of the myriad other games that celebrated murder and prostitutes, and for that Andrew was glad. Better to have a son who liked frogs than automatic machine guns. Andrew himself had played gentle video games and read three-inch-thick fantasy novels about mice. They were two of a kind, he and Harry, soft on the inside, like underbaked cookies. It was what people always wanted, wasn't it?

'Harry,' Andrew said again. He closed the refrigerator door and stood quietly. 'Harry.'

The game noises stopped. 'I heard you the first time, Dad,' Harry said. 'Let's just order a pizza.'

'You sure?'

'Why not?' The noises started again. Andrew pulled out his phone and walked through the doorway into the living room, Iggy following behind. It was still light outside, and for a moment Andrew felt sad, looking at his gentle son, so happy to stay indoors on a beautiful June evening. No solo penalty kicks in the park, no pickup basketball, not even any contraband cigarettes on a secluded bench. Harry looked pale – Harry *was* pale. He was wearing a snug black sweatshirt with the zipper pulled all the way up to his neck. 'Want to play?' Harry asked. He looked up, his brown eyes shimmering, and then Andrew put his sadness away in a deep, deep pocket and sat down next to his son. Iggy Pop jumped on to his lap and curled up. The frog winked, and the music began.

It was someone's job to write that music – a tinny little melody that played in the background on repeat. It was someone's job to write the music that played behind actors' dramatic pauses on soap operas. Cell-phone ringtones. Someone was getting paid, maybe even cashing royalty checks. Andrew had never been a very good bass player, but he had always been good at coming up with melodies. It was probably the only thing he'd ever really loved doing, professionally speaking, even though it was never exactly professional. Still, whenever he was feeling low, which was more often than not, Andrew would think about his own royalty checks, his and Elizabeth's, and how they were paying for most of Harry's tuition at private school, and it would cheer him up a little. There was always someone doing better, especially in New York City, but fuck it, at least he'd done something in his life, something that would be remembered.

'Dad,' Harry said, 'it's your turn. I'll order the pizza.' Harry pushed the hair out of his eyes and blinked like a baby mole seeing sunlight for the first time. He was such a good kid, such a *good kid*. They talked about it all the time, ever since he was a baby – Andrew and Elizabeth would huddle together in bed, cozy and content, the baby monitor between them, listening to his coos and hiccups. He'd always been easy. Their friends all warned them that the next kid would be the doozy, here comes trouble, but the next one never came. And so it was just the three of them, steady as anything. At first people would ask why they'd had only one child, but the longer you went, the more people assumed it was by choice, and let it go. Even their parents had stopped asking by the time Harry was six. And who needed more grandchildren when Harry would climb into his grandmother's arms and kiss her on the cheek without being prompted? Who could ask for more than that? Some people in the neighborhood – not really their friends, just people they waved at when they were taking out the trash – had three or four kids, and it always struck Andrew like something out of the last century, where you needed as many small hands as possible to milk the cows and hoe the fields. What did you do with that many kids in Brooklyn? Were their genes that good, that important to the human race? He understood when it was for religious reasons – the Lubavitchers up in Williamsburg, the Mormons in Utah – they were in it for the endgame. But he and Elizabeth? They were just doing their best, and their best was Harry, sweet Harry. Andrew half wanted him to bomb the SATs and live at home forever. But of course he'd ace those, too, thanks to the purple prose of the novels he loved. Even when he was a baby, Harry had loved multisyllabic words – 'this is exTRAWdinary,' he said before he was two, about the fountain at Grand Army Plaza, which shot jets of water high into the air.

'Love you, buddy,' Andrew said.

Harry was staring into his phone, pushing buttons. 'Ordered.'

Three

Ruby hated the fucking SAT as much as she fucking hated high school. Both were examples of the patriarchy's insistence on male domination and total sexist bullshit like that. Whitman was a good school by Brooklyn private-school standards – not the best, but not the worst. Maybe one kid would get into an Ivy, but maybe not. Most people would go to places like Marist or Syracuse or Purchase. But not Ruby. Ruby was taking a gap year. That was the polite way to put it. The truth was that she had gotten into exactly none of the five schools she'd applied to, and her falsely optimistic mothers were convinced it was her SAT scores that were to blame, not her bad attitude or bad grades or shitty essays about being a black Jew with lesbian moms (the essay that everyone incorrectly assumed she would write), and so she was going to have to take another prep course, the summer after her senior year. Who even did that? Nobody did that. It was a joke, and she was the punch line.

Her phone vibrated on the bed: MEET ME AT PLAYGRND AT 10? Dust was nineteen, with a chipped front tooth and a shaved head. He was one of the church kids, the tiny gang of skaters that spent all day kick-flipping off the church steps right across the street from Whitman. None of them went to school, as far as Ruby could tell, not even the ones who were under eighteen. The Whitman security guards sometimes chased them away, but they weren't doing anything illegal, and so it never lasted long. Dust was their leader. He wore jeans that were the perfect size – not so tight they looked girly, but not too baggy so they looked like somebody's dad's. Dust had muscles that looked like they had occurred naturally, like he was a 1950s greaser who spent a lot of time working in a garage. Everything Ruby knew about the 1950s was from *Grease* and *Rebel Without a Cause*. Basically, being a teenager was the worst for everyone, unless you were John Travolta, who was obviously twenty-nine years old, and so it didn't matter anyway. The only kids at Whitman who ever spontaneously burst into song were the musical-theater geeks, and Ruby hated them as much as she hated the athletes, who were even more pathetic given that Whitman barely had a gymnasium. Then there were the regular geeks, who did nothing but study for tests, and then there were the do-gooders, who were always trying to get you to sign their petition to kill the whales or save Ebola or whatever. The church kids were really her only hope, sexually.

CAN'T, she wrote back. MY MUM'S BOOK CLUB IS HERE. PARTY TIME/SHOOT ME.

IT'S COOL, he texted, and then nothing.

Calling her mother 'Mum' wasn't a British affectation – there were two of them, Mom and Mum, and so she had to call them different things. Anyway, it didn't matter about the book club. That was only the most recent excuse. Ruby wouldn't have gone to the playground regardless. She'd broken up with Dust three weeks ago, or at least she thought she had. Maybe she wasn't clear. There was the time they went to Purity Diner on Seventh Avenue, right by school, and she wouldn't let him pay for her french fries, and then two days later, she was leaving school and Dust was across the street on the church steps and she pretended not to see him and walked straight to the subway instead of letting him walk her into the park, where they would do as much fooling around as one could possibly do in public, which was a lot.

The thing about Dust was that he wasn't smart or interesting except if you were counting skateboarding or oral sex. For a few months, his messed-up teeth and his bristly head and his crooked smile were enough, but after the effects of those wore off, they were left talking about *American Idol* (which they both hated) and the *Fast and the Furious* franchise (which Ruby hadn't seen). The problem with Ruby's moms was that their restaurant was three blocks from their house, and so you never knew when one of them was going to be home. What Ruby knew for sure was that she didn't want them to meet Dust, because them talking to each other would be like trying to get a dog to speak Chinese. Dust was not made for parents. He was made for street corners and nuggets of hash, and Ruby was over it. She slumped off the bed and on to the floor and crawled over to her record player. While her mom was no one's idea of cool, with her kitchen clogs and her barbershop haircut, Ruby's mum had her moments. The record player had been her mum's in college, in the days when the dinosaurs roamed the earth, but now it was Ruby's, and it was her most prized possession. If Dust had been worth her time, he would have known all the bands she loved to play – the Raincoats, X-Ray Spex, Bad Brains – but he only listened to dubstep, which was obviously one of humanity's greatest atrocities.

Ruby pushed through the pile of records on the floor, spreading them out like tarot cards, until she found what she was looking for. Aretha Franklin, *Lady Soul*. Aretha had never had a zine and probably hadn't pierced her own nose, but she was a fucking badass anyway. Ruby put on side A, waited for the music to start, and then lay back on the rug and stared at the ceiling. From the floor, she could hear the book club starting to cackle more. Honestly, it was like no one over thirty had ever gotten drunk before, and they were always doing it for the first time. Pretty soon they'd start talking about their spouses and their kids and her mum would whisper when she said anything, but Ruby could always hear her, could always hear everything – didn't parents get that? That even when you were on the other side of the house, your children could hear you, because they had hearing like a fucking bat and you only thought you were whispering? The summer already sucked, and it hadn't even started yet.

Four

It was almost eleven, and the only women still at the party were all in the kitchen helping Zoe clean up. Allison and Ronna were both new to the neighborhood and eager for details. Elizabeth had sold them both their places – a lovely old fixer-upper on Westminster between Cortelyou and Ditmas for Allison, and an apartment on Beverly and Ocean for Ronna. They were in their thirties, married, no kids. But trying! Young women loved to tack that on, especially to real-estate agents. Elizabeth had been a therapist, a marriage counselor, a psychic, a guru, all in the name of a quicker closing. There were things you weren't legally permitted to discuss – the strength of the local public schools, the racial breakdown of the area, whether or not anyone had died there. But that never stopped people from trying. They were so excited to meet each other, too, giggling about looking for faucets and wallpaper hangers. Elizabeth kissed them both on the cheek and sent them off to inspect each other's kitchens.

Zoe stood at the sink, her wet hands sending sprinkles of soapy water across the floor every few minutes. 'You got me,' Elizabeth said, brushing some water off her arm.

'My deepest apologies,' Zoe said. 'Well, that was nice. What was the next book, again?'

'*Wuthering Heights*! Chosen by Josephine, who has never finished a book in her life! I wonder if she thinks she'll just rent the movie. In fact, I'm sure that's exactly why. There's probably some new version of it that she saw on her HBO Go, and so now she's going to pretend to read the book. She's going to spend the whole night talking about how it takes place on some beautiful Caribbean island.' Elizabeth picked up the stack of clean plates and put them back in the cupboard.

'You really don't have to help, Lizzy,' Zoe said.

'Oh, come on. That's what you say to people when you want them to leave.'

Zoe laughed. Elizabeth turned around and leaned against the counter. 'There actually was something I wanted to talk to you about.'

Zoe turned off the sink. 'Oh, yeah? Me, too. You first.'

'Someone is making a movie about Lydia, and they need the rights. Our rights. To the song, and to us. Someone famous is going to write it, someone good, I forget their name.' Elizabeth made an excited face, and then gritted her teeth. In ancient times, before Brooklyn and before kids, Elizabeth and Andrew and Zoe had been in a band, and in addition to playing many, many shows in dingy basements and recording their songs into a pink plastic cassette deck, they had sold exactly one of their songs, 'Mistress of Myself,' to their friend and former bandmate Lydia Greenbaum, who then dropped out of college, dropped the Greenbaum, got signed by a record label, released the song, became famous, had her hair and clothes copied by all the kids on St Mark's Place, recorded the sound track to an experimental film about a woman who lost her right hand in a factory accident (*Zero Days Since*), shaved her head, became a Buddhist, and then dropped dead of an overdose at twenty-seven, just like Janis and Jimi and Kurt. Each year, on the anniversary of her death, 'Mistress of Myself' played nonstop on every college radio station in the country. It was the twentieth anniversary, and Elizabeth had been expecting something. The call had come in that morning. They'd been asked before, but never by people with actual money.

'What?!' Zoe grabbed Elizabeth's elbows. 'Are you fucking kidding me? How much do we get paid?'

'Oh, I don't know yet, but Andrew wants to say no. Technically, they need all of us to sign our life rights, and they need us to agree to have the song in the movie. . . .'

'And they can't make a movie about Lydia without the song.'

'Nope. I mean, they could, but what would be the point?'

'Hmm,' Zoe said. 'Who could play her? Who would play you? Who would play *me*? Oh, my God, Ruby, obviously! Oh, my God, it's too perfect, I love it, yes, give me the forms, I say yes.'

Elizabeth waved her hands in the air. 'Oh, I think that part doesn't matter as much. I'll have the woman send you the thing to sign. I'm pretty sure they'll just make us into one giant composite, like Random College Friends One, Two and Three. But Andrew's never going to agree to give them the song. It stirs it all up for him, you know?' For the past ten years, Elizabeth and Andrew had quietly been writing songs again, just the two of them, mostly during the afternoons when Harry was in school if they didn't have to work. They sat on two chairs in the garage and played. Elizabeth couldn't tell if their new songs were any good, but she enjoyed singing with her husband, the way intimate bodies could be feet apart and still feel like you were touching. No one else knew. Andrew wanted it that way. 'Anyway,' she said, 'what was your news?' There was half a pecan pie on the counter, brought over by Josephine, who baked it every month, even though it was totally unseasonable and therefore largely ignored by the book club. Elizabeth picked at it with her fingers.

'Oh,' Zoe said. 'We're talking about getting a divorce again.' She shook her head. 'It seems kind of like it might really happen this time, I don't know.' Bingo, Zoe's ancient golden retriever, lumbered out of his hiding place under the dining-room table and leaned sympathetically against her shins. Zoe squatted down and hugged him. 'I'm hugging a dog,' she said, and started to cry.

'Honey!' Elizabeth said, and dropped to her knees. She threw her arms around Zoe, the dog wedged in between them. There were good questions to ask and bad questions. One was never supposed to ask why, or to appear either surprised or the reverse, which was actually more offensive. 'Oh, no! What's going on? I'm so sorry. Are you okay? Does Ruby know? Are you talking about selling the house?'

Zoe raised her head from Bingo's back, a dog hair stuck to her wet cheek. 'Me, too. Yes. No. Well, maybe. Probably. And I think so? Oh, God.'

Elizabeth petted Zoe's head and plucked the dog hair from her face. 'I'll help. With any of it. You know that, right?' Zoe nodded, her lower lip puffing out in a pout, its pale pink inside the color of a seashell.

Five

Whitman Academy was a small private school, with only sixty-eight students in the senior class. Ruby was one of twelve students of color in her grade: three African-American, four Latino, five Asian. It was pathetic and depressing, but that was private school in New York City. Zoe felt conflicted about sending Ruby – she wanted her daughter to be surrounded by a diverse student body, but all the private schools were just as bad, the public schools in their zone were appalling, and Whitman was the closest to home. It was what it was.

The graduation ceremony took place after dark, which made the working parents happy, and made the students feel like it was more of a red-carpet affair, as if such measures were to be encouraged. The school was on Prospect Park West, which meant that it was always impossible to find a parking spot, but Ruby had worn heels, and refused to walk from the subway. They should have taken a taxi, but it was raining, and trying to get a cab in the rain in Ditmas Park was like trying to hail a polar bear. It just wasn't going to happen. Zoe sat in the driver's seat of their Honda, idling in the driveway. They had twenty minutes to get there. Jane had taken the night off, which meant that she was probably standing in their kitchen instead of the restaurant's kitchen, on the phone ordering twenty pounds of heirloom tomatoes from a purveyor in New Jersey, chewing on the end of a pen until it looked like the gnarled root of a tree. The radio was tuned to NPR, which Zoe wasn't in the mood for, and so she hit the button to find the next station, and the next. She stopped when she heard the chorus to 'Mistress of Myself' and Lydia's signature shrieking. It was a good song, sure, but really it had just been the right song at the right time, sung by the right mouth.

At Oberlin, Lydia hadn't been anything special. She was a little doughy, like most of them, a few new layers of fat added by the cafeteria food, the soft-serve ice cream and Tater Tots they ate at every meal. They'd all been in the same dorm, South, which was across campus from where most of the freshmen lived, but housed lots of conservatory students. When her parents dropped her off, Zoe had watched a girl and her mother maneuver a full-size harp up the staircase. But Zoe and her friends weren't musicians, not compared to the conservatory kids, all prodigies who'd been chained to their instruments since birth. Zoe could play piano and guitar, and Elizabeth had been taking guitar lessons since she was ten. Andrew was a rudimentary bass player at best. Lydia was supposed to be their drummer, but she didn't have a drum set, just a pair of sticks that she would bang against whatever was closest. Back then, her hair was brown and wavy, like the rest of the girls' from Scarsdale. Of course, once Lydia became Lydia, she wasn't from Scarsdale anymore.

Zoe heard some shouting from the house. She shut the radio off and rolled down the window. Ruby and Jane both hustled out the front door, Ruby in the white fringe dress and Jane in a mask of disbelief.

'Are you kidding me with this?' Jane said, poking her head into the passenger-side window.

'Mom, God, it's just a *dress*,' Ruby said, slumping into the backseat.

'That is definitely not an entire dress.' Jane let herself collapse into the car, her heavy body rocking the small car as she pulled the door shut and buckled her seat belt. She spoke without turning to face Zoe. 'I can't believe you agreed to let her wear that.'

'I'm right here, you know,' Ruby said.

Jane kept staring straight ahead. 'Let's just go. I can't even.'

Zoe put the car in reverse. She caught Ruby's eye in the rearview mirror. 'We're so excited for you, sweetie.'

Ruby rolled her eyes. It was an involuntary gesture, like breathing, an automatic response to whatever her mothers said. 'I can tell,' she said. 'You could always just drop me off with Chloe's family, they're going to the River Café for dinner.'

'The River Café isn't what it used to be,' Jane said. 'Those stupid Brooklyn Bridge chocolate cakes. It's for tourists.'

'I know,' Ruby said, and turned to look out the window.

When they got to the school, Jane hopped out and switched places with Zoe – someone was going to have to circle the block to find a parking spot, and they both knew that Ruby would have a meltdown if she had to drive past her school three hundred times before going inside. All the seniors and their families were milling around in front and in the lobby, everyone dressed like they were going to the prom. Whitman didn't have a prom, of course – that was too square, too suburban. Instead they had a party with the entire faculty in a converted loft space in Dumbo. Zoe was waiting for the e-mail to go out that the students and teachers had been caught having a group orgy in the bathroom. Most of the teachers looked like they could have been students, maybe held back a couple of grades. The young men almost always grew scruffy little beards or goatees, probably just to prove that they could. Ruby had skipped the party, 'Because eww,' which Zoe secretly agreed with.

Zoe let Ruby lead her through the crowd in front of the school, weaving in and out. She nodded and waved to the parents she knew, and squeezed the arms of some of the kids. It was a small school, and Ruby had gone there since she was five, and so Zoe knew everyone, whether or not Ruby deigned to speak to them. Ruby's intermittently loving and cruel cluster of girlfriends – Chloe, Paloma, Anika and Sarah – were already inside, posing for pictures with their parents and siblings, and Zoe knew that Ruby was likely to ditch her and Jane for her friends as soon as possible. Impending-graduation hormones made regular puberty hormones seem like nothing – Ruby had been a lunatic for months. They went inside through the heavy front door, and Zoe saw Elizabeth and Harry across the lobby.

'Hey, wait,' she said to Ruby, pointing. Ruby reluctantly slowed to a stop and crossed her arms over her chest.

'Ruby! Congratulations, sweetheart!' Elizabeth, bless her, couldn't be stymied by Ruby's death stares. 'That dress looks phenomenal on you. Yowza!' Zoe watched her daughter soften. She even managed to squeeze out a tiny smile.

'Thanks,' Ruby said. 'I mean, it's just high school. It's really not that big of a deal. It's really only a big deal if you *don't* graduate from high school, you know what I mean? Like, I also learned how to walk and to use a fork.'

Harry chuckled. 'I can tie my shoes,' he said. He kicked his toe into the floor for emphasis, and also to avoid looking Ruby in the eye. Even though Harry and Ruby had grown up together, had lived three houses apart for most of their lives, things had changed in the last few years. When they were children, they'd played together, taken baths together, built forts and choreographed dances. Now Harry could barely speak in front of her. Mostly, when he was standing next to Ruby, all Harry could think about was a photograph that his mother had on her dresser of him and Ruby when he was one and she was two, both of them standing naked in the front yard. His penis looked so tiny, like the stubbiest baby carrot in the bag, the one you might not even eat because you were afraid it was actually a toe.

'Exactly.' Ruby scanned the room, looking over Harry's head. 'Oh, shit,' she said. Zoe, Elizabeth and Harry all turned to follow her gaze. 'Mum, stay here.' She hustled across the room, elbowing people out of her way.

Zoe craned her neck – the room was getting more and more crowded. 'Who is she talking to, Harr?'

'It's Dust,' Harry said, and immediately regretted it. He'd seen them kissing in front of school, and on their street after dark, standing in between parked cars. Dust was obviously not the kind of boy a girl would bring home to her parents, even if her parents were cool, like Ruby's. There would be too many questions. Dust was the kind of guy, if life had been a sitcom, that Ruby's moms would have tried to adopt, because it turned out he couldn't read and had been living on a park bench since he was twelve. But in real life, Dust was just kind of scary, and Ruby should have known better. Harry had lots of good ideas about who she should go out with instead, and they were all him.

'Dust?' Elizabeth asked.

'Is that a name? Does he go to school here? How old is he?' Zoe said.

'What?' Harry said, waving his hand by his ear. It was getting loud in the school's lobby, and he was sweating. It was better to pretend he hadn't heard. Ruby was going to be so mad at him. Harry felt a deep, sudden longing for the indifference she'd shown him since the ninth grade.

The head of the high school came out and shouted for the seniors to get lined up, and the crowd began to disperse. Excited parents took photos of each other with their phones, and a few with real cameras. Teachers wore ties and shook hands. Elizabeth cupped Harry's shoulder. 'I'm sure it's fine. Should we go get seats? Zo, you want me to save you and Jane spots?'

'Hang on,' Zoe said. Now that people were filing into the

auditorium, it was a straight shot through the lobby to the door, where Ruby was having an argument with the boy, who looked like a skinhead. Were there still skinheads? He was taller than Ruby and was stooped over to talk to her, his shoulders rounding like an old man's. Ruby looked furious, and the boy did, too. His face was pointy and sharp, and his chin jutted out toward her daughter's sweet face. 'Harry, spill it.'

Harry felt his face begin to burn. 'Shit,' he said. 'He's her boyfriend.'

'Is his name Dust or Shit?' Elizabeth asked. 'What's the story?' Chloe and Paloma were inching across the room toward Ruby, teetering on their new heels like baby dinosaurs.

Harry opened his mouth to answer – he'd never been good at lying – but just then Ruby let out a little scream, and before he could think about what he was doing, Harry was running across the room. He threw his entire body at Dust, and the two of them hit the floor with a thud. Harry felt Dust roll away and then saw him scurry up and out the door like a hermit crab, on his hands and feet. Ruby stood over Harry with her own hands on her mouth. For a second she looked actually frightened, and the dangly white tassels of her dress shook a tiny bit, almost like she was dancing. It was the most beautiful dress Harry had ever seen. It wasn't just a dress; it was a religion. It was an erupting volcano that would kill hundreds of pale-faced tourists, and Harry was ready for the lava to flow. Ruby regained her composure and looked around the room. A half circle had formed around them, and their mothers were cutting through it, mouths open like hungry guppies. Ruby turned toward the crowd, smiled, and did a pageant-winner wave, her elbow gliding back and forth. Both Chloe and Paloma made mewling noises and reached for her with grasping fingers, but Ruby ignored them. 'My hero,' she said archly to Harry, and extended her hand to help him up from the floor.

Six

Elizabeth and Andrew's bedroom was too warm. All three windows were open, and a large oscillating fan swiveled its face from left to right, but the room was still hot. Iggy Pop had forsaken his usual spot on their bed in favor of one of the windowsills, and Elizabeth was jealous. The air conditioners were in the basement. It was one of Andrew's points of pride to wait as long as possible before putting them in. One year, before Harry was born, they'd waited until July 15. Elizabeth kicked the top sheet off her body, and rolled on to her side.

'I thought rain was supposed to make everything cooler,' she said.

'The planet is dying,' Andrew said. 'You'll appreciate it more in January.' He nudged her with a toe, teasing.

'Oh, stop it,' Elizabeth said. She wiped her forehead. It was almost midnight. 'I can't believe Harry attacked someone.'

'It sounds like it wasn't really an *attack*,' Andrew said. 'Rescue, maybe? You're right, though, it doesn't sound like him. Maybe there was some kind of wasp and he was trying to get the kid out of the way.' Andrew rolled on to his side, too, so that he was facing his wife. 'That doesn't sound much like him, either.'

'No, Harry dove for this kid like he was a grenade about to

explode. He was running, and then he was in the air. It was like an action movie. I have never seen him move so fast in his entire life.'

'Weird.' Andrew sat up and took a few gulps of water. 'I can't believe it's going to be him next year.'

'Let's just hope that no one tackles him. That kid also looked about twenty-five. I bet he was held back three grades. Remember being held back?' Elizabeth flopped on to her back and let her legs splay out to the side. 'Anyway,' she said, 'want to talk about Lydia? I told them I'd give them an answer as soon as I could.'

'Can we not? I'm tired, okay?' Andrew said. Elizabeth grumbled. 'Let's talk about it tomorrow. Love you.' He clicked off his bedside lamp and kissed Elizabeth on the forehead. 'Good night.'

Elizabeth stared at the back of her husband's head. His dark brown hair was going gray at his temples and in seemingly random spots around his head, but his hair was still thick and curly at the ends when it had been months since his last haircut, like now. She listened to his breath even out until it was involuntary and soft, inhale and exhale, inhale and exhale. Andrew had his share of anxieties, but sleep had never been one of them. He was like a robot – when it was time, he just closed his eyes and he was done.

It was funny to think about Lydia. When they'd all met, they were just two years older than Harry was now, a year older than Ruby. Elizabeth could remember so much about that time – how she felt when she walked into parties, what her skin looked like after three days of beer and no showers, sleeping with new people for the first time. Sleeping with people for the only time! She always assumed that she would have more years of exploration, of awkward mornings with strangers, but she and Andrew had met so early, and then she was done. Five men. That was Elizabeth's entire sexual history. It was pathetic, really. Her friends who hadn't met their spouses until they were in their thirties had easily slept with twenty people, if not more. Taylor Swift had probably slept with more people than she had, and good for her. Most of the parents at Whitman were a decade older than she was – she and Andrew had started too early, probably, before they were even thirty, an act that seemed horrifying to the other parents she knew, as if she'd been a teen mother. But Zoe and Jane, only two years into their romance, had Ruby, and Elizabeth had suddenly felt her biological clock (or her inner keeping-up-with-Zoe clock) ticking like mad, and they were right behind them, screwing every day between one period and the next.

Elizabeth was happy in her marriage, she really was. It was just that sometimes she thought about all the experiences she'd never gotten to have, and all the nights she'd listened to the sound of her husband's snores, and wanted to jump out a window and go home with the first person who talked to her. Choices were easy to make until you realized how long life could be.

It was flattering, the way her song had stayed relevant. Some hits aged badly – no one felt that 'Who Let the Dogs Out' accurately described their inner workings – but 'Mistress of Myself' had aged better than most. Pissed-off young women, sensitive young men, teenagers of any description as long as they were angsty, breast-feeding mothers, everyone who had a boss he hated or a lover she wasn't getting enough attention from – the song was applicable in a surprising number of categories. She'd written the lyrics quickly. It was the fall of her sophomore year, and she was sitting in one of the round orange chairs in the school library. Designed in the 1960s, they were called 'womb chairs' because they were deep enough to crawl into, round and cozy, and surely there had been at least one student who had tried to stay in one for nine months at a time. The insides were upholstered, and it was best not to think about how hard they were to clean. Elizabeth liked to curl up in one of them and read or write in her notebook. Everyone else at Oberlin was all hot and bothered about Foucault and Barthes, but she was far more interested in Jane Austen. She was reading *Sense and Sensibility* for pleasure, and that's where she saw it – on one of the very last pages, when Elinor Dashwood was trying to prepare herself for a visit from Edward Ferrars, with whom she was deeply in love but who she believed had forsaken her. 'I *will* be calm; I *will* be mistress of myself,' Elinor thought.

Elizabeth understood it completely: the desire to be in control, the need to speak the words aloud. No one in St Paul, Minnesota, had ever been truly her own mistress. Elizabeth's mother and her friends all went to the same hairdresser, shopped at the same stores, sent their kids to the same schools. She was pretty sure that they all ate the same things for dinner, except maybe Purva, whose parents were Indian, and Mary, whose parents were Korean. Elizabeth swiveled the chair around so that it was facing the window, and opened up her notebook. The song was finished fifteen minutes later. She showed the lyrics to Zoe and Andrew and Lydia later that afternoon, and the rest of the song was done by the time they went to bed. The band was called Kitty's Mustache, a hat tip to Tolstoy's heroine. They were regular college kids, in love with the idea of their own cleverness. No one had ever thought of anything before. It was the best night of her life to date, easy.

She and Andrew weren't serious. They'd slept together three or four times, almost always when they were drunk, or, once, on some Ecstasy that she thought was probably just aspirin with a tiny bit of cocaine sprinkled on top, like Parmesan on a lasagna. Andrew was quiet and a little angry, an irresistible combination. He only wore black. Black Dickies, black T-shirts, black socks, black shoes. There was something rigid about him that Elizabeth liked, but she wasn't sure. His parents were rich, and he hated them – it was an old story. Elizabeth was nineteen, Andrew was twenty, and it didn't really matter. But then she was twenty, and then twenty-two, and then twenty-four, and then they were married. When Lydia asked the rest of the band if she could license the rights to the song, to actually record it and put it out, Elizabeth didn't even need to think about it.

She'd never had the chance to be the mistress of herself, not really. None of them thought Lydia could sing – empirically, she couldn't. What could it possibly matter?

It had been hardest for Andrew, watching Lydia's version of the song take off the way it did. Elizabeth believed that songs – great songs, perfect songs – belonged to the universe. Did it matter who wrote 'They Can't Take That Away from Me' when both Ella Fitzgerald and Billie Holiday could sing the hell out of it? Good songs deserved to be heard. It was better to be sanguine about your own output. Why did it have to be emotional? She'd written it, she'd put it on the page. Lydia did a better job putting it out into the universe. Andrew was more of a hoarder. Zoe knew from her parents that the whole music industry was fucked, and she wanted nothing to do with it.

Since they'd graduated from Oberlin, Elizabeth had had three jobs. First she'd worked as an assistant to a former associate of her father's, a lawyer who worked near Grand Central. Getting there from Ditmas Park had taken forever, and she worked so many hours that she often fell asleep on the subway home and woke up at the last stop, in Coney Island. Her second job was also as an assistant, but this time to an art-book publisher in Chelsea. Her boss was in the midst of selling her town house and moving to Brooklyn, and it was Elizabeth's job to help. She was measuring walls and taping up boxes of books, packing and unpacking. That was how she fell into real estate. It was so long ago now that the job felt like a part of her soul, like being a teacher or an artist who made things out of sand. You never really saw the results – you just trusted that you knew what you were doing and that everything would work out okay in the end. Sure, every once in a while a television actress would buy a house from her and there would be photos of it in a magazine, but that wasn't Elizabeth's triumph, not really. It was a modest career, like being a flight attendant. She helped people get from one place to another.

It was hard to say what Elizabeth liked most about selling houses –

she liked the imagination that was required. She liked walking into a space and considering the possibilities. She made a good percentage of her income selling apartments, some of them new and glossy and soulless, but what she really loved was selling old houses to people who appreciated them. Elizabeth swung her legs out of bed and slid forward until her feet hit the wood floor. The floorboards creaked, because the house was a hundred years old, and that's what floorboards did. She got up and walked over to the window, over on Andrew's side of the bed, and looked out on to Argyle Road.

'I will be *calm calm calm calm calm*,' Elizabeth sang in a breathy shout. 'I will be *calm calm calm calm calm*!' The words sounded funny coming out of her mouth. They had felt so vital at the time, as if a channel inside her had opened up and some beam of raucous feminist light was pouring through her – she wrote the lyrics in her notebook in her small, orderly handwriting, the letters getting messier as she wrote faster and faster. As soon as it was down on paper, Elizabeth knew it was good. She didn't know – couldn't have known – what would happen next, but she knew that the song was the best thing she'd ever done. Andrew snored. Elizabeth stared out at the street until Iggy Pop jumped off the windowsill, landing with a yowl on the hardwood floor, distraught that something was amiss. She picked up the cat, held his thin body against her sweaty chest, and climbed back into bed.

Seven

Jane had taken to sleeping in the guest room. Now that Ruby knew that they were having problems, problems that might actually end their marriage, it felt both better and worse in the house. She and Zoe didn't have to pretend that everything was fine, but Jane had enjoyed pretending. She enjoyed it so much that she would often make it all the way through the day and evening and only remember when she got home after the dinner rush and Zoe glared at her from her spot on the couch. Jane couldn't turn on the television; she couldn't change the music. She could choose to sit quietly and not bother Zoe, but if Jane was on her laptop, getting work done, she'd get shit for that, too. It was as if Zoe thought that they were all just swimming through oceans of time, endless vast amounts of time. Who sat in one place for three hours reading a book? Maybe that's why they were talking about getting divorced. Dr Amelia, the couples therapist they'd seen years ago, said that all marriages went through rough spots, and that it didn't mean the union was faulty or unsound. It just meant that you had to kick a few tires, or tighten some bolts, or adjust the seasoning. Dr Amelia hadn't been afraid of metaphors. Sometimes, when they were sitting on the low orange sofa in her office, Dr Amelia would tilt her head back and go through long lists of them, trying to find the right one.

It wasn't like the beginning, when they spent their days eating their way through the Chinese shopping malls in Queens, or when they opened Hyacinth and they were both on their feet fifteen hours a day, too exhausted to fight, or when Ruby was born and they were too in love to have to. Now Zoe spent so much time hunched over her computer, working on the payroll and the schedules and the billing, that Jane took it as a silvery stop sign. Somehow, now that they weren't needed in the space every second of every day, instead of having more time together they had less. Jane went to dinners at the James Beard House by herself, she drank whiskey with the cooks after closing at the bar down the street. For the first time in her life, Zoe went to bed early. There were big problems and little problems, the latter of which seemed to multiply in the night like rabbits. Jane cared about Yelp comments too much, she drank too much. She didn't care about Zoe's friends. She didn't care about her own friends. She didn't have friends! She was too bossy, she wasn't bossy enough. She didn't care about Patti Smith. When they met, Zoe was wild, and Jane had felt like a steadying force – her sturdy body anchoring Zoe's rangy limbs to earth. That's what she still wanted to be. It wasn't the word, or the feeling, of failure, which is what Jane's mother was so mopey about, having to call her aunts and uncles and cousins, and tell them that it hadn't worked. Her mother acted like it was an affront to Jane's gayness, the divorce, like she'd been granted the right to vote and then slept through the election.

The guest-room bed was full size, a lumpy leftover futon. Until recently, they'd kept it folded up unless Ruby had a friend sleeping over, and then they'd drag the mattress on to the floor of her room and the girls could jump and flop all over it. Kids didn't care. Jane cared. Her back felt terrible, and so did her knees. Standing up at the restaurant was bad enough, but sleeping on a piece of glorified cardboard was worse. Every morning, she rolled off to one side and had to come up through hands and knees, as if she'd just crawled across a desert. She felt like she was a hundred years old. Meanwhile, Zoe was always dipping in and out of Pilates classes. She'd been wearing makeup, a glittery dusting on her eyes, some bright pink on her lips. It was hard not to feel as though Zoe was dancing on her grave. It wasn't as if Jane had ever kept Zoe from doing whatever she liked – it didn't make sense. Jane liked it when things made sense. It wasn't even a question of rocking the boat – Zoe was carving the boat in half with a chain saw. God, she was as bad as Dr Amelia.

They were just moving into true summer – tomatoes were perfect, round and sweet. Soft-shell crabs were perfection. Corn was everywhere, so fresh you could just peel the silk back and eat the kernels right off the cob. Hyacinth was less busy in July and August, when so many people left the city, but June was still brisk, and Jane woke up thinking of specials to add to the menu. She almost always opened her eyes to visions of food – not breakfast, never breakfast – things she could serve at the restaurant. A dessert with strawberries and peppercorns. A salad with enormous watermelon radishes and fat wedges of avocado. Fresh pasta with asparagus pesto. And then she'd think about Zoe.

They'd always talked about what would happen when Ruby left home – when she was little, it seemed like a hilarious nightmare, the idea that this tiny, helpless creature would ever be able to pay her own bills or pull open the fridge door. When she was five or six and in school every day, Zoe had flipped out. At first, it was thrilling – so many hours in the day! such freedom! – but then she began to complain about how much time Ruby was spending with other adults, worrying that she was going to be influenced by them. 'They're *teachers*,' Jane would tell her. 'That's what we're paying them for.' It didn't matter – Zoe was always five or ten minutes early to pick Ruby up, pacing back and forth in front of school, as if she thought that her daughter might have forgotten her in the hours she'd been gone. In those years, Zoe clung to Jane like a loving barnacle. They were a power couple, rich in kale and quinoa and fizzy glasses of rosé.

Jane rolled on to her side. The ceiling fan was on, whirring around in circles. The house was quiet, but there was some construction going on outside. Jane could have sworn there used to be rules about jack-hammers on weekends, but there they were. It was so strange to be in her house, sleeping in another bed. She felt embarrassed, and ridiculous. What did any of this have to do with sleeping arrangements, anyway? All she wanted was her normal, easy life. She thought it wasn't anything they couldn't fix. Maybe once Ruby left home, things would be easier. There would be more space for them to talk – to argue, even. It wasn't as if Zoe were prone to the idea of divorce – her own parents had stayed married through the seventies and eighties and cocaine and all the rest. They were still married and drank gin and tonics together in front of the fireplace, though Los Angeles was usually too warm for them to turn it on. Jane loved Zoe's parents for many reasons, but that's what it boiled down to – she loved that they were happy, utterly devoid of neuroses.

She and Zoe were a mixed marriage, both racially and religiously speaking – Jane was a Jew from Long Island who'd been taking ulcer medication since she was a teenager, and Zoe was a Martian who never worried about anything, who believed that Chaka Khan played *everyone's* sweet sixteen. They'd always balanced each other out, but now Jane felt like instead of balance, she'd just been a brick tied to Zoe's ankle, a rusty anchor trying to drag her under. Maybe, after all this time, it turned out that Zoe was right, that working hard and having fun were all that mattered, and everything else should just vanish in a puff of smoke. Ruby's clothes, Ruby's grades? The server at the restaurant who was always high, like Hyacinth was the Odeon and Bret Easton Ellis was about to walk in the door? Her mother's latest fight with her postal worker about how she was stealing her magazines? She wanted to let it all go. All Jane wanted was to look at Zoe's beautiful face every day for the rest of her life.

'Zo?' Jane said. She stood up slowly, her knees creaking. 'Rube?' She walked with stiff legs into the hall and peered into the other bedrooms. There was no sign of either her wife or her daughter. 'Guys?' she called, her voice loud and clear. The house was empty. This is what it would be like for the rest of her life – calling into empty rooms and waiting for responses that weren't coming. Getting married was the easy part, even though they'd had to wait until Ruby was twelve to do it legally. When they got together, it was all balloons, all hope. Now that they knew what the future held – what the future looked like – it was much harder. Why couldn't everyone stay young forever? If not on the outside, then just on the inside, where no one ever got too old to be optimistic. Zoe would have laughed at her, standing like a mope in the middle of the hallway in her pajamas. Jane had no idea what time it was. Was it too late? She rested her forehead against the wall.

Eight

The SAT prep course was held on Saturday mornings in a karate school on Church Avenue, the northernmost thoroughfare in the neighborhood, populated by Laundromats, bodegas, and the occasional coffee shop that sold freshly baked scones and croissants to the laptop crowd. The class was two hours long, every week for eight weeks – two whole months. Harry didn't mind much. He didn't have anything better to do, and it was nice to get out of the house, almost healthy. Taking tests didn't scare him, and he was pretty sure that he didn't have to get a perfect score in order to get into the schools he wanted to go to – maybe Bard or Bennington, somewhere small like Whitman but without any of the people. Reed sounded good. A little crunchy, but good. Being far away was a bonus.

Harry pulled open the door to the studio. There were folding chairs set up facing a dry-erase board along the back wall, and a projector screen was already showing off the crowded desktop of somebody's laptop. A few other kids were milling around, and about half the chairs were occupied. Harry ambled over to the back row and sank into a chair. He recognized two girls from his grade sitting in the front row and pulled his hood down over his eyes.

'Hey,' someone said, smacking him in the back of the head.

Harry put his hand up to protect himself, spinning around as quickly as he could. Ruby stood behind him, smiling.

'Oh,' Harry said. 'Hey.'

They hadn't spoken since graduation. After the Dust incident (girls like Eliza and Thayer, now four rows ahead of him, had christened the event '#dustup' on Instagram, which they thought was hilarious until Ruby threatened to kill their parents), Ruby and Harry hadn't even been in the same room. Harry had walked by Ruby twice, once when she was sitting on her front porch with her dog, and the other when she was standing on line at the grocery store on Cortelyou, buying milk and the same hippie deodorant that his mother used. He hadn't said hello either time, because it was much easier to stare at the ground than it was to figure out what to say, but he had spent a lot of time smelling his mother's deodorant.

Ruby picked up someone's backpack that had been sitting in the chair next to Harry and moved it over one. 'Mind if I join you? I hear the shrimp cocktail is out of this world.'

'And the Martinis,' Harry said. 'Very good olives.' He had a momentary panic that Martinis didn't have olives, and that he sounded like an idiot.

Ruby let her bag drop to the floor with a thud and then slid into the folding chair. 'Are they going to dim the lights? It is definitely my nap time.'

'I don't know,' Harry said. Ruby was six inches away. Her breath was toothpaste-minty. 'I'm sorry about the other day.'

She looked surprised. 'Why? That was fucking awesome.'

'No, I mean, I'm glad and everything. I'm just sorry that that guy was being such an asshole. At your graduation. That sucks. And I'm sorry that I had to tell your moms about him. I just hope . . . you know, that I didn't get you into trouble.' Harry was sweating. The plastic folding chair was digging into his back. He pushed his hood off and then pulled it on again.

'It's cool, man,' Ruby said.

A woman with glasses and a large Starbucks iced coffee walked to the far side of the room, the direction they were all facing, clapping her hands like they were a roomful of kindergartners. She waved a stack of paper. 'Hey, guys, I'm Rebecca, and I'll be your SAT prep tutor for the next eight beautiful Saturdays! I went to Harvard, and you can too! Let's get started! Who's down with some vocab quizzes?'

'Oh, dear Lord,' Ruby said.

'Want me to tackle her too?' Harry said. Ruby laughed so loudly that Eliza and Thayer both turned around, saw who it was, and quickly snapped to attention.

'I like your energy!' said Rebecca, flashing a double thumbs-up.

Ruby let her head loll back and pretended to hang herself.

Nine

It wasn't a kind first thought, and it wasn't a very hopeful one, but it drove Elizabeth slightly bonkers to think that Jane was going to profit from Zoe's foresight and investment and commitment. That was marriage, agreeing to share bank accounts and bookshelves, even when you didn't want to, even when it made things messier in the case of an eventual split. In her years as a real-estate agent, Elizabeth had come across several couples with separate checkbooks, which seemed like a red flag. Too cold-blooded, too pragmatic. It was like announcing that you hadn't decided if you were going to stay married or not. Take me, take my overdraft charges! Take me, take my embarrassing number of books with teenage vampire protagonists! Elizabeth had never considered the alternative – it was as bad as signing a prenup. Why bother getting married, going through with all the pomp and pageantry, if you didn't think it was going to last? It was far easier to live in sin and not have to deal with the paperwork.

She knocked on the door – Zoe was on the sofa reading a magazine and waved her in through the window. Elizabeth opened the door and glanced up – the ceiling in the vestibule was cracked and needed a new coat of paint. Looking at the house was easier than looking at Zoe and telling her what was broken and needed fixing. They had always been close – in college and even more so in the years after, when they'd lived together inside these very walls – but after marriage and crawling children there wasn't an easy way back. Like many, their friendship had slipped a disc somewhere along the way. Yes, sure, they would sometimes have dinner, just the two of them, and then they'd have a Big Talk about everything in their lives, but that was only once every three or four months. Their friendship was still there, but it also felt like it was a million miles away, viewable only through a time machine and a telescope.

'Do you want to talk?' Elizabeth asked. It had been her idea to come over. Zoe had expressed some interest in knowing what the house was worth, just in case. 'Do you have a piece of paper? I want you to write it all down so that you can talk to Jane about it, about what needs to be done, okay?' Elizabeth had been in the house a thousand times – more, maybe – had lived here, had slept on the couch, had thrown up in the toilet. She had a good idea of what needed to be done, but she needed to show it all to Zoe. It was impossible to really see a space when you'd lived there for so long. All the eccentricities began to seem normal – the way you'd never properly rewired the doorbell, and so you had to push it extra hard to the left; the way the guest bedroom was two different shades of cream, because . . . well, why was it? It was a mistake, just a part of life, but now someone else was going to buy that mistake, and that someone was going to offer a hundred thousand dollars less because of it.

Elizabeth was in her work clothes. In Manhattan, the agents wore outfits that looked like they could double as evening wear: tight black dresses and heels. Luckily, no one in Brooklyn wanted that. It made people uncomfortable, that much gloss, but she still had to step it up a notch. Her biggest concessions were ditching her clogs for a pair of flats and putting on actual pants in place of jeans. It was important to show respect for the fact that people were plunking down their entire life savings for three thousand square feet. Sometimes, because it was

New York, people spent all their money on five hundred square feet. That's when Elizabeth wore heels, when she felt a little bit guilty.

'You look nice,' Zoe said.

'I had to,' Elizabeth said. She dusted off her blouse. 'I have a closing today, a house up in Lefferts.' She wondered how bad she normally looked. Her hair was straight and naturally blond, which is to say a light, innocuous brown, and cut short, just below her ears, with little bangs like a schoolgirl's. She liked to think that she looked like a gamine, but that probably wasn't true anymore, if it ever had been.

'Hmm,' Zoe said, not really listening. 'Shall we begin the processional death march?'

No one was ever interested in the business part of Elizabeth's job – all anyone ever wanted to know was if she found people's sex toys or whether the sellers were getting a divorce. No one wanted to buy bad juju. If she were a better liar, Elizabeth would always have told prospective buyers that the sellers were retiring and moving to Florida after several happy decades in whatever space she was trying to sell, with entirely redone mechanical and electrical systems. That's what people wanted – the promise of a satisfied life with very little work to do. Of course, no one in New York City was ever satisfied. It's what kept her busy. Even people who liked where they lived kept an eye out for something better. Shopping for a new place to live was easier than shopping for a new husband or wife, and less traumatic than going into analysis.

They started on the ground floor – the kitchen was old but sweet, with a nicely expensive stove, well used. House shoppers would be impressed, even if the cabinets hadn't been painted in twenty years. The dining room needed paint, too, and less furniture – Jane had stacks of chairs in all four corners, in case of an impromptu dinner party for thirty, which Elizabeth knew they often had. The living room was okay – ditch the family photos, the vintage knickknacks they'd so lovingly acquired at yard sales, Ruby's piles of clothing everywhere. The staircase needed a little love – nails were poking up all over the place, and the skylight on the landing hadn't been cleaned in a decade. Upstairs, all the bedrooms needed paint jobs, and Ruby's needed a hazmat expert. The two bathrooms were pretty terrible, but not worth doing. Throw out the mildewy curtains, get all the dog hair off the floor. Whoever came in with that much money was going to want to do things their way. Elizabeth and Zoe stopped in the master bedroom.

'You want to talk about it?' Elizabeth asked.

Zoe sat on the edge of her bed, which was low to the floor and rumpled. Bingo padded over and sat down on her feet. 'It's been coming forever,' she said. 'You know that. After Ruby was born, I didn't think we'd last two years. Then, when we opened the restaurant, I thought we were done for sure.' She ran her hands back and forth over Bingo's stomach. 'But then when Hyacinth started doing well and Jane was always there, it didn't seem as pressing. How sad is that? We were too busy to split up.'

'So why now? Why do it?' Zoe wasn't the first to get divorced – slowly, Elizabeth and Andrew's circle of friends had come closer and closer to the national average. At first, it was just one couple, then another and another. Now half of Harry's friends had parents living apart from each other, and the kids bounced back and forth like tennis balls. Andrew sometimes expressed worry about it, whether Harry was absorbing some of that stress and angst from his friends, even though it had never seemed like an issue.

'The last time we had sex was in January.' She paused. '*Last* January.'

'Sex isn't everything,' Elizabeth said. She took another look at the bed that Zoe was sitting on. It looked like the bed in a hipster hotel, streamlined and Danish, a more expensive Ikea model – Zoe's choice, clearly – the kind of bed where people did nothing *but* have sex or maybe read each other some translated poetry. Zoe had always had scores of lovers at school, and afterward – she'd had women chasing her down streets and out of dance clubs, throwing their phone numbers at her like so much confetti. Jane had sleep apnea and sometimes slept with a special mask that Zoe said made her look like the villain in a science-fiction movie, and yet it was Jane who had stolen Zoe's heart at a bar, the kind of place where you were supposed to meet one-night stands, not wives, and Jane who had stolen her from Elizabeth.

Zoe shook her head. 'It's not nothing. I don't know. I think we both finally came around to the idea that we could be happier apart. It's one thing to be in a lull, but it's another thing to stare down the next thirty years of your life and just be filled with depressing fucking dread. I don't know if it'll really happen, but it sure seems like it.' She gave Bingo a few good pats on his head. 'As long as this guy comes with me, I'll be fine.'

'Okay, so we need dog-friendly.' That ruled out certain buildings in the Slope and Cobble Hill. It was easier to think about Zoe and Jane this way, in terms of concretes, especially in an area where she could really help. Zoe needed her; it was nice.

'Dog- and old-queer-lady-friendly, yes.'

'Easy.' Elizabeth leaned against the wall. 'So where would you want to move? Would you want to stay in the hood? Leave?' They'd been pioneers in Ditmas, planting the flag before the neighborhood had any decent restaurants or a good public school or a bar with a cocktail menu. Before tree guards, before block parties with bouncy castles.

'God, I don't know. I mean, why am I here, right? It was sort of random, and now it's home, but I don't care about the outdoor space or a stupid lawn. That's why people move to the city! I want that. I want to move somewhere where I can walk to a good movie theater by myself at nine o'clock at night, and eat pad thai, and buy jewelry on a whim. Does that exist? I want Ruby to think it's cooler than wherever Jane goes. Jane's talking about moving into a studio above the restaurant. She'll be a monk until she finds someone else to be her housewife.' Zoe flopped backward on to the bed. 'I need a massage. And some acupuncture. And a yoga class.'

'When did you guys do the roof?' Elizabeth ran her finger along the windowsill, gathering dust. The view was almost exactly the same as from her own bedroom, only a few degrees shifted. She could still see the Rosens' place, with its red door and folding shutters, and the Martinez house, with its porch swing and the dog bowl. She'd heard once that what made you a real New Yorker was when you could remember back three layers – the place on the corner that had been a bakery and then a barbershop before it was a cell-phone store, or the restaurant that had been Italian, then Mexican, then Cuban. The city was a palimpsest, a Mod Podged pileup of old signage and other people's failures. Newcomers saw only what was in front of them, but people who had been there long enough were always looking at two or three other places simultaneously. The IRT, Canal Jeans, the Limelight. So much of the city she'd fallen in love with was gone, but then again, that's how it worked. It was your job to remember. At least the bridges were still there. Some things were too heavy to take down.

'Five years ago, maybe? Shit.'

'It's okay,' Elizabeth said, turning back to face Zoe, who had covered her face with a pillow. 'It's okay.'

Ten

Harry's room was painted dark purple, and it was a little bit like sleeping inside a gigantic eggplant. He could have asked his parents to paint it another color, but it didn't really matter, seeing as the purple only peeked out here and there between the edges of the posters and other things he'd taped to the walls. He was going for one complete layer, like the people who got tattooed over their entire bodies, even their eyelids. Harry didn't care about everything he'd put on the walls, but at some point he'd cared enough to put it all up there, and he respected his own process. It was okay to grow out of things and keep them around. He liked being reminded that he'd been obsessed with Rugrats and Bart Simpson and, for a few inexplicable months around his thirteenth birthday, Kobe Bryant. He didn't even like basketball. Mostly the walls were covered with pages ripped from magazines and things he'd printed out, pages from books that he'd copied at school. It was like Tumblr, only 3-D, with no scrolling. The narrow strip of wall next to his closet was completely covered by pictures of sandwiches. Teenage girls got all the credit for being angsty and weird, and it wasn't fair. Even at Whitman, which was supposed to be progressive and artsy, the boys bragged about the time they went to a shooting range with their grandfathers in Connecticut or Virginia. They wanted to learn how to drive and listened to hip-hop. Harry wasn't interested in any of it. Luckily, his father wasn't the kind of guy who insisted on things – everything Harry had ever done was because he wanted to, like the child sultan of a palace with only two servants.

Going to one school from age five to age eighteen was like being buried in amber. It wasn't even like his walls, which were covered with layers of things – you had to be the same person from start to finish, with no big cognitive jumps. Harry was quiet and sweet and did his homework. He had three close friends, two boys and one girl, and he wasn't particularly fond of any of them. He didn't vape or drink malt liquor, because there were other kids who did that and he wasn't one of them. He had smoked weed a few times, but he knew that his parents did, too, so it didn't seem that bad. Harry lived in a monastery built of his childhood likes and dislikes. His parents loved it, and he never got into trouble, and it made him want to scream.

His phone vibrated in his pocket: COME OUTSIDE. It was from a number he didn't have in his phone. Harry walked over to the window and pulled the curtain to one side. Ruby was leaning against a parked car, holding her phone over her face, with her giant dog leaning against her legs. Harry's parents were in bed, or working – their bedroom was upstairs, and his mother often worked late at the small desk in their room. BE RIGHT THERE, he texted back. Harry changed his T-shirt twice and then tiptoed down the hall. The route to the front door was creaky but clear.

'What's up?' Harry said once he was a few feet from Ruby. She hadn't moved. Her hair was spread out over the passenger-side window like big purple jellyfish. Bingo sniffed genially in Harry's direction.

'Walk with me, my moms are being total dicks.' Ruby pushed herself back to standing and pulled Bingo's leash in the direction of the park. Harry put his hands in his pockets and followed. She pulled a pack of cigarettes out of her pocket and stuck one in her mouth. 'Want one?' she said through her teeth.

Harry shook his head and watched Ruby cup one hand around the end of her cigarette and flick a lighter with the other. He was amazed at how brazen she was – smoking on their very own block, where they knew the people inside every house, all of whom could have picked up the phone and called her mothers. Very few kids at Whitman smoked. It wasn't like when their parents were young, when everyone had packs of ciggies in their back pockets instead of cell phones. Now everyone understood about lungs and cancer and how the tobacco companies were trying to appeal to youth. It seemed borderline pathetic to give in, not that Harry could have thought that anything Ruby did was pathetic. It looked bad on other people, was all. The small contingent of smokers at school went around the corner to do it, or crossed the street and sat on benches in the park. Harry had never smoked a single cigarette – he'd actually never been offered one before. That was how small Whitman was. It wasn't even a question. Harry Marx didn't smoke. It was a fact.

They walked three blocks straight up Argyle, until they hit the soccer fields and the back of the tennis center. It was dark, and the park was closed, but there were still a few people kicking around a ball. 'Rebels,' Harry said, and Ruby laughed. They crossed Caton Avenue and walked into Prospect Park proper. Harry didn't like going into the park at night, even though there were always people running or biking around the main loop. It just seemed like one of those things that people did right before something bad happened to them, like running upstairs instead of out the front door in a horror movie. At least they had the dog with them, even if Bingo was geriatric and had permanent tearstains under his sad eyes. Ruby nudged Harry toward the bridle path, a soft dirt road that went a little bit farther into the park than Harry would have liked, but she moved with such confidence that he didn't want to be lame. Bingo seemed to know where they were going. Finally, after a few minutes, Ruby plopped down on a bench. They were completely alone, staring out at the lake.

'People fish here, have you seen that?' Ruby asked. She lit another cigarette, and this time didn't bother to ask Harry if he wanted one. 'You couldn't pay me a million dollars to eat a fish that was born in Brooklyn.'

'I'm pretty sure no one is paying anyone a million dollars to eat anything that was born in Brooklyn,' Harry said. He watched the red end of Ruby's cigarette move up and down to her mouth. It got brighter when she inhaled, and for a second Harry imagined that he was the cigarette, his entire body, and when she drew the smoke into her lungs, he felt himself slip inside her throat and slide down into her body. He felt the softness of her lips and the thick velvet of her tongue. 'So that SAT lady is pretty bad, huh.'

'Um, yes,' Ruby said. She gripped the cigarette in her teeth and pulled her hair to one side and wove it into a thick braid. 'She's a fuck-ing psycho.' Bingo opened his mouth in a wide, stinky yawn.

'Speaking of psychos, has Dust called you? Do I need to hire a bodyguard?' Harry tried to make his voice sound as light as possible, but he had been worried. Dust seemed like the kind of guy who had a lot of scary-looking friends who knew how to do things like get into fights, which Harry definitely, definitely did not.

'Oh, he's totally harmless,' Ruby said. 'I'm pretty sure.'

'What about your moms?' Harry said. There were ducks in the lake, swimming from one side to the other, and Harry wondered when ducks slept, and how long they lived with their parents. Then he wondered if kids who grew up in Manhattan thought ducks were mythological creatures, like cows, things that existed only in picture books and in cheese commercials. Or maybe they had ducks there, too, in the park. There were some kids at Whitman who took the train from the city every day, which seemed beyond stupid, like walking up the stairs to the top of the Empire State Building. There were easier ways to accomplish the same thing.

'They're probably getting divorced. I don't officially know that yet, but I know your mom does, so maybe you do, too.' He didn't. Ruby shrugged. 'It sucks.'

Harry had heard his mother tell his father about Ruby's mothers, but he hadn't been told directly, and so it was easy enough to pretend. 'I didn't know,' he said. 'I'm sorry.'

'It's their marriage, not mine,' Ruby said. 'I'm a modern girl. I know it's not my fault.'

'Still,' Harry said.

'Still,' Ruby allowed. She took another drag.

'Can I have some?' Harry asked.

Ruby cackled. 'Oh, shit,' she said. 'I thought you didn't smoke.' She held it out to him, upright, like a candle.

'I don't,' Harry said. He plucked the cigarette from between her fingers and put it up to his lips. The filter felt rough against his tongue. Was he supposed to lick it? Probably not. Harry inhaled – he had smoked weed before, after all, he wasn't a total noob. The smoke flooded his lungs, sharp and harsh. He coughed once and tried to swallow a few more, which just made him cough harder. Ruby hit him on the back. The dog offered a sympathetic snurfle.

'Ride that pony!' she said, laughing. 'Ride it!' Harry thrust the cigarette back at her, but she waved him off. 'No way,' she said. 'Not until you tame that beast.'

Harry waited for his breathing to return to normal and for his eyes to stop swimming, and then he tried again.

Eleven

In the age of the Internet, when his son couldn't walk three steps without checking his phone, Andrew appreciated a Xeroxed advertisement stapled to a telephone pole. Usually it was just ads for the nerdy guy who taught guitar lessons or for lost dogs or cats, but Andrew always looked. He was between jobs. Between careers, if you wanted to be specific. There was enough family money that he didn't have to worry too much, plus the royalties, plus Elizabeth's income, and so Andrew had spent his adulthood to date following his inspirations. A decade ago, he'd taken a cinematography course at the New School and had worked on some short films, including one about an abandoned mental hospital in the Palisades. Before that, he'd taught English as a Second Language at a high school in the Bronx, but that had only lasted a year. More recently, he'd been working on a lifestyle magazine for Brooklyn fathers, doing some editing and soliciting but mostly acting as a consultant. It was good to be around younger people – kept the blood flowing. Next, Andrew thought he'd do an apprenticeship at a butcher shop or with a woodworker. Something with his hands.

His usual routine was to get up with Harry and Elizabeth, send them off to school and work, and walk down to Cortelyou to get some coffee. Now that Harry was out for the summer, Andrew felt like it was even more important to keep busy. He ordered a small coffee and walked back out on to the street.

Ditmas Park was great in the summertime. The sycamores and oaks were full and wide, leaving big pools of shade along the sidewalks. Families were on their porches. Kids were throwing balls around and learning how to ride their bikes. Neighbors waved. Andrew ambled to the corner and waited for the light to change, feeling happily aimless. Harry would stay in his room for much of the day, taking SAT practice exams or playing video games or reading books, bless him. Even though that was the point of parenthood – to raise smart, happy, self-sufficient people, Andrew mourned the loss of the days when Harry cried out 'Daddy!' every time he walked in the door, even if he'd only been gone for ten minutes. Andrew was staring into space, thinking about Harry's two-year-old body, the hugs he would give at night before bed, when a flyer stapled to the pole next to the crosswalk caught his attention.

It was a drawing of a lotus flower, like the logo of a yoga studio, with hand-drawn petals. Underneath the flower, large block letters spelled out 'WE ARE HERE. ARE YOU?' Below that there was just an address on Stratford Road, three blocks from where Andrew was standing. No hours, no phone number, no website.

'Huh,' Andrew said. He thought about ripping it down so that he could hold on to it, but that would look bad. He didn't want any of his neighbors to see – they'd think he was either for or against it, when he didn't even know what it was. Instead, Andrew typed the address into his phone and crossed the street.

It was definitely going to be woodworking. The more he thought about it, the more sense it made. Butchering would mean vats of blood, saws, bones. Andrew wasn't squeamish, and he loved the idea of knowing more about where his food came from, but a rooftop vegetable farm was probably more his speed. That didn't appeal, though. Vegetables took too long. Andrew had always liked a simpler equation;

he wanted to see the payoff before an entire season had passed. When he and Elizabeth met, he'd worked in the school's bike co-op, fixing old beaters that careless students had left locked outside over the summer, and he'd loved his dirty, greasy hands at the end of the day. The spinning wheels. Woodworking – carpentry – would be like that. He would have calluses and maybe burns. He would whack a fingernail by accident, and it would turn black. That was just what he was looking for. He'd build a desk for Harry, a new pair of end tables for their bedroom. Maybe they could do it together.

Elizabeth's professional problem was the opposite – instead of Andrew's searching, she had the answer but chose to ignore it. It was a lost cause at this point, though he did coax her to start playing again by saying that he wanted to do it. She would do it for him, he knew, but not for herself. His wife was a true talent – unusual, smart, gifted – all the words that places like Whitman loved to throw around to describe perfectly ordinary students. But Elizabeth wasn't ordinary. She was incredible, and she had stopped playing for such practical reasons, as if practicality had anything to do with it.

Instead of turning right and walking back home, Andrew turned left and walked to Stratford. He never walked in that direction – it was toward the gas stations and the one bar that had recently opened that he hadn't been to yet. Come to think of it, the bar wasn't that new anymore, it was probably a year old, but he still hadn't been. Andrew turned right on Stratford and walked another block – he was now parallel with his own house, only two blocks east.

The house had once been white but was now the color of dirty city snow. The windows were old; Andrew could tell just by looking at the outside. He'd learned a lot about houses from Elizabeth, what to look for. Together, they'd been inside most of the houses in the neighborhood. The steps were sinking in the middle, and the floorboards of the porch were cracked. It wasn't a hard fix, but it would be expensive, especially if they got soft enough that the mailman fell through and decided to sue. Andrew hovered for a minute on the sidewalk, not sure what he was going to do. He should go home and start his day. Zoe knew a guy who built things, some kid from Maine who lived in the neighborhood and built dining-room tables for people in Cobble Hill and Brooklyn Heights. Andrew was going to give him a call. The door to the house was open, and Andrew could see another flyer taped above the doorbell. He took one step toward the house, and then stopped. He could see a man inside. The guy had a beard, not quite ZZ Top but heading that way. It was impossible to tell how old he was. The man turned toward the door, saw Andrew, and waved as if he'd been expecting him. Andrew waved back, then climbed the stairs to introduce himself.

'Welcome,' the man said. From close up, he looked younger than Andrew had thought, maybe not even forty. His beard was speckled with red and gray hairs, like a duck egg that was so beautiful and complicated that you couldn't believe it just happened that way, with no intervention from a design team.

'I saw your poster,' Andrew said. Inside, the house itself was nothing special – sort of falling down, really, but the floors were clean and painted white, as were all the walls. The thin curtains were pulled to the side, and light came pouring in. Andrew immediately felt at home.

'This is EVOLVEment,' the man said. 'I'm Dave. Come on in.' He spoke softly, the way that people did when they knew others were going to listen. There was no reason to speak loudly, not in this house. Andrew got it right away. This was calm. This was a sanctuary. He thought about the monks he'd seen in Tibet, and upstate, when he'd gone for silent retreats. This was one of those special places, or it was going to be, and right here, in his own neighborhood.

'What can I do?' Andrew asked. His hands were empty. He wanted to help.

Twelve

Hyacinth sat forty-two people. On a good day, the restaurant was half full at lunch and then busy from six p.m. until nine thirty p.m., with stragglers hanging around the long, narrow bar until eleven, when they closed. Even ten years after opening, Jane couldn't charge what she wanted to charge – no one would pay twenty-seven dollars for skate this deep in – but she got by. There was a small desk right next to the hostess stand, and that's where Jane liked to sit when she wasn't in the kitchen, or upstairs in the office, or downstairs checking the walk-in, or walking the floor, which the servers hated. Jane had to wedge her body in between the wall and desk to keep from getting elbowed by the hostess, but she didn't mind.

She had sous-chefs now, good people whose taste buds she trusted, but there was no substitute to being in the room herself. Jane liked to sweat, and to yell, and there was no better place to do that than in a tiny restaurant kitchen. Elizabeth had found the space – they had looked for months, waiting for the right place, and Elizabeth had taken it on like her own little pet project. They didn't just look in Ditmas, though that's what they wanted, of course. There would be less foot traffic, but they both loved the idea of helping make the neighborhood a place where people wanted to *live*, not just sleep. Jane and Zoe had fallen in love eating food, talking about food, about what they dreamed of eating down the block from their door. Zoe was old-fashioned and wanted to open a French bistro, somewhere to eat steak frites at night and soft eggs during the day. Jane wanted to do Thai, or better yet, Vietnamese. There was nothing in the neighborhood but pizza and a Chinese place with bulletproof glass in front of the cashier. There were so many holes, and they wanted to fill one.

They'd looked everywhere – in Williamsburg, in Carroll Gardens. Nothing was right. But when Elizabeth called and said she'd found the space, Jane could hear in her voice that she was right – she and Zoe walked over holding hands, giddy. Hyacinth was one of their girl names, for when Ruby had a little sister, but Ruby was already in first grade and it didn't seem like she was going to get a sister after all, so Hyacinth went up on the wooden sign and got painted in gold leaf on the door, and they were open for business.

Jane was in charge of food, and Zoe was in charge of everything else. She picked out the chairs and the water glasses, the flatware and the floral arrangements. She did the payroll and the billing. She dealt with the staff, which was the worst part of owning a small business – someone was always getting fired, or showing up late, or hitting on too many customers, or on drugs. As long as they didn't need money or sleep, life was easy. Ruby's babysitter would bring her straight to Hyacinth after school, and when they couldn't afford the babysitter anymore, Ruby would come on her own, and sit at the bar with her homework. Elizabeth and Andrew would pat her on the head, and she'd join them for some french fries. The regulars loved it – their own little Brooklyn Eloise. After dark, Zoe would take her home and put her to bed and then come back if they were really in the weeds. They had an elderly neighbor who fancied herself the mayor of Argyle Road, and both Jane and Zoe felt sure that she would never let anything bad happen to Ruby while they were out.

It was early, just after nine. They didn't open for lunch until eleven. Jane shut the window with her menus and her lists for the purveyors and opened the Internet. She wasn't really looking for a new place to live, not yet. Once Ruby left, wherever and whenever that happened, and when Zo found a place she liked, then she'd look. If it really happened. Jane wasn't in a rush. If it were up to her, they'd stay married forever. So what if they weren't as happy as they'd ever been? They were adults, with a nearly grown child. 'Happy' was a word for sorority girls and clowns, and those were two distinctly fucked-up groups of people. They were just wading through the muck like everyone else.

At twenty-four, Zoe Bennett was the sexiest thing Jane had ever seen. They met at Mary Mary's, on Fifth Avenue, a proper lesbian dive bar that was always full of service professionals, especially after midnight. Jane went two, sometimes three times a week and rarely did more than drink beer with her friends, but one night, this electric little nymph shows up at the end of the bar, pirouetting around like she owned the place, and by the end of the night, she did. Jane was working as a garde-manger at the Union Square Cafe, and Zoe was a hostess at Chanterelle. They didn't even talk that first night – Jane swore that Zoe fell on to her lap while singing along to a Bonnie Raitt song on the jukebox, but Zoe didn't remember doing any such thing. They were both lushes, ready to eat and drink until the reservoir was empty and the lights were on. Three weeks later, Jane moved in.

The bell over the door rang, and Jane looked up. Johnny, her UPS man. He wheeled in a tower of boxes – paper towels, toilet paper, all the things she never wanted to have to think about. That was Zoe's job, keeping them stocked and ready for the apocalypse. They hadn't figured that part out yet – what about Hyacinth? It would be strange for Zoe to keep doing her job, but it would be stranger for her to stop. Everything was in both of their names. They didn't need to be married for them to keep working together, of course, but what if Zoe started sleeping with Allie, the adorable hostess? They always joked about her, about how she was in love with Zo, but now, if she were single, what if it were true? Jane could see it so clearly – peeking out of the kitchen and seeing Zoe touch Allie on the back, or tuck her hair behind her ear. Maybe Jane would fire her before Zoe got the chance – she wasn't great at her job anyway. It wasn't part of Jane's job, dealing with personnel, but she was the chef – everything was her job, really.

'Hey, hey,' Johnny said. He nodded toward the supply closet. 'Want it over there?'

'Please,' Jane said. She wasn't just talking to him, she was beseeching the universe. When Johnny was gone, she locked herself in the bathroom and cried. It was the only room with a door that locked. She'd told her mother that they were considering splitting – not any friends, not the staff, no one else. Jane thought that if no one ever found out, it might not really happen, the way they didn't tell anyone that Zoe was pregnant until she was four months along, or like when Jane was sixteen and knew she was gay but didn't come out until she was twenty. If it really happened, her parents were going to be crushed – they'd always loved Zoe, her mother in particular. Maybe Jane could avoid talking to them entirely for a few months, or a year. Maybe they didn't have to speak until Ruby got married, at which point they might be eighty and hard of hearing and not fully understand. Maybe she could wait until they were dead.

Someone knocked on the door to the bathroom. 'Yeah,' Jane said. She stared at herself in the mirror. She was over fifty, with moles she'd been meaning to get checked out and a lone chin hair that sprouted up again every time she plucked it. Life was a fucking disaster, but it was time to organize the lunch prep and to call the butcher, and so Jane unlocked the door.

Thirteen

The Mary Ann O'Connell Realty Group was a boutique firm, with just five agents. Elizabeth was the only one who didn't have the last name O'Connell – in addition to eighty-three-year-old Mary Ann, there were her two children, Sean and Bridget, plus Sean's wife, Deirdre. The office was on the corner of Cortelyou and East Sixteenth Street, half a block from the rumbling Q train. Elizabeth and Deirdre shared a desk, which Elizabeth had always found a bit odd, that Sean would rather share a workspace with his sister than with his wife, but the O'Connells were nothing if not odd, and so it was to be expected. Family businesses were deeply complicated organisms, and it was almost always best to stay as far away from the decision-making processes as possible. Elizabeth would happily have worked from home, as she had when Harry was young, but Mary Ann got nervous when she didn't see her crew hard at work or hear the jingle of keys as they left for a day of showings. Her office was in the back, and the door was never closed. When you came in or went out, even if it was just to get a sandwich, Mary Ann's white corona of hair would begin to vibrate slightly, like a rung bell. Deirdre liked to joke that her mother-in-law had been struck by lightning as a child and the jolt reappeared whenever she thought she was about to make money. She also liked to joke that the only reason she and Sean were allowed to get married was that on paper she (born in Trinidad) sounded as Irish as he did. Deirdre was the only O'Connell whose company Elizabeth actually enjoyed.

It was a glorious day outside – not yet the full summer warmth, but balmy enough for people to bare their arms and legs without the fear of goose pimples. Those windows of time were so short in New York City, which was in all ways a place of extremes. They'd thought about leaving, for that reason among many others, but the steadiness of California's seventy-two-degree days didn't appeal either. It was good to have things to complain about, to build character. Elizabeth leaned back in her chair and admired what she could see of the day through the window. The three desks were arranged by seniority, which meant that Elizabeth, a company veteran of only a decade, was sitting three feet from the sidewalk outside.

Sean walked in from lunch after a morning full of showings – early summer was always their biggest season, and inventory was high. The bell tinkled, and Elizabeth heard Mary Ann start asking Sean questions before he'd passed fully through the doorway. He nodded a greeting at Elizabeth and kept walking into his mother's office. Her cell phone rang, and Elizabeth answered without looking at the caller ID.

'Hello?' she said. There was a pause, then a click.

'Holding for Naomi Vandenhoovel,' a young woman on the other end said.

'Excuse me?' Elizabeth said. She put a finger in her right ear to block out a fire truck roaring down the street. 'Hello?'

'Lizzzzzzzy,' another voice said. 'Thank you so much for speaking with me. I so appreciate it.'

'I'm sorry, who is this?' Elizabeth swiveled her chair away from the window. The whole office dotted with sunspots. 'This is Elizabeth Marx,' she said, wondering if someone had called the wrong Elizabeth, scrolling quickly through the E section of her contacts.

'Elizabeth, it's *Naomi*. Naomi *Vandenhoovel*. I've been in touch about the rights for the Lydia biopic. I work for the studio. We've e-mailed.'

'Oh, Naomi, yes,' Elizabeth said. She turned back around and opened her e-mail, frantically searching for Naomi's most recent missive. 'I've been meaning to get back to you.'

'Listen, Elizabeth, I know it seems crazy, after all this time, to just sign over the rights to your work and to your story, but this is a go picture. Do you know how hard it is to get a movie made these days?' There was a whooshing sound. 'Sorry, I'm in my car. Let me close the window.'

'But how did you call me from your car? Your person just had me on hold!' Elizabeth was asking a serious question, but Naomi only laughed.

'I know, right?' she said. 'Anyway, we really need the song. You know we need the song. And the life rights. I know that sounds scary – like, *LIFE RIGHTS*, but it's just a fancy term for agreeing for there to be a character who may or may not have anything in common with you. Really. I can give you a few more weeks to work on your husband, but that's really it. They want to start shooting in the fall. Don't you want millions of teenage girls to go to the movies and see some badass fucking chicks playing rock 'n' roll? Like, wahhhhhhh on the whammy bar, or whatever, you know? Don't you want to be an inspiration? Forget about Lydia – just think about a girl in the middle of nowhere who thinks life is sucky and boring and then she sees this movie at the mall and she goes and buys a guitar and starts writing songs in her bedroom.'

Elizabeth closed her eyes. She hadn't been able to talk to Andrew about Lydia at all. He'd gone to extraordinary lengths to avoid the conversation – he'd booked dentist appointments, taken their otherwise neglected car in for an oil change. This imaginary girl in her bedroom, though. That might work. Her life saved by music, by the movie, by them! It was certainly working on Elizabeth. She felt tiny tears forming, as suddenly as with a truly excellent Kleenex commercial. 'I'll try.'

'I'll send over the forms again. The world needs to see this story, and to hear your song. Anecdotally, it's my favorite song of all time. I'm sure you hear that a lot, but it's true. I have the chorus tattooed on my rib cage.'

'You don't,' Elizabeth said, though it wasn't the first time she'd heard of such a thing. Once she'd seen a whole slide show of them on BuzzFeed.

'I do!' Naomi said. 'I'll send you a photo.'

'You really don't have to,' Elizabeth said.

'Oh, I want to! It looks fucking great!'

Elizabeth's e-mail dinged, and she swiveled around to look. Sure enough, there was a rib cage with the words *I will be calm calm calm calm* in cursive. 'Wow,' Elizabeth said. 'Wait, how did you just send that, aren't you driving?'

'I was so tan this summer, it was sick,' Naomi said, ignoring the question. California was a terrifying place. 'Anyway, sign the forms and get them back to me as soon as you can, okay? Thank you so, so much.'

'I will,' Elizabeth said, not meaning to agree, but just that she'd let her know. She was nothing if not polite. Harry was always teasing her for calling to cancel restaurant reservations or appointments at the Apple Store Genius Bar. *No one cares, Mom,* he'd say, but Elizabeth believed in courtesy. She waited for Naomi to say more, but realized she was already gone.

Fourteen

The garage was unfinished – unlike some of their neighbors', who had converted the spaces into playrooms or offices, and put in plumbing and heat and wood floors, Andrew and Elizabeth had the old-fashioned kind, with rusting shovels and half-empty cans of paint. They pulled the car in only when huge snowstorms were expected – otherwise, the large center of the space was empty, with a rug from Andrew's parents' house and two creaky wooden chairs. Elizabeth's small Marshall amp was on her side, and Andrew's boxy Orange amp was on his. Andrew rolled the garage door high enough for them to walk under, and then slid it halfway back down to the ground. People walking along the sidewalk could see their legs, maybe, but only if they were really looking, and there were far more exciting things to look at. Middle-aged rock 'n' roll hobbyists were about as thrilling as old ladies gardening, and significantly more embarrassing. Andrew knew how things looked.

He had his notebook with him. He'd been writing things down, not whole lyrics but ideas for songs. Elizabeth was much better at making things sound good. She had a notebook full of lyrics, too, or at least she used to. Now her notebook was filled with this couple or that's likes and dislikes, their contingencies, the size of their bank accounts.

'Want to play that one from the other day, the bum-bum-bum-*ting* one?' Elizabeth asked. She settled into her chair and pulled her guitar on to her lap. She plugged it in and slid the strap over her shoulder. Andrew loved the way his wife looked with a pick between her teeth. It went straight to the very essence of him. Once, in high school, his history teacher had gone on an epic tangent about how Barbara Stanwyck was his 'sexual profile,' and everyone got extremely creeped out, but that was how Andrew felt about women who played the guitar. It didn't matter if they were really good or really bad or just holding one. If they could really play, forget it – he was done. It was deeply sexist, and so he'd never said it out loud (that was what Oberlin had been good for, teaching him that most things men thought on a daily basis were rooted in sexism), but it was true. With Elizabeth, it wasn't just that she could play, but that she was really fucking good at it.

'What?' Elizabeth said, the pick still between her teeth.

'Nothing,' Andrew said. He grabbed his bass by the neck. 'Sure, let's play that one.'

'Actually, honey, I meant to tell you – the people called about Lydia again.' Elizabeth puckered her lips. 'Can we talk about it? We're supposed to let them know soon.'

A garbage truck clattered down the street, its brakes squealing every thirty feet. Andrew let go of his bass and ran his fingers back and forth through his hair. 'I just don't like the idea of signing a piece of paper that hands over the control to some giant corporation. Next it'll be in a Kleenex commercial.'

'I'm pretty sure that we can stipulate exactly how they can use it,' Elizabeth said. 'The movie is about Lydia, not about us. They don't care about us, honey.' She leaned the smooth back of the guitar against her sternum.

'That's exactly my problem,' Andrew said. 'You didn't write those words for Lydia to sing. We didn't write that song to have teenage girls in the mall in New Jersey pretend to be punk.'

'You mean like teenage boys who grew up in Manhattan pretended to be punk?' She rolled her eyes. 'Pot, kettle.'

'It was the eighties! I wasn't pretending! I was fucking angry, and the fact that my parents were Reagan-loving demons had a lot to do with that. Come on, Lizzy.' Andrew crossed his arms over his chest and took a few deep breaths. 'I just don't want to contribute to some soft-focus portrait of Lydia Greenbaum as some kind of folk hero. Why should we help them?'

'Because they'll give us money?'

'Are you really that cheap?'

Elizabeth felt the words as acutely as a slap. 'Excuse me? Andrew, I understand that you and I feel differently about this, but the fact that I am willing to get paid a very healthy additional fee for work I did two decades ago does not make me cheap. Harry is going to go to college, you realize. Soon. This house needs twelve new windows. Our basement is a resort for cockroaches. We could use this money – the Marx family trust doesn't have to pay for our lives, you know. I'm not being greedy.' She started to sweat. 'And it's not just about Lydia, you know, or us, even. It's about being inspiring to young women, to girls who feel like maybe they could play music, too. Like that Girls Rock Camp or whatever.'

When they'd met, in Ohio, so far away from their families and from their real lives, there was no way to tell that Andrew had money and that she didn't. Everyone was exactly the same. They all wore thrift-store clothes and carried bags from the army/navy supply shop. Elizabeth had always thought her parents' house was normal – nice, even – until Andrew reluctantly brought her home for a visit during their senior year's winter term.

They drove Elizabeth's car – Andrew didn't have a license, nor did he seem to have a sense of how to get around. He kept directing Elizabeth to go one way and then cursing when he realized he'd sent them in the wrong direction. They spent an extra hour driving in circles in

New Jersey before finally finding the Lincoln Tunnel, then another hour crawling through traffic to the Upper East Side. Elizabeth drove with her shoulders hunched over the wheel, looking for a parking spot on the quiet, dark streets.

'This is where your parents live?' she'd asked, when he pointed out the building. It was on the corner of Seventy-ninth and Park Avenue, with a giant metal sculpture of a cat out front. They lugged their bags into the lobby, all marble and spotless black countertops. A doorman with a cap hurried to help them and greeted Andrew by name.

'Yeah,' he'd said, mortified. That night, when they curled up together on his childhood bed, in a room that overlooked Central Park, he'd told her how he fantasized about running away, about hopping on trains or sleeping on a bench in Tompkins Square. At Oberlin, Andrew majored in religion and was doing his senior thesis on Hindu goddesses. He wanted to move to Nepal. He wanted to sleep on the floor. He told Elizabeth over and over again how little his parents' wealth mattered to him, and when she said that she was hungry, he called a diner on Lexington Avenue and had them send over scrambled eggs.

'I'm sure your parents have eggs in the kitchen,' she'd protested, but Andrew insisted that the diner's were better. Elizabeth thought about those eggs on an annual basis, if not more often – still warm, and yes, delicious – and how they told her more than Andrew ever could about how he'd grown up. Sometimes even the brightest people had truly no idea.

'We don't have to decide today,' Elizabeth said, shaking her head. 'You play, I'm going to make lunch.' She put her guitar back on its stand, clicked the amplifier off, and walked out of the garage.

Fifteen

This time, Eliza and Thayer didn't even pretend to say hello to Harry. They turned, saw him walk in with Ruby, and continued their conversation with no visible break. Rebecca, their fearless leader, was shuffling papers on her makeshift desk beneath the projection screen. Thick blue mats that the karate school used to teach people how to not get murdered by ninjas were still out, and a few kids in the class were doing somersaults.

'Oh, they are *totally* getting into Harvard,' Ruby said.

'I think that one looks more like a Yalie,' Harry said, pointing to one guy who had toppled over on to his side. 'Maybe Princeton.'

'Barf,' Ruby said.

This was the only way that Ruby would talk about the future. She knew that Harry must be wondering why she was taking the class – no one took an SAT prep class for fun, especially not after their senior year – but Ruby never volunteered any information. She made fun of everyone who was going to good schools, but she also made fun of everyone who was going to big party schools and everyone who was going to tiny liberal-arts schools. It was open season on everyone but her. It wasn't anyone's business. So what if she'd applied to eight schools and not gotten into any of them? It didn't make her a bad person, it made the admissions committees look like idiot snobs who deserved to be covered in honey and walked into the bear cage at the zoo. There wasn't even really a point to going to college, not anymore, not for her. The thought of sitting through another four years of bullshit lectures about things that happened and books that were written hundreds of years ago was the world's biggest waste of time and money. Ruby's personal essay had been to that effect, and it appeared to have accomplished its goal. If either of her parents had thought to proofread her applications, they might not be in this pickle. She'd written the essay half as a joke, but then the joke had turned into her actual life. Ruby was sure that someone would stop her eventually. When she clicked the button to send in her applications, knowing what the attached documents looked like, Ruby kissed college good-bye. She wasn't surprised when the applications were all rejected. At first, her mothers didn't even know, because they were waiting for letters to show up in the mail, not realizing that nowadays letters only showed up if the news was good.

'Wait, that's actually the best idea,' Ruby said.

'What is?' Harry asked. They were standing four feet inside the door. Rebecca clicked on her computer, and a drawing of a cat taking the SATs popped up on the projection screen.

Ruby folded over herself, her hands clutching her stomach. 'Oh, no,' she said. 'Rebecca, I really need to go home, I think I'm going to throw up.'

Thayer and Eliza turned around, their mouths open. Harry folded over in sympathy. 'Are you okay?' he said, their faces both upside down. Ruby winked.

'Is it okay if I make sure she gets home?' Harry said, righting himself. Rebecca hustled over with some handouts. Ruby made a sound, dark and low and rumbling, that sounded like an approaching subway. No one wanted to see what was on that train.

'Of course,' Rebecca said, pulling the corners of her mouth down into a cartoon pout. 'Feel better, okay!' She patted Harry on the back.

Ruby grabbed on to Harry's wrist. 'We have to get out of here right now, or else I am going to puke all over the dojo,' she said. 'What belt would that get me?' Harry let her lead him out the door. Ruby kept moaning until they'd crossed Church Avenue and rounded the corner. Even though they were now out of sight, Ruby went over to a waiting mailbox and pretended to vomit into it, complete with sound effects. Then she stood straight up and took a deep, graceful bow. Harry looked at her with awe, and Ruby saw the rest of her summer in his face: he could be her project, her hobby, her doll.

'I'm hungry,' she said. 'Do your parents have food?'

'Your parents own a restaurant,' Harry said.

'Which is exactly why they never have food. I can tell you right now what's in the fridge: yogurt, three different kinds of fish sauce, and pâté.' Ruby had once searched online for a support group for children of those in the food-service industry, for kids like her who'd never been allowed to eat milk chocolate or Cheez Whiz or Marshmallow Fluff or the extra-sweet supermarket peanut butter, but she hadn't found anything.

'I think we have some chips and salsa,' Harry said.

'That'll do.'

The living room was empty when they walked in. Harry called out 'Hello?' but his parents didn't respond. It was nine forty a.m. 'My mom's got some open houses, I think,' Harry said. 'I don't know where my dad is.'

'Whatever,' Ruby said, and walked straight into the kitchen. 'If he comes home, just tell him that I got sick, and that your house was closer, so we came here.'

'Like fifty feet closer.'

'If you're barfing, fifty feet is a lot of feet.'

'I guess that's true.'

Ruby loved being in other people's kitchens. Her mothers were such total freaks – the salt had to be a special kind of salt, unless it was for baking, in which case it had to be some very particular kind of normal salt, that sort of thing. Elizabeth and Andrew were just regular. They had Diet Cokes and a giant block of orange cheddar cheese. Ruby took the jar of salsa and the bag of chips off the counter. 'Want to go to your room?'

'S-sure,' Harry said. Iggy Pop slowly climbed down from his perch over the refrigerator, and Harry scooped him up and held him like a baby. Ruby walked past the two of them toward the staircase.

Ruby hadn't been upstairs in the Marxes' house since she was little, but not much had changed. The walls were still a very pale orange, like a melted Popsicle after a rainstorm, and the same pictures were on the walls. There was one painting hanging by the door to Harry's bedroom that Ruby had always liked, a village scene, with a Japanese woman watering some flowers in one corner and some free-range chickens in another. The Marxes' house was always neat. Everything had its place. Unlike Ruby's mum, who came home from every trip with some colorful trinket to put on a shelf to gather dust forever and ever, Elizabeth and Andrew seemed to have no useless objects. Ruby wandered down the hallway, poking her head into rooms.

'My room's over here,' Harry said, behind her.

'I know,' Ruby said, still walking. 'What's this?' She stopped in front of an open door – the smallest room in the house.

'It's the guest room,' Harry said. 'The couch folds out. Plus, it's just, like, storage, I guess.'

Ruby walked in, and over to the metal shelving along the wall. There were big clear plastic bins, each of them labeled. She ran her finger along the bins. 'Wow, your mom is kind of OCD, huh.' Harry shuffled in after her and sat down on the couch, his hands in his lap. Iggy Pop, who had darted up the stairs after them, jumped into his lap.

'I don't think so,' he said. 'She's just organized.'

'Is this what that looks like?' Ruby asked. 'Oh, shit, wow!'

Harry stood up quickly, sending Iggy back to the ground. 'What? Is there a mouse?'

Ruby turned around to look at him, her purple hair flying. 'Why would I say "wow" if I saw a mouse, you weirdo? No, look, it's all Kitty's Mustache stuff.' She pulled one of the bins on the top shelf down to the floor and unlatched the lid. The box was filled with stuff – flyers and cassettes and seven-inches and posters and zines and college newspapers with reviews of their shows. Ruby leafed through the pile on top and pulled out a glossy photograph. 'Check this shit,' she said.

From left to right, it was a picture of Lydia, Andrew, Zoe and Elizabeth. None of them smiled or looked at the camera. Her mum was wearing a suede jacket with fringe and had a cigarette dangling out of her mouth, like a pissed-off movie star who'd just come back from a bender in the desert. Elizabeth was wearing a floor-length black skirt, with dark lipstick, her then-long blond hair tucked behind her ears, her body pointed toward the rest of the band. Andrew wore a white shirt and a flannel tied around his waist, his hair curling past his shoulders. Lydia was sitting cross-legged on the ground, holding her drumsticks in an X over her head.

'When is this from?' Harry said, taking the picture out of Ruby's hands.

'Ninety-two,' Ruby said, pointing to the date in the corner, in Elizabeth's handwriting. 'OCD.'

'They're so young,' Harry said. 'It's kind of horrifying. Look at my dad's jeans. And his hair!'

'Look at my mum's boobs!' Ruby pointed. Zoe wasn't wearing a bra, and her nipples were clearly visible, even across time and space and this many years. Harry covered his eyes. 'And look at Lydia.'

It was weird, knowing that your mother had had a life before you were born, but everyone had to deal with that eventually. Everyone's mother had had sex at least once, and lots of people's mothers had gotten drunk and been wild. Ruby knew she wasn't alone. But it was extra weird to know that your mother had been drunk and wild with someone famous. And not someone famous for no reason, like the stars of a reality show, but someone actually famous and important because she was really good at what she did and people loved her. Ruby pretended that she didn't care about Lydia because she knew that her mum would find it . . . annoying? Amusing? Her mum would have thought it was adorable. That was the worst fate of all, for your parents to look at you with their parent eyes and to call your inner turmoil cute. Zoe would have loved it if she knew that Ruby had Lydia's two solo albums on her phone and that she listened to them when she walked down the street by herself, that they made her feel invincible and angry, but there was no way in hell that Ruby was ever going to tell her.

Ruby shuffled through the stack of posters and photos on top. There were a few more of the band, including one with Lydia standing in the middle with her mouth open in a scream, the rest of the band standing diagonally behind her. Unlike the others, this photo actually looked like Lydia, the real Lydia, the Lydia whose face would be taped on bedroom walls and printed on T-shirts.

'Do you know how much money we could get for this on eBay?' Ruby said. Her mum sometimes sold her old clothes on eBay, vintage dresses she'd had for decades and finally decided she didn't need.

'No,' Harry said.

'Well, good thing you have me,' Ruby said. Her hobby was paying off already.

Sixteen

Andrew had waited until Harry left for his class, and then slid his feet into his rubber-bottomed slippers and walked quickly to Stratford Road. This time, he didn't hesitate before walking up the stairs and into the house. The sign was still outside – WE ARE HERE, ARE YOU? – but now Andrew knew the answer. He was.

Dave was in charge, if anyone was in charge, but it wasn't that kind of place. EVOLVEment was a co-op, and everyone who lived there worked there, too. It wasn't about ownership, or hierarchy. It was about people, and mindfulness.

A young man with a beard and skinny legs said hello and offered Andrew a cup of tea.

'Is Dave around?' Andrew asked.

'Have a seat wherever you like, make yourself comfortable,' the man said. Normally, Andrew would have been annoyed that the guy hadn't actually answered his question, but that was how things worked around here, he got it. There were stacks of cushions on the floor. Andrew took one, plopped it down next to a wall, and sat. He was happy to wait. A few other young people flitted around quietly, all of them in bare feet. Andrew pulled off his slippers and tucked them under his knees. After a few minutes, there was some laughter at the top of the stairs, and then Dave was walking toward Andrew with a huge smile, like he'd been expecting him.

'Nice to see you again, Andrew,' Dave said. He was short and stocky, like a gymnast, densely packed. Dave lowered himself down next to Andrew and touched him on the shoulder. They were only a few inches apart, as close as you'd be to a stranger on the subway, but in the big, open room, it felt remarkably intimate, as if Dave had stroked Andrew's cheek with the back of his finger.

'Sure,' Andrew said. He felt himself blush a little bit. 'I'm interested.'

And he was – Andrew was interested in philosophy, and the mind-body connection. He was interested in getting out of his own house and his own brain, seeing if he could link up to something outside, like the cables that ran between houses. He was interested in channeling his anger into something else, into a color, into air, into positivity. It was that kind of talk that Andrew's parents hated: they didn't give a shit about process, they only cared about the bottom line. His whole childhood had been wasted that way, bouncing from one after-school enrichment class to another, from one prep school to the next, as if those places were actually preparing him for anything other than a corporate job, where he was sure to be surrounded by all the same people he'd grown up with. Those people made him feel sick to his stomach, their chinos and boat shoes, their scuffed leather luggage with their initials on the side. No one cared about anything except whether the boat was going to be ready for Memorial Day. They were shitty to women and to the people hired to help their lives run smoothly. All Andrew had ever dreamed about was living somewhere with the barter system, someplace where money meant nothing unless it was all in the collective pool. His Oberlin co-op had been his wet dream, everyone cooking tofu together and baking dense little brown loaves of bread. If Elizabeth had been less type-A, and if they hadn't had a baby, they'd still be living like that, with Zoe or whomever. Not that he'd trade a moment with Harry for anything in the world – if he'd done one thing right in his life, it was being a dad, Andrew knew that much for sure. Everything else was the problem. Andrew wanted to push every angry feeling he had down into his stomach and cover it with mulch and love until it was a goddamn flower bed.

The house – Dave's house, the collective – was really coming together. The front rooms were used for yoga and meditation classes, open to anyone. If you came to class, or to meditate, or to qigong, someone would slide a finger with essential oils over your temples and you'd go home smelling like lavender and orange and eucalyptus. They were working on getting the permits or the licenses to serve food, but that seemed legally complicated. It might just be juice. Dave was from California, and it showed. He talked like the words were stuck in the back of his throat and he had to coax each one out individually. In his most secret thoughts, Andrew believed that he should have been born to a surfing family, the kind who traveled up and down the California-Mexico coast, sleeping in a Winnebago on the beach. Dave didn't say, but Andrew was sure that was his story. Sand in a sleeping bag, the waves crashing at night.

A few young women in yoga clothes came into the room. Dave said hello to them, and the women began to roll out a number of yoga mats at the other end of the room, gently placing blankets and blocks beside each place. The women looked no older than Ruby, but then again, Andrew was always surprised by people's ages now. When he was a teenager, anyone over the age of twenty looked like a grown-up, with boring clothes and a blurry face, only slightly more invisible than Charlie Brown's teacher, but life had changed. Now everyone looked equally young, as if they could be twenty or thirty or even flirting with forty, and he couldn't tell the difference. Maybe it was just that he was now staring in the opposite direction.

'We're about to have class,' Dave said. 'You should stay.' He patted Andrew on the shoulder again and then stood up and walked over to the women at the front of the room, crouching between them and touching them both on their shoulder blades. Then Dave stood up again and pulled off his T-shirt, displaying his bare chest. He picked up a blanket off a stack, unfolded it, refolded it in a different way, and dropped down to his knees. Dave cupped his hands together on the blanket, nestled the crown of his head into the web of his fingers, and then slowly raised his legs up behind him until he was standing on his head.

The two women turned around and nodded at Andrew. One of them pulled her hair into a ponytail, and the other began to stretch, shifting her body this way and that.

'Okay,' Andrew said, not sure what was about to happen. He crawled forward on to one of the yoga mats on the floor. More people filtered in and took the spaces around him, and pretty soon the room was full – ten people, maybe twelve. At the front of the room, Dave lowered himself back down and came to a lotus position. He lit a few candles and began to chant so quietly that Andrew wasn't sure if it was him or a passing car, a low rumble that got louder and louder until all the other voices joined in and Andrew could feel the room begin to vibrate. He closed his eyes. Elizabeth would have laughed, but Andrew loved it. It reminded him of when he was little and his older cousins would use him as their hairdressing doll, braiding and brushing his hair for what felt like hours, how good their fingers felt on his scalp. Andrew had tried reiki before, and that's what was happening in the room: energy was being pushed around and manipulated in order to heal. He was being healed, even before Dave stopped chanting and asked them to put their hands on their knees and set an intention for their practice. Andrew's intention came to him, clear as a bell: Be here. Be here. Be here. And when Dave asked them all to move into downward-facing-dog pose, Andrew did. He was the oldest person in the room, and he was going to be whatever he was told. Maybe EVOLVEment needed some shelves built for the yoga equipment, or a small table for the candles so that they didn't sit on the floor. Andrew was going to meditate on it.

Seventeen

Elizabeth backed out of her driveway and drove the four-second commute to Zoe's house. She didn't even need to put the car in park – Zoe was waiting out front, wearing a sundress and a large, floppy hat, and she bounded into the front seat like an excited puppy.

'So, what's up first?' Zoe took off her hat and held it in her lap. 'I feel very weird about this, but I really want to do it, so just pretend that I'm a regular client and not just your friend having a midlife crisis, okay?'

'You're the boss, boss. First up are two apartments in Fort Greene,' Elizabeth said. 'Very different vibes. The first one is in the Williamsburgh Savings Bank, with a view to die for, very mod. The second one is a floor-through in a brownstone on Adelphi. Both are really, really nice.' She turned on her blinker and made the left on to Cortelyou, heading toward Flatbush. 'Close to the train, close to restaurants, all that stuff.' She looked over at Zoe. 'And if you want to stop, we'll stop, okay?'

'Sounds good to me,' Zoe said. She twisted the rings on her fingers. 'What else can we see?'

'There are a couple of condos on the water in Williamsburg, and one in Dumbo.'

'I think I'm too old for Williamsburg.'

'You're retro,' Elizabeth said. 'You're like a cassette tape. They'll go crazy for you.'

Zoe slumped over, pretending to be wounded. 'Ack,' she said. 'Thank you.'

'No, come on,' Elizabeth said. 'You're just going to get the lay of the land, see what feels good. It'll be fun.'

'Okay,' Zoe said. She flipped down the mirror and patted the skin under her eyes. 'Do I look really tired? I have been sleeping like shit. Like absolute shit.' She turned toward Elizabeth. 'Tell me the truth.'

Elizabeth waited for a red light and then swiveled as much as she could in the driver's seat. Zoe did look tired – but they all did. It felt like a minute ago that they could stay up until two in the morning and still look like normal, well-adjusted human beings the next day. Now when she didn't sleep, no amount of drugstore makeup could disguise the bags under her eyes, and that's how Zoe looked, too, even beautiful Zoe.

'You do look a little tired,' Elizabeth admitted.

'Fuck, I knew it,' Zoe said. 'I swear to God, it's all a plot. Jane is trying to make me look like a hideous monster so that no one will ever want to sleep with me ever again, and I'll just pretend to forget that we're unhappy, and then nothing will ever change, and we'll just be sad, lonely eighty-year-olds before you know it.'

A dollar van cut in front of them and Elizabeth honked her horn. 'I hate driving in Brooklyn.'

Zoe rolled her eyes. 'You sound like my mother.'

They drove to the first appointment of the day, an apartment on the sixteenth floor, overlooking the Barclays Center. Zoe's house would sell quickly if they priced it right, and Zoe wanted to have a better sense of where she wanted to go before they put the house on the market. If they wanted to sell. If they actually split up. It was the kind of maneuvering that would have driven Elizabeth totally crazy – a complete waste of her time and energy – if they hadn't been friends, but they were, and so it seemed like the least she could do. It was the equivalent of fantasy football, she guessed – people who couldn't actually play pretending that they had some semblance of control over the outcome of games on television.

'I could have a sofa over here,' Zoe said, gesturing toward the windows.

'Or over here,' Elizabeth said, gesturing toward the wall opposite.

'The kitchen's a little small,' Zoe said, and she was right, it was just a corner of the room with a few cabinets from Ikea and a cheap, glossy black countertop. She ran a finger over the lip of the stove. 'This is a piece of garbage.'

'Not everyone is married to a chef,' Elizabeth said, wanting to make light of it, but it wasn't light at all, and Zoe turned her back.

'Not even me, pretty soon,' she said, and it was time to leave.

The next apartment was better, warmer. Elizabeth unlocked the door and walked in first, half a step ahead. As soon as she crossed the threshold, she could feel how much more Zoe would like it. No matter what she claimed to want, Zoe liked old things, and no shiny apartment building was going to be the right choice. The second apartment had moldings and curved doorways and hundred-year-old windows with wavy glass. She loved it.

'And there's a shared garden,' Elizabeth said, pointing out the back window.

'And we're three blocks from BAM!' Zoe clasped her hands together, her silver rings little punctuation marks between her fingers. 'This is a good one, Lizzy.'

Elizabeth waited in the front room while Zoe poked around the closets. 'Do you want my measuring tape?' she hollered, but Zoe didn't respond.

When she was young, Elizabeth had imagined that she would live in a number of houses as an adult – a garret in Paris, overlooking a cobblestone street; on the beach in California. She and Andrew loved to talk about the possibilities. That was one of the things she'd always liked about her husband, how open he was to ideas. Peru? Sure! New Zealand? Why not?! But after Harry was born, and they found their house, it was harder to travel, to be bohemian in the way they'd always imagined they might be. All their money was in that house, in its bricks and plaster, and if they sold it, they would have to ask Andrew's parents for money to move anywhere more desirable, and no one wanted that. Not Elizabeth, not Andrew, not his parents. They'd made the trip from the Upper East Side to Ditmas Park eight or nine times, full stop. There were nominal reasons, as if they needed them: Andrew's father walked with a cane, and his mother couldn't be in an enclosed space without the fear of a panic attack, and so had been on the subway only a handful of times in her life. Of course they could take a car, but the distance was too much, psychologically. It was easier to make an annual pilgrimage in the other direction, up to the limestone and the army of doormen and the manicured medians of Park Avenue.

Was it too late for them to leave? Once Harry was out of high school, they would be free to make another choice, to move to an adobe house in Santa Fe, but could they make friends? At fifty? Maybe it was better to wait until they were seventy-five, old enough to move to a retirement community, a place on the coast of South Carolina that offered shuffleboard and karaoke. Andrew would rather die. Marfa, maybe, or a place upstate, near the Omega Institute. No place where they'd be surrounded by people like his parents. Sometimes Elizabeth looked at her husband and for a split second, he looked identical to the way he did as a twenty-four-year-old, with his sharp chin and his hooded eyes. He was so much angrier than Harry, even now, after decades of trying to be the opposite of how he was raised. Sometimes it worked, and sometimes it didn't. When Andrew got upset, she could see the fury rise in his face like on a cartoon, red-red-red-red until his head exploded. Most of the time, he was able to dial it back down, but sometimes, rarely, he still exploded. Harry had only seen it happen a few times in his life, and every time, he had immediately burst into tears, the fire extinguisher to his father's four-alarm blaze. They worked in both directions, actually – whenever Harry was undone, by a broken toy or a skinned knee, Andrew swooped into action, calm and comforting, a perfect nursemaid. Elizabeth was grateful for that, for their joint sweetness. It was so hard to tell when a child's personality would harden and fix, but it seemed true that Harry was kind and quiet, a good boy.

'Whew,' Zoe said, appearing at Elizabeth's side. 'I like this one a lot.' She bent forward at the waist and touched her toes. 'I could live here, I think.'

'That's great,' Elizabeth said. 'I mean, you can't live here, unless you want to move before you sell your house, or unless you want to buy this place and keep it empty for six months, but it's good to know what you're looking for.'

'Oh,' Zoe said. 'Right.'

'Or the timing could work out – you never know how slowly people are going to move. We could hurry up with your house and drag our heels over here, and if you're not bidding against multiple other offers, it could work.'

They hadn't talked about a real schedule. Once the balls were in the air, things were going to get messy. The room got a little bit wobbly for a second, while both Elizabeth and Zoe suddenly imagined the fantasy becoming a reality. But 'fantasy' was the wrong word – a fantasy was a thatched hut on a faraway beach, a fantasy was a white horse and a castle. The idea of Zoe actually getting divorced – of her being *single* – was actually horrifying. It was a choice people made all the time, to end a marriage, but it had never happened to them, and they looked at each other for a minute, both grim-faced. If Zoe and Jane could do it, so could she, Elizabeth thought, the notion flickering across her brain quickly and vanishing like a phantom mosquito.

'Can we just sit here for a while?' Zoe asked.

'Sure,' Elizabeth said. They had other appointments, later in the day, but mostly she just had keys to empty apartments, like this one, and spending a few extra minutes wasn't going to throw off their schedule. This was how decisions got made in her business – sitting in empty rooms, listening to people's daydreams about furniture and imaginary children.

They sat down on the floor of the living room, or what would become the living room when someone moved in. Elizabeth sat with her legs stretched out in front of her, crossed at the ankles, and Zoe leaned against the opposite wall, with her knees bent. The wood floors were gleaming, with defiant dust bunnies forming in the corners of the room. It was nearly impossible to keep an empty space completely clean.

'I've been walking through the house, making imaginary lists of what's mine and what's hers,' Zoe said. 'It's surprisingly easy.'

'Oh, yeah? Like what?'

Zoe ticked the items off on her fingers. 'The nice rugs are mine, the kitchen stuff is hers. The trunk we got at the flea market is mine, the records are mine, mostly. The ugly fucking lamp that I've always hated is hers.'

'Plus Bingo.'

'Bingo is nonnegotiable.' Zoe rolled her head back so that Elizabeth was looking at her throat. 'Ruby, on the other hand . . .'

'What's going on with Rube?'

'It's all so typical.' Zoe shifted her head forward again and smacked her lips. 'Teenage girls are teenage girls. Do you remember what giant assholes we were? Or, you weren't, but I was. Ruby is kind of a giant asshole right now. Not always. When she has a stomach ache or the flu and she feels awful, then she'll still crawl into bed with me and cuddle up and let me pet her, but otherwise? Forget it! She treats me like a warden. Not even the nice warden who gives you extra soap, but the mean one, with the nightstick. It's horrible.'

'What about Jane?' Elizabeth had often observed Ruby acting like an asshole over the course of her life, but it was an awareness she tried to suppress. Not liking your friends' kids was worse than not liking your friends' spouses. And it wasn't that Elizabeth didn't *like* Ruby – she was often funny, and dark in a way that Elizabeth found amusing – but there was a touch of the asshole there, it was true. You couldn't ever say that, though, no matter how true it was. When the kids were little, she and Zoe had been friends with another mom in the neighborhood, and this lady's kid was so horrible that they both mentioned it to her, that he seemed like a miniature serial killer in training, and she stopped speaking to them. Pretty soon she moved out of the neighborhood, and Elizabeth guessed it was to move closer to whatever prison facility her son was bound to wind up in. People just didn't want to hear it.

'Jane is hopeless. She doesn't even try. Which, of course, makes it so much easier. Jane and Ruby can go eat a thousand chicken wings together and not say more than three words, and they're fine, like a couple of frat boys. Ruby never says she hates Jane. She only hates me.'

'Ruby does not hate you, Zo,' Elizabeth said.

Zoe crossed her fingers. 'Remember when all you had to worry about was how much breast milk they were eating, and what their poop looked like?' She laughed. 'Parenthood is the only job that gets progressively harder every single year, and you never, ever, ever get a raise.'

'I'll give you a raise,' Elizabeth said. She stood up and offered Zoe a hand. 'Harry said he'd been hanging out with her in their SAT class, did you know that?'

'I am more likely to learn about my daughter from the mailman than I am to get any information directly,' Zoe said. 'But that's nice. Chivalry, I guess?'

'I suppose,' Elizabeth said. She started to describe the look on Harry's face when he'd mentioned it – though he tried so hard to be casual, his cheeks were tight with disbelief and happiness – but she stopped herself. Ruby, like Zoe, had a long life of adoration ahead of her, and Elizabeth didn't feel she needed to fuel the fire. No matter how old you got, there were certain things that clung from childhood – a cool-girl meanness or a nerdy girl's pining for someone who wouldn't want her back. Elizabeth saw so much of herself in Harry, even in his silent crushes, the secrets he thought he kept. It was hard to be a boy, just like it was hard to be a girl. 'Let's go,' Elizabeth said, and she opened the front door, happy to have the noise on the street come into the apartment and fill it with something other than her own thoughts.

Eighteen

Ruby didn't love the idea of working at the restaurant, but her mothers didn't really give her a choice. It was either work as a hostess at Hyacinth or get a job somewhere else, and anywhere else would require (at the very least) a résumé and an interview, not to mention the clothes she would have to buy at Banana Republic or wherever else lame people with boring jobs bought their gray pantsuits and white button-down shirts. Chloe was in France all summer, and Paloma was at her parents' country house for the month of June, until she left for a month in Sardinia at her parents' 'cottage'. Ruby didn't miss them. Sarah Dinnerstein was around all summer, and Ruby wished she weren't. As soon as graduation was over, Ruby knew that the whole thing had been a setup – not the ceremony itself, but the years preceding it. She wanted to go into a witness-protection program somewhere in the middle of Wyoming, learn to break horses, maybe marry a cowboy, spit in a can for fun. Anything to get out of Brooklyn and her own life. But here she was.

Allie, the current hostess at Hyacinth, who had also been Ruby's babysitter, seemed to have left abruptly, but that happened a lot in the service industry. Her mom said they needed someone fast, and nothing was faster than Ruby. She agreed to work the lunch shift (which was always slow during the week) and then the brunch shift plus dinner (after her class on Saturdays, and from ten a.m. to three p.m. on Sundays), which was always like being an infantry soldier on a very crowded battlefield. Ruby herself found brunch to be an infantilizing meal, but as her mothers loved to remind her, those long afternoons of eggs and mimosas paid for her tuition. The least she could do was show people to their tables and tell them to enjoy themselves. She didn't have to like it.

The hostess stand was near the door, across from the bar. Jorge, the daytime bartender, was also a stand-up comedian, and he liked to practise on Ruby while she sat and waited for people to come in. He was an okay bartender but not a very good comedian. The current bit was about how no one watched commercials any more, and though Ruby wasn't really paying attention, it seemed to have something to do with a bunch of old white guys sitting around a boardroom table complaining. Jorge was going to be a bartender forever. Ruby laughed charitably when he stopped talking, because she assumed he was finished. She had her phone behind the stand and was playing Candy Crush, level 24.

'Hello? Did you see him or not?' Jorge was drying off glasses with a dish towel, twisting and stacking, twisting and stacking.

'What are you even talking about?' Ruby glanced up from her phone.

Jorge pointed to the left corner of the window. 'Look over here. You know this white kid, Casper the ghost? He's been walking back and forth for like five minutes, just staring at you.'

Ruby shut her phone off and hopped down from the stool. She tiptoed to the end of the bar and peeked out the window. Dust was standing with his skateboard perched on his toe, leaning against the storefront of the Mexican bakery next door. 'Oh, shit,' Ruby said, and scurried back to her post.

'You know him?' Jorge asked. 'Do I need to go tell him to scram?'

'*Scram?* Are you still pretending to be an old man? I can't tell. No, thank you. I can handle this myself. I'll be right back.' Ruby tossed Jorge a stack of menus. 'Just in case.'

She tucked her hair behind her ears and pulled open Hyacinth's heavy front door. 'Hey!' she said to Dust. He was smoking and staring off into space, two of his favorite hobbies. 'What are you doing, you stalker?'

Dust saw her walking toward him and smiled. He opened his arms wide for a hug.

Ruby smacked his hands away and crossed her arms over her chest. 'What are you doing here?'

'I wanted to see you, and I heard you were working.' Dust licked the pointy edge of his chipped tooth. 'I was around the corner – it's not some weird stalker shit.'

Dust did have a friend who lived on Westminster. His name was Nico, and he grew marijuana in his closet and in the window boxes outside his bedroom. 'Fine,' Ruby said. 'Now you've seen me.' She didn't move.

'So is that kid, like, your boyfriend now? Your little private-school ninja bodyguard? Looked kinda young for you.' Dust cocked his head to the side. 'You don't miss me?'

Ruby did miss Dust, sort of, but she would rather have been eaten alive by sewer rats than admit it. Mostly she missed his body, and that broken tooth. It was fun to talk to someone who knew how to flirt, and how to flirt while riding a skateboard. Harry had no idea how to flirt. That was entertaining, too, in its own way, but sometimes Ruby got tired of feeling like Mrs Robinson. She had already decided that she would kiss Harry back if he ever tried anything, but now it was getting to the point where Ruby had to decide if she actually wanted to kiss him enough to do it herself. Whitman was small – if Harry had ever kissed anyone before, she would probably know it. There was no hiding anything – the whole school was packed so tight that you had to squeeze past couples making out by their lockers, not like in the movies, where there were bleachers and football fields and stuff. The back staircase was where you could see real action, and Ruby herself had done some serious business there. Harry Marx, on the back stairs? That would be like seeing Dust in an SAT prep course. It just didn't compute. But maybe with some practice.

'I have to go back to work,' Ruby said.

'Text me,' Dust said. He winked at her and dropped his board to the pavement and was zooming away before she could say no.

Nineteen

Elizabeth didn't like to think of herself as anal, but she did like things to be a certain way. She could have been an architect, if she'd cared more about math. It was why she was good at her job – there were so many offer sheets, comp sheets, pages and pages of contracts – and Elizabeth's were always in spotless order. It just felt good, to have everything in its rightful place. She wasn't sure about godliness in general, but if she were, then cleanliness would definitely have been next to it. She was organizing the guest room when she noticed that her storage boxes were in the wrong order. Everything was chronological – her childhood things, Andrew's childhood things, Kitty's Mustache memorabilia, files of old letters, Harry's childhood things. The Kitty's Mustache box was all the way to the right-hand side of the shelf, three spaces over from where it should have been, and the top had been put on backward. Elizabeth slid the box out and set it down on the floor.

She knew every piece of paper in the box: every press clipping, every photo. At first she saved things just because it seemed like a special time in her youth, but after Lydia died, it seemed more important than that. No one else had pictures of Kitty's Mustache's first practice, or of Lydia with her drumsticks sitting on a dorm-room floor. No one else had pictures of Lydia smiling, wearing a sweatshirt, with a ponytail. These were cultural artifacts. Like dinosaur bones, they were proof of previous life, and as precious to Elizabeth as her wedding pictures.

There were a few pictures missing – two band photos, including Elizabeth's selfish favorite, the one where she thought she looked like a high priestess, with the dark lipstick and the long black skirt. She'd bought the dress for seven dollars at the Elyria Salvation Army, and it was so long that it dragged on the ground behind her, which meant that the polyester began to unravel and wear after a few months of constant contact with the sidewalk.

'Andrew?' Elizabeth called.

'Yeah?' It sounded like he was in the kitchen.

'Can you come up here?' She leafed through – there were three things missing in total, she was pretty sure.

'Hey,' Andrew said, eating an apple. 'What's up?'

'Did you go through my pictures, take anything?' Elizabeth held up one of the band portraits. 'Remember your flannel phase?'

Andrew shook his head. 'God, I haven't looked at those in forever.' He stepped into the room and plucked the picture out of Elizabeth's hand. 'Man, we look fucking cool. Right? Or do we not? You look incredible.'

'I think we do. Or did. I think we did. You still look like that.' She kissed him on the cheek. Andrew handed the photo back and took another bite of his apple, sending a juicy mist into the air.

'Don't spray my memories,' Elizabeth said, wiping off the photo on her shirt. 'It's so weird, but I'm pretty sure there are some things missing. You don't think Harry would have taken them, do you?' She lowered her voice. 'Is he in his room?'

Andrew nodded. Elizabeth tucked the picture back in the box and stood up, dusting off her fingers. She squeezed past Andrew and knocked on Harry's bedroom door. Once she heard his muffled reply, Elizabeth turned the knob and opened the door.

Harry was sitting cross-legged on his bed, an SAT study guide splayed open in front of him. He had his giant headphones around his neck, which made his head look shrunken, as if he'd gotten into a fight with a voodoo shaman.

'Hey, Mom,' Harry said. There were dark circles under his eyes. Elizabeth had never seen him look that way before, like he hadn't been sleeping enough. She wanted to scoop him up in her arms and rock him back and forth, even though he probably weighed as much as she did.

'Hi, honey,' Elizabeth said. She didn't know why she was asking him – Harry had never taken anything that wasn't his, not a pack of gum from the supermarket, not an extra piece of Halloween candy out of a neighbor's bowl. He didn't fib. Harry was their little golden ticket. Whenever she got together with other mothers of kids in his class, she would listen to them complain and rail against the demons living in their houses, and Elizabeth would just smile and nod politely. 'This is probably silly, but did you happen to be in my storage boxes?' She pointed to the wall. 'You know, in the guest room?'

Harry would have made any poker player very, very happy. His face melted instantly, and his lower lip began to wobble. 'Um,' he said.

Elizabeth took another step into the room, her hands on the edges of the door. 'Honey, what is it?'

He was trying not to cry. 'It was just a couple of things. I didn't know you'd miss them. If I'd known, we wouldn't have done it.'

'Who's "we"?' Elizabeth asked. Harry's friends were the sort with glasses and dirty sneakers, the sort of boys who'd worn sweatpants to school long after they should have. Arpad, Max, Joshua – those boys weren't thieves. Together, they were a motley crew, like the geeks she remembered from her own high-school days, with squared-off glasses and overbites.

'Me and Ruby,' Harry said. 'She thought they were worth a lot of money.' He temporarily brightened, thinking this information might scuttle him out of trouble. 'And she was right! We're already way past the reserves, look!' He opened his laptop and clicked some keys, then spun the computer screen toward his mother. Sure enough, there were her photographs on eBay, each going for over two hundred dollars already.

'Harr,' Elizabeth said. It was unlike him in so many ways – too entrepreneurial, too sneaky, too thoughtless.

Andrew poked his head in. 'Did you find them?'

'Oh, we found them all right. Ruby Kahn-Bennett put them on eBay.' She grabbed the computer from Harry's bed and showed Andrew the screen.

'Are you kidding? What are you going to do next, sell the television set for drug money?' Andrew frowned, his forehead creases deepening into hard lines, as even as ruled paper.

'I'm sorry,' Harry said. He shrugged. 'I mean, I guess I knew I shouldn't, but Ruby thought that it wasn't a big deal, and that we'd make all this money. . . .'

'Which you were going to do what with? Buy your mother flowers?' Andrew's voice was veering close to a shout, which made Elizabeth's ears ring. He never yelled at his son – maybe three times in the last sixteen years. Elizabeth knew how important it was to him to keep his temper in check. It had been a problem in their youth, Andrew always flying off into the stratosphere with rage over something totally inconsequential, but since the birth of their son, it had vanished almost completely.

'I don't know,' Harry said. 'I hadn't thought that far ahead.' His cheeks were bright red.

'Andrew, relax,' Elizabeth said. She was upset that Harry had taken the pictures, but it was so clear – so perfectly obvious – that it wasn't his fault. He was under Ruby's spell. 'It was Ruby's idea.'

'And that makes it better? I'm going to call Zoe. Right now.' He slid his phone out of his back pocket and dialed Zoe's cell. In the band, there had been two distinct teams: Elizabeth and Zoe, and Lydia and Andrew. It wasn't that Andrew and Zoe weren't friends, officially, it was just that they weren't friends, actually. Sometimes Elizabeth wondered what her life would have been like if she'd hit it off with Lydia instead of Zoe, what dominoes that would have sent knocking together.

'Oh, my God,' Harry said. He dropped his face into his hands.

'It's not your fault,' Elizabeth said. He'd been taken hostage, simple as that. In the hall, Andrew's voice got louder and louder, and Elizabeth walked over to the bed and put her arms around her son.

Twenty

After screaming at Zoe (and then Jane) about their delinquent daughter's theft, Andrew took a walk around the block, walking away from the Kahn-Bennetts', just in case the three of them were staring out the window and ready for a rematch. He could feel his blood pumping in his ears. Andrew exhaled loudly through his mouth, once, and then again. Harry's offense wasn't so horrible, he knew that, but it was sneaky and wrong, and it was because Zoe was as shitty a mother as she was a person. She'd always been totally self-centered, and Elizabeth couldn't see it, the way Zoe treated her like a dog. Worse than a dog! Zoe loved her dog, but Andrew wasn't sure she felt the same way about his wife.

Andrew was at EVOLVEment before he realized that that's where he was headed. He took the stoop steps two at a time. The door was open, and there was a meditation group in session. A girl with two braids pinned to the top of her head motioned him in, pointing to a blanket toward the front of the room, where Dave was sitting. Andrew climbed over everyone as quietly as possible and sank to his seat. He closed his eyes and felt better already. He sat in silence for an indeterminate amount of time – it could have been fifteen minutes, it could have been an hour. Dave rang a singing Tibetan bowl to reawaken the room, and they all started to move their bodies, sliding their hands over their knees and faces. When Andrew opened his eyes, Dave was looking right at him, smiling.

He hadn't seen the upstairs, and was excited when Dave offered the full tour. Like the first floor, the stairs and the upstairs hall had all been painted white, and the only rugs and curtains were white as well, which made the space seem much more open than it really was. Most of the houses in Ditmas were Victorian, which was code for small, dark rooms with lots of wood, but this house had been ripped apart by enough owners that none of the original millwork remained. Young people walked around barefoot, the soles of their feet making gentle sucking sounds. It wasn't like one of the yoga studios in the Slope, where everyone was wearing ninety-dollar yoga pants, all the logos on their asses lining up perfectly when they were in downward-facing dog. These kids were wearing whatever they wanted, shorts and T-shirts and filmy little dresses. One kid standing near the kitchen was wearing a headband with flowers on it and an open robe, a millennial Hugh Hefner. Andrew ran his hand up the banister. He and Elizabeth had always been on the minimal side of things, but being in EVOLVEment made him want to get rid of everything unnecessary – he wanted blank walls, open windows.

'This is one of the body-treatment rooms,' Dave said. 'Reiki, massage. We have so many talented body workers in our community.' He kept walking, with Andrew a half step behind. 'This is another treatment room.' A young woman was lying on her back while another dripped something on to her forehead. 'Ayurveda.'

'So who lives here?' Andrew asked.

'Right now there are six of us – me, Jessie, who I think you've met' – Dave pointed toward the girl with the braids – 'three artists-in-residence, plus Salome, who leads the cosmic trances on Friday nights. She's amazing, you should come. The vibes in this house are incredible. I swear, for three days after, the whole place is still vibrating.'

'I will,' Andrew said.

There were more rooms – bedrooms filled with potted ficus trees and rubber plants, rooms with futons and candles and musical equipment. Every so often, a young woman or man would squeeze by them slowly, touching Dave on the arm and then smiling. Andrew never wanted to leave.

'Do you need help building things around here?' he asked. 'I've been getting into woodworking. I'd love to help.'

Dave clapped Andrew on the back. He smelled like sage and sandalwood. 'That would be great, man. We'd love that. And if you ever need to crash here, go right ahead. There is always room in a bed.'

'Thanks,' Andrew said. It wasn't clear if the beds Dave was offering already had people in them or not, but it seemed like it. Jessie, the girl with the braids, walked quickly toward them, her feet in ballerina turnout. She held a small cup in each hand.

'You guys have to try this juice I just made,' she said. They each took one and raised it to their lips.

The juice was green and pulpy, leaving stringy pieces in between Andrew's teeth. Dave seemed to have no trouble sucking it down. 'What's in it?' Andrew asked, after he swallowed. There was a funny taste, medicinal, lingering in the back of his throat.

'Kale, chili peppers, anise, apple, orange, St-John's-wort, a few other things. It's good, right?'

'Delicious,' Dave said. He pulled on his beard. 'Mmmm.'

'That's right,' Jessie said. She took a few tiny steps forward and kissed Dave on the mouth. Then she pirouetted around and walked back the way she'd come.

There was nothing about youth that was fair: the young hadn't done anything to deserve it, and the old hadn't done anything to drive it away. Andrew thought about Harry and the stolen photos and Ruby and her purple hair, and even though part of him wanted to call Zoe and Jane back and yell at them even more, mostly he wanted to know how it was that he wasn't the child anymore, how his baby boy had become a teenager, and how it was possible that he – Andrew Marx! – would soon be fifty. It didn't matter what any listicle said, about how fifty was the new thirty. Harry was going to start having sex, and Andrew was going to be a grandfather, and then Andrew was going to be dead. It was a chain of events that he couldn't stop, even if he had all of his parents' money. They had tried – the sports cars in the garage at the country house in Connecticut, the 'skin treatments' his mother had every three months in an attempt to erase the lines and spots from her face – but it was all a pathetic Hail Mary. Andrew just wanted to pause time for a little while, to pretend that he was still young enough to do something that mattered. He wanted to drink juice and sit in a quiet room and wait for all the young bodies around him to dance.

Twenty-one

Harry had been weighing the decision for weeks – three weeks, every day since Ruby's graduation. He was going to kiss her, with tongue. If that's what she wanted. If she let him! It was unclear how exactly to make a kiss happen. They had to be alone, obviously, and they had to be sitting close enough together that Harry didn't have to lunge across the room like a zombie, eyes closed and mouth open. Other than that, though, he really wasn't sure.

He and Ruby hadn't spoken since the Grand Theft of 2014. Harry's parents had gone crazy, as if Ruby had taken nuclear-bomb codes from the president's briefcase. It really didn't seem like that big a deal, or at least it hadn't before they'd been discovered. Harry hated being in trouble, but he also hated that Ruby was now going to think he ratted her out. He'd been trying to figure some casual way to tell her that he hadn't narced on them, but so far all he had was a text that said HEY with the emoji for a bomb and the ghost sticking out its tongue. It wasn't quite there yet.

It was Friday morning. He'd done nothing all week. On Wednesday, he went to see a crappy movie with Yuri, one of his few friends from Whitman who wasn't off doing something glamorous all summer long. Most kids were at their summer houses, or backpacking across New Zealand or Israel or France. Yuri lived in Windsor Terrace and was working at a Starbucks and made Harry free iced coffees when he visited. On Friday, Harry and his parents went to the Tibetan restaurant by the train. The entire time, all week long, Harry had been thinking about walking into his SAT class and worrying about whether Ruby would still sit next to him.

There were three houses for sale in their neighborhood, and his mom was working them all – one down by Newkirk, one at the end of their block, and one over on Stratford. Sometimes she dragged Harry along when she was setting up for things. He liked to fill the giant glass bowls with the Granny Smith apples, that kind of thing. It all seemed so goofy, but his mother swore that it worked, as if someone would say, *I freaking* love *apples. I need to buy this house.* Mostly, though, it meant that his mother was AWOL most of the time and so was his dad.

Because the bidding wasn't over yet, Elizabeth was able to take down the listing on eBay. Zoe and Ruby had brought the pictures back, and Zoe stood there in the doorway while Ruby apologized to Elizabeth. Harry sat on the stairs, cringing. It was his fault, too, and he was technically in trouble, but everyone involved knew that he never would have done it without Ruby. Her voice was flat and even, just this side of insolence. Elizabeth nodded and offered her terse thanks, and then Zoe and Ruby were gone. Harry thought he saw Ruby wink at him quickly on her way out the door, but he was probably seeing things. He held his phone in his hand all night long, waiting for a message, but none came.

Harry slid out of bed and pulled on his jeans, still sitting in a crumpled pile on the floor, as if he'd just evaporated out of them. He swabbed some deodorant under his arms and shuffled into the hallway.

'Dad?' There was no answer. Harry poked his head up the stairs, toward his parents' bedroom. 'Dad?' Still no answer. His father was almost always home. When Harry was small, he actually believed that his father didn't sleep but instead just sat in a corner of a room, waiting to be played with, like the biggest toy in the house.

Harry walked slowly up the stairs. His parents' room was empty, except for Iggy Pop, who was still curled up in a ball at the foot of the bed. Harry wondered if Ruby had gotten grounded, or if she'd ever been grounded. Being grounded was such an ancient concept, like feudalism, or jazz being cool. It had no place in modern society. Parents couldn't even take away phones or computers, not really, because then how could you call for help if you were run over by a bus on the way to school, and how could you turn in your reading logs and science worksheets? It would be like giving your kid an abacus and sending him off to his calculus final exam.

His mother's laptop was sitting open on her small desk, which was against the far wall, away from the windows. Harry sat down and clicked the mouse. Her computer woke up, a photo of Harry and Iggy asleep on the couch together a few years ago as the background. Without thinking about it, Harry clicked the mail icon on the bottom of the screen, and Elizabeth's e-mail in-box leaped up, alert and dinging.

He wasn't a snoop – his mother's e-mails were boring. Of the fifty or so e-mails in her in-box, half of them were from work, and the rest seemed to be junky things that she should unsubscribe from. Harry tried to tell her how to do it, how easy it was to click a few buttons and not get a hundred e-mails a day from the Container Store or whatever, but she didn't listen. Ruby was right – his mother was obsessive, but not about everything. Her e-mail in-box looked like it belonged to a hoarder with an online-shopping addiction. He scrolled through for a minute, checking to see if Ruby's moms had written, if they'd said anything about him. It wasn't like him to read someone else's private correspondence, but Harry felt bad – felt bad that Ruby had probably gotten into trouble and all he'd gotten into was a hug. His parents were so sure that he'd never do anything wrong, that he wasn't capable of it, and all that love and trust made Harry want to rob a bank. And so he started reading. It was a low-level crime, but it was a crime, and that's what counted.

There was one from Zoe, but the whole e-mail thread was just about apartments. He copied down some of the links so he could show them to Ruby, but there wasn't anything juicy. It was sad, the idea of one of her mothers moving out – which one would go? Would Ruby get to stay? Or would they both move? Even so, Harry pictured Ruby rolling her eyes at the notion of real estate as juicy information. A truly cutting-edge wooing tactic for a teenage boy. He kept scrolling.

About halfway through her in-box, there were a few flagged e-mails from someone named Naomi Vandenhoovel. The first one had the subject 'MY TATTOO MISSES YOU,' which made it look like it was written by some weird bot, but she'd written again and again – subjects 'MISTRESS OF MYSELF FILM VIP VIP VIP,' 'HI AGAIN, CONTRACT DEADLINE FOR KITTY'S MUSTACHE,' 'HI HI HI HI HI IT'S ME NAOMI.' The last one seemed to be dictated via Siri.

Harry read them all, one after the other.

This is what he put together: A crazy woman named Naomi was trying to get his mother and father to agree to sell the rights to 'Mistress of Myself' for a movie about Lydia. A biopic. Like *Ray*, or *Walk the Line*. The kind of movie that would win someone an Oscar, especially if they really sang. And it wasn't even like they'd have to actually be a good singer, to sing like Lydia. Harry had never liked the way Lydia sounded. His mom was a much better singer, technically. Anyone who had ever watched *American Idol* or *The Voice* knew when someone was singing out of tune, and that was Lydia's specialty, sliding in and out of tune and screeching like she'd just dropped a toaster into her bathtub. So far, Elizabeth had been putting her off, but crazy Naomi (he couldn't lie, the tattoo picture was kind of hot) was persistent as hell. No wonder his mom had been going through the Kitty's Mustache stuff.

Most of the time, Harry didn't think much about how his parents had been cool. It mattered to his daily life significantly less than English muffins, slightly more than the existence of remote-control helicopters. He was glad that they were interesting and interested, that they read books and went to the movies, which wasn't true for all of his friends' parents. His friend Arpad's father was a surgeon, and no one ever saw him. It was like he was a ghost who left expensive things lying around the house in an attempt to get you to solve his murder. Harry's parents were present; they were nice to him. It was boring, in a good way. And so Harry wasted very little time thinking about how, when they were his age, they had actually been cool. It sucked to feel as if your parents – your embarrassing, dorky parents – had been invited to parties that you would never get invited to, had done drugs no one had ever offered you, had stayed up all night talking to other cool people just because they wanted to. Harry wanted to stay up all night. He wanted to out-Dust Dust. He wanted to take Ruby's hand and lead her somewhere she'd never been, and to do it with such confidence that she never once questioned that he knew where he was going. The past was the past. Harry was ready to be someone new. What was the masculine form of 'mistress'? The 'mister.' He was going to be the mister of himself, starting now. He wrote his parents a text that he was going to spend Saturday night at Arpad's, that he was going there right after his SAT class. His mother texted back some smiley faces and some kisses. He had a day to change the entire trajectory of his life. Simple as that.

Twenty-two

Elizabeth was in the mood for chicken. It was also the only thing they had in the fridge, so it was what they were having for dinner. She'd often thought that being as close as they were to Jane and Zoe should yield some high-level kitchen skills, but so far, it hadn't. Elizabeth could appreciate good food – she'd been to most of the city's best restaurants with her in-laws, Andrew always pulling at his shirt collar like an awkward bar-mitzvah boy – but she could never figure out how to replicate those beautiful meals using her own two hands. There were only so many ways to cook things – boiling water, pans, oven – and yet other people seemed to do it so naturally. Whenever she dropped by Zoe's house for lunch, one of the three of them would be eating some bowlful of brown rice and hard-boiled egg and sautéed kale, with an avocado-miso dressing that they'd just whipped up. Leftovers, they'd say, sheepish, as if it weren't something that could easily be on the menu at Hyacinth. When Elizabeth felt sheepish about her food, it was because she was an adult with a teenage son and she still counted frozen pizzas among her chief food groups.

It wasn't easy to have a best friend who seemed so much better at so many of life's important skills. Maybe it was that she and Andrew had been together so long, or gotten together when they were still so young, or that they'd started out as friends, but Elizabeth couldn't remember ever experiencing the all-consuming, life-eating early love that Zoe had found with Jane. They'd disappear into Zoe's bedroom for days, they'd play cutesy and irritating games of footsie at restaurants, they'd go away for long weekends without a moment's notice. Not to mention the kissing. Elizabeth had never seen so much kissing. In taxicabs, in their kitchen, on the sofa – never mind if there were other people present. Next to their romance, Elizabeth felt like she and Andrew were an incestuous brother and sister, or maybe close first cousins. They had always enjoyed sex, but even Andrew had never seemed to *need* her body the way that Jane *needed* Zoe and vice versa. On the one hand, it had made the slide into long-term marriage easier, because they were already comfortable with a lower level of intensity, but Elizabeth had sometimes wondered what it was like to feel that kind of desire and to send it back, gulping, even if it meant for a sharp letdown in the years to follow. Because no one could keep that up, not even Zoe.

Harry zipped through the kitchen, head down, hurrying toward his backpack, which was in its usual slump by the coatrack.

'Hey,' Elizabeth said. 'Where are you going? Hungry?'

'Not right now,' Harry said. He grabbed his bag and ran back up the stairs.

Elizabeth rinsed off the chicken breasts in the sink and put them on a plate. Even before she'd married Jane, Zoe had been good in the kitchen. When they'd lived together at Oberlin, Elizabeth had once washed Zoe's cast-iron pan with a sinkful of dishes, scrubbed it for hours with a soapy sponge, and when she realized what Elizabeth was doing, Zoe had given her a look like she'd just shaved off her eyebrows while she was sleeping. The Bennetts were California gourmets, all farm-raised and organic before it was cool. Elizabeth thought about her childhood diet of Oreo cookies and jars of Skippy peanut butter and felt embarrassed all over again. Her parents were fine – they were good enough people and she loved them, but her mother had always liked gin more than vegetables. Her father cooked a bloody steak on the grill every Sunday, and that was it. He took pills to make the bad cholesterol go down and the good cholesterol go up, and he had never told her that he loved her, not directly. They never listened to music. Her mother read novels, but only love stories starring beautiful blind girls or war widows. There was so much that Elizabeth had had to figure out on her own.

Andrew came quietly down the stairs and hugged her from behind.

'Hi,' he said, and laid his head against her shoulder.

'Hi,' she said. 'Are you okay? I feel like you've been MIA.'

'I actually feel great,' Andrew said. He slid one hand into Elizabeth's waistband, and she wriggled away.

'I have raw chicken hands,' she said.

'I'll take a little salmonella.' He kissed her neck.

'Oh, stop it,' Elizabeth said, elbowing him gently but happy for his nuzzling affection. 'Where have you been?'

Andrew paused. 'There's this new place, over on Stratford. A yoga studio, sort of. I went to a class today.'

'Oh, yeah? That's good, we need a new one.' Elizabeth was always looking for new businesses to add to her roster. There was nothing that young home buyers wanted more than yoga studios and restaurants, as if they'd be young forever and looking for ways to fill their days. 'Hey, so, have you thought about it at all? About the Lydia thing?' She turned toward her husband. He'd always been weird about Lydia – they were buddies, but as soon as she left school, Andrew never mentioned her again. It was as if she'd died, and then when she did die, he'd bristle at the sound of her name. Lydia's death had made Elizabeth feel softer toward her, weirdly – as if there were nothing she could have done, as if it weren't just that Lydia had never liked her, it was that she had much bigger problems. It wasn't exactly nice, but it was comforting. Maybe if he saw the movie, he'd understand – he'd see how young they all were, how beautiful and ridiculous.

Andrew leaned against the stove. She watched his face cloud over, as quickly as a thunderstorm in July. 'I really don't want to do it,' he said, finally. 'I really don't. I know you think it's stupid, but it means something to me.'

'But I wrote the song.' Elizabeth was usually careful not to phrase things this way: bands were about equality, marriages too. It rarely did any good to claim complete ownership. Feelings were hurt and resentment so easily built. In this case the division of labor was clear: *Elizabeth Johnson, lyrics; Andrew Marx, Lydia Greenbaum, Zoe Bennett, and Elizabeth Johnson, music.* She owned more of the song than anyone else did.

'You wrote the words, yes.' Andrew shook his head. 'But you don't get to decide for the rest of us.'

'They have Lydia's permission – her mother said yes. They have Zoe. And they have me. I think it'll be exciting. And weird, yes, probably really weird. But I think we should do it. I want to do it.'

'Why? So you can watch some skinny teenage movie star scream "Mistress of Myself" a hundred times? Are you that much of a narcissist?' Andrew's cheeks were starting to flush.

'A *narcissist*? Because I don't want to stand in the way of someone making a movie about someone else? What are you talking about?'

Andrew pursed his lips and closed his eyes. 'You're really not thinking about the big picture, Lizzy.'

'I'm pretty sure I am, actually,' Elizabeth said. She turned back around to her chicken. The idea was to rub it with garlic and ginger and to stir-fry it, or something. She'd lost her train of thought. Elizabeth heard the front door shut and realized that Andrew had walked out.

There were two choices: make dinner or not. Who knew what

Harry would eat if she didn't cook? And so Elizabeth kept cooking, her blood pressure making her a little fast and loose with the spices. Dried parsley? Why not. Black pepper? Sure. The chicken breasts looked like little Jackson Pollocks as she slid them into the hot pan. She watched the chicken turn from pink to opaque, checking the door every so often to see if Andrew was going to walk back in. She stepped out on to the porch, in case he might just be sitting on the front steps, but he wasn't. Debbie from across the street waved, and Elizabeth waved back. Being the neighborhood real-estate agent meant never being in a bad mood, never arguing in public. It was like being a very low-level celebrity, where you knew your actions would have repercussions, that people would be watching. Elizabeth retreated back into the house and shut the door.

Half an hour later, dinner was done and Andrew still wasn't home.

'Harry! Dinner!' Elizabeth called. She set the table for three, as usual, even though she seemed to be the only one eating. She wasn't even hungry.

After a few minutes, Harry clomped down the stairs, his eyes wide. 'Whoa,' he said, looking at his dinner plate. He slid into his chair, and Elizabeth into hers, across from him. There were the expressive chicken breasts, plus a shredded-carrot and couscous salad. 'This looks weird, Mom.'

'Eat it, Harry,' Elizabeth said. She picked up her fork and knife and started shoveling food into her mouth. As she chewed, she felt hungrier and hungrier, as if each bite emptied out her stomach. Harry watched, and eventually followed suit.

'It's good,' he said. 'Where's Dad?'

Elizabeth spoke with her mouth full. 'Yoga class.'

'Oh,' Harry said, satisfied.

They ate the rest of their meal in silence, both deeply engrossed by their own thoughts. Harry carried his plate over to the garbage and scraped it clean. He put the plate in the sink and ran back upstairs.

'I have to pick something up at the grocery store, sweetie,' Elizabeth said, before he'd completely disappeared. 'I'll be back in ten minutes, okay?' She put her plate on top of Harry's in the sink and slipped her feet into her flip-flops. Andrew had said Stratford Road.

It was a perfect night – the end of June, when even Brooklyn had to admit that nothing was the matter. It was past seven and still not yet quite dark. Elizabeth was wearing a T-shirt and the stretchy yoga pants that she wore to bed. She tucked her hair behind her ears as she walked. She hated fighting with her husband. Even now, after so many years together, she sometimes had the thought – abrupt and sharp, like a bolt of lightning – that she'd made the wrong decision, all those years ago, and ruined her entire life. Andrew was smart and serious and handsome. His family money drove him crazy, but it also meant that they never really had to worry, especially about Harry. The Marx money was stretched under Harry's crib like a fireman's net, ready to catch him if necessary. All their friends, if asked, would say that Elizabeth and Andrew were a great couple. They were seamless; they were united. They alley-ooped each other's punch lines at dinner parties. But sometimes, she wondered. Probably everyone did. Probably that was marriage. But on the nights when they fought and he walked out the door, which had happened maybe four times in their entire relationship, including college, when walking out the door was a much easier feat and wouldn't have required an attorney, Elizabeth was sure that it was over, and that no matter how much she loved her husband, he was lost to her forever.

The house on Stratford was easy enough to find – she'd guessed which one it was. Corcoran had sold it, it hadn't been her listing, but she'd been inside it before. Elizabeth rounded the corner from Beverly and walked south. It had been called a 'fixer-upper,' politely. In the office, Deirdre had referred to it as a 'crack house.' It hadn't really been a crack house, at least not officially, but there were boarders and renters and strange locks on all their bedroom doors, with stained carpets. Those were easy fixes, but not everyone could see past them.

Elizabeth put her hands on her hips and stopped walking. She was two houses away. It was on the left, toward Cortelyou, with a nice wide porch that the owners would have to sink about twenty grand into, if they wanted to do it right. What was she going to do, walk in? What if he wasn't there? What if he was sitting at the bar at Hyacinth, talking to Jane? What if he'd apologized for overreacting and they were clinking small tumblers full of top-shelf whiskey, complaining about their wives? She was just taking a walk, that was all. Elizabeth tucked her hair behind her ears again and walked the rest of the way to the house.

She heard it before she saw anything – loud music, the kind of music that played in the background of dream sequences in bad television shows, with layers of sitar over something more contemporary. It was dance music, what they used to call techno, electronic and repetitive. It was loud enough that she could hear it from the porch. Surely the neighbors were going to complain, once it got late. Ditmas Park was nothing if not swift with a noise complaint.

People were dancing. They all looked like sweaty versions of Ruby, twirling themselves around with their eyes closed. Elizabeth nudged herself closer to one of the large windows. There were shades down, but the shades were gauze and it was lighter inside than out – she could make out everything. The main room was crowded with bodies, all of them smiling and jumping. She saw hands on asses, hands on faces, lips on lips. 'My God,' she said, out loud. 'It's a fucking rave.' Elizabeth was just about to turn away and walk toward Hyacinth, so sure now that she would find her husband there, tucking into some beautifully prepared dish, and then she saw him.

Andrew was drenched in sweat. His T-shirt clung to his thin chest. His head was thrown back, lolling a little bit from side to side. He hadn't danced that way in years. She felt like her very own Ghost of Husbands Past, like she was watching herself and Andrew when they were nineteen and on Ecstasy and licking each other's faces all night long just because their tongues felt so funny. Only Elizabeth wasn't in the room, she was standing outside it, and she wasn't licking her husband's face. To his credit, no one else was either, but Andrew looked as if any number of the young men and women pressing past him and against him could easily have slipped their little bodies into his mouth and he wouldn't have objected. This was not the face of propriety. This was not the face of marriage. This was one man, midlife, losing his shit.

Twenty-three

Ruby couldn't believe it – the SAT class was ten minutes under way, and she was sitting in the back row alone. Harry had ditched the class, and she hadn't, and faking another stomach flu would have made the Queen Dork call her mothers for sure. She sat with her bag on the seat to her left and her jean jacket on the seat to her right, just in case anyone got any ideas about sitting too close. Rebecca smiled and waved, and Eliza and Thayer made a couple of stinkfaces in her direction, and Ruby ignored them all. She flipped over the first handout – 'Turn Similes into Smiles!' – and started drawing Bingo with a superhero cape and a cigarette.

The class was interminable. Three hours of practice tests and tricks for how to answer multiple-choice questions when you didn't know the answer. Ruby had bombed the SAT so efficiently the first time that she thought she could teach the class better than Rebecca, a simple Do the Opposite of Whatever I Say methodology, where you got extra points just for not skipping every third question. Tomorrow it would be July, and the class would be half over. She tried to think of it as meditation. Her body had to be in this room, but her mind did not. She tried astral projecting but found Thayer's gum chewing too distracting. Ruby filled in bubbles in the shapes of fish eating smaller fish.

It wasn't that she was *against* college, per se. Ruby just felt that the world held too many unique experiences for her to be pinned down to doing one thing for so many years, especially when she'd spent her entire life up until this point doing that exact thing. When was her boxcar-jumping period? Her life as a carny? Reality TV and PETA newsletters had spoiled many things, but they couldn't kill her dreams about being a loose woman in the United States of America. What if she wanted to work as a stripper someday? She didn't, but what if? What if she wanted to get ill-conceived tattoos with brand-new friends? Ruby had two tattoos already. Her mothers knew and didn't even pretend to care. One was a small star in the space between her right armpit and her boob, and the other was a *B* for Bingo on her left big toe. Her mum was so jealous of the *B* that she got one, too, but only because Ruby made her promise that they would never bare their toes at the same time in front of anyone Ruby knew.

The kids in the row ahead of her stood up, shoving handouts into their bags. 'Fabulous,' Ruby said, at full volume, and followed suit. She waved to Rebecca, gave the finger to Eliza and Thayer, and was the first person out the door.

Harry was standing outside, wearing sunglasses. He had a very full tote bag slung on his left shoulder and a beach umbrella leaning against his right. 'Ready, mademoiselle?' he said. 'Dirty hipster beach in the Rockaways. I found it on the Internet. Taxi's waiting. And by taxi, I mean the subway. It's going to take us a hundred years to get there, but I swear to God, it'll be worth it.'

'For fuck's sake, yes,' Ruby said. She raised her arms in victory.

PART TWO

Jane Says

Yoga Evolves on Stratford

EVOLVEment owner David Goldsmith hadn't spent much time in Ditmas Park before opening his brand-new yoga and health center on Stratford Road. 'I'd been looking around Brooklyn – mostly in Williamsburg and Bushwick – when a friend tipped me off about this place,' he told us. 'Like a lot of people, my first thought was, whoa!' EVOLVEment offers yoga classes, massage services, and serves juice and other beverages. Goldsmith says that he's interested in getting involved in the neighborhood, so stop by and check them out! Drop-in classes are $11, cheaper with a class card. We tried a ginger-kale-apple juice, and it was delicious!

Twenty-four

It was more fun than he'd had in years, though 'fun' wasn't precisely the right word. Salome called the dance parties 'cosmic trances,' and they were fucking cosmic, absolutely. Andrew had never been a dancer – in high school he had occasionally pogoed into his friends in the pit at shows, and at Oberlin he had grinded his body against beautiful girls with short hair and nose rings when he was fall-down drunk, but he had never really liked to dance. He was far too self-conscious. Zoe was in the dance department, always flinging her body against the wooden floor and calling it choreography. That was how she got all the girls. Elizabeth was more like him, happier to stand against a wall and bob her head, preferably holding a red plastic cup in front of her face so that she could whisper things to whoever was standing next to her. Andrew hadn't realized he was so tired of whispering.

At first, when Salome had started playing music, they were all sitting down or giving each other little back massages. Andrew closed his eyes and sat on a pillow in the corner of the room. He wanted to let go of his body, to let go of his mind. He'd tried talk therapy, but it wasn't for him. You couldn't change anything by sitting in a room with a stranger and telling him your side of the story. Andrew liked interaction, and healing from the outside in. The music was interesting, rhythmic and wobbly. He couldn't tell if he was listening to guitars or synths or nothing at all, just some computer-generated tracks made by a kid in his basement. Probably the latter. Did anyone even learn how to play an instrument anymore? No, he wasn't going to think about that, he wasn't going to be Clint Eastwood telling kids to get off his lawn. And so Andrew relaxed, and waited.

It was three a.m. when he finally walked out the door. He was soaked with sweat – his own and everyone else's. EVOLVEment had turned into a greenhouse, all of them their own individual hothouse flower. The air on Stratford Road felt cool and refreshing, just like the glasses of cucumber water that the EVOLVErs had been passing around and then pouring over one another's heads.

Elizabeth was going to be pissed, if not worried. Andrew didn't know which was worse. Worry could remove some of the sting of anger, if she was happy to know that he was all right. Of course, he wasn't her child – why would she assume that something had befallen him? Andrew thought about explaining why he liked EVOLVEment but couldn't come up with anything that didn't sound like he was about to start sleeping with a nineteen-year-old.

It wasn't that. Andrew had no interest in having sex with the beautiful young things. There were unbelievable-looking girls everywhere in the house, making juice and dancing and kicking up into handstands, giving you a peek of their stomachs and underwear all over the place, and it only made Andrew feel like a latter-day Humbert Humbert, or like a more Jewish version of Sting. Andrew didn't care. The only nineteen-year-old he wanted to have sex with was himself. He wanted to go back in time and watch himself take off his clothes, so terrified of the world that he couldn't stop snarling, even when he was about to make love to someone for the first time.

He and Elizabeth had known each other from the dorms. They'd had a few classes together – an intro creative-writing class, plus The Story of the Dinosaurs, the science class that all the humanities kids took – and they were friends, a bit. If they saw each other outside the library, they would sit on a bench and smoke cigarettes. Elizabeth was so sweet, so suburban – Andrew had liked her from the start, even before they were in the band together and he saw what she could really do. She had none of the jaded bullshit that his friends from home had. She wasn't spoiled. She could knit. They went bowling, and Elizabeth got strike after strike – it turned out she'd been on her high school's bowling team. What kind of high school had a bowling team? Andrew thought it was possible that Elizabeth had grown up in the 1950s and been teleported to Oberlin through space and time. Lydia, on the other hand, had been as familiar as a sibling. She was from Scarsdale, which wasn't so far from the Upper East Side. She had rich parents and her own car and a credit card that she wasn't afraid to use. Just like all of his high-school friends, Lydia was mean as a snake, something she'd no doubt learned from her parents. She would have been the easy choice. His mother would have loved her.

Andrew hadn't been outside at three in the morning since Harry was a baby, and they would take walks around the block to try to coax him back to sleep, the three of them like a tribe of zombies, he and Elizabeth making shushing noises and bouncing in unison, no matter which one of them was wearing the baby in the Björn. Ditmas Park was always quiet, but this close to Coney Island Avenue there were more trucks and horns, even in the middle of the night. It was true what they said about New York and sleeping – Andrew had forgotten that. He turned right on Beverly and started walking back toward Argyle. A breeze made the sweat on his forehead feel cool. Summer was the only season that mattered – the only reason for winter to exist was to increase the gratitude that Andrew felt for the month of June at this exact moment in time.

He unlocked the door to his house quietly and slipped his shoes off next to the front door. Iggy Pop was asleep on the sofa, and Andrew scooped him up and carried him up the stairs. The cat arched his back into Andrew's shoulder, still mostly asleep. The bedroom door was open a crack, and Andrew could see from the hallway that Elizabeth had left her bedside lamp on. He nudged the door open a few more inches with his toe, and gently set the cat down on the bed.

Elizabeth stirred. She'd never been a hardy sleeper, but in the years since Harry was born – even well after he stopped waking in the middle of the night – she'd been prone to waking when cars drove past, at distant sirens, at barking dogs. He knew this only because she told him in the morning – Andrew himself was always fast asleep. It was something they fought about, in a low-level way, that she was awake and he was asleep and he had missed whatever it was that had annoyed her. Andrew slid off his shirt and his shorts. His sweat had dried to a thin film of salt – he smelled a little bit, but Elizabeth had never minded that.

'Where have you been?' she asked, her voice low. She rolled over to face him.

'At the yoga place. They were having a party.' Andrew sat down on his side of the bed. Elizabeth's foot peeked out from under the sheet, and he put his hand on her arch.

'A party.' She narrowed her eyes at him, and Andrew tried to decide if it looked more like sleepiness or contempt. He clicked off the light.

'A party.' Andrew pulled back the sheet and slid underneath. He inched closer to his wife in the darkness. Elizabeth's body felt like the ocean, vast and cool. First he kissed her arm, and when she didn't shove him away, he kissed her shoulder, and then her cheek. By the time Andrew kissed his wife's mouth, she was moving her body back and forth like a snake about to strike, and he knew that whatever happened next, it would be good. This is what it was like when they were kids: playful, nibbling. Elizabeth had been an eager lover, like the student athlete she'd been in high school, cheeks flushed and full of energy. They rolled and stretched like two lion cubs, biting and pawing at each other's body parts. After a few minutes, they settled into a familiar position – they knew what worked. His ears were still vibrating from the party, and the room sounded like a subway platform. 'Am I being too loud?' he asked Elizabeth, now flat on her back, his hands wedged under her hips with his face between her legs.

'Harry's at a friend's house,' she said. 'Get to work,' shoving his face back against her body.

Twenty-five

It was almost two when their feet actually touched the sand. Harry dropped the umbrella and his two enormous bags with a satisfying thud. Ruby leaned down to grab one of the beach towels, but Harry put out his arm to block her. 'Please,' he said. 'Allow me.' He stretched out two towels, stuck the umbrella in the sand between them, and then gestured for Ruby to sit. The sand was grimy, with candy wrappers and cigarette butts poking up here and there, but the water looked clear, and people were swimming. Harry's mother had always told him that New York City beaches were toxic-waste zones and to be avoided at all costs, and he was glad he hadn't listened. What other things were out there, just waiting to be enjoyed? Elizabeth didn't like bacon, and so they never ate it, never. Harry was going to order a BLT with extra bacon – a BBLT – at the next possible moment.

'What else is in those bags?'

Harry dug around in one and pulled out a plastic pail and shovel.

'Okay,' Ruby said, giggling. 'What else?'

Harry reached back down and pulled out a little insulated cooler. Inside were two tiny cans of champagne. It had taken Harry an hour and forty dollars to convince some young woman walking down Cortelyou to buy them for him. 'Cheers,' he said, popping one open and handing it to Ruby, who took such a small sip that Harry knew she was impressed.

The beach was filled with old Russian ladies holding hand weights as they walked up and down the boardwalk, avoiding the packs of guys with beards and dark sunglasses and girls wearing tiny shorts and cutoff T-shirts.

'It's like an American Apparel billboard,' Ruby said. 'But with beer and sand.'

Harry couldn't tell if that was a compliment or not, but Ruby seemed to be enjoying herself, and so he didn't respond other than to nod and say, 'Yeah.'

They took half naps, they splashed in the water. Neither of them had a bathing suit, but it didn't matter. Ruby peeled off her dress. Her stomach was a soft, creamy brown, just like the rest of her, of course, though every inch gave Harry a new thrill. She had a perfect little outie belly button right in the middle! He could see more than the outline of her breasts through her thin, lacy bra, and when she walked away from him, toward the water, wearing nothing but her bra and underwear, Harry tried not to have a heart attack. He took off his shirt and his jeans and went in his boxers, praying the flap stayed closed. There was a burger place just on the other side of the board-walk, and Ruby waited on their towels while Harry got them food. She licked a spot of ketchup off her hand. It was the most beautiful beach anyone had ever seen, ever, even with the planes going overhead to JFK and all the seagulls and the noise and the people. There were towels everywhere, and Dominican families, and hipsters with ironic mustaches, and old men wearing Speedos, and fat women in bikinis. Harry thanked God that his parents had never moved to the suburbs, or to France, or anywhere else in the world. Ruby got the giggles after the champagne, and she let him put sunscreen on her shoulders. Harry took as long as possible, painting little designs and taking pictures with his phone before rubbing them in.

The burger place was getting rowdy. On their walk back to the train, Harry and Ruby stood outside for a few minutes and watched people dance and chug beers.

'I feel like I'm watching a movie,' Harry said. 'About people who kill a hobo while they're drunk-driving.'

'Yeah, and this is part of the montage that we keep seeing in flashback,' Ruby said. 'Totally.'

Harry let Ruby carry the smaller tote bag, which was less heavy now that there were no drinks and snacks in it, and he had lost a few of the beach toys, which he was fine with. They were more of a joke anyway, even though he really had liked watching Ruby build a sand castle. It was the kind of thing he wouldn't have done for fear of looking too babyish, but Ruby obviously never worried about that. They got on the train and sat in a two-seater facing the direction they were going, with Harry against the window and Ruby on the aisle. As soon as they sat down, she let her head drop against his shoulder and put her arm around his waist.

'I had a good time,' Ruby said. 'Almost good enough to stop being mad at you for ditching our stupid SAT class this morning.'

'Me, too,' Harry said. He sat as upright as possible and tried not to move, just in case Ruby took his fidgeting as a sign that he didn't want her there. At the next stop, someone started to sit in the seat next to them, which would've crushed Ruby's knees and made her have to shift positions, so Harry gave the best death stare of his entire life, and the guy moved away.

'I feel like we must smell bad,' Ruby said. 'No one wants to sit near us.'

'You do smell bad,' Harry said, softly, into her ear. 'You smell like toasted garbage.' He paused, afraid he was taking the joke too far. Everything still seemed precarious, as if Ruby might just sit up and look at him and see the truth, that he was still Harry, just Harry, no one she wanted to cuddle with on the subway.

But Ruby said, 'Mmmm,' and snuggled closer. 'My favorite kind.' She was asleep in a few minutes and slept all the way until they had to change trains to get the Q home. When they finally got off at the Cortelyou stop, Harry was nervous. Ruby seemed rested and happy after her siesta, and the bridge of her nose was a bit burned, despite Harry's artistic efforts with the sunscreen. She bounded up the stairs and started walking toward Argyle. Harry stopped.

'Hey,' he said. His voice was quiet – his mother's office was a few doors away, and he didn't want to cross in front of it, just in case she happened to be sitting at her desk.

'What?' Ruby said.

'This way,' Harry said, using his head to point behind them.

'Okaaaaay,' she said. 'You do know that our houses are both the other direction, right? Did you have some kind of brain injury while I wasn't paying attention?'

'Just trust me,' he said, and started walking.

Convincing someone to buy him champagne was easy – part B of the plan had been much, much trickier. Elizabeth kept the keys to all her properties at the office, except on weekends when she was having a few open houses – then they lived in a zippered pouch that hung from a hook above her desk. The summer was always busy, and she was running from one place to another every day – right now there were a few houses a bit farther south, closer to Brooklyn College, and one on East Sixteenth Street, a really big house that backed up on to the train tracks. She was showing the two houses on Sunday, and had shown the subway one that afternoon. Harry knew it was a risk to take the key, but he had, and the hardware store made him a copy in five minutes. The house's owners had moved to Florida. It was just sitting there, with their enormous old-people furniture, all dark, heavy wood and formal dining chairs. One of the smaller bedrooms had had a doll collection, which Elizabeth had shoved into a box and hidden in the basement. The subway running through the yard was enough of a handicap – they didn't need to give people nightmares, too.

The porch was dark, and Ruby hesitated before following Harry up the stairs.

'Whose house is this?' She was whispering.

'Ours,' Harry said. He knew there wasn't an alarm, even though there were stickers on the windows and a sign in the lawn saying that there was. According to his mother, that was true for 70 per cent of the houses in their neighborhood. Ruby hurried up behind him.

'Are you serious?' she asked, but Harry had already opened the door. He pulled her in and shut the door behind them. 'Whose house is this?' she asked again. 'You're fucking crazy!' It was crazy, a little, and he knew that they could get into massive amounts of trouble, and his mom, too.

'I told you. It's ours.' Harry wasn't sure if he could pull off mysterious, but he was having fun trying. Ruby was an inch taller than he was, maybe more. She sucked in her lower lip and looked around. 'Come here,' Harry said.

'Where?' Ruby asked. She peeked around the corner, into a dark kitchen.

'Here,' Harry said. He took a step forward, closing the gap between them, and kissed her. Ruby was good at it, of course. They stopped and started and stopped and started and stared at each other. Her mouth opened and closed, and she flicked her tongue against his, and Harry let out a moan that sounded like Chewbacca, and he didn't care. A SWAT team with machine guns could have broken down the door and taken him to a federal prison and he wouldn't have cared – it was a hundred per cent worth it. Ruby pulled away, took his hand, and started walking farther into the dark house.

'Let's go explore,' she said. All day long, Harry had been trying to convince his penis to stay down, to be quiet, but now it was a lost cause. His erection pressed against his jeans, and when Ruby's wrist accidentally brushed past it, she said, 'Oh, hello there,' which made it even bigger. If this was what came from a life of crime, Harry was ready to sign up.

Twenty-six

The house on East Nineteenth Street was going to sell fast – there were three bids after the open house, and now it was a matter of who was willing to pay. Elizabeth loved the rush of multiple bids – they were all under ask, but once buyers knew there was competition, they'd come up, and pretty soon, they'd be sailing over the $2 million mark. The sellers were going to be thrilled. Their condo in Boca had probably cost under a million. This was the kind of money that paid for grandchildren's college educations. It wasn't all greed. She leafed through the offers on her desk at work. Deirdre looked over Elizabeth's shoulder.

'Not bad,' she said. Deirdre had chopped off her hair, so that people would confuse her with Halle Berry, she said. Deirdre was a gorgeous size fourteen, and Elizabeth thought she actually did look like a movie star. She always wore tight sweaters the colors of emeralds and rubies. The O'Connells were dazzled by Deirdre, and Elizabeth didn't blame them. Mary Ann and her kids were pasty, with freckles all over, even on their arms and legs. Every one of them always looked like they had a very mild case of the chicken pox.

'It's great!' Elizabeth said, holding up one of the offer sheets. 'I really like this couple. Young, friendly. Totally book-club potential.'

'Do your clients know that you're just scouting for your personal friends?' Deirdre raised an eyebrow and then laughed. 'It only works if your friends have big checkbooks! I'd sell a house to an asshole if the check wouldn't bounce. I like 'em rich and heartless.'

'You do not,' Elizabeth said. Before Deirdre could respond, Elizabeth's phone rang.

'Holding for Naomi Vandenhoovel,' someone said.

'Oh, shit,' Elizabeth said. 'Not again.'

'Lizzzz-eeeeeeee,' Naomi said. 'I'm in New York! Come and have coffee with me! Come to the office! I want to show you what we've got put together so far. I think you'll go craaaaaaaazy for it.'

'Hi, Naomi,' Elizabeth said. 'How are you?' She rolled her eyes at Deirdre. *It's nothing,* she mouthed.

'I'm freezing my ass off because the air-conditioning in the office is on autopilot, but other than that I'm perfect,' Naomi said. 'I'll e-mail you the address. Come today, my afternoon is totally clear. You need to see our Lydia. Ciao-ciao!' She hung up.

Elizabeth set the phone back in its dock and looked at the pile of paper on her desk. She'd already done her work for the day – she'd responded to all the agents and all the clients. Everyone had their marching orders. There was more to do in the office, of course – there always was. But no one would mind if she took a few hours to go into the city.

Naomi was set up in a conference room in the Fifties, on Fifth Avenue. Elizabeth had had to give her name to three different people sitting at desks, each of whom whispered into a phone and looked her name up on a computer. The last gatekeeper, an effete young man wearing a bow tie, told her to wait and that Naomi's assistant would be right out. A girl with a small, neat Afro and bright red lipstick came swanning out a few minutes later.

'Elizabeth?' she said, sounding bored. 'Follow me.'

They walked past stainless-steel half walls and glass-enclosed offices. Elizabeth peeked into each of them, just in case there were any visiting movie stars. The studio released prestige movies, award winners. Naomi was no slouch. Finally they reached a door. Elizabeth saw Naomi inside, talking to another young woman, whose back was turned. Elizabeth stopped – even from behind she could see it – this woman, whoever she was, was their Lydia. And if Elizabeth didn't know better, she would think that it was her Lydia, too. The hair was just right – thick and dark and wild, as if it had never been brushed. It wasn't just fashion – Lydia didn't own a brush, or a comb, or a blow-dryer. She'd practically set those things on fire when she moved to Oberlin for school. Scarsdale was in her rearview mirror, and she was never going back.

'Hiiiiiiiiiii,' Naomi said, opening her arms wide. 'It's the genius!' She was taller than Elizabeth expected, with thick-framed glasses and perfectly straight California-blond hair down to the middle of her back.

'Who, me?' Elizabeth asked. She let Naomi embrace her, inhaling a cloud of sweet perfume.

'Yes, you!' Naomi pulled back, holding Elizabeth's arms out. 'Darcey, this is Elizabeth Marx, who wrote "Mistress of Myself." She fucking wrote it. Can you believe that? Like, it didn't exist, and then Elizabeth wrote down the words, and it was a fucking song.'

Darcey stood up and turned around. It wasn't just her hair that looked like Lydia's – it was her eyes, her cheeks, her chin. Elizabeth understood immediately why Naomi had wanted her to come.

'Oh, my God,' Elizabeth said.

Darcey did whatever actresses do in place of blushing. She smiled, and turned her face from side to side. 'I know,' she said. 'I was literally born to do this. If I had a dollar for every person who ever told me I looked like Lydia . . .'

'You wouldn't even have half your salary for this movie! Ha!'

Naomi pulled Elizabeth closer, and then pushed her toward a white leather office chair.

Darcey sat back down in a chair opposite Elizabeth. Elizabeth tried to look away but couldn't, which Darcey seemed to enjoy, smiling widely every time she caught Elizabeth staring.

'I also found this,' Naomi said. 'You've seen it, of course, but we did a little work. Check it out.' She grabbed a remote control and aimed it at the ceiling. Curtains slowly lowered, making the whole room dark. A screen illuminated on the far wall, and with another button push, a familiar song started to play.

Kitty's Mustache had made three music videos. They were all shot by an Oberlin kid named Lefty, whose real name was Lawrence Thompson III. He had a good camera and was in love with Zoe. She'd slept with him once or twice, Elizabeth suspected, just to keep him in the band's employ, or maybe she just let him see her naked. The first two videos, for 'Frankie's Lament,' a song Elizabeth had written about their landlord, and 'Magic Lasso,' a song about Wonder Woman, were both okay, shot in and around campus, mostly in their grimy apartments and in empty classrooms and in the arboretum, but for the 'Mistress of Myself' video, they'd spent the day on a cold beach on the banks of Lake Erie.

There they were – in full goth mode, all of them dressed entirely in black, standing side by side on the beach. Small snowbanks were in the foreground. It was Lefty's masterpiece, his Swedish art film. 'How did you get a copy of this?' Elizabeth asked. Lydia's hair whipped around her face. They'd brought out some of their instruments, but Lefty decided they should leave them in the car. It was like 'Wicked Game,' except instead of Chris Isaak and Helena Christensen, it was all Elizabeth's screaming mouth. At one point, Zoe lay down in the sand and rolled around. Lydia scowled. Andrew spent half the video with his back to the camera, which he claimed was his silent protest of his own role in the patriarchy.

Elizabeth leaned forward. It was a close-up of Lydia's face – only it wasn't Lydia. It was Darcey. 'Wait,' she said. 'How did you . . . ?'

'I know, it's seamless,' Naomi said. 'Our guys are fucking great. Once they retouched a birthmark on Angelina Jolie's boob for a three-hour movie. They added a birthmark! She refused to do makeup, said it was something to do with child labor, or maybe with her children, needing more time or something. Makeup can seriously take hours every day, so it was worth it to let her sleep in with all her kids and then just spend an extra million on Photoshop or whatever. It's amazing, right?'

'How did you get this? The original, I mean?' Elizabeth had a copy on VHS, but she'd heard through friends that Lefty had burned all his films after he decided to go into the family investment-banking business, so as to set himself free from his artistic dreams. As far as she knew, hers was the only copy.

'Not for nothing, Lydia's archives are in surprisingly good shape for someone who died of a heroin overdose,' Naomi said. 'She kept everything. If you didn't know better, you'd think that she was a librarian. Seriously. Color-coded, in chronological order, the whole nine.'

'That is so strange,' Elizabeth said. 'The Lydia I knew was a mess. She didn't even know how to balance her checkbook.'

Naomi's assistant laughed. 'Checkbooks. That's like a flip phone, right? But for money?'

'I'm serious,' Elizabeth said.

Naomi nodded. 'I think this is something you're really going to sink your teeth into, Darce – on the outside, she was this wild child, you know, this fuckup, but on the inside, she was always plotting for her historical legacy.'

'I totally get that,' Darcey said.

Elizabeth folded her hands in her lap. Her Lydia wasn't a wild child or a fuckup. Her Lydia was self-centered, and unreliable, and kind of a jerk. Her Lydia had never been interested in having female friends, at least until pretty famous actresses started coming to her shows, and then she seemed to be one of the gals. But Elizabeth knew that those pictures – or her Buddhism, or whatever she called it – didn't really mean that she had changed. Elizabeth had tried with Lydia; they all had, especially Andrew. At first, it had made Elizabeth jealous, all the nights that Lydia would just happen to be curled up with Andrew on his couch, her socked feet tucked under his legs. This was after Elizabeth and Andrew had made it clear to the band and everyone that they were a real couple, and still, there Lydia would be, batting her eyelashes and asking Andrew for help putting air in her bicycle tires, as if she were ever going to ride that stupid fucking bicycle.

'I want to see this movie,' Elizabeth said. It would only be part of the story, of course, but maybe there was more to Lydia than she knew. If Lydia had been hoarding Kitty's Mustache ephemera, then maybe she was also taking notes. 'Did she have diaries?'

'For every day of her life, starting at fifteen.' Naomi smiled. 'She did all the work for us, you know?' Naomi uncapped a pen and handed it to Elizabeth. 'Need another copy of the form? Ashley?' The assistant was at her side in less than a second.

Elizabeth didn't think about Zoe, who she knew would be happy enough either way. For the first time in a long time, she really thought about Lydia, her long-lost, faraway friend. Twenty-seven was such a dumb time to die. But more than Lydia, she thought about Andrew, and herself. The imaginary girl that Naomi had talked about, that was her – both then and now. She wanted to see herself pick up the guitar and write that song. She wanted to watch Andrew fall in love with her on the spot, once he knew what she was capable of. She wanted it for both of them, and signed her name. 'Give me one for Andrew, too,' she said. When Elizabeth left Naomi's office, she went into the bathroom, dried off the countertop with a paper towel, and forged

Andrew's messy signature, just as she'd done a thousand times on school permission forms and credit-card receipts. In their family, she was in charge of the paperwork, and so that's all she was doing, taking care of their joint business. It wasn't a big deal – just two seconds of ink on a sheet of paper. In another two seconds, she'd be in the elevator, and then she'd be in the subway, and then she'd be back in the office, and she'd fax it in, just like she faxed a thousand other forms all day long. Nothing to see here, nothing at all.

Twenty-seven

At home, Zoe's piles of stuff migrated from surface to surface, stacks of unread magazines and bobby pins, but at Hyacinth, all the counters belonged to Jane. Everything was labeled with masking tape, everything was face out. All the salts were next to one another, fine to coarse to flakes.

What people didn't understand about chefs was that it was only partially about cooking. It was about having a vision, a voice, a set of personal beliefs that were so strong that you needed to build something around them. There was literally no reason to open a restaurant if you felt like someone else was doing it better than you could. After twenty-five years of working in kitchens and ten years in her own place, Jane was still sure that no one else was doing Hyacinth better than she was. The restaurant was a glorious machine, and she was its engine – the mastermind. And all she wanted was to be the mastermind of the rest of her life, too.

Jane had a headache, and the headache's name was Ruby. Zoe had it worse in terms of direct combat, that was true, but they could also cuddle up and go play dress-up in Zoe's closet and talk about obscure bands that no one else had ever heard of, and it was all fine. Jane was the baddie. She was always the one who had to tell Ruby she couldn't have another ice cream, or that she couldn't force all of her preschool friends to call her the Queen and do her bidding. Jane was the boss, and the boss never got to cuddle.

Her own teenage years had been remarkably easy. Massapequa was a fine place to grow up. She played on all the teams, and went out for pizza with her friends, and had crushes on movie stars, just like everyone else. Everyone was a virgin, so it didn't matter that she was a lesbian virgin. What was the difference? They all had bad haircuts and listened to Z100. The summer before she left for the NYU dorms, Jane had spent every day in the local pool, avoiding little kids because they were obviously peeing at all times. She had freckles everywhere, even between her toes.

All summer, her parents treated her like she was made of glass, and she didn't understand why until it was over and they were packing the car full of pillows and boxes and books. Unlike Ruby, Jane had siblings – two brothers and a sister, all younger than she was. Like Ruby, Jane had had no idea what it meant for her parents to have their oldest child get ready to leave home. Leave home! It sounded so final. At the time, Jane had thought her mother was experiencing some very prolonged kind of stroke, where she was always blinking back tears and staring at Jane like she was the new episode of *Dallas*. But she understood it now. Children wanted to go. Children knew that they were old enough – it was prehistoric, baked-in knowledge. Only the parents still thought they were kids. Everyone else – tobacco, the voting booth, porn shops – said otherwise.

Jane moved through the kitchen slowly. She rotated jars so that they were facing the right way. The bell rang over the door, and Jane looked up to see her sous-chef, Clara, striding in. Clara was good – as solid as they came. Someday she'd want her own place, too. There were always more children to leave. Jane could feel herself drifting into the danger zone, and cleared some space on the counter. She grabbed the bread flour and the salt and the yeast, and when Clara walked in, Jane nodded hello. Baking bread for no reason had always been Jane's favorite form of stress relief, and Clara knew well enough to go about her own work instead of asking questions.

Twenty-eight

Andrew was happiest when he was busy. Ever since the night of the party, he and Elizabeth had been great. It was as if she understood that he needed her to just be on his side, to support him, and he understood that she needed him to be present and supportive like always, and so they were. It didn't hurt that they were having sex more often – it wasn't quite back up to trying-to-conceive levels, which had been exhausting for both of them in the several years after Harry was born, when they were so intent on giving him a sibling, but it was good, really good for people who had been together for two decades. It was a part of their relationship that had always been satisfying, a gentle reminder that they still knew how to do things right. Not that Andrew actually knew how often anyone else had sex. He assumed that Elizabeth knew whenever Zoe or any of her close friends had an orgasm, that she got a text message automatically, but guys weren't like that, even guys like him.

Tuesday mornings were the guided-meditation group, Wednesdays were yoga, Thursdays were dharma talks, and Fridays were the cosmic trances. Andrew knew he probably wouldn't be able to go every week, not without giving Elizabeth some big, drawn-out explanation. He could invite her, maybe, but she might hate it or poke fun, and then he'd have to explain to Dave how his wife wasn't into getting transcendental. Elizabeth had always been supportive of his various endeavors, but for now, he wanted to keep it to himself.

Most days, Andrew walked over after Elizabeth left for work. They'd set up a woodshop in the garage, and Andrew was building some bookshelves for the rooms upstairs. Dave would wander in and out, half dressed. Sometimes he looked like he'd just woken up, with tiny clusters of sleep still in the corners of his eyes, and sometimes he looked like he'd been up all night. They'd talk a bit, just one rung up from basic office watercooler chitchat. Lately Dave had been talking about a boat – a floating EVOLVEment.

'In the summer, it could be here in Brooklyn. Maybe docked next to the Brooklyn Bridge, where Bargemusic is, all decked out so the tourists want to know what's going on. And then in the winter, we sail south – Vieques, Saint Maarten, maybe.' Dave had his arms crossed over his bare chest. He had a patch of hair in between his pecs, a fleur-de-lis of brown curls.

'Do you sail?' Andrew asked. He was sanding a giant piece of wood, a shelf that would run the length of the main yoga room. He knew enough to do that – he was good with his hands. Dave had never asked if he was an expert craftsman. That wasn't the vibe – if you thought you could do it, you could do it. One of the young guys with short dreadlocks and a wide smile popped into the garage and said he had some tools in the trunk of his car, and he could help Andrew put the shelf up when he was done.

'When I was a kid,' Dave said. 'Here and there. It's all muscle memory, though.' He tapped a finger against his temple. 'It's all still here.'

'Me, too,' Andrew said. He didn't like to talk about his family, but it just came out. 'I took sailing lessons every summer, near my parents' house on Long Island. We spent three days on land just tying and untying knots, before they even let us get our feet wet. I tried to teach my son, and he could not have been less interested.'

Dave laughed. 'You're a real polymath, man, I love it.'

'I don't know about that,' Andrew said, 'but I guess I've been able to do a lot of different things.'

'Did you do any racing?'

'Sailing races, you mean? No. In my father's fantasies, yes. He would have loved a good regatta trophy or two around the house, but I was never that kind of kid, not really. It was always a great disappointment to my parents that I was more interested in Buddhism than in country clubs.'

Dave made a sympathetic *mmm*. 'You ever go to India?'

'Once, yeah, when I was nineteen.' Andrew put the sander down. He'd licked out a small groove by mistake, and the wood looked like a cresting wave. Dave didn't seem to notice. 'I spent some time traveling around. Jaipur, Kerala.'

'Nice,' Dave said. 'That's what I'm picturing – totally different vibe than the house. I want it to be *pink*, you know? Bright. Colorful. Like nothing else. And people could stay for a night, or maybe for a week, as it sailed around, doing treatments, working with our people. Like a floating retreat. EVOLVEBoat. BoatMENT? Not sure what it'd be called yet.'

'That sounds amazing,' Andrew said.

'I'm glad you're into it,' Dave said. 'We should talk more about it later.' He clapped Andrew on the shoulder. 'This is beautiful, man. Wabi-sabi, right?' He nodded at the piece of wood and turned back toward the main house.

'Right,' Andrew said. The garage was cool and quiet. There was some faint music coming from inside – he couldn't quite make out what it was. The Kinks? Big Star? A young couple came out of the back door with plates full of rinds and peels for the compost bin. Andrew gave a friendly salute, and they waved.

What did he look like, their dad? Their cool older brother? He really didn't know. When he and Elizabeth were in their garage, sitting on their rickety wooden chairs, Andrew sometimes felt like a tooth-less old man in some Appalachian folk song. Elizabeth closed her eyes when she sang, and sometimes it made her look just like her mother, half-cocked on two glasses of Chardonnay. Which was better than looking like his mother, whose face had been pulled back toward her ears so many times that it was a wonder she still had cheeks.

There were probably guides on the Internet for building a boat. Andrew could see it, the giant whalebones of the hull coming together beneath his hands. He wanted to make something that could take on the open water, something buoyant and beautiful.

Twenty-nine

Weekday lunches were so boring that Ruby had started drawing a graphic novel about Bingo's secret life as a hairdresser in New Jersey. Eventually she stopped laughing at any of Jorge's jokes, and so he would just stare at her mournfully from behind the bar while muddling mint and squeezing oranges. Every time someone came in and wanted a table, Ruby would pretend to be from a different country. She was French, she was Japanese, she was Mexican. She thought at least one person would be offended and/or amused, but no one seemed to notice. Most of the customers were women in their thirties wearing clogs for no good reason, and so they were obviously not the most sophisticated audience for Ruby's performance art.

Her mum was in and out, bringing in flowers for the tables and boxes of dish soap from the trunk of the car. They were acting literally ridiculous, her parents. Ruby sometimes thought about sitting them down and explaining that all they had to do was act normal and that everything would be fine. Zoe was behaving like she was on Rumspringa on steroids, all cute outfits and glasses of rosé in the middle of the afternoon, and Jane was groaning like the Abominable Snowman. Ruby wouldn't want to be married to either of them, but that was their problem, not hers. At this point, what was the difference between being married and divorced? They still went over all the

Hyacinth stuff together. The only reason that the restaurant looked half decent was that Zoe had picked out every tile, every paint chip, every chair, every salt shaker. Running a marriage really couldn't be that different from running a restaurant. Whatever. Plus, being someone's parents meant that they would be linked for the rest of their lives anyway. There was no getting out, not really, and plus it didn't even seem like it was really that bad. Ruby had it much worse than they did. She was probably going to have to become an organic farmer or an exotic dancer, or something else that you only needed hands-on experience for, but hey, if they wanted to ignore her to focus on their own stupid problems, fine. She drew a hideous, glitzy ball gown like someone on *The Bachelor* would wear to get out of the limo and then added Bingo's head on top.

It was two forty-five p.m. They stopped seating for lunch at three. With only fifteen minutes left, Jorge would turn people away, and she could go home. Harry said he was going to pick her up, though, and so she was going to wait until he showed.

They'd hung out three times since the night at the house, twice just at night, on walks with Bingo, and once in the afternoon when Ruby's mothers were out. Harry was a quick learner. He seemed to know that the clitoris existed, even if he didn't know precisely where to look, and unlike some guys, he took instruction well, and wasn't offended when Ruby offered some tips. That was the one piece of sex advice her mum had given her – that it should feel good for her, too – and thank God.

It was easier in the relative dark, always. That way you could fumble around and touch a new body part without fully admitting that you wanted to. *Oh, was that me? Oh, is that you?* Ruby liked to take off her clothes and watch Harry's eyes get enormous. No matter how dark it was, she could still see those giant circles, like in a cartoon. It was extremely gratifying. She drew a picture of him with flying saucers instead of eyeballs. The bell over the door rang, and Ruby looked up, expecting to see Harry.

Dust held his skateboard against his chest like a shield. Over his shoulder, on the sidewalk, Ruby could see Sarah Dinnerstein, her Whitman classmate and a fellow devotee of Dust and his army of church-step kids. Sarah had been pretty straitlaced until senior year, when she got her nose pierced and the inside of her lower lip tattooed with the word LOVE. People said she was on heroin, but mostly it seemed like she was on Nico, who, like Dust, had no real school affiliation and might have been twenty-five. No one knew for sure. In the fall, Sarah was going to Bennington. Ruby couldn't actually believe that Sarah Dinnerstein, who had four brain cells in her entire head, had gotten into college and she hadn't. The world wasn't fair. Sarah Dinnerstein had probably never had an orgasm. She probably thought female orgasms were a myth, like the Loch Ness Monster.

'What do you want?' Ruby asked.

'I come in peace,' Dust said. He leaned against the hostess stand. 'Nico is having a thing today. All day, all night. We just came out to get some more drinks. Sarah wanted a Gatorade.'

Outside, Sarah was twirling around in the sunlight. She had heavy, babyish cheeks and a dress that was too short. 'Jesus,' Ruby said. 'Is she tripping?'

Dust licked his teeth. 'Molly. You want some?'

The bell rang again. Harry did a double take at the sight of Dust but kept his head high, which made Ruby happy. 'Hey,' Harry said, nodding at her.

'Hey,' Ruby said. She held out her fingers like a crab. Harry turned sideways to slide past Dust and let himself be pinched. Ruby slung her arm over Harry's shoulder, pulling him close. 'So, maybe we'll come by, Dust.'

Dust raised an eyebrow. 'Okay, man. You know where I'll be.' He dropped the board to the floor with a clatter, making Jorge jump. 'Later.' He nudged the board out the door and did an ollie on the sidewalk, to Sarah Dinnerstein's great delight.

'We're not really going to a party with Dust, are we?' Harry asked.

Ruby shrugged. 'I don't know. My friend Sarah is going. And Nico is cool.'

'Okay,' Harry said. 'If you want to go, I'll go.'

Ruby slid off the stool. 'Let's blow this pop stand.' She wanted to see if Harry's cheeks turned pink when she said the word 'blow,' and they did.

Despite having dated him for six months, Ruby had no idea where Dust lived, not really. His mom lived in Sunset Park, maybe, and his dad lived somewhere in Queens, but it was all sort of fuzzy. Nico, on the other hand, lived in a big house around the corner from Hyacinth, and she'd been there a hundred times. Nico's house was a semi-mythical place. His parents didn't exist. There weren't bags of lentils in the cupboard or eggs in the fridge. There weren't any photographs on the walls. The curtains were always closed. Harry was walking slowly, his hair falling in his eyes. Ruby brushed her hand against his arm.

'These dudes are not my friends,' Harry said. 'I mean that specifically and also generally, you know, like in a philosophical sense.'

'They're not that bad,' Ruby said, even though they were actually worse than Harry could imagine. Ruby wasn't sure why she wanted to go to the party – it certainly wasn't to hang out with Sarah, whom she had never liked, and it also wasn't to make out with Dust, which is the only reason she would have gone before. It was definitely the most racially diverse social group she was a part of, which she liked. Everyone at Whitman were whiter shades of pale, as if all of them were in a competition to see who could be the most clueless about their own white privilege. The church-step kids were fuckups, but at least they weren't as bad as that. And she did enjoy the idea of making Dust jealous, and she enjoyed the idea of showing Harry what her life was like, or at least what it had been like before. Now that she had graduated, everything seemed different – she wasn't a cool fuckup, she was maybe just a fuckup. Maybe she wanted to go because she was afraid that she and Dust were more similar than she thought. Maybe she wanted to go because she was afraid that Harry would get scared off and then she'd be left with Dust and Nico and Sarah, which is all she really deserved anyway.

There were a few kids smoking on the porch – Ruby knew them and waved. She reached for Harry's hand and entwined their fingers, even though holding hands in public was not something they'd done before. She looked back at him, and Harry smiled the way you smile at a YouTube video of a baby lion making friends with a baby porcupine, like you just can't believe how good the world can be. Ruby felt instantly guilty, but it was too late, and so they walked in.

Thirty

Dr Amelia was on vacation. Every other shrink in the world went away in August, but Dr Amelia went away in July. Zoe had called three times and left messages, and finally Dr Amelia called her back.

'Zoe,' she said. There were seagulls in the background. 'I'm in Cape Cod. It's as pretty as a picture. It's the picture of health! What's up?'

Zoe was under the covers. Jane was at the restaurant, and Ruby was wherever Ruby went. She'd stopped trying to keep track when Ruby was fifteen and came home with a tattoo. She was a good girl, mostly, and Zoe trusted her. It was smart to give kids a little rope – that's what Oprah said. Of course, Oprah didn't have any children. Maybe she'd been talking about puppies. 'Oh, nothing,' Zoe said. She felt her voice begin to waver.

'Jane called, too,' Dr Amelia said. 'I'll be home in three weeks, so why don't you guys come and see me then?'

'Okay,' Zoe said. She crawled downward, so that her head was closer to the foot of the bed, and collided with Bingo. 'I was just hoping to talk for a minute, if that's okay.'

'What's on your mind?'

'How do you know when you should get a divorce? Do you have

some sort of chart? I thought I was sure, but I don't really know. You've seen us – what do you think?'

'You know I can't tell you whether to stay married or not, Zoe.' More seagulls.

Zoe closed her eyes and pictured Dr Amelia in a bathing suit. It would be a colorful one-piece, maybe with a little skirt, the kind her grandmother used to wear. Dr Amelia was probably wearing prescription sunglasses and a straw hat. Why *couldn't* she tell Zoe that? Everyone else was full of advice – Zoe's mother in Los Angeles, Zoe's aunts back in Michigan, people on the street. Why couldn't a therapist just give you a simple yes or no? Maybe Zoe needed a psychic instead, or one of those little paper fortune-tellers. Cootie-catchers. Yes or no.

'Are you renting, or with friends, or what?'

'You know I'm not going to tell you that, either.'

'How are the oysters?'

'Delicious.' Dr Amelia exhaled heavily. 'What's up, Zoe?'

'I think I'm good at my job,' Zoe said. She was trying not to cry. 'And, you know, if we get divorced, will I have to find something else to do? I'm almost fifty.' The number scared her. Jane had turned fifty five years ago, and they'd had a giant party, and everyone had stayed up too late dancing. Ruby had fallen asleep on the bar, like a proper street urchin, little Brooklyn food-service Eloise. But when Zoe thought about her own birthday, which was still two years away, she wanted to crawl into a hole and die. Fifty was fine, but not if you were suddenly adrift. Fifty was fine only if you were in great shape and still got kissed at least once a day.

'You guys can sort out the business stuff after you sort out the marriage stuff. It doesn't have to all happen at once. No one is going to get excommunicated. One thing at a time. When was the last time you signed a really complicated contract? Divorce is a business, too.'

'But how do I know if that's really what I want?' Zoe was

whispering. She wanted to ask Elizabeth if she ever felt this way around Andrew, but saying the words out loud seemed cursed, like if you'd ever even thought them, if you'd let them pass through your brain and then lips, then your marriage was doomed. She didn't want to be doomed, and she didn't want to admit to Elizabeth that she was doomed.

'Do you love your wife?'

Zoe's ear and cheek were slick with sweat from the phone. 'Of course I do. We have a daughter, we have a life. We just never have fun, you know? I feel like I have a roommate and I have to do her laundry. Sometimes when Jane kisses me, I forget that she's allowed to do that, like she's a homeless person on the bus or something.'

'Maybe you should try having some fun,' Dr Amelia said.

Zoe wiped the sweat off her face. 'Yeah,' she said. 'Any suggestions?' She poked her head out of the covers, knocking Bingo on to the floor.

'When was the last time you went on a date?' Dr Amelia said. 'Maybe you need to kick the snow off your boots. Kick the tires. See if you can pump a little air into the bicycle.'

'I gotcha,' Zoe said. 'We'll book an appointment when you're back. Thanks for calling. I'm sorry to bug you on your vacation.'

'That's what telephones are for. It's fine. You take care.' And then Dr Amelia was gone, and Zoe and Bingo were alone in the house again. There was a thump downstairs, and Zoe called out 'Hello?' but no one answered. The house had its own problems.

Thirty-one

Elizabeth hadn't seen Iggy Pop all afternoon. She'd been in and out –
into the office, to the grocery store, to the coffee shop – but Iggy usually rotated through his sleeping spots throughout the day, and so it
didn't seem strange until she realized that it had been nearly all day.
Harry was playing a video game in the living room, an SAT book
splayed open on the coffee table. 'Igs?' she said. 'Iggo Piggo? Pop
Pop?' Elizabeth walked in circles around the kitchen.

'Have you seen the cat?' she asked.

Harry shook his head without taking his eyes off the screen.

'Hmm,' Elizabeth said. She checked all the beds and the bathroom
sinks. Sometimes when it was hot, Iggy went from sink to sink, trying
to stay cool by pressing his body against the porcelain. Andrew was
at EVOLVEment again.

Elizabeth wasn't interested in being a nag. She loved that Andrew
was in touch with his feelings. She never wanted a husband like her
father, who could have been on fire and wouldn't have called for help.
But she didn't love that Andrew seemed to have chosen to be an intern
at a yoga studio instead of finding an actual job, even if that actual
job had been an internship as a woodworker. Andrew had never cared
about money – he'd never had to – but for most of their adult lives, he
had at least respected the appearance of having a job.

There were tons of kids at Whitman in similar situations – the children of actors and hedge-funders, the grandchildren of people whose names were on the sides of public buildings. Brooklyn wasn't the same as it had been when they'd moved, a city next door, with its own rhythms and heartbeats. Now it was all Manhattan spillover – the Russian oligarchs were buying up Tribeca and the West Village, and so Brooklyn was the next-best thing. It was her job to support this, but Elizabeth didn't like it. She would have been happier making smaller commissions and keeping the borough full of middle-class families. She'd sold so many houses to public-school teachers – Center Slope town houses – and those houses were now worth absolutely stupid amounts of money. Sometimes she thought about moving upstate, somewhere pretty along the Hudson. Maybe when Harry graduated, she and Andrew could cash out for good. Sell the house, sell the life. If they weren't in the city, then maybe Andrew wouldn't ever have to pretend to have a job again. He could just go on meditation retreats and build sculptures or throw pottery or take tae kwon do classes. She could sell country houses to the rich people who were buying $2 million houses in Brooklyn – she'd ask the O'Connells to let her open a branch office in Rhinebeck. Harry could spend summers at home, living in the apartment over the garage. What did it mean about their self-worth if they needed to be in the city for no reason? Was she that afraid of what her friends would think of her, if they'd say she was a quitter? Was she a quitter?

'Mom?'

'Sorry, what?' Elizabeth blinked. Harry was staring at her, the scene on the screen paused with his detective frog in mid-jump.

'Do you want help looking for the cat? It's going to get dark soon.'

Elizabeth rubbed her hands together. 'Yes, oh, sweetie, yes, let's do that. Can you check the basement? I'll do one more search down here, and then maybe we'll walk around the block?' Iggy Pop wasn't supposed to go outside – there were feral cats in the neighborhood, and he was no fighter – but the back screen door was easy enough to shove, even for a cat. He'd gotten out a few times before, and they'd always found him stalking around the flower beds in the yard, a determined look on his face.

Elizabeth opened and shut cupboards in the kitchen and peeked under the dining-room table.

'Not in the basement,' Harry said, coming up the stairs.

'No,' Elizabeth said. 'I didn't think so.'

They started in the garden, Elizabeth walking clockwise and Harry counterclockwise. No sign of Iggy.

'Let's walk around the block,' Elizabeth said. They walked down the driveway to the sidewalk and turned right, checking under the parked cars and in the flower beds.

Harry needed a haircut. His curls were starting to creep down his neck the way they had when he was a baby. Elizabeth resisted the urge to reach out and put her finger inside one of the ringlets.

'So, are you spending time with Ruby?' Since the eBay incident, Harry hadn't mentioned her, but Elizabeth saw his phone light up more than usual, and then his whole face, and so she knew that Ruby was still hovering around. She wasn't against it, not really – she loved Ruby. She loved Zoe. She loved that Harry was spending time with a girl, whether what they were doing was romantic or platonic or, most likely, somewhere in that giant, hazy, in-between zone.

'I guess,' Harry said. 'Yeah, we hang out. I mean, after our SAT class, and stuff. Sometimes.'

'That's nice,' Elizabeth said. She didn't want to press. She had never once talked to either of her parents about her love life as a teenager, or as an adult. When she and Andrew had decided to get married, her father had made a joke about the marital bed, and Elizabeth had felt nauseous for days. It was Harry's business. Ruby was a little bit wild, but Elizabeth very much doubted that her sweet son was up to Ruby's romantic standards. Zoe had been like that – happy to flirt with anyone who looked her way, but much harder to pin down. It was funny to see how things repeated. Not funny ha-ha.

When Zoe and Jane had started talking about having a baby, it wasn't clear how they'd do it. Zoe was younger, but also more squeamish. Jane's mother had had four kids at home with a midwife and no drugs; her genes seemed promising. It was a logistical conundrum – they would both be mothers, of course, but who was going to carry the child, who was going to breast-feed, who was going to have her hormones and pelvis put through hell? They were both open to it. If they were going to have more, then maybe Jane should go first? But how could they know if they were going to have more? Neither Zoe nor Jane had elaborate fantasies about big families. And then, of course, they had to figure out the sperm.

It was what people always wanted to know – and what Elizabeth had been afraid to ask too many questions about, even as close as she was. Were they going to get it from a friend or a sperm bank? If it was from a friend, would they actually have sex, or go for the turkey baster? Elizabeth hated to think about how Ruby probably got asked all those questions – at school, at summer camp, by bigots and friends alike. Before Zoe had Ruby, Elizabeth had never thought about how easy it was for a heterosexual couple – even though she and Andrew had had a horrible time getting pregnant, both before Harry and after, it was their private trauma and heartbreak and no one else's. No one ever asked how they were planning on having a baby, what elaborate measures they would have to take.

It was amazing to think that that sperm – Jane's younger brother's, if you must know – had eventually turned into Ruby, who had been a full-cheeked baby, who had been a mermaid child, who had been a sullen tween, who had graduated from high school. Elizabeth had wiped her bottom dozens of times, had bathed her in the sink. And now Harry blushed at the sound of her name.

'She doesn't know what she's going to do next year,' Harry said, unprompted. They'd made it to the corner and turned right, still with no sign of Iggy.

'No? Zoe told me she was going to take a year off. In Europe, practically everyone does. I think it's a great idea.'

'Yeah, but she doesn't even know what she wants to do, like, at all.'

Elizabeth looked at her son. 'Next year, you mean? Or for the rest of her life?'

'Either. Both.'

'I didn't know what I wanted to do for the rest of my life when I was eighteen.' Elizabeth waved to an elderly neighbor across the street. 'I still don't. And your father *certainly* doesn't.'

'What do you mean?' Harry looked stricken.

'I mean, it's never too late to decide to do something else. Becoming an adult doesn't mean that you suddenly have all the answers.' Elizabeth stepped over a large crack in the sidewalk and then stooped down to check under a few more cars.

'I know,' Harry said. 'I wasn't raised in an igloo. But what do you mean that Dad *certainly* doesn't?'

'Oh,' Elizabeth said. 'That. I just mean that he has a lot of interests, and that he hasn't had a conventional career path, you know, moving up the corporate ladder.'

'Oh, yeah,' Harry said. He seemed satisfied. They got to the next corner and turned right again. 'Maybe we should make signs.'

'For your dad?'

'For the cat.'

'Right.' Elizabeth put her hands on her hips. The sun was setting. The neighborhood looked prettiest at dusk, as did the rest of the world. Sometimes she wished she could take all the photos for all the houses just before sunset, when every room looked alive with beauty and possibility. Harry's curls were outlined with gold. She wanted to kiss her son on the mouth the way she had when he was a baby, and to remember every second of their lives together, like some sort of robot. Andrew was better at that, at remembering all the tiny moments of Harry's development, what day of the week it was when he first smiled, and when he learned how to ride his bike without training wheels. There wasn't enough time in the world, not for the things that mattered most, even counting all the endless days when Harry had a fever and was home from school and they didn't move from the sofa. Even counting the days the three of them had spent marooned indoors during blizzards. Even counting the days before he was conceived and she and Andrew wanted nothing, nothing, nothing more than a wick to light and hold.

Thirty-two

The house was a mess, with Ruby's clothing everywhere, and dog hair, and half-empty abandoned glasses of water. Zoe knew how it must look to Elizabeth; like she wasn't sure what to do next, as if the likeliest result would be for her to end up like the Collyer brothers, buried under mountains of her own junk. That morning, she'd weeded out the bookshelf next to her bed and her underwear drawer. She wasn't sure if she was clearing things out in order to begin to think about maybe selling the house (she couldn't even *think* about it de-claratively) or whether clearing things out was a way of procrastinat-ing even doing that much.

It was her favorite time of day, the window of time between lunch and dinner. All was quiet at home, and Hyacinth was recharging its batteries, the cooks readying everything for the evening rush and making staff meal, something large and comforting to feed everyone from the cooks to the waiters and the runners and the busboys. Zoe had always preferred staff meal to anything on the menu. She'd had everything so many times over the years – a bite here, a bite there, spoonfuls of everything at home – that even with the changing of the seasons, she couldn't stomach another plate of Hyacinth's polenta and mushrooms or shaved asparagus with pecorino. Staff meal could be anything – fried chicken, moo shu, burgers smothered in blue cheese. She wasn't always around Hyacinth to eat, but Jane was cooking tonight – she'd been inspired and signed herself up – and Ruby was working, and so she went. All she was doing at home was moving things from one room to another, and she was happy enough to get away from it for a little while.

It took six minutes to walk to the restaurant. Ruby was sitting at the table in front of the window, her legs crossed underneath her and her long purple hair falling in her face. Zoe knocked gently on the window to get her attention, and Ruby stuck out her tongue.

Inside, Hyacinth smelled like basil and peaches and brown sugar. Zoe folded herself into the chair next to Ruby, and waved hello to the servers setting the tables.

'Hi, sweets,' she said, and tucked Ruby's hair behind her ear.

'Mum,' Ruby said. 'Please.' She untucked it.

There was a bowl of sugar snap peas in front of her, and Zoe popped one into her mouth.

'Hey,' Jane said, coming up from behind them. She was in her kitchen clothes, a stiff white jacket unbuttoned at the collar. Zoe loved seeing Jane in her chef coat – it had always been a turn-on. It was her formal wear, her version of a ball gown, when she looked most like herself, and most in charge. Jane had always seemed like an adult, even when they met, when Zoe was twenty-three and Jane was thirty. Unlike Zoe, who'd never had to work a job, who paid her rent late because she was disorganized but not because she didn't have the money, Jane was already a grown-up. When she'd told Zoe that she wanted to open a restaurant, Zoe knew that she would make it happen. There was nothing adolescent about her, nothing wishy-washy. Jane put her hands on Ruby's shoulders and squeezed.

'Hi,' Zoe said. 'What's for dinner?'

'Carnitas, baby. So rich, it tastes like chocolate. Watermelon salad. So good.'

'Sounds delicious.' Zoe loved it when Jane talked about food. She wasn't one of those chatty chefs who killed a whole meal by telling you where every grain of rice was born. Jane cared about that, of course, but she'd rather just sit across from you and nod at your happy moans. She was more den mother than sommelier – she didn't care whether or not you could identify the sage or the saffron, she just wanted to know that you liked what she'd given you. She'd cooked for Zoe early and often in their courtship – when Zoe thought about falling in love with Jane, she thought of the two of them sitting naked at Jane's kitchen table, dragging their fingers through brownie batter and twisting their forks into perfect orange yolks, sending tendrils of richness down over handmade pasta. Jane was fresh out of the CIA and liked to practise her techniques. Fresh croissants, sometimes stuffed with almond paste. Zoe licked her fingers every day. She gained ten pounds in the first six months they were together. Whenever she'd lost weight in the intervening years, Jane would take it as a personal slight. It was a good quality in a wife.

Jorge waved from behind the bar. 'You want a glass of something?'

Zoe shook her head, but Jane ducked back around the bar and returned with two glasses of cava. 'Come on,' she said to Zoe. 'Live a little.' Jane handed her own glass to Ruby. 'Not the whole thing – I'll get arrested. You're sitting in the window.' Ruby slurped a little off the top. Zoe pursed her lips and then smiled.

'How's your SAT class going? I haven't really heard that much about it,' Zoe said. Behind Ruby, Jane rolled her eyes – but it was never a good time to have a conversation that a teenager didn't want to have, so Zoe forged ahead. 'You think you'll be able to take the test again?'

'As I've already told you, Mothers, the score was not the problem.'

Ruby gritted her teeth. 'My scores were fine. Like, better than half of my stupid friends'.'

'But not as good as the other half of your stupid friends'?' Jane sat down.

'They're not actually stupid. My friends are smart. I'm just calling them stupid because I hate them.' Ruby closed the book in front of her.

'Gotcha,' Zoe said.

'And yes, I can take the test again, if you want. I really don't think it matters, though. Mom didn't go to college, and she's fine.' Ruby turned toward Jane. 'Right? Are you fine?'

'I went to cooking school,' Jane said. 'If you want to go to a trade school, that counts.'

'And what did you do in college, Mum, except smoke cigarettes and play in a band?'

Zoe laughed. 'Hey, I was an art major! I also made prints!'

'You guys are really not selling this idea.' Ruby shook her head. 'No wonder neither of you gave a shit about my applications. It's a waste of time and money, and you know it! Come on, admit it, part of you is relieved that you're not going to have to spend like fifty grand a year for me to learn how to weave baskets, or whatever you did at Oberlin, or make a soufflé.'

'You already know how to make a soufflé,' Jane said proudly.

'Again, not the point.' Ruby swiveled in her chair and looked back toward the kitchen. 'Are the tacos ready? I'm starving. It was a long day of doing absolutely nothing in here.' She pushed back her chair and walked into the kitchen.

Jane slid over into the empty chair. 'Did we do everything right, or did we do everything wrong? Sometimes I can't tell.'

Zoe let herself fold against Jane's shoulder. 'If you figure it out, let me know.' She smelled like pork and garlic and chocolate, and Zoe breathed it all in. If things were always this easy, they'd just be together. If the restaurant weren't a tug-of-war, if Ruby weren't a gorgeous ball of anxiety that grew in the pit of her stomach every day. Zoe wished that marriage were just the good parts, just the parts that made you happy, but it wasn't. Even she knew that.

Thirty-three

It was an official date, as far as Harry could tell. The singer from the Aeroplanes lived in the neighborhood and ate lunch at Hyacinth every day, and so he was friendly with Ruby's moms. The guy put them on the list for the show at the Barclays Center, good seats, too. Ruby asked via text, like it wasn't a big deal, but Harry knew it was. He would have to tell his parents, and she would have to tell her parents, and one of them would probably pick the other one up at the door and sit in the living room for two minutes and make small talk. Harry really, really hoped that his parents would let him go over to Ruby's, but he wasn't surprised when they were both sitting in the living room, waiting for her to arrive. They said they were just making signs with pictures of Iggy Pop to put up around the neighborhood, but Harry didn't believe them. They were lingering.

'What?' said Elizabeth. 'I just want to see her! It's just Ruby!'

Harry was pacing back and forth, stopping every time he heard a noise on the sidewalk. Andrew watched, amused, which was the worst. He leaned back and peeked out the window. 'She's coming,' he said.

Harry zipped into the kitchen and opened the fridge. He needed the cool air, and also not to be staring at the door as Ruby walked in. The party at Dust's friend's house had been pretty dumb, not that

Harry had much to compare it to. There were lots of kids sitting around smoking, and he'd followed Ruby from room to room. Every now and then, they'd stop to say hi to someone, and when they moved on, Ruby would tell him how she didn't really like that person, no matter what she'd said to their face. Eventually they'd found an empty corner and just sat on the floor, Ruby ashing her cigarette into a discarded Snapple cap by their feet. Dust ignored them, and Harry was relieved. Parties were way less eventful than in the movies. No one was dancing, no one was barfing, at least not until the end, when Ruby's friend Sarah ducked into the bathroom and some pretty gross sounds came from the other side of the door. The only exciting thing that happened was that Ruby held his hand, even if their hands were tucked behind their knees, out of view of passersby. That didn't matter. What mattered was that after they got home, she sent him a text asking him to go on an actual date.

'Hey, Ruby, how are you?' Harry heard his father greet her. He closed the fridge door and wiped his hair out of his eyes. Ruby was hugging his father, then his mother. She'd done something different to her hair – it was all braided tight against her scalp for a few inches, when it exploded into curls.

'Whoa,' Harry said. 'When did you do that?'

Ruby twirled a curl around her middle finger. 'An hour ago.'

'I *love* it,' Elizabeth said. She scrunched a handful of Ruby's hair. 'You look like your grandmother. For most people, that's a weird compliment, but you really do.'

'I was going for post-apocalyptic sun goddess, but I'll take grandmother, I guess.' Ruby smiled. 'Thanks.'

'We should go,' Harry said. 'We don't want to miss anything.'

'Right,' said Elizabeth. 'You guys have fun. Tell the boys we say hi!'

Harry stopped with his hand on the doorknob. 'Mom, I am not telling anyone that you say hi.'

'Fair enough.' Elizabeth blew a kiss, which Harry waved away, as if he could push it back through the air on to his mother's lips. They were out the door before she could say anything else. Ruby didn't take his hand on the walk to the train, but she did once they were on the Q heading toward the concert.

The Barclays Center was enormous. Harry didn't care about basketball, and so he hadn't been before. From the outside, the arena looked like a spaceship had just landed on Flatbush Avenue, and on the inside it was all gleaming black floors, like being inside an evil crystal ball. Ruby had been to a couple of concerts with her mum, and she pulled him through the crowd toward the will-call windows. Most of the concertgoers were in their thirties, with unseasonable beards and knit caps, which made Harry rethink his plain white V-neck. Ruby was dressed, as she'd said, as some kind of goddess, with her new hair surrounding the back of her head like a halo, and a flowy little dress over some giant heavy black boots. She scowled at everyone who came within three feet of her, which was about a hundred people a minute. They finally found their seats, which were in a roped-off section of the floor, only a few feet from the left-hand side of the stage.

'Um,' Harry said. 'This is close. These guys must really like your mom's food.'

'My mom did the food for the singer's wedding,' Ruby said. 'It's cool. They're like, whatever. They're not that famous.'

Harry gestured to the rest of the arena. 'I'd say they're pretty much famous, not that that means anything in any real sense, but it does mean that they sold a lot of tickets to this concert.'

'Fair enough,' Ruby said. She snuggled her nose against Harry's neck. 'I don't really like their music. It's for sad boys and dads.'

Harry could almost picture a day when Ruby's touching his neck wouldn't give him an instant boner, but today was not that day. 'I may or may not fall into that category,' he said.

'I know, that's why I invited you,' Ruby said. 'That and the fact that I wanted to make out with you in public in front of ten thousand strangers.'

'I accept,' Harry said, but before he could say more, Ruby's tongue was pressing against his lips and her hands were on his face. The Aeroplanes walked out on to the stage, and everyone in the crowd screamed, and Harry felt the entire wall of sound inside his body. For the rest of his life, no matter where he was or what he was doing, hearing the first few chords of that one song would bring him back to Ruby's tongue and to feeling like the luckiest boy in Brooklyn.

The band played. All the people around them stood up and swayed or bopped around in their seats, and when they felt like participating, so did Harry and Ruby. Harry found that Ruby would just make fun of the people around them and/or the band if he wasn't kissing her, and so he felt like it was his civic duty to do that as much as possible. About halfway through the show, the singer in the band, a tall, scrawny-looking guy with greasy black hair that hung down to his ears, said, 'This next song isn't one of ours, but I think you'll know the words anyway,' and then the guitar player launched into the opening lick of 'Mistress of Myself.' Ruby and Harry pulled away from each other and started laughing. The entire crowd – thousands upon thousands of people – sang along.

'This is so weird!' Harry said, shouting over the noise of the crowd.

'I know,' Ruby said. She bobbed her head and mouthed the words. 'I think the singer has a crush on Zoe.'

Harry shrugged. A lot of people did. It was sort of a joke in their family, Zoe's sex appeal. When Harry was young, before he understood about lesbians, he'd once asked his father if he'd ever had an affair with Zoe. She was so beautiful, and she was always around.

Maybe it was like bumper cars, being a grown-up, just crashing into whoever was closest. He didn't know. Andrew had laughed, and Harry had felt instantly ashamed, having clearly misunderstood something important.

The singer writhed around, bending in half and jerking back up. It was like watching someone be electrocuted over and over again. Ruby threw her hands in the air and danced. 'Don't tell my mum,' she said, bouncing up and down.

Harry shook his head. 'Not in a million years.' They didn't kiss or even touch again until the song was over, because otherwise it would have felt like their parents were watching them, like the song was a radio transmitter and something in both of their houses would start beeping and show their parents what they were doing. Like incest, almost. It wasn't like that – sure, they'd grown up in tandem, Harry in his house and Ruby in hers, on the same block, and sure, there were those old photos of them standing naked together, but that was before life was real, before Harry could actually remember. What Harry could remember was feeling nervous when Ruby walked by, and her not paying attention to him once they were in middle school. Their families didn't all hang out like they used to, in and out of each other's houses. Everyone was too busy now. That was when they were someone else, some babies who looked like them. They weren't kids anymore, they were actual people. Harry worried that his parents would never notice that he'd stopped leaving his dirty underwear on the floor, or that he'd started eating avocados. Almost everything about him had changed, or was changing, and they had no idea. Harry had watched porn, he'd smoked weed, he'd jerked off a thousand times. In their house! Sometimes he felt like he could build a robot out of old pictures of himself and his parents would never know the difference.

All Harry wanted was to have sex with Ruby, preferably all day long, for at least a week. They'd gotten close – or at least he thought so. In the house, she'd given him a blow job, his first, and since then it had been mostly hands-over-the-pants-type stuff, which was obviously a huge improvement from staring at her surreptitiously down the hallway at school, but after her actual mouth had been (he could hardly believe it) on his actual dick, there was no going back. Ruby had invited him to her house, but Zoe was always around, and she didn't seem to knock, and Harry wasn't ready for his very first coitus to be interruptus, too. His mom had more open houses coming up. Or it didn't have to be like in some high-school movie, the deed taking place underneath a fluffy pink duvet, the guy all cautious and serious and asking 'Is this okay? Is this okay?' every two seconds. It could be anywhere. Even just being around Ruby made him feel braver than he'd been before – like with Dust, at graduation. Harry had never dreamed of hitting anyone before, ever – but it was for Ruby, and so he could do it. He could do this, too.

'Let's go,' Harry whispered in Ruby's ear.

'What?' she asked, still dancing. He put out his hand, and she took it, and this time he was the one leading her through the crowd.

The arena was enormous, and the Aeroplanes had been on for only an hour, so when they made it out into the halls, it was mostly empty except for vendors selling beer and T-shirt stands.

'This is your new thing, huh, like, International Man of Mystery?' Ruby said.

Harry looked around until he saw the exit. 'Maybe it is,' he said.

'Maybe I like it,' Ruby said.

Thirty-four

There was a playground tucked just underneath the bottom of the park. Ruby had always preferred it to the tiny one on Cortelyou, because the one in the park was big enough to get lost in. Someone's parent was always wandering through, calling a kid's name. Ruby and Harry opened the little metal gate and hurried inside. Unlike the rest of the park, which was 'open' until midnight, playgrounds were technically closed after dark, but that still didn't mean they were actually locked. There was a row of swings running along the right-hand side, closer to the street, and then there were big fiberglass cutouts of animals on a squishy floor, soft enough that little kids could fall and not actually hurt themselves. The playground was empty, except for the two of them.

Harry walked around a large purple elephant, running his hand along the elephant's back. 'Would you do that to my hair?' Harry said, without looking up.

'You want to look like a disco goddess?'

Harry ruffled his hair and fluttered his eyelashes. 'Yeah. And maybe cut it shorter?' He pulled up a curl, stretching it out straight from the top of his head.

'I'll cut it, I'll bleach it, whatever you want. Full service.' Ruby walked around to Harry. They'd probably played together, right here.

She just hadn't seen him recently. She'd *seen* him, sure, on the block and at school, but that was just his familiar face, like his father and mother shrunk down in some sort of machine. The machine of procreation. They were robots, all of them, built with eggs and sperms and covered in goo. Ruby had seen the photos of herself coming out of Zoe's vag – some friend of her moms who'd been in the room for that exact purpose, to snap pictures of Zoe's vagina and Ruby's hairy little head and all the blood and the goop and the whatever. And then there you were, this tiny person, a doll that would grow and grow and grow until you were standing in a playground at ten o'clock on a Wednesday in the middle of the summer and you were about to slide your undies off and kick them to your old friend, your new boyfriend, whatever he was.

Cars drove past, but Harry and Ruby didn't once stop looking at each other. Harry held her underwear in his hand, his fingers loose around the cotton. Ruby walked up to him, waiting until their lips were touching, and then she pushed him lightly backward until they were both lying on the ground. She reached down for his zipper and took him out of his pants.

'I don't have anything,' Harry said, stammering. 'If I wasn't afraid to walk through the park by myself right now, I would run to a Duane Reade and buy every condom in the store just so that I would never, ever be in this particular situation again.'

'I do,' Ruby said. She reached into her bag and pulled out a condom. 'In fact, I have more than one, in case this goes well. Or fast.'

Harry coughed. 'Ruby,' he said. His cheeks were pink – even in the dark she could see it. That was one thing she loved about boys as pale as Harry – it was so easy to make them turn color, like a chameleon trying to blend itself into a tree.

'I know,' she said. Ruby unrolled the condom on to Harry gently. He was already convulsing when she climbed back on to him and slid him into her body.

'Oh, fuck,' he said. Harry pulled her torso down to his and kissed her. Ruby rocked back and forth, enjoying Harry's little spasms of delight. 'Oh, fuck,' he said again, and Ruby felt him come. She kissed him and gave her Kegels a squeeze, which elicited another great big moan.

'Oh, my God,' Harry said. 'Did that just happen?'

Ruby laughed, and kissed him. 'Um, yes. That's why I brought more than one.'

'No,' Harry said. 'I don't mean. Well, yeah, I guess that is what I mean. But I also mean, wow.' He looked up at her with astonishment.

Ruby had slept with four people, including Harry and Dust. That was only counting actual sex. If you counted other stuff, the list was longer. But out of the four guys, only Harry had ever looked at her like this. Even with Mikhail, who she'd lost her virginity to when she was fourteen, Ruby had never felt like she was doing anything that really mattered to anyone. Jamal, who had been her second, had been an RA at her summer program, and she was pretty sure that having sex with the campers was exactly what he was not supposed to do, which didn't seem like a great sign. Not that the boys she'd slept with hadn't enjoyed it, or hadn't wanted her – and she had wanted them, always, she wouldn't have done it otherwise – but Ruby had never, until this second, felt like she was watching herself become a part of someone else's story. She could see the whole thing: no matter what happened with Harry, even if they never slept together again, even if she got hit by a bus when they walked home, even if she moved to the North Pole and they only communicated via Santa Claus, Harry would always remember this playground, and her face, and the fact that she had agreed to be his first.

There weren't very many differences to having gay parents, or parents of two races. It wasn't like being raised a pagan or a Wiccan or whatever conservatives wanted their constituents to believe. No one was being indoctrinated. In fact, it was the opposite. Most of Ruby's friends with straight parents grew up assuming they'd be straight, too, and that they'd marry someone who looked pretty much the same way they did. If you had two moms, though, or two dads, or your parents weren't the same color, then you were born knowing that there wasn't actually a default setting. Ruby was open to being attracted to anybody. She'd thought a lot about being a lesbian, even though she knew she was attracted to boys. Sometimes she wondered if that was just her wanting to be different from her parents, or buying into the societal pressure pushed on her by Barbie dolls or whatever. There were a few out girls at Whitman, two little baby dykes who wore bow ties and dress shoes and one pretty junior who had a girlfriend already in college, which Ruby found creepy from a purely statutory standpoint. There was one other family she knew at school with gay parents, but those kids were still in middle school, and so Ruby wasn't about to ask them what they thought about the whole thing. She was pretty sure that she was straight, but maybe not. Maybe she'd change her mind later, who knew? Her mum had been with guys when she was a teenager, too. Her mom wouldn't have had sex with a guy in one trillion years. Everyone was different.

Sex wasn't a big deal. Sex was the biggest deal. 'Wow yourself,' Ruby was about to say, but then there were flashlights and a voice coming through a megaphone, and she and Harry were scrambling away from each other like cockroaches when you turned on the light.

Thirty-five

Wednesday nights were slow at Hyacinth, and so Jane and Zoe were home early. Jane was on the couch, watching something dumb, and Zoe was upstairs in bed. They were both pretending that they weren't waiting up for Ruby to come home. Jane's phone began to vibrate on the coffee table, and when she didn't recognize the number, she ignored it, reaching for the remote instead. A minute later, she heard Zoe's phone ring upstairs, and Zoe said, '*What?*' Her feet thumped to the floor. Jane sat up straight, suddenly at attention. She debated checking upstairs to find out what was going on, but Zoe was hurrying down before she had the chance.

'We have to go to the fucking police station,' Zoe said. She had a scarf wrapped around her hair, and it looked like she'd dozed off, with a pillow line running across her left cheek. 'Ruby and Harry were fucking *fucking* in the fucking park. In the fucking playground!'

Jane slipped into her clogs and patted her pockets. 'I have my keys. Let's go.'

The 67th Precinct was not one of the glittering bastions of justice like on *Law & Order: SVU*, with computerized screens everywhere and cops with good haircuts. The floor was dirty, and the desks were messy. Jane had been there a number of times before, in the early days of Hyacinth, when they couldn't seem to go a month without an incident of one kind or another – a stolen credit card, a break-in, a shattered window. The cops were overworked and exhausted. She nodded hello to Officer Vernon, whom she knew from his work with the neighborhood watch. Zoe was hysterical, her silver bracelets jangling like a thousand bells. Jane took her hand. 'It's going to be fine,' Jane said.

'I'm going to murder her,' Zoe said. 'As soon as I know she's okay. If Harry had been rolling around with some white girl, they would have sent him home. I am going to murder *everyone*.'

They stopped at the desk, and Jane peeked around the side – she could see Ruby's legs through an open office door in the back.

'We're here to pick up our daughter,' Jane said, pointing. 'Ruby Kahn-Bennett?'

The woman at the desk nodded, and reached for the phone. They stood there for another minute, and then another female officer came clomping down the hall to get them.

'I'm Officer Claiborne Ray,' she said. 'Come on back. The other parents are already here,' she said, beckoning for them to follow. Zoe hurried in front, as if they were walking into a Cambodian prison and she might never see Ruby again.

The office was small, and seemed even smaller, because in addition to Ruby, Harry, Elizabeth and Andrew, there was another police officer sitting behind a desk. The guy was young, maybe twenty-five, with a smug look on his face. He was, no doubt, the one who had caught them. Jane wanted to slap him. As if he'd caught actual criminals. He'd probably been promoted from animal control and had just stopped rescuing cats from hoarders' apartments.

Andrew was rocking back and forth in the chair, which made an irritating squeak. Elizabeth had an arm wrapped around Harry's shoulder. Ruby was picking at her nails. They all looked up when Jane and Zoe walked in. Ruby waved, unable to force even a fake smile. Andrew shook his head and clenched his jaw.

'Come in,' Officer Ray said.

Zoe dropped quickly into the chair next to Ruby and squeezed her knee. There were no more seats, and so Jane leaned against the wall. She felt Andrew's and Elizabeth's angry stares boring into the side of her face so acutely that she put her hand on her cheek.

'What exactly happened?' Jane asked.

The young male officer cleared his throat. 'These two were having sexual relations in the playground.'

'Sexual relations? Who are you, Bill Clinton? You mean you actually saw them?' Zoe's voice was high and loud. Zoe got angry so rarely that when it came out, it was like a volcano after a hundred years at rest. 'I really doubt that. Ruby, please. Can you tell us what actually happened? I very much doubt that you caught them doing anything. So they were in a playground after dark. Fine. Fine! Please.' She was breathing out of her nose like a bull about to charge.

The officer cleared his throat again. 'The young lady was on top of the young man. Her underwear was on the ground. There was a used condom. I'm not making this up, ma'am.' The little prick was practically smiling. 'This is a serious offense.'

'A used condom?' In comparison to Zoe's, Elizabeth's voice was tiny, as if her lips didn't want to let the words out. She took her arm off Harry's shoulder and leaned back.

'That's right, ma'am.' He crossed his arms over his chest. 'And Ms Kahn-Bennett is over eighteen, which makes this much more serious.'

'Oh, come on,' Harry said.

Elizabeth covered her face with her hands.

'Ruby, is he telling the truth?' Zoe leaned in, offering her daughter her ear.

Ruby shrugged. 'I mean, I guess so. Mr Marx and I were not

having sex when we were so rudely interrupted by these fine officers, but we could have been, and it is humanly possible that we very recently had been, so I guess I can't really say anything other than I deeply apologize for so rudely using the park after dark for my own purposes.'

Harry stifled a laugh, and his mother put her finger in his face. 'Do not.' Elizabeth shook her head. 'I just can't believe this,' she said.

'Well, I think we all know whose fault this is,' Andrew said. He raised his palms. 'Harry has never been in any kind of trouble before, Officer, not once. Whereas Ruby . . .'

'Oh!' Zoe said. 'Oh! I see how this is!'

'Am I making this up?' Andrew turned to Elizabeth for confirmation. She looked queasy.

'It doesn't really matter whose idea it was,' the female officer said. 'Let's not get bogged down. This is the first time that either of them have ever been in here, and seeing as both Ms Marx and Ms Kahn are leading members of the local community, we are willing to let this go with a warning and a fine. But I do want written apologies from both of you kids on my desk tomorrow.'

'Thank you,' Jane said, extending her hand to the officer. 'We really appreciate that.' She clamped her other hand on Ruby's shoulder. 'This will *never* happen again, I promise you that.'

They gathered their things and stood up. Jane watched as Elizabeth mouthed *I'm sorry* to Zoe. Then they made their way back out on to the street in single file, the Kahn-Bennetts first with the Marxes behind.

When they were all on the sidewalk in front of the station, Zoe was starting to usher Ruby toward their car, as if shielding her from paparazzi. 'Hang on,' Jane said. She stopped and turned to Elizabeth. 'What exactly are you sorry for?'

'What?' Elizabeth put on her best naïve face, the face of a choir girl.

'Inside, you just told Zoe that you were sorry. I want to know what you're sorry for. Are you sorry for the fact that my daughter had sex with your son? Because I have really had it with this bullshit. You think that you guys have this perfect kid and this perfect shit, but you're just as messed up as the rest of us, I promise you.' Jane felt her heart beating faster. She wanted to wrestle Elizabeth to the ground, to fold her skinny limbs up and throw her away.

'I really don't know what you're talking about, Jane,' Elizabeth said. The night air was cool, and there was a wind picking up, blowing trash at their feet. 'I never said we were perfect.' They had never been perfect, not she and Andrew nor she and Zoe. Lydia popped into her head, Lydia, who had been arrested half a dozen times before she died. She would have laughed hysterically at all of this. How bourgeois! How parental! They couldn't even commit their own crimes.

'Oh, right.' Jane cracked her knuckles. She didn't mean to be threatening, it was just a habit, but she saw Elizabeth jump back a bit at the sound and wasn't sorry about it. 'You think I can't see the way you look at Zoe, and me, and Ruby? Like you're above it all and looking down on us from your little throne?'

'Mom,' said Ruby. 'Whoa.'

'Jane,' said Zoe. 'First of all, please relax. Second of all, this is totally crazy and not at all true. Third of all, can we please not have this conversation in front of a police station? This is turning into an episode of the Maury Povich show.'

'I was apologizing for Andrew implying that this was Ruby's fault,' Elizabeth said. She stuck her hands in the pockets of her sweatshirt. 'As for the rest of it, I'm really sorry that this is all happening at once, with you guys, and everything that you're dealing with, and

I'm sorry! I'm just sorry, okay? I love you guys! Come on! You know that.'

'You're apologizing to *her* about *me*?' Andrew asked, incredulous. 'Are you serious?'

'Fine,' Jane said, raising her hands in surrender. 'Fine.' She stalked back toward the car, kicking a newspaper off her leg and into the street, cursing under her breath, happy at least to know that they were not the only ones going home to have a fight.

Thirty-six

Oberlin College (population: 3,000) had more lesbians than all of Wellesley, Massachusetts (population: 27,982), if you weren't counting the all-women's college, which Elizabeth wasn't going to apply to because it would mean that she could never leave home. Lesbianism was one of the things she always assumed she'd try in college, like a tofu scramble, or a cappella. She'd kissed a girl once, during a particularly good session of Truth or Dare at a party her senior year of high school, but the girl was just some random drunk sophomore who had dissolved into giggles immediately, and so it didn't really count.

Then there was Zoe Bennett. Elizabeth sometimes thought about the improbability of her life, starting the way it did, all in a dormitory that looked like a cellblock. What if Andrew hadn't lived on her hall? What if Zoe hadn't lived downstairs? Oberlin was a small school, but there were certainly people whose paths she'd never crossed, and people she met years later. She and Andrew had met during their freshman orientation, and she'd met Zoe that first week, when she was sitting in front of the dorm smoking. Lots of people had bleached-out hair, but not many of them were black girls in enormous goth platform boots. Elizabeth had lost her key to the building and was waiting for someone to come out so that she could get back inside. It was the first day of September, and Ohio was beautiful, flat and sunny and full of flowers. Zoe sprang up and opened the door, and then walked Elizabeth all the way to her dorm room, as if she were the resident bellhop. They became friends so quickly that Elizabeth sometimes thought that Zoe must have confused her for someone else, someone prettier and funnier, someone with better stories and a higher tolerance for alcohol.

They hadn't had sex.

They hadn't done anything at all.

It was almost true. Elizabeth and Andrew were already together, more or less, kissing at the end of the night and never talking about it during the day. Kitty's Mustache was playing shows at house parties once or twice a week, their flyers up all over campus. '*MEOW,*' they'd say, and then the address. Two dollars for the keg. Everyone knew who they were. Both Zoe and Andrew were living off campus now that they were allowed to, Zoe in a one-bedroom apartment next door to Oberlin's crumbling movie theater, the Apollo, which meant that the neon marquee lit up her living room every night after dark until about ten o'clock. They were a funny match – even once they were in the band together, Elizabeth still felt like an amateur next to Zoe – an amateur woman, an amateur college student, an amateur cool kid. Even so, they had more fun together than seemed possible. They went to the Salvation Army and bought bags of clothes for ten dollars, they went bowling and came out reeking of cigarette smoke and french fries, they went to the movies and got drunk and laughed all night long. Elizabeth wanted to be Zoe's best friend, to wear matching necklaces and everything. They were almost there, maybe, but Zoe had so many friends already, from so many corners of the campus, that it was hard for Elizabeth to know where she stood.

Elizabeth was embarrassed at how well she remembered it – Zoe probably had forgotten it by the time she went to sleep that night. She and Elizabeth were lying on the couch in Zoe's apartment, watching a movie – *Bonnie and Clyde*, with Warren Beatty and Faye Dunaway. Zoe was waxing rhapsodic about Faye's clothes. They were head to foot, overlapping at their stomachs, but then, near the middle of the movie, Zoe said she was getting tired and did a half somersault, half flop, so that she was lying right behind Elizabeth, both of them facing the small television. Zoe looped her arms around Elizabeth's middle and snuggled up against her back.

'I'm going to sleep,' she said. 'Wake me up if Bonnie's going to die.'

But she didn't go to sleep – at least Elizabeth didn't think so.

On-screen, Faye Dunaway was leaning against a car, smoking. Zoe's nose rubbed against Elizabeth's spine. The sky was vast and cloudy, flat and endless. The room glowed green. Zoe's hand moved flat against Elizabeth's stomach.

Despite her open mind and abstract curiosity, Elizabeth still hadn't found a girl to kiss. She thought it would just happen eventually, the way it happened with boys, that someone would flirt with her at a party and then they'd find themselves tumbling against a wall and maybe going back to one dorm room or the other, hands over the clothes, hands under the clothes, mouths on skin. But it hadn't. There were a few other boys, and then there was Andrew, but that was it.

Elizabeth didn't think she was a lesbian. She just thought that it was a possibility, like a groundhog seeing its shadow. Despite the fact that she'd slept with several guys, Zoe said that she'd always known, since she was a child. She said it was like knowing whether you were right- or left-handed. Obviously you didn't get to choose – Elizabeth knew that much – but she wasn't sure about anything, not even what she wanted to have for lunch, so how could she be so sure about this?

Zoe's right hand, the hand that was slung over Elizabeth's shoulder. Zoe's mouth, now on the back of her neck. Elizabeth didn't move – if she moved, Zoe might stop. If she moved, she might wake Zoe up. Zoe was probably dreaming about someone else, one of the girls from the co-op down the block, the ones with nose rings and sourdough starters and special woven baggies for their Ecstasy that they wore around their necks. The room was getting warmer. Downstairs, the movie theater was showing *The Bodyguard*, and there were probably beer bottles rolling down the sloped floor under everyone's feet. She and Zoe had gone to see it the night before, everyone laughing at Whitney Houston until she opened her mouth and sang, and then they all got quiet and just listened. That's what Elizabeth wanted to do now, to lie still and listen. If she tried hard enough, she thought she could hear the squirrels in the park across the street, or the airplanes flying overhead. It was kissing, what was happening to her neck. Zoe was kissing her, and Elizabeth felt it all over her body, like a hundred electrical sockets all licked at once.

Someone knocked at the door – this happened a lot when you lived across the street from the only bar in an otherwise dry town. Zoe stopped what she was doing, and they both waited for a moment. Whoever it was knocked again, more insistently.

'Hmm,' Zoe said.

Elizabeth sat up and turned her face away from the door. 'I should go home anyway,' she said.

'Just let me see who it is,' Zoe said. She crawled over the edge of the couch to the door and reached for the knob. Elizabeth pulled on her shoes.

'Zoeeeeeeeeeeeeeeee, open the door!' The door swung wide, knocking Zoe over. It was Zoe's friend TJ, a girl with enormous tattoos up and down both arms. She was a senior, older than both of them, and rough in a way that Elizabeth didn't like. Zoe crawled clear of the door, and TJ stepped over her. 'Do you have any cigarettes? Gibson's is closed.'

'I'm going to go,' Elizabeth said. She couldn't look Zoe in the face, and so instead she inspected the filthy carpet, which had probably never been cleaned, ever.

'Are you sure?' Zoe said, her voice soft. She stood up slowly. Elizabeth squeezed by her and into the hall, being careful not to touch. She heard TJ turn off *Bonnie and Clyde* and put on music instead.

'I'm sure,' Elizabeth said, even though she wasn't. She got all the way to the top of the stairs and then down the first few before she looked behind her. Zoe was still standing there, waiting, her head poking out. It would have been so easy to run back up those steps. Elizabeth's whole body was pumping with blood. She felt like she was in the middle of a relay race, running between places she'd never been. Zoe must have felt it, the elastic cord between their chests. Before the pull got too strong, Elizabeth hurried down the rest of the stairs and out the door, into the clear night.

Thirty-seven

There were no two ways about it – Andrew refused to compromise. Harry was not allowed to see Ruby other than in their SAT class. After the tiniest flicker of pride that his son had made his (likely) sexual debut in a public place, with a (face it) really beautiful girl, Andrew had swiftly moved on to more practical parental feelings. As far as Harry was concerned, Ruby Kahn-Bennett was his invisible neighbor, a ghost girl, a memory. If her parents had been good at any part of their jobs as mothers, Ruby would have been leaving the nest soon, flying off to some second- or third-rate college, where she could terrorize all the local ruffians with her winning combination of insouciance and innate grace. But Ruby was probably going to live at home forever, working at her parents' restaurant. Andrew didn't care. Ruby wasn't his problem – that was what Zoe and Jane got for being distracted and loose. Ruby had slept in their bed, in between them, until she was three. That's what you got. So many people were wishy-washy with their kids, softer than butter, and all it did was ensure that you were going to have bigger problems down the road.

It was easier to focus on positive things. He and Dave were going over the plans for the boat. Ideas, really. The garage at EVOLVEment had turned into more of a coffee klatch than a workshop, but Andrew didn't mind. He didn't know how to build a boat big enough for people to live on. At first, Andrew thought Dave might be annoyed, but he wasn't – Dave was remarkably cool about the whole thing. It was actually better this way – the kid with the tools had taken over the shelf project, and instead, Dave and Andrew spent afternoons talking and meditating. One afternoon, after a quick juice, Dave asked Andrew to go with him down to the Rockaways. There were some herbalists with a little shop right off the beach, and he needed some supplies. Andrew thought it sounded like he was talking about weed, but he didn't want to be rude and ask. There was a lot about EVOLVEment that he didn't understand, and that was okay. Sometimes the whole top floor of the house stank like bong water, but that didn't mean it was Dave's finger on the carb. Even if it was, what did it matter?

The communal EVOLVEment car was a truck with paneled wood sides. The air-conditioning was broken, but it didn't matter, because it was cool enough with the windows rolled down. Andrew tapped the base of the window as they drove down Bedford Avenue toward the water.

'So you and your family have lived in Ditmas a long time, huh,' Dave said. He was wearing aviator sunglasses, a shiny contrast to his dense, dark beard.

'A really long time. Maybe even too long?' Andrew didn't mean anything by it.

'You thinking about moving?' Dave asked. 'We just got here, man.' He smiled.

'Oh, no, no, we're not going anywhere,' Andrew said. The fact that Zoe and Jane were probably going to get a divorce and move was a silver lining, not that he could admit that to Lizzy. When they were kids, Zoe was fine – smart, funny, sexy, all that. It wasn't that he didn't like her – it was that Elizabeth liked her too much. Whenever she came home from a dinner with Zoe, he could feel the prickly edges poking up, the remnants of whatever Zoe had said about him.

Elizabeth always denied it, but he knew it was true – Zoe loved talking shit, and she always had, and when you got old and married, what else was there to talk shit about, except your marriage? Jane was fine – she was solid. He liked her food, and he liked that she was chill. Jane was not the problem.

So much made him angry. The traffic, the congestion, the population. Harry had one more year of school. Then things would be different. When Harry was young, when he was a child (which Andrew supposed he wasn't anymore), they would troop up to the natural-history museum to look at dinosaurs, they would ride the Staten Island Ferry back and forth. They had fun. Being the parent of a teenager meant that not only were you no longer having fun, you stood for the opposite of fun. Andrew wondered how long that had been true – God, they were so *stupid*, he and Elizabeth. How long had Harry been this other person, capable of sex and lies? How long had it been since he was a baby? There was no way to tell. Andrew closed his eyes and stuck his head closer to the window. The breeze felt like cool water on his forehead.

'I see what you're saying,' Dave said, even though Andrew wasn't saying much. 'A couple of years ago, I was in Joshua Tree with a couple of friends, including a healer, and we took ayahuasca every night for a week. When I went in, I thought, how do I know how my body will react? Maybe I'll just call a cab and go back to L.A., you know? After the first night, I knew I was in for some real magic. Have you ever done it? It's like opening your third-eye point for six straight hours. Everything just comes pouring out.' He drummed his fingers against the steering wheel. 'That's when I knew I had to make EVOLVEment a reality.'

'What were you doing before?' He didn't mean to be impertinent – it felt a bit like asking your therapist what *her* problems were, but it was hard to imagine Dave at a desk job, or even at a non-desk job where he had to wear real clothes. As far as Andrew could tell, Dave didn't own a pair of socks or a single pair of pants with a zipper.

'Some body work, some life coaching. Taught yoga. You know, the circuit.'

'Of course.'

'What about you, Andrew? What circuit are you on?' Dave smiled. He had great teeth, the kind of teeth that orthodontists probably dreamed about – big and white and perfectly straight, with the tiniest gap in between his front two. Preacher teeth. Talk-show-host teeth. Guru teeth. Andrew had always thought that gurus would look sort of like Gandhi or, at the very least, Ben Kingsley. Under the beard, Dave looked like an amiable frat boy, a lacrosse player.

'I guess I'm not really sure,' Andrew said. 'I was on the music circuit. Then I was on the documentary circuit. The dad circuit, for sure. I was good at that one. Killed it at the playground. Then the magazine circuit. I think right now I'm in the figuring-shit-out circuit.' He paused, and exhaled through his mouth. 'Is there a list I can look at?'

Dave reached over and patted him on the leg. 'It's cool, man. I have a feeling that it's all going to come together. It's about being in the right place at the right time, you know? Energy. It's about preparation, and energy. And you have it – I could feel, like, buzzing around you, like. The second you walked into the house, I just knew.' The car was slowing down. Andrew looked around – they were already in the Rockaways, that funny little toothbrush of Brooklyn (or was it Queens?) that stuck out into the water, parallel to the mainland. Dave pulled over and stopped the car. For a split second, Andrew thought Dave was going to kiss him. That was what gurus did, wasn't it? Gain followers and then sleep with them all? Andrew wouldn't have been surprised if Dave had slept with every girl at EVOLVEment and half the boys. They were all so gorgeous, their bodies so strong and toned.

Their bodies were meant to be used! Andrew wasn't sure what his body was for. They were parked in front of a slightly ramshackle house with wood-shingled walls that reminded Andrew of his parents' summer cottage on the Vineyard, a house he hadn't visited in almost twenty years. To the left of the house were four smaller identical houses, like little ducklings following their mother down the street.

'This is it,' Dave said. 'This is what I wanted you to see.'

'This is where the herbalist lives?'

Dave laughed. 'No, the herbalist lives in a shitty apartment near the taco place. This is the next phase.' He held up his hands so that his thumbs almost touched and leaned over so far that he was almost lying across Andrew's lap. 'Do you see it, man?'

'See what?' Andrew scooched over in the leather seat and leaned out the window. 'Good breeze. How close are we to the water?'

'One block,' Dave said. 'One block to the waves. The Waves! Maybe that's what we call it.'

'Call what?' The houses were sweet. The windows and doors looked weathered but solid. He liked it out here. Maybe this would be their next act – a beach house in Brooklyn. He could finally learn to surf. Elizabeth could sell condos to the hipsters from Williamsburg. Harry would be off at school, and he'd come back to visit and they'd both be tan, wearing flip-flops.

'Our hotel, man.' Dave reached into the pocket of his T-shirt and pulled out a joint.

Thirty-eight

According to Ruby, all Zoe and Jane did was take turns yelling at her. Jane usually yelled at the restaurant, in the guise of giving Ruby things to do: 'Clean the bathroom! Really do it this time!' or 'Wipe down Table Six. Get the broom – there are Cheerios everywhere. This is not a Chuck E. Cheese!' Zoe chose to yell at home. Those outbursts were more erratic, but she couldn't help it: sometimes she was angriest that Ruby had left the shampoo bottle right side up instead of upside down, which meant that it took longer for the shampoo to come out, and if the cap was open, the bottle would fill with water. Sometimes she was the angriest when she thought about Ruby's body exposed in public after dark, how anything could have happened to them, to both her and Harry, that they were in danger and they'd put themselves there. Sometimes she was angriest about the college applications, and Ruby's SAT score, and the fact that it was the middle of July and there was nothing on the horizon except more of the same. It was hardest to yell about that, so that's when she made popcorn, covered it with some nutritional yeast, and left it in front of Ruby's bedroom door instead.

What made Zoe feel even worse (and what she wouldn't admit out loud, not even to Jane) was that she was also relieved. If Ruby had been leaving for school, then she and Jane would be forced to sort through their shit without any breaks, with no pauses for good behavior while Ruby was at the dinner table. Right now, it felt like their marriage talk was on pause, and Zoe was okay with that, for a little while. It wasn't like she was *dying* to get divorced. It just seemed inevitable – because how many downgrades could one marriage get? From lovers to friends to roommates to fond acquaintances? Things could always get worse. Elizabeth and Andrew seemed to be hovering somewhere below fond. How many years would it take for her and Jane to start poisoning each other with arsenic, or to 'accidentally' run over each other's toes in the driveway? How many years would it take for them to end up a Lifetime movie, based on real facts? Zoe wasn't sure how much further down she wanted to go. Jane had always been jealous, of Elizabeth and other friends, and of everyone else she'd ever loved and/or touched. It didn't matter if the relationship was sexual or platonic or somewhere in the middle – Jane was a fucking gorilla, and she wanted her woman close. At first it had seemed so sweet, almost old-fashioned. Jane held Zoe's waist when they crossed the street, she carried her over the threshold when they got married, she knew and worshipped every inch of Zoe's body, every mole, every notch. Now Zoe wasn't so sure that was a good thing.

When Elizabeth complained about Andrew, it was about him having to go off somewhere, to some hippie-dippie shit, or to climb some mountain with his own special Tibetan Sherpa. Jane never left the neighborhood. All Zoe wanted was some goddamn space. And attention. She wanted Jane to miss her when she was gone, but she never went anywhere except to bed.

'Jane? You here?' Zoe knew she was. She grabbed an orange off the counter and walked up the stairs. It was just before noon, which meant that Ruby was at the restaurant and Jane was probably in her pajamas. She knocked on the door to the guest room and opened it after Jane growled a response.

Someone had once told her that you should never marry anyone you wouldn't want to divorce, but Zoe had always thought that Jane's ornery qualities were among her most attractive. She didn't give a shit about how she looked. She didn't make small talk. She didn't pretend to like people she didn't, which Zoe thought probably saved about a dozen years of wasted time. Bitchy Whitman parents? Jane looked right through them. She was rough, and she was fair. She was a junk-yard dog that made popovers for no reason, just because she was in the mood. Zoe poked her head into the room.

'Can we talk?'

Jane rolled over, the futon nearly rolling with her. She scooted backward until she was leaning against the wall. Her head knocked on a low-hanging picture frame, a drawing of Ruby's from kindergarten. 'Sure,' she said, rubbing her eyes.

'Elizabeth is not the problem.'

'I know that.'

'You went straight-up Hulk at the police station.' Zoe sat down on the floor next to the futon.

'I know that, too. But I also know the way she looks at you, like you're her fucking chocolate ice cream cone and she wants to eat your brains and live inside your body.'

'Are you saying that she wants to lick me, or that she wants to kill me? I'm confused.' Zoe peeled her orange, sending sprays of citrus into the air.

'Maybe both? Both.' Jane paused to consider. 'I don't actually think she wants to kill you. But I do think there's some weird shit happening over there, and I wouldn't be surprised if she thinks about you when she jerks off.'

'I don't think Elizabeth jerks off.'

'Exactly my point. There's some weird shit going on over there. Listen, that was nothing, okay? It was nothing. I was just tense, and worried about Ruby, and then I saw Elizabeth making her stupid Eliza-beth faces at you, and I just went crazy. I'm sorry, okay? I'm sorry. I know things have been low for a while, but I've actually been feeling so much better, haven't you? Or am I crazy for thinking that, too? How are we doing? Are we okay? Should I stop asking you so many questions?'

Zoe laughed. She offered Jane a section of the orange, her fingers wet and sticky. When they met, Zoe had been in all kinds of relationships: good ones, bad ones, short ones, long ones. But nothing serious, not ever. She thought she'd been in love before – with a girl in high school, with a couple of girls at Oberlin and one after – but as soon as she met Jane, she knew she was wrong. Everything else had been make-believe, practice for the real thing. She'd learned how to say all the romantic words, and how to use her tongue just so, but it had all been pretend. Training wheels. With Jane, the wheels were off, and Zoe was flying.

She'd never thought about getting married: it seemed so square, so boring. But when she met Jane, so determined and purposeful, she understood: it was the acknowledgment of steadiness and trust, the shouted-out claim. Jane was already an adult, whereas Zoe and all her friends were still acting like teenagers. *Oh*, Zoe had thought. Marriage was something that grown-ups did, and if she grew up, she could do it, too. Jane made her want to stand up straight and stop referring to herself as a girl. When Jane's fingers reached the orange, their hands touched, Zoe smiled.

Thirty-nine

Harry had been looking forward to the SAT class all week. His mother had been taking his phone whenever he was home, which was like living in pioneer days, but only during mealtimes and when he was playing video games on the Roku in the living room. Elizabeth didn't quite seem to understand that his computer did everything his phone did except make phone calls, and who wanted to talk on the phone anyway? He'd been playing by their rules, though, and hadn't been in touch with Ruby since leaving the police station. It all felt very Romeo and Juliet, minus the suicide. Still, he understood. If they'd gotten caught having sex in his bedroom, it would have been one thing, but in public, the police station – that was worth some punishment. His parents had never been strict or unreasonable – his father in particular had always been willing to sit down and have lengthy conversations about why Harry had to wait until Hanukkah for a new Thomas the Tank Engine train or whatever. This seemed fair.

Iggy Pop had been gone a week. They'd put posters up all over the neighborhood, at bus stops and on telephone polls, plus on corkboards at the three different coffee shops on Cortelyou. Iggy had never been gone longer than a day before, and Harry was starting to imagine the more bleak possibilities. He'd told his friend Arpad about both the cat and having sex with Ruby in one phone call, and Arpad had only asked about the cat, assuming the latter was a joke. Harry wasn't sure what the bigger joke was – that he'd gotten to lose his virginity to the girl of his dreams, or that he was never, ever going to have sex ever again, at least not with Ruby. There were no other prospects. There had been other girls at Whitman whom Harry had stared at across the library, but now that he'd touched Ruby's body, now that he knew what was possible in the universe, he wasn't going to settle for just anybody.

His parents had been clear: he was in trouble for the first time in his entire life, and his punishment was not being allowed to sit next to Ruby, or to speak to her unless absolutely necessary. But they also weren't going to be there. Harry was jittery on the walk to the karate studio. He was running through all the different ways he could say hello – he could saunter in and pretend not to notice her, but sit right next to her as usual and then pass a note. He could kiss her right on the mouth in front of the Queen Dork and Eliza and Thayer and everybody. He could wait to see if she said anything to him first. Maybe she was secretly glad to be rid of him – after all, nobody wanted to have to teach her boyfriend how to have sex. Not that he was her boyfriend. Was he her boyfriend? Or rather, had he been? Harry wanted a neon sign in the sky, anything that would tell him what to do.

Ruby wasn't there yet – of course not. That was good – that meant that where she sat was up to her. Harry took his regular seat in the last row and pulled his notebook out of his backpack. In a funny way, having Ruby in the class had made him significantly less stressed out about taking the SATs. He did take notes, at least as often as he and Ruby passed notes back and forth, and he did feel like he had learned a few things. College was the light at the end of the tunnel, and Harry wanted that light so badly. He thought he probably wanted to go somewhere small but not small – Amherst, maybe, or Wesleyan. But fuck! Maybe he wanted to go to Deep Springs or whatever it was called and learn how to be a farmer and a gentleman poet. He swiveled around in his chair every time he heard the door open. Everyone else seemed to have made friends with one another – Harry hadn't noticed. The rest of the class could have been taught in Chinese and he wouldn't have noticed.

Rebecca opened her computer and projected an image of a geometry problem. An isosceles triangle, the easy kind. Harry tuned out as she started to talk. He knew enough to get by. Class had started, Ruby was late.

He smelled her shampoo before he saw her. Rebecca turned the lights off to make the screen easier to see, and then Ruby slipped into the chair next to him, giving him the quickest, blink-and-you-missed-it kiss on the cheek. Harry turned toward her, smiling with all his teeth. Ruby reached over and into his mouth and gave his tongue a soft pinch. She loudly let her bag drop and rifled through it, like a dog digging for a bone.

'Is your bag just full of random loose-leaf paper?' Harry asked.

'Shh,' Ruby said. 'Yes.' She found what she was looking for and slapped it on Harry's desk. It was her mothers' schedules for the next two weeks, printed off their joint calendar. 'Dr Amelia,' she said. 'That's their sex doctor. And now she's our sex doctor, too, if you know what I'm saying. Her office is in Park Slope, which means we have at least two hours from the minute they walk out the door. And that's a meeting with their purveyor in Jersey, which means they'll be gone for like five hours, sniffing tomato plants or whatever.' She pointed at the name. It was still six days away, but there it was. Their next date. Harry felt his whole body relax. Maybe he'd just go to Brooklyn College. How could he leave? He could rent an apartment, and Ruby could live with him and just hide in the closet when his parents came over. He'd say that he had some other girlfriend, someone who traveled a lot, a Rhodes scholar! He was dating a Rhodes scholar who was in Barcelona for the year, and so he was holding on to her stuff, which was why there were two toothbrushes in the bathroom and purses hanging off the doorknobs. Maybe they would be over it by then and understand that Ruby wasn't some bad girl in the first place, but the best girl – the only girl. It was all going to be fine. It was all going to be perfect.

'I love you,' Harry said, louder than he meant to. A kid with a stupid haircut in the row in front of them snickered, and Harry kicked the back of his chair. 'I mean it, Ruby, I love you.'

'I know you do,' Ruby said. She reached over and pinched him on the arm, and that was enough for now.

Forty

Elizabeth was genuinely worried that Iggy Pop was dead. Either dead or adopted by some stupid kid in the neighborhood who couldn't read and/or look at signs on telephone poles. It happened a lot – someone puts out a bowl of cream and a cat thinks it's discovered a higher plane of existence. At least a few times a day, Elizabeth would see something out of the corner of her eye and she would think, *Oh, thank God, Iggy's right there*, but then it was always a dust ball or a wadded-up T-shirt. When she walked to and from the office and to her listings in the neighborhood, she kept peering down driveways and on to front porches, even more than she usually did. Deirdre thought cats were disgusting pets and had very little sympathy.

'They're *wild*,' she said in between forkfuls of salad at their desk. 'Cats were never meant to live with humans. I've heard about people who were killed – *murdered* – by their cats. That's why we only have fish.' Deirdre plucked a walnut out of the salad with her fingers. 'This place is so stingy. There are four walnuts in this entire salad.'

'Iggy Pop isn't going to murder me,' Elizabeth said. 'The worst he does is when he walks across your face in the middle of the night. But I'm usually awake anyway.'

'See, if I had a cat and it walked across my face in the middle of the night, I would take that as a warning sign. I think your cat isn't missing – he's out there gathering enough sticks and bones to build an army, I'm telling you.'

'I appreciate your concern.' Elizabeth leaned back in her chair. There was a lot to be done – she had to draw up contract information for the house on East Nineteenth, and for an apartment on Newkirk. She had to get another big house on Ditmas Avenue ready for its first open house, and the dining room still looked like an episode of *Hoarders: Beanie Baby Special Edition*. 'I think right now I'd welcome his tiny army, though. I just want him to come back.'

Deirdre reached over and gave Elizabeth's knee a quick pat. 'I know, sweetheart. We'll find that mangy little killer.'

The office phone rang, and Deirdre spun around to answer it. Elizabeth rubbed her temples with her fingers.

'It's for you, I think,' Deirdre said. She had a funny look on her face, which meant only one thing.

Elizabeth picked up her extension. 'Hello?' she said.

'Still holding for Naomi Vandenhoovel,' someone said.

'Right,' said Elizabeth.

What the hell? Deirdre mouthed.

'Trust me, I barely understand it myself,' Elizabeth said.

'Hellooooooo from Ohio!' rang out Naomi's voice.

'Are you actually filming at Oberlin?' Elizabeth couldn't picture Naomi in Ohio. Not even Cleveland. Not even the Ritz-Carlton, Cleveland, where Andrew's parents had stayed for graduation, despite the fact that it was a solid hour's drive from school. She hadn't realized that things were going to happen so fast – she'd sort of forgotten about it, on purpose, since signing their names, assuming that it would be ages before she'd have to tell Andrew. Maybe by then he'd have come around? It wasn't a great plan, but it was all she had.

Naomi laughed. 'No, no, of course not. We're in Pasadena. But you should see it! We're shooting so muddy. It's very 1990.'

'That's great,' Elizabeth said, though she was feeling flustered. She was still in the office, after all, and couldn't suddenly have a freak-out with Deirdre and the rest of the O'Connells bearing witness. 'What can I do for you?'

'All business! I like it! Hang on,' she said, and then Elizabeth listened while Naomi ordered a coffee with almond milk and three extra shots of espresso. 'I was watching you and Lydia write this song, and so I wanted to call you! You look great! Very skinny, really great hair. Kind of a big mouth. Not like Steven Tyler big, but maybe Liv Tyler big. Actually, you know, you look a lot like a blond Liv Tyler. Young you, I mean.'

Elizabeth quickly moved her free hand to her head. 'Oh, God,' she said.

'Don't even worry about it! You look amazing! Just wanted to give you an update! The girls are so cute together. They're, like, all over each other's Instagrams already. You should check it out.'

'I will,' Elizabeth said. She thought for a moment, about herself and Lydia. Lydia, who had never liked her. It wasn't like with Zoe, who was clearly in a class above in terms of sophistication but somehow found Elizabeth amusing anyway. Lydia had practically turned her back when Elizabeth entered a room, like a haughty cat or a sullen teenager. Which she had been, of course. 'Wait, Naomi?' Her stomach sank.

'Mm-hmm?'

'It's so funny that I haven't thought to ask this before – what's the time frame of the movie? I assumed it was mostly Lydia at the peak or . . . you know, up until the end. There isn't a *lot* of college stuff in there, is there?' In her mind, her part of the story was a sliver at the beginning, before Lydia became LYDIA, and the movie really began. She'd wanted to see them all larger than life, which is how everything felt right at that moment anyway, but Elizabeth had assumed that the movie would have briskly moved on to the more glamorous stuff. But now she was faced with the sudden, terrifying thought that she had no input whatsoever about how their shared youth was going to be portrayed, and that Andrew was not going to be happy, not one bit, no matter how she tried to spin her misguided hope. She had wanted it for him as much as for herself – Elizabeth knew how much Andrew had loved the band, and Lydia, and her. Yes, that was part of it, too – Elizabeth wanted Andrew to see the movie and to remember how much he had loved her, once upon a time, when they were still kids and life was an endless, open ocean, stretching out at once in all directions.

'You know, I can't really talk right now,' Naomi said. 'But do you want to see the script? I'll have my assistant send it over. Okay?'

'So is that a yes or a no?'

'Yes, totally.'

'Yes there isn't a lot of college stuff, or yes there is? And you know that Lydia did not write the song, like, at all, right?' Elizabeth's neck polka-dotted with big red blotches. 'Hello?' But Naomi had hung up. Elizabeth removed the finger from her ear and handed the phone back to Deirdre to hang up. Deirdre was staring at her, her eyebrows so high they looked like part of her hairline.

'I'm ready when you are,' Deirdre said. She crossed her arms expectantly.

Elizabeth had meant to tell Andrew about the movie, about signing his name. She'd thought about calling Zoe, to practise on her, but she was too ashamed of herself. Elizabeth was always waiting for something, and then, after Harry got in trouble with Ruby, it just felt as if things were too tight, too stressed. Andrew wasn't good at managing balls in the air unless they were all made of helium. Good news could pile on all day, but if the news was bad, it was best to measure it out slowly, like antibiotics.

'It's a very long story,' Elizabeth said, 'but this is good – I'll use you as practice.'

Deirdre unwrapped a stick of gum, as excited as if Elizabeth had just agreed to do a striptease.

Forty-one

Andrew was sitting on the porch when Elizabeth got home. It was hot outside, inching toward the part of the summer when Brooklyn was thick and airless. They had air conditioners in the bedrooms and one in the dining room, but they didn't do much, especially on the first floor, where the rooms were large and open. The dark stone porch was often the coolest place in the house.

'I took the fans out of the basement,' Andrew said. 'I put one in the living room and two upstairs.'

'Thanks,' Elizabeth said. 'Can I talk to you about something?' She wasn't good at this part, even after so many years of marriage. It was her parents' fault, of course. She had never once seen them have an argument – it just wasn't in their nature. And so Elizabeth had spent her entire life avoiding unpleasant situations as much as humanly possible. It meant a lot of swallowing and smiling and apologizing for things she wasn't truly sorry for, and it meant never, ever starting conversations she didn't want to have. But if she didn't tell Andrew, the movie would come out, and there would be fake Lydia's face everywhere, and he would see it. She briefly considered suggesting that they go to Italy or somewhere for a year, just because, but things were probably too universal now anyway – his e-mail in-box would light up like the Fourth of July no matter where they were.

'Sure,' Andrew said. He patted the cushion next to him. He was wearing an old T-shirt that had little scalloped holes around the neckline, one that he'd had almost as long as he'd had her. Instead of sitting beside him, Elizabeth leaned against the porch banister.

'You know that movie about Lydia?'

'Yeah,' Andrew said, already wary.

'They're doing it. I said yes.' Elizabeth watched Andrew's jaw clench.

'But I never said yes,' he said. His eyes narrowed. Sometimes Andrew reminded Elizabeth of a cat, the way cats' other secret eyelid closed when they were asleep. With Andrew the secret eyelid closed when he was angry. 'They wanted me to sign the form, and I never did.'

'I know that,' Elizabeth said. It was semantics, she knew, but it was all she had. A technicality. 'But the lyrics are mine, and I let them have it. I was the manager. I agreed on your behalf.'

'What exactly does that mean, you agreed on my behalf?'

'It means . . .' Elizabeth paused, considering how best to get the words out of her mouth. 'It means that I signed your form. I signed your name.'

Andrew shook his head. 'Meaning that you forged my signature? Are you fucking kidding?' He stood up and dusted off his jeans. 'This isn't a credit-card receipt at a restaurant, Lizzy! This is actually serious! I can't believe you did that. It's going to be total garbage, you know that? Garbage that doesn't even tell the whole story.'

'You're worried about *Lydia*?' Elizabeth waved to a neighbor across the street, offering a tight smile.

'I'm worried about you, Lizzy, not Lydia. At least Lydia was always up-front about what she wanted. She might have been kind of an asshole, but at least she didn't pretend to be something else. Everyone else thinks you're so sweet, so nice.' Andrew rolled his eyes, and pulled his phone out of his pocket. 'I have to go.'

'Time for another yoga class?' Elizabeth rolled her eyes back at him – it was involuntary, a contest to see who could devolve the fastest.

'You have never understood me,' Andrew said. 'And obviously, if this is something that you are capable of, I have never understood you.'

Elizabeth crossed her arms and cocked her head to the side. 'That is a crazy thing to say.'

'Crazier than saying yes to something like that without talking to me?' She hated it that he made sense. 'Harry's going to see that movie, and he's going to think he understands us better, you know? And what is he going to understand? He's going to think that the version of Lydia on the screen is what she was really like. And what are the odds of that happening? It's going to be about Lydia the martyr, which is the most bullshit thing ever. Do you remember the last time we saw her?' Andrew turned around so that they were both facing the house, with their backs to the street. Elizabeth remembered.

They were at Veselka, in the East Village, having an early dinner of pierogies and apple sauce. Harry was six months old, asleep in the car seat, which sat on the floor between them. He loved ambient noise – people talking, forks clinking – and so they brought him everywhere.

The rules about celebrities were clear: you were not supposed to notice, and if you did, you were honor-bound to ignore whoever it was. There was a ripple in the room, a game of telephone. Whispers bounced off the walls and the ceiling. Elizabeth, sleep-starved and leaking milk, scooted as far to the right as she could and looked toward the front of the restaurant.

The crowd parted like the Red Sea, into two distinct human walls three feet apart – the only people who didn't care about Lydia were the Polish waitresses. Everyone else stood still, eyes wide. Elizabeth waved, but Lydia didn't see her, so focused on making her way across the room. 'What's going on?' Andrew said, swiveling around in his chair. 'Oh.'

She was nearly abreast of their table. The room had quieted to a hush. Andrew cleared his throat, which he always did when he was nervous. Why was he nervous? She was their friend, she had been their friend.

'Lydia!' Elizabeth said. She pushed her chair back and stood up. All around them, diners in pseudo-punk garb looked on, appalled at the breach of conduct. They'd already horrified everyone by bringing the baby, but this was a whole new level of misbehavior.

Lydia's eyes were swimming, murky and red. She turned slowly toward the sound of her own name, clearly half meaning to ignore it the way she probably did most of the time. Her eyes finally settled on Elizabeth, standing, and on Andrew, still sitting across the table, his fork in hand with a pierogi speared on top. Lydia smiled and spread her arms open wide, bypassing Elizabeth and going straight for Andrew, who hugged her awkwardly with his fork still in hand. The punky kids at the table next door were trying not to turn into girls at a Beatles concert – and doing a terrible job. Lydia either didn't notice them or managed to ignore them entirely without seeming rude. There was a force field of fame around her, thick as Pyrex. She stroked Andrew's face with her thumb.

'How are you?' Lydia cooed. She turned her gaze toward Elizabeth. 'Your cheeks look different.'

'I just had a baby,' Elizabeth said. 'We just had a baby.'

'Breeders!' Lydia said, and laughed. Her entourage laughed, too. She patted Andrew on the chest. 'Look at you, Daddy.'

'Congratulations on the warehouse movie,' Andrew said. 'Or is it about a factory? We haven't seen it yet, but I hear it's great.'

Lydia shrugged. 'They tell me it's good,' she said. 'But they tell me everything's good, so . . .'

Under the table, Harry began to cry, little hiccupping bursts of sound. Elizabeth bent down to pick him up and quickly jostled him sideways until he latched on to her breast. She was still standing in the middle of the restaurant, and everyone was looking at her. At Lydia and now at the pink cushion of her nipple, which slipped in and out of Harry's mouth as he fussed.

'God, he's like a cannibal,' Lydia said, and pretended to gnaw on her own hand. 'That is so scary.' She kissed the air. 'Good to see you,' she said, looking at Andrew. She made a loud munching noise at Elizabeth and turned away. A waiter pointed her and her friends to a table in the far back corner, and once she was sitting, the noise in the restaurant rose up and swallowed them. Elizabeth sat down again and found herself blinking back tears.

'What's the matter?' Andrew said.

'Nothing,' Elizabeth said. 'Let's just go. When he's done, let's just go.' She looked down at Harry's sweet face, sucking away. A year and a half later, Lydia was dead.

I'm sorry,' Elizabeth said. It had all been a mistake. She couldn't even blame Naomi for talking her into it – Elizabeth could see herself nodding along at the idea, so eager to sign on the dotted line. It was like an O. Henry story, only she'd sabotaged herself. She had been her own sacrifice. 'It was for you,' she said, knowing that he wouldn't see it that way. 'I did it for you.'

'Did you?' Andrew said. 'The door is unlocked. I'll be back later. And just so you know, what I'm doing over there isn't just yoga. It's self-care. I'm not pretending that it's a present for you. You should try it sometime.' He slipped his feet into his sandals and flopped down the stairs and on to the sidewalk.

Forty-two

The Waves was going to be gorgeous – it would help revitalize the Rockaway community, it would be an emissary of deep Brooklyn values, it would be less expensive to renovate than a hotel in Manhattan. It turned out that Dave had been planning it for a while – it was all part of the EVOLVEment plan. Dave had taken a couple of meetings with architects, some EVOLVEment yoga practitioners who lived in the neighborhood, just to get a sense of time and money. Now he wanted Andrew to come along – he really 'got it,' Dave said. They were meeting at one of the coffee shops on Cortelyou, a few doors past Hyacinth. Dave and Andrew walked down from EVOLVEment.

'I hear that place is good,' Dave said.

'It is. The couple who owns it are our good friends,' Andrew said.

'Should we meet there instead?' Dave stopped.

'No,' Andrew said, and kept walking.

They were in front of the café, and Dave waved to a guy sitting in the window. He held up a finger – *One minute* – and then turned so that his back was facing their date.

'I've been meaning to ask you this,' Dave said. 'And there's no really good way. I don't want you to feel awkward, or like there's any pressure coming from me. You know that I am all about comfort and good vibes, and if this is not your thing, man, that is *cool*. But I think it might be your thing.'

Andrew squinted into the sunlight. 'Uh-huh,' he said.

'I want to bring you on as an investor. For the Waves. I think that it would be a really amazing project for us to do together. What do you think? Do you want to be partners?'

'How much are we talking? I mean, in terms of money, how much?' Andrew could see it so easily – himself as a hotelier. Picking lamps and records for the guest rooms, talking to reporters at the *New York Times* about giving back to Brooklyn, about introducing people to places beyond the bridge, beyond Williamsburg.

'It's hard to say,' Dave said. 'We could probably get the whole thing going for under a million, give or take. The place is on the market for seven hundred thou.' He ran his hands over his beard, giving the whole thing a squeeze. 'There are other investors, of course, but they don't really *see it*, you know, which makes the whole thing way more of an uphill battle.'

'Of course,' Andrew said. It could be his new circuit – he could sit in the back during guided-meditation classes and look over lists of vendors they needed to contact. He could write checks – he could make something new. 'I'd love to,' Andrew said. He put out his hand, but Dave dove into his body for a hug instead, giggling.

Forty-three

Elizabeth was forgetting things everywhere – she forgot her dressy shoes at the office, she forgot the keys to her listings at home. She'd texted Zoe to make a dinner date but hadn't heard back. She and Andrew weren't talking, and she reluctantly understood why, even though he was obviously the one acting like a crazy person. Signing his name on one piece of paper wasn't betrayal. Still, she understood: marriage was supposed to be a sacred covenant, and if that wasn't quite achievable on a daily basis, marriage was about always getting the okay from the other person before doing something major. Want to go bungee jumping, or switch health-insurance policies? Want to pierce the kid's ear? Want to buy a new sofa, book airline tickets to France? You had to confer. It wasn't the same as asking permission, nothing so archaic – it was about being on the team, being equal partners. She wanted to blame the fact that she'd said yes on being the kind of woman who wanted to be accommodating to everyone, but that was only part of it. The other, larger reason was that she really did want to see the movie. Elizabeth imagined seeing it by herself, in the middle of the afternoon, and weeping into a bucket of popcorn. That was what she wanted – to celebrate and mourn her youth simultaneously.

Elizabeth wanted to take some photos of Zoe's house, mostly for her own reference. They still hadn't pulled the trigger, and maybe they never would, but she wanted to take a few pictures for herself. The house had never belonged to her, of course, but Lydia had never belonged to her either, and they both had helped to build whatever it was that made up Elizabeth's life. She wanted to walk around the house without Zoe, for the first time in a hundred years with no actual purpose – not because she'd agreed to walk Bingo or to watch Ruby or to bring in the mail. She just wanted to think about the house, and about Andrew. It was easy enough to convince herself that it was a business visit – no matter how well you knew a house, pictures were important – and that way, eventually, she could talk to Deirdre about the list price, just to get a second opinion.

Zoe hadn't said anything about moving forward lately – in fact, she'd been a little hard to pin down – but she didn't hesitate to give her blessing for Elizabeth to pop over and poke around. It was all a part of her figuring out what she wanted to do; that's how Elizabeth saw it. She didn't want to feel like an angel of death, hovering over her friends' marriage – she was just trying to be helpful. If Jane and Zoe could split up, it could happen to anyone. They'd always been stable, and happy enough, happy as anybody. Sure, Zoe sometimes complained about Jane, but no more than Elizabeth complained about Andrew. Having someone close to you decide to quit – or even seriously consider it – was axis-knocking. *Why them?* Elizabeth found herself wondering. *Why now?* Zoe didn't seem clear herself, which was the scariest part.

Elizabeth had always had keys to the Bennetts'. The Kahn-Bennetts'. Would Zoe go back to being just plain Bennett? There were so many things to worry about, enormous and tiny – it was too much to bear. Elizabeth jogged up the steps and unlocked the door. Zoe had told her that they'd all be out – she and Jane doing some restaurant thing and Ruby at Hyacinth. Bingo was asleep on the living-room floor and raised his head and offered a genial sniff.

It was always better to be in someone's house without them – that's when you could really look at the cracks in the ceiling, the sticky cabinets, the floors of the closets. No one wanted to spend that much money for someone else's dirt. If Zoe really went through with it (with the breakup, with the sale – these things were separate and they were together, kissing cousins), Elizabeth would have to bring in a real cleaning crew, at least twice, once for the official photos and once for the first open house. She knew two Salvadoran women who could make any house look like the Vatican – she'd have Zoe call them for sure if the house actually did go on the market.

Mostly, it looked the same as it had a hundred years ago, when she and Andrew had shared the house with Zoe and the other guys from Oberlin. Elizabeth closed her eyes and could see the Indian-print tapestries that had hung on the walls, the full ashtrays on the coffee table. Disco money paid for the house, and there had been traces of it in various spots: records everywhere, some framed on the walls, old hilarious photos of Zoe's parents with giant Afros and glittering jumpsuits. Those were gone now, replaced with pictures of Ruby as a baby, and the elder Bennetts appeared in their civilian clothes.

Elizabeth snapped the kitchen, which had the best stove in Ditmas Park. People wouldn't understand how much it cost by looking at it – she'd have to explain in the listing. The living room and its endless piles of magazines, the dining room and its endless supply of chairs. She photographed the staircase from below and the pretty sconces that were original to the house. On the second floor, she flipped on the light switch in the hallway and took pictures in the bathroom. She paused outside Ruby's room, which Elizabeth had once shared with Andrew. That was the first time she ever really felt like they were a couple, like they were adults who had chosen to be together. He was so good at everything then, so good at building them shelves out of bricks and boards, so good at kissing her shoulders before they went to sleep. He liked showing her his city, the good parts and the bad parts, the museums and the parts of Central Park he had explored alone as a teenager. His hair was still long, and he would tuck it back behind his ears over and over again, a nervous tic, as they sat across from each other in bed, eating take-out Chinese food. He made her laugh. He danced. Elizabeth turned the knob to Ruby's room and opened the door, flicking the light on.

'Mum, Jesus! Knock much?!' Ruby said. Elizabeth saw a flash of a bare breast. There was some scrambling.

'Oh, I'm so sorry, sweetie, it's Elizabeth, your mum said that no one would be home,' Elizabeth said, covering her eyes with her hand. 'Wait a second,' she said, and slid her hand back down.

'Hi, Mom,' Harry said, and pulled the sheet up to his chin. He and Ruby were sitting side by side, all red cheeks and knotty hair sticking up at odd angles. The room smelled like sweat and dirty clothes and other identifiable things that Elizabeth refused to let herself name.

'Harry,' Elizabeth said. 'What are you doing here?' She covered her eyes again. 'Can you please get dressed?' There was more scrambling. Elizabeth heard the sound of a belt buckle and couldn't keep herself from groaning.

'Okay, it's fine,' Harry said a minute later, sitting on the edge of the bed. Ruby had pulled on a dress and piled her hair on top of her head with a giant clip, the braids from the concert already gone. Harry looked so old, too old – he looked like his father, and Elizabeth felt her nose start to run, which always happened right before she burst into tears. 'Shit, Mom, I'm sorry. It's a messed-up situation, I guess, but it's really not that bad. We're using, um, protection and everything, I swear.'

Elizabeth blinked quickly. She felt a bit faint, as if she'd just inhaled a can of paint thinner. 'Do you mind if I sit down, Ruby?' She looked around and saw the telltale lump of a beanbag chair underneath a small mountain of clothing. Ruby pointed and nodded. Harry's cheeks seemed to indicate he would rather his mother leave the room where he had, until very recently, been naked with a girl, but he wasn't going to say that.

'Okay,' Elizabeth said. 'So. Here we are.'

'Want a glass of water?' Ruby said. She crawled to the edge of the bed like a puppy, her cleavage amply visible.

'Sure,' Elizabeth said, turning her face toward the ceiling. Ruby padded out the door and down the stairs.

'Mom,' Harry said, 'I'm really sorry.'

'Sorry about which part, love? Sorry about not staying away from Ruby or sorry about growing up?' Something was digging into her back – Elizabeth reached behind her, pulled out a chemistry textbook, and tossed it on to the floor.

Ruby pushed the door back open with her elbow and handed glasses of water to both Elizabeth and Harry. 'Let's just be real about all this, okay?' She looked to Harry, who simultaneously nodded and curled his lip, no doubt as afraid of what Ruby was about to say as Elizabeth was. 'Harry and I are not trying to be sneaky assholes, Elizabeth. We just like spending time together. It is totally my fault that we got in trouble, but it's also totally his fault, and that's okay.'

'I know,' said Elizabeth. 'I don't care anymore.'

'What?' said Harry.

'I don't care that you two are an item. I'm sure no one says that anymore. I don't care that you're hooking up, or on lock, or on the down low. It's fine with me. It's healthy! It's just also really sad, for reasons I can't quite put into words.'

She looked at Harry. 'You're my baby. I just want to know that you're safe, and that nothing bad is going to happen to you.'

'Mom, I'm seventeen.' He was blushing.

'And you'll be my baby when you're thirty-five and when you're fifty.' She was sweating. 'I think I'm having a hot flash, is that possible?'

Ruby and Harry both looked uncomfortable.

'Listen,' Elizabeth said. 'I'm not going to tell your father, Harry, or your mothers, Ruby. But you two have to promise me something.' She was hot, and tired. She felt like she was a hundred years old, like a wrinkled old crone in a fairy tale.

'Anything,' Harry said.

'Depends,' Ruby said.

'Help me figure out what your father is doing, and how to get him out of there. You'll be my little Nancy Drew and Hardy boy. Will you?' Harry looked startled at her request, but Elizabeth kept talking. 'I just need a little help. Can you two give me a little help?'

They nodded, solemn-faced. Elizabeth gulped down her sweating glass of water. 'I'll put this in the sink on my way out. And clean your room, Ruby. It looks like a deranged hobo is squatting in here, okay?'

'Um,' Ruby said.

'See you at home, Harry,' Elizabeth said. She pushed herself up to stand and walked slowly into the hallway. She pulled the door shut behind her and waited for a minute, to make sure there was no laughter. When she was satisfied, Elizabeth stepped gingerly down the stairs and back out on to the street, her head up high, as if she were walking on a balance beam.

Forty-four

Zoe had texted Jane late that afternoon: DINNER TONIGHT? CHINESE, SUNSET PARK? It was what they used to do when they wanted to talk business over a meal. They couldn't go anywhere in the neighborhood, because they knew every single person who owned every single restaurant (there were only half a dozen, after all), and eventually whoever it was would come over and sit with them, and they'd all be talking about purveyors and farms and about which servers had drug problems. Jane texted back, PICK ME UP AT EIGHT, and at eight o'clock on the dot she was standing in front of Hyacinth, hands in her pockets, waiting for Zoe to appear at the corner and then pull up in front. The car appeared at 8:03 p.m., not bad for her wife. Jane still loved saying 'wife.' If that was the Long Island in her, so be it. She had no interest in being transgressive. She loved living in the only neighborhood in New York City that felt like the suburbs, and she loved living there with her wife and her kid and her garage and her walk-in pantry. Zoe slowed to a stop, the windows rolled down.

Jane got into the car and buckled her seat belt. 'Hey,' she said.

'Hiya,' said Zoe. She was wearing a dress that Jane liked, a blue swirly thing that tied around her waist. 'How are you?' They'd spent the day talking about vegetables and orders and menus, but that wasn't what she meant.

'Not bad. This is a nice surprise.' Jane rubbed her hands on her knees.

'Yeah, well. I was in the mood for Chinese food.'

'Sounds great.' Jane crossed her arms over her chest, then shifted back to her hands on her knees.

'Relax,' Zoe said. She reached over and cupped her hand over Jane's. 'It's just dinner.'

'If it were just dinner, we'd be at home.' Jane fiddled with the door lock. They'd turned up Coney Island Avenue.

'Fine, it's a date,' Zoe said. 'Happy?'

Jane let out a little snort. 'If you must know, yes.' She slid her phone out of her pocket and plugged it into the car stereo. The night had cooled down, and the air that blew in through the car's open windows was brisk enough to give her tiny goose bumps on her forearms. Jane scrolled through her music until she found just the right song and then turned up the volume. Zoe's parents' biggest hit of 1978, '(My Baby Wants to) Boogie Tonight,' blasted through the speakers, and Zoe laughed. They were having a good time already.

Forty-five

Ruby spent her evenings at Hyacinth pondering the future. It was a slow night, with only a few tables lingering over dessert in the garden. It was almost ten. Neither of her mothers had been around, which was nice, because it meant she could be terrible and lazy at her job. It was a cool night for the end of July, and she wished she'd brought a sweater. She stole Jorge's hoodie from behind the bar and put it on, knowing that he wouldn't mind. It didn't exactly look professional, but it was deep Brooklyn on a Wednesday night, and so who really cared?

The way Ruby saw it, she had a few different choices: she could stay at home and apply for school again in a year; she could go on one of those intense semi-abusive programs where you hike through the desert for three months with no toilet paper; she could move to New Orleans and shuck oysters for tourists. At this point, she could do any of it – it was just a matter of deciding what she wanted. Harry would be in Brooklyn for another year, which was something, but not if they couldn't be seen together without his parents losing their minds. Ruby wandered over to the door and pressed her nose to the glass.

Her pocket buzzed. She pulled out her phone: PARTY @ NICO HOUSE WHEN UR DUN WORKIN.

Dust had no plan, and he seemed fine with it. When they were dating, he had told Ruby that he never wanted to have a job that paid him more than fifteen dollars an hour, and that he never wanted to work more than ten hours a week. His only jobs had been at a skate shop and at a skate park, neither of which he'd done for more than a few months, and so he seemed to be doing a pretty good job of accomplishing his goals thus far.

If Ruby went into the garden to reclean already clean tables, which she sometimes did to try to hurry along customers, she might have been able to hear the party. Nico's house was only a quarter of the block down, and when it was nice outside and people were in the yard, voices carried. Tonight, though, she wasn't interested. She'd seen Sarah Dinnerstein traipsing down the street earlier that afternoon, wearing shorts that even Ruby would have thought twice about, and she really didn't need to see how a few hours of sun and booze had added to the effect.

One of the couples from the back was chatting behind her, drunk on mediocre wine. 'Sorry,' they said, squeezing past Ruby to get out the door.

'Come back soon,' she said, as monotone as possible. By the time she walked back to her post, the other couple was finally paying and, after a few long, wet kisses, up on their feet and walking to the door. The server on duty, a tall guy named Leon, rolled his eyes at Ruby as he ran their credit card.

'Let's get the fuck out of here,' he said. 'No offense.'

'None remotely taken,' Ruby said. She organized the menus and started piling the chairs on the tables, and Leon grabbed the broom. They got the garden cleaned up, as they'd already done everything else. She could hear the party, or what sounded like it, and the whole garden smelled like weed and Sarah Dinnerstein's Rastafarian essential-oil perfume that she bought from a guy with a card table set up outside the Union Square subway station. Jorge and Leon closed the two registers while Ruby waited outside with the keys for the roll-down security gate. Once all three of them were outside, Ruby locked the padlocks. She would text Harry when she was closer, check and see if he was still awake. It was kind of cool that Elizabeth hadn't turned them in, but it was also weird and sort of freaky. Ruby's parents had always been relaxed, too relaxed, and she had always thought of Elizabeth as the Good Mom, the one who always knew where her kid was, and who had regular food in the fridge, and who knew all the best bedtime songs. Elizabeth was not supposed to be drinking a glass of water on Ruby's beanbag chair, her eyes all crazy.

In the very back of the restaurant, something flickered. A firefly, probably. Ruby squinted through the gate. There was something red in the corner, along the wooden fence, but she couldn't quite see what it was. It was probably nothing. It was late, and Ruby was tired. 'Okay, guys,' she said to Jorge and Leon, giving each of them a high five. 'See you later.' They walked toward the corner together, but instead of turning left, to go home, Ruby turned right and walked toward Nico's house. When she was a few car lengths away, she crossed the street and slowed down. There were a few people on the porch, but she couldn't tell who it was. The party seemed to have died down, at least out front.

Ruby squatted down in between two cars and leaned against a bumper. She could see the porch, and the little floating red dots of people's cigarettes in the air. Chloe had texted her that morning – Paris was in some other time zone, and Ruby had no idea if Chloe knew that she was writing at six a.m., or cared. It just said HIIIIIII I MISS YOU! with a long string of hearts. It was bullshit. Everything was bullshit. All of Ruby's friends were about to leave her forever. Who was actually friends with people from high school? Everyone loved to say that people who peaked in high school were stupid and lame, and didn't that mean that by holding on to those people, you were also stupid and lame? Wasn't everyone trying to trade up? Chloe would join a sorority and live in a house with a gaudy chandelier, and then she'd go to law school, and then she'd get married, and then she'd have three kids, and then she'd move to Connecticut, and then they'd see each other at their twentieth Whitman reunion, and they'd hug and kiss and pretend that one of them was going to get on Metro-North so they could see each other. Paloma was the same but worse – she might be interesting. At least Dust and Nico were going to stay the same forever. It made Ruby feel less pathetic about her own life choices, or lack thereof.

People on the porch were laughing. A few months ago, Ruby would have sauntered up the steps, pulling a cigarette out of someone's mouth and sticking it in her own, the queen of the goddamn place. Now what was she? She was a hostess. She recommended the crostini and the house-made aioli for the french fries. Her boyfriend was a recent de-virgin who took practice SATs for fun. Ruby imagined crossing the street and getting run over by a truck. Ruby imagined crossing the street and having a giant gate come down right in front of Nico's front steps. She imagined her friends – her former friends – ignoring her while she walked through the house like she was invisible. Ruby imagined seeing Dust fucking Sarah Dinnerstein on Nico's invisible parents' bed. 'This is so stupid,' she said. Her knees hurt from pressing against somebody's bumper. She got up slowly, like an old lady, and stooped over to walk back down the block. The breeze was even smokier than before – it no longer smelled just like weed, or patchouli, or Marlboros – now it truly smelled like fire. 'What the shit,' Ruby said. When she got to the corner, there were a few people standing in front of Hyacinth, staring in the windows, all of them on their cell phones. She started to run.

PART THREE

Mistress of Myself

THE Q AT CORTELYOU: DITMAS PARK'S
NEIGHBORHOOD BLOG

Posted at 11:37 p.m.

Anyone else smell smoke? We've been out on the street for half an hour, trying to trace the origins of the fire. Seems to be coming from the south. Reply in comments with any info.

Forty-six

Jane's phone rang, then Zoe's. Their phones were both sitting in the car's cup holders, in between the front seats, but Jane and Zoe were in the backseat. Zoe's underwear was slung around one ankle, and Jane's right hand had vanished up her dress. They had bellies full of dumplings and mouths full of each other. The cloth seats in the Subaru had seen worse.

'Who the hell keeps calling?' Jane said, into Zoe's neck. It was probably Elizabeth, calling Zoe to ask her which side she should fall asleep on, which hand she should use to hold her toothbrush. She didn't care, let the phone ring.

Food was always the way back in. Why hadn't she thought of it? Jane liked fine dining as much as the next girl, but really she always wanted something salty and fried that could be eaten with chopsticks. Zoe's skin was as delicious as a bowlful of MSG, and Jane was trying to lick her from top to bottom, every inch she could reach without pulling a muscle. It had been a solid decade – if not more – since they'd fooled around in the backseat of a car. There was one long late-night cab ride from Union Square to Ditmas Park that Jane could remember, with at least three orgasms apiece, but man, it had been a long time. Her body pulsed, and so did Zoe's. They were breathing in unison, the air thick and shared.

'I just hope it's not the police again,' said Zoe. She laughed a little but then paused. She scooted out of Jane's reach. Jane rolled back against the seat while Zoe squeezed through the front seats to grab her phone. 'It was Ruby,' she said. 'And Leon. Oh, my God.' Zoe reached down and stuck her other leg into her underwear and climbed into the front seat, giving Jane a glorious view, a single moment of pure pleasure, like looking at a Renoir in person. 'It's Hyacinth.'

They double-parked in front, right behind the fire engine. The fire-house was only two blocks away, so they'd arrived fast – Ruby hadn't even called, she'd just run over and banged on the door until someone opened up. Ruby, Leon and Jorge were still out front, the three of them sitting on a little silver bench one storefront away, taking turns popping up and smoking on the corner. Ruby had a cigarette in her mouth when her mothers got there, and Jane plucked it out and threw it on the ground.

'What happened?'

Ruby started to blubber, and Leon put his arm around her.

Jane shook her head. 'Goddamn it, will someone tell me what is going on?' She craned her neck to see past all the firemen into the restaurant.

One of the firefighters came over, slow in his enormous suit. 'Ma'am, are you the owner?'

'Yes, we are,' Jane said, pulling Zoe close. 'What happened?' There was smoke in the air.

'It seems there was a fire in the backyard behind the restaurant, and it spread into your building. Luckily, your daughter was here before the fire had reached all the way through – there is heavy damage, but the building is salvageable. Come and see.'

Jane and Zoe stepped gingerly through the open doorway – the glass had been shattered and covered the entrance, shards reaching nearly to the hostess stand. Inside, the smoke still felt thick, and the air smelled like a wet campfire. The floor, where it wasn't covered with broken glass, was slick with water from the sprinklers and the firefighters. Jane pulled the neck of her T-shirt up over her nose and mouth and held it there. There was a large black shadow printed all the way along the wall of the dining room. The ceiling was in pieces, flaking off like a sunburn, and the glass doors out to the garden were broken, too. Jane clenched her fist, ready to hand someone, anyone else, the bill. But when she looked outside, she knew the answer: in any game of rock-paper-scissors, fire beat everything.

The wooden tables in the garden were all ruined and would have to be replaced. The chairs were gone, too. The back wall, a wooden fence, looked like it had been eaten by an angry shark.

'Shit,' Jane said.

'Shit,' Zoe said, coming up behind her. She rested a hand flat against Jane's back.

The firefighter shrugged. 'At least it didn't get all the way inside. You're really lucky that your daughter was here – another few minutes and the whole place would have been up, gone.'

'Thank you,' Jane said, and shook the firefighter's hand. After he walked away, she turned to Zoe. 'Seems like we're really making the rounds lately, huh? What's next, the coast guard?'

'Don't even joke,' Zoe said. 'How long before we can open again, you think?'

'A month? Two? God, I don't know. Oh, man.' The power was off – everything in the walk-in would be ruined. There was gorgeous fish, beautiful marbled steaks. All those stupid tomatoes. Enough fresh mozzarella for three days of caprese salads. Everything would go to waste. She should take home what they could eat now, while anything was still good, *if* anything was still good. 'Shit.' She hadn't even checked the damage in the kitchen yet. That's where the sprinklers would have gone off first, no matter what, but Jane made a mental list of all her beautiful equipment, all her jars, all her fucking salt – everything.

'It's okay,' Zoe said. 'It's just money.' She pulled her phone out of her pocket and started taking photos. 'Go check on Ruby.'

Jane made her way back to the street, glass crunching under her sneakers. Ruby had lit up another cigarette and was pacing back and forth in front of the health-food store on the corner. She was wearing someone else's sweatshirt, with the hood pulled tight around her face, her purple hair hanging out the sides like a psychedelic waterfall. Jane approached her slowly.

'Mom,' Ruby said. Her voice cracked. 'I'm so sorry. It was my fault, I should have caught it sooner. I thought I saw something when I was locking the gate.' Ruby's eyes were red. She took a long drag of her cigarette and bounced nervously on her toes. 'I'm sorry that I'm smoking, too, but I can't help it. Otherwise I'm going to start pulling all my hair out.'

Jane reached over and took the cigarette out of Ruby's hand. Instead of dropping it on the sidewalk, she put it to her own lips and took a drag. 'Don't tell your mum.'

Ruby exhaled loudly and fell into her mother's arms.

Forty-seven

Elizabeth was groggy. She'd slept terribly, rolling around all night. Andrew had fallen asleep upon impact, as usual, and watching him sleep while they were fighting was ten times worse than watching him sleep when they were getting along. The window was open, and at midnight some drunk person had been yelling on the sidewalk. At three, a car alarm went off, over and over. There were the usual sirens, backdrop to the city life, insistent and wailing. Elizabeth had finally fallen asleep around four, she thought, but it was equally possible that she'd been awake until just before six and finally conked out for an hour, until Andrew woke her up with a cough. When she opened her eyes, he was standing on his side of the bed, looking at her. Her cell phone was in his hands.

'What?' she said. 'What is it?'

Harry was sitting on the couch hunched over a bowl of cereal. Elizabeth pulled her robe tight around her waist and sat down next to him. 'Honey,' she said, 'I just heard from Zoe. There was a fire at the restaurant last night. Everyone is fine, but I thought you should know.'

'I know,' Harry said. 'Ruby texted me last night. Like, when the firemen were going in. She said they broke the door with axes, even though the fire wasn't even near the door.' He slurped up a spoonful of milk.

'You *knew*? How could you not wake me up?' Elizabeth stretched her fingers toward Harry's neck and pretended to strangle him. 'God! Harry!'

'What were you going to do? Run down there with a bucket of water?' He raised the bowl in front of his face as a barrier when Elizabeth glared at him. 'Sorry! I should have told you, fine!'

'I'm going to pop down there and see if they need anything. You stay here and out of trouble, okay?'

Harry waved good-bye with his spoon.

The front door was open, and Elizabeth poked her head in, knocking on the doorframe. Zoe was sitting at the dining table, her phone to her ear, a stack of paper in front of her. Ruby and Jane were both in the kitchen, with their backs to the door. The whole house smelled like pancakes and bacon.

'Hey,' Elizabeth said. 'Can I come in? I just heard.'

Zoe glanced up and waved her in, but a look passed over her face that made Elizabeth stop just inside the door. 'I can come back, if now isn't good,' she said, half-whispering. Zoe waved her in again, more vigorously.

'I'm on hold, endless hold,' she said. 'It's shocking, I know – insurance companies are surprisingly hard to get on the telephone when a place burns down.'

Jane muttered something, and Ruby laughed. 'Oh, hi, Elizabeth,' Ruby said, swiveling around in a clumsy pirouette. She winked.

Elizabeth scuttled over to Zoe and gave her a quick hug before gently lowering herself on to the next chair over. 'I can't believe it,' she said. 'Are you okay? Can I help?'

Zoe raised a finger. 'Hang on, I think I have an actual person now. Hello?' she said into the phone. 'Yes, hello, hold on, thank you so much.' She mouthed, *Sorry*, and then covered her left ear with her hand and walked up the stairs.

Jane set an enormous platter of pancakes – thick, fluffy, generously studded with blueberries – in front of Elizabeth. 'Stay,' she said. 'I always make too many.'

Ruby threw herself into the chair opposite Elizabeth and forked four huge pancakes on to her plate.

'Oh, I shouldn't impose,' Elizabeth said. The pancakes smelled like Hyacinth on a Sunday morning. Her stomach growled.

'Really,' Jane said. 'You know Zo never eats more than two. Better you than Bingo.' She smiled and handed Elizabeth a plate.

'Okay,' Elizabeth said. For someone whose restaurant had just been knocked out of commission for an unknown period of time, Jane seemed remarkably upbeat. Elizabeth edged off a small bite of pancake with the side of her fork. 'Oh, my God,' she said. 'These are insane.'

'I know,' Jane said, and smiled even more broadly, like the cat who had eaten not only the canary but the nest, too. 'No hard feelings about the other night, right?'

'Sure,' Elizabeth said. 'Of course not.'

'I forgot the syrup!' Jane said. 'What are we even doing?' She hustled back over to the kitchen and came back brandishing an oversized bottle of syrup. Jane poured giant puddles on to everyone's plate.

'You are extra goofy today, Mom. Is there Prozac in these?' Ruby said.

'Ha-ha,' said Jane. 'Maybe.' She stuck a quarter of a pancake into her mouth. 'Tastes good, doesn't it? Nice and medicinal.'

Ruby rolled her eyes but was looking at her mother with affection. Elizabeth was tempted to back away slowly and open the door again, just in case she'd accidentally walked into an alternate universe.

Zoe thumped back down the stairs, as quick on her feet as Ruby.

'Hey!' she said. 'Sorry about that! I think we have a good guy over there, Jane. Shouldn't be too bad. I mean, it'll be terrible, and God knows how long it'll take us to fix everything, but we're covered, and they know it, so at least all we're losing is time and money, you know?'

'Right,' said Jane. 'Great. You hungry?'

'Always,' said Zoe. Instead of scooting behind Ruby, which would have been the most direct route to her chair, Zoe walked the long way around. Elizabeth pretended not to notice the way Zoe gave Jane's earlobe a gentle tug as she scooted behind her, and then she pretended not to hear the low little noise Jane made in response.

'Did you make these with ricotta or yogurt or melted butter or all three?' Elizabeth said, instead of what she wanted to say. When Zoe finally sat down again, Elizabeth widened her eyes and gave her a look, but Zoe only smiled, beatific and sweet and full of it.

Forty-eight

The plans came together remarkably quickly – Dave was organized. Phillip, the architect they'd met with at the coffee shop, drew a few different scenarios and priced things out, and then they were interviewing contractors, the three of them. Dave introduced Andrew as 'his right hand, his partner,' and every time he said it, Andrew felt better about the whole thing. Sure, it was a lot of money, but this was what money was for – investing in things you believed in. If it all went well and the other investors came in the way Dave thought they would, they'd be in construction by the fall and then spend the winter working on the inside, decorating and programming and finishing. Next summer, the Waves would be up and running. He could see all the photos now, he and Dave leaning casually against a rustic wooden check-in counter. Hotelier! His mother would no doubt find the career a bit gauche, but Andrew liked the thought of it. Purposeful, with a sprinkling of glamour. It was a good plan.

The first check wasn't huge – a hundred grand. Dave said that they could squeak by with seventy-five, and that one-fifty would be ideal, and so Andrew thought an even hundred was a good place to start. He and Elizabeth had an accountant in the Slope and an investment person in the city, but he handled only their retirement accounts and Harry's college fund. That's where all their savings went. The big money – Andrew's family money – was taken care of by a junior guy in the Marx family arsenal of suits. He and Elizabeth touched the money only in case of emergencies – when they had to replace something in the house or when they occasionally had to borrow from the fund to pay Harry's tuition. It was just sitting there – not an endless Scrooge McDuck–size swimming pool, but a good-size puddle of money.

Andrew lay on his back at the far end of the EVOLVEment studio. It was relaxation meditation co-practice time, which meant that Dave offered a guided meditation while Salome walked around giving miniature head and shoulder adjustments and massaging everyone's forehead. Andrew didn't have to pay for classes anymore – Dave insisted. He was part of the team.

Kitty's Mustache was the only other team Andrew had ever been on. A marriage was a partnership, and a family was a team of sorts, but those didn't count, not really. The band had had meetings and practices and voted on things. There was no voting in a marriage – everything always had to be a double compromise. Parenting was an absurd job, mundane and sublime in equal measure, and once Harry had learned to talk, walk and use the toilet, Andrew and Elizabeth had largely split up their days so that each of them could have some time 'off.' When you were in a band and you wanted time off, it meant that you were quitting, and who cared, really? There was always another mediocre bass player.

'Imagine every breath you take is a white light,' Dave said, 'and the light travels in through your nose and through your sinuses, across your cheeks and up into your head. Now imagine the light is a ball in the world's softest pinball machine and it bounces around inside your head until your whole head is full, every inch of it, with that light. I'm moving the flippers on the machine, and the ball is pinging all over the place. Light! Light! Light!'

One of the best things about Elizabeth was the way that she willingly overlooked people's bad qualities. It was as if she could see how terrible someone was and then redoubled her efforts to be kind to them, as if every asshole she encountered was an abused child she was trying to stop from setting animals on fire. It's how she was with Lydia, who certainly never deserved it. Andrew had never been able to equal that goodness, that generosity. It was hard to reconcile that good-hearted kindness with what Elizabeth had done, but Andrew was trying. The white light was surrounding her face, making her blond hair glow even brighter. But Dave's cool white light couldn't seem to knock out Lydia, no matter how many deep breaths Andrew took.

Kitty's Mustache was the most popular band at Oberlin – they played shows at the Grog Shop in Cleveland, opening up for bands on tour from New York and Chicago, and when they played at parties around campus, the houses would turn into glorious fire hazards, the packed rooms overflowing into front yards until a neighbor called the police. Zoe and Andrew were the same year, one class ahead of Elizabeth and Lydia, and they had endless conversations about what to do when half the band graduated. Andrew was in no hurry to get back to New York. He wanted to stay to be with Elizabeth, just live off campus and work at the bike shop – it cost almost nothing to live there, and Elizabeth could steal enough food from the dining halls and the co-op kitchens to feed them fine, if the parental well ran dry. But the well wasn't going to run dry, and so Andrew wasn't worried. It all would have been easy, except that Zoe wanted to get the hell out of Ohio, and how the hell were they supposed to practise without her? They had a seven-inch already, *Kitty's Mustache and the Male Gaze*, which an indie label had pressed three hundred copies of, and Andrew and Elizabeth were anxious to finish a whole record.

That was when Elizabeth wrote the song. It was a fucking hit –

there were no two ways about it. Even if Elizabeth had never shown it to anyone, had only played it for herself in her bedroom, it still would have been a hit. Songs were like that – freestanding monuments. When she came back to their practice space from the library, she played it on the guitar and sang, with Andrew, Lydia and Zoe all sitting on the floor in front of her. Lydia drummed her sticks on the floor, keeping time. By the time Elizabeth got to the second chorus, Zoe was on her feet, singing along, and Andrew knew that she wasn't going anywhere. They stayed late, doing it over and over again, until their cheeks were flushed and their fingers were red.

When they were done, it was midnight, and the bar in the shitty hotel across the street from Zoe's apartment would be open for another two hours. They walked over together, giddy. Elizabeth and Zoe got a table in the corner, Andrew went to the bar to get a pitcher of beer, and Lydia went to the bathroom, which was in the lobby. The entire first floor of the hotel stank of cigarettes (the rooms probably did, too, but Andrew had never actually been in one) and stale popcorn, which was free at a machine in the corner. Zoe knew all the bartenders, enormous guys with motorcycles and terrible teeth, and every other pitcher was usually free. Andrew was buzzing – he always liked the band, and they had other good songs, including ones that he'd written, but this was different. He got the pitcher and sloshed it over to the table. 'I have to take a piss,' he said.

'I was dying to know that, thank you,' said Elizabeth, who was always more sarcastic when Zoe was around. Both the girls laughed.

Andrew gave them each a middle finger and headed into the lobby. The bathrooms were behind a half wall, as if the hotel were nice enough to pretend that people passing by didn't walk in and use them all the time. Andrew pushed through the swinging door and relieved himself loudly at the urinal, sighing. He walked out again, whistling 'Mistress of Myself' but only made it one step back into the hall before Lydia got to him.

'I was waiting for you,' she said, her eyes mostly hidden under her bangs. 'Come with me.' Lydia pulled him by the hand out the front door of the hotel, well out of view of the bar. It was April, and not yet warm, though the flower buds had started to push through in the park across the street.

'Fucking good song tonight, huh?' Andrew said. He felt drunk, even though he hadn't had a sip yet, and rubbed his belly. They stood on the dark street corner, and Lydia wrapped her arms around his body. She was small, just over five feet, and her head fit under his armpit in a way that he liked. Elizabeth was taller than he was, and he liked that, too, but Lydia made him feel like he was 30 per cent handsomer, like the star quarterback on a high-school football team.

'What's up?' Andrew said, petting her head affectionately.

'I don't want to go back to the bar,' she said. 'I just want to be with you.'

'But we're celebrating!' Andrew pulled back and put his hands on Lydia's shoulders. 'Come on, it'll be fun!'

'That's not the kind of fun I want to have,' Lydia said, and she grabbed his face and kissed him.

It wasn't unexpected. Was it ever? Elizabeth had teased him about Lydia's flirting, and Andrew had always said it was nothing, because it was easier than telling Elizabeth the truth. They'd slept together a handful of times – only when they were both really wasted, and when Elizabeth was elsewhere for the night. Lydia seemed to know exactly when she would be gone, and she'd present herself on Andrew's door-step with a bottle of not-terrible wine and no underwear. They never talked about it after the fact, which made it feel less like a secret and more like a shared fugue state. It had nothing to do with Elizabeth; Andrew loved Elizabeth. She was a glass of whole milk, fresh from the cow – undiluted goodness. Lydia was something separate. Something spiked. It was like Betty and Veronica. Archie loved them both, and they loved each other, too, even though they tugged him back and forth. When Andrew imagined Elizabeth finding out, that was a part of his defense. It wasn't much, but it was something. He hoped he'd never have to use it, that Lydia would just disappear one day and make his life easier. It wasn't like he and Elizabeth were married. They weren't even living together. It was worse than jaywalking but not as bad as a root canal. Worse than throwing up in a taxicab but not as bad as going to the DMV.

'Come on,' Andrew said. 'Let's go back.'

'Fine,' Lydia said, sticking out her lower lip and squinting at him. 'Or I could just blow you right here.' They crossed the street into the park, and Andrew unzipped while Lydia crawled half under a bush and then pulled him to his knees.

Would that scene be in the movie? The white light didn't exist. Andrew's head was filled with Lydia. They slept together a few more times, and then the semester was done, and Andrew moved in with Elizabeth, and it was over. Lydia swore to him that he wasn't the reason she was leaving school, that she actually fucking hated it there and he wasn't even remotely that important to her, but he never knew for sure. That summer he helped her load a U-Haul truck, and when she hopped up into the driver's seat, she shook her head, giving him that same look she gave him a thousand years later at the restaurant, after Harry was born. She looked at him like he was a fool, like he'd made the wrong choice and she knew it. It was never so clear to Andrew – nothing was. All he wanted in life was for something to be as clear as everything had always been for Lydia. She had wanted him, and when she didn't get him, she was out. Whenever Lydia sang that song, that fucking, perfect, beautiful song, it was all Andrew heard. She was calm, and she was gone, and he was left with her voice and Elizabeth's words, and Andrew was sure that he heard exactly what Lydia wanted him to. It was the thing in his life that he felt the guiltiest about, and when Lydia died, Andrew's first emotion had been relief. No one else knew, and now he'd never have to tell Elizabeth. That relief was the second thing he felt guiltiest about. It was a guilt sandwich, with Lydia in the middle.

Andrew felt Salome ruffle his hair and heard her crouch down behind him. She pressed her thumbs against his shoulders, grounding him into the floor, and then she rubbed little circles on his forehead. Her hands smelled like lavender. Andrew breathed it in and breathed out as much Lydia as he could. There was always more. She was sticky inside him, a thin coating of lust and regret stuck to his insides like tar. There was never enough white light, but he kept breathing, hoping that it would change.

Forty-nine

Now that her job was on indefinite hiatus, Ruby had more time for being a creeper for Elizabeth. It was fun, like pretending she was Harriet the Spy, and more than anything, it gave her something to do. The first step was going to a yoga class, which Ruby thought sounded relatively low-impact, in terms of spy missions. The EVOLVEment website was garbage – just a bunch of photos of pretty girls with their eyes closed, smiling like someone's tongue was on their clit – but there were class schedules on pink pieces of paper in a clear plastic box on the porch. Ruby put her hair in a ponytail and stole Zoe's mat from the hall closet. 'Just see what it's like in there,' Elizabeth had said. 'Just see if there's anything weird going on. You know, talk to people.' Ruby was on it.

The classes were fifteen dollars for drop-ins. Ruby paid cash and signed a waiver under the name 'Jennifer Lopez,' which seemed both funny and within the realm of possibility. 'Call me Jen,' she planned to say to whoever was teaching the class, before launching into a long soliloquy about her youth as a gymnast and her tight hamstrings.

The preplanned speeches were unnecessary – unlike most studios, which were pretty empty during the day, EVOLVEment was packed, and the woman teaching the class didn't even introduce herself. She was a lissome blonde, and she stepped on the tiny slices of hardwood floor in between the mats, touching everyone as she made her way around the room. Ruby unrolled her mat in the front row – she had to be an eager student if she was going to get any intel – and Om'd loudly when called upon to do so.

'Welcome to EVOLVEment,' the woman said. 'My spirit sees you.'

'My spirit sees you,' everyone in the class said back.

'Let's do this!' the blonde said. She turned around, whipped out an iPhone, and pressed a button, immediately filling the room with Afrobeat music. 'I want to see your beautiful bodies *moooove*!' If Andrew was in trouble, it certainly wasn't with this idiot. Ruby did as many upward-facing dogs as she could before collapsing on to her mat and waiting there for the class to be over.

When they were all rolling up their mats, Ruby sauntered casually up to the teacher, who was drinking a tall glass of something frothy and green.

'Good class,' Ruby said. 'I ran six miles yesterday, and my body just needed a little break. But really good class.'

The woman lifted her thumbs to her forehead and offered a micro bow. 'Thank you so much,' she said. 'My spirit could tell that your spirit needed a rest. That's so important, really – it's, like, the number-one thing that you learn in teacher training, that the hardest thing to do is to just listen to your own body and not care about what else is going on in the room.' She put her hand on Ruby's arm. 'You are my greatest teacher today.'

'I feel exactly the same way,' Ruby said, and put her own thumbs to her forehead. '*Namaste*.' She looked around the room, which had finally thinned out. There were still a few bendy-looking people loitering, giving each other back rubs, complete with appreciative moans.

They reminded her of Dust and the church-step kids, only with better skin and clean livers. 'This place is so great,' she said. 'Do you teach here a lot?'

'Oh, we're all teachers here,' the woman said. She leaned in. 'You know, I think that you could really be an interesting part of this place. I'm Lena. Can I show you around? Want some kombucha? We make it here, it's so good. Have you had it before? It's kind of like iced tea, only funky.'

'I'd loooove that,' Ruby said, trying to ignore how sore her thigh muscles were when they started climbing the stairs.

Fifty

The tops of Dr Amelia's feet were tan except for the crisscrossing flesh that had been hidden underneath the straps of her sandals, which made her look like she was sitting in the shadow of venetian blinds. Zoe thought someone ought to tell her that her whole body needed SPF 30, not just her face and arms, but it seemed awkward to give a doctor medical advice, and so she kept her mouth shut.

There was a lot that Zoe wanted to keep her mouth shut about – she knew that Ruby and Harry had been fooling around whenever they thought she and Jane were asleep, and she didn't care. She and Jane had been fooling around whenever Ruby was out, which was like when she was a baby, and they'd have sex during her naps because they were too tired and/or busy after she went to sleep for the night. She didn't want to tell Elizabeth about Jane, which was ridiculous, because Jane was her wife and Elizabeth was her friend – but Zoe was worried that Elizabeth would be disappointed if she and Jane stayed together, like she was chickening out.

Dr Amelia liked to sit cross-legged in her Aeron chair. 'How's it going, guys?' she asked. 'Seems like it's been a good summer?'

'We just had a fire at the restaurant,' Jane said. 'The restaurant itself, actually.'

'And Ruby still hasn't gotten into college,' Zoe said, and then corrected herself. 'Isn't going to college, I guess.'

'And she got hauled into the police station for having sex in Prospect Park,' Jane added.

'Oh,' said Dr Amelia. She wrote something down on her notepad. 'And are you two getting along? That seems like a lot of additional stress.'

'We are,' said Zoe. She looked at Jane, who was sitting to her left. Jane hated therapy – her mother was a therapist and had seen patients in her home office in Massapequa, and it had soured her on the whole thing, all those afternoons when she and her siblings weren't allowed to watch television because the den was connected to her mother's office with French doors. But now Jane looked completely happy to be there, even smiling for no particular reason.

'And have you talked about the problems you were having? It's great to get in a good spot, of course, but I want to make sure that it's not just a passing mood – have you two spoken about the issues that caused the space in the first place?'

Jane closed her mouth.

'Well, we haven't really had time,' Zoe said. And they hadn't – after the fire there was a lot of busy work to be done, and meals to be cooked, and they were two seasons behind on *Damages*, which they were watching on Netflix. Every day, Zoe thought about having a Talk, but every day she thought better of it.

'We've been really busy,' Jane said. 'And plus, I don't know, it feels like it would be a jinx or something. Rock the boat. You know what I mean.'

'I do know what you mean,' Dr Amelia said. 'You're afraid to frighten the natives. To muddy the water. To poke the bear.' She tapped her pen cap against her chin.

'Right.' Jane clasped her hands in her lap. 'Something like that.'

'Well,' Dr Amelia said, 'why don't we start now? This is a safe space, remember, and all feelings are valid. Zoe, do you want to start?'

'Okaaaaay,' Zoe said. She crossed her legs one way, then switched. Her hair was in her eyes, and she tucked it back behind her ears. 'I guess I feel like things have been going really well, but maybe my fear is that it's because Jane is maybe afraid of being lonely? And so she's more interested in me right now than normal? And in a little while it'll just die down again? And then we'll be right back where we were?' She covered her eyes. 'Don't kill me,' she said to Jane.

'I'm not going to kill you,' Jane said. 'You're right. I don't want to be lonely. But the reason I don't want to be lonely is because I love you. It's not just that I want to have *someone* around, I want to have *you* around.' She rolled her eyes. 'You're really making us do this here?' Jane cleared her throat. 'I think we should talk about Elizabeth.'

Zoe was genuinely surprised. 'You're joking.'

'I'm not saying it's sexual, Zo. But I do think there's some weird stuff there. Is that a thing, Dr Amelia, even if it's not about, like, doing it?'

'Of course,' Dr Amelia said. 'There are all kinds of betrayals – physical, emotional, spiritual. What exactly do you think is going on, Jane?'

'We used to fight about this, years ago. I just think that Zoe has someone else to go to, for whenever she's upset, or happy, or whatever. I know it's not as big a deal as it used to be, but still, I think that it's messing with us. There's a reason people don't live close to their parents, you know, or next door to their best friends. It's weird. People need space. Or at least I need space.'

Zoe scrunched up her mouth. Space was her line.

'What?' Jane said. 'Do you really think I'm so off base?'

Dr Amelia waited expectantly, her toes wiggling with excitement.

'I think that's completely ridiculous,' Zoe said, and then she tried to slow down and think about whether or not she actually did. She felt herself heat up for an argument, the way matadors probably felt before striding into the bullring. The more she thought about it, the more she realized that Jane was a lot like a bull – angry and immovable, sharp and prone to snorting. Zoe knew that it wasn't only Jane's fault, though, whatever had happened to them. And maybe she was right. Zoe thought about all the times she'd gone to Elizabeth instead of her wife, for any number of reasons. It hadn't happened that often recently, except to talk about the house, really, but years ago it had happened all the time. When she and Jane were first together, she and Elizabeth had been inseparable, and Zoe had often started sentences, 'Well, I was just telling Elizabeth,' or 'Elizabeth just told me . . .' which was obviously tedious and annoying. She thought about how she would feel if Jane had someone like that, a confidante she really loved, and if that person lived next door. They weren't in college anymore – they weren't Jerry Seinfeld and his bachelor(ette) friends, always popping in and out with no notice or reason. They were adults, with families and taxes and mortgages. Zoe had the horrifying realization that her wife might be right. The specifics were all wrong, but Jane was right that Elizabeth had always been there, hovering at the edges, eager to answer the phone.

'I think we should set up a few more appointments,' Zoe said. Dr Amelia nodded and made a note.

Fifty-one

Dave could surf – he was from Southern California, as Andrew had suspected – and Andrew agreed to give it a try. Dave had a friend who rented boards and wetsuits a few blocks from the hotel property, and they had everything they needed in fifteen minutes. He recommended a nine-foot foam soft top, and Andrew nodded like he knew what that meant. 'We're gonna get you right up, man,' Dave said.

He'd taken a lesson once before, when he and Elizabeth went to Hawaii for their honeymoon, which was otherwise nothing but reading paperbacks in the sand, stopping every now and then to kiss each other and twirl their rings. More than anything, Andrew had spent his days feeling *lucky* – lucky that Elizabeth, so light and good, had chosen *him*, this lump of coal. He was sure from the start that he didn't deserve her, but he was going to try, and that was how they'd spent their honeymoon – having sex and getting sunburnt and walking nowhere, holding hands. Maybe they should go back – maybe Harry could stay at home. He was old enough. Andrew was still upset about the movie, but maybe if he looked deeper into it, he *could* see what she was trying to do.

They – EVOLVEment, Andrew, Dave, the Waves, whatever they were going to be called – had made an offer on the hotel. There was some due-diligence zoning work to be done, so the process would take a few months. Dave and Phillip were taking care of everything. The first check had gone to the realtor's escrow account, along with some other money from investors, where it would sit until they signed the contract. In the meantime, Andrew had written a second check, this time straight to Dave, for another fifty thousand. EVOLVEment was growing so fast – they needed money to pay for the teachers and for the equipment, cases of bottles for the kombucha and reams of plastic cups for the juices, and to continue to make improvements to the house – and all of Dave's capital was earmarked for improvements to the hotel. He'd asked so sheepishly, as if Andrew would object, when EVOLVEment was the clearest and easiest of all his responsibilities.

Together they paddled out into the water. Andrew quickly remembered the feeling from so many years ago, all those dormant muscles in his chest and shoulders suddenly squeaking awake. It was hard to keep the board flat underneath him – he felt like a Weeble Wobble, only with no weight keeping him down. They made it past the break, and Dave gave him a few pointers – not to try to leap up to stand but to sort of drag his feet into place, which sounded easier but wasn't, not really. Leaping was for people like Dave, whose stomachs were circuit boards of muscles, each tiny piece clicking together with purpose.

'It's not about instruction,' Dave said. 'It's just about feeling it, you know? The wave, the vibe. That's what surfing is all about. The ocean tells you when it's your time, and then you go.'

'Right,' Andrew said.

Nearby, a surfing school was teaching lessons, and three girls in matching wetsuit tops and bikini bottoms giggled as they watched one another slide off their boards and into the shallow water. A large wave began to roll in, and Dave nodded at it, squinting. 'That's mine,' he said, and began to paddle. He was on his feet in another minute, his back flexing as he shifted his weight.

Andrew was on his stomach, bobbing up and down with the waves. August had come so quickly this year – the city was empty, but the beaches were full, dotted with people young and old. Andrew wished he'd taken Harry to the beach more as a kid – they went every so often, maybe once or twice a summer, but that was it. It struck him as a grand injustice, a wrong he had done. The kids playing on the sand were digging holes, they were building castles with plastic buckets. Harry was just like Elizabeth, prone to indoor activities, and Andrew thought it was all his fault for not intervening. They'd never gone camping without a car. They'd never driven a Winnebago. They'd never gone down a zip line or made a bonfire. Andrew wanted to cry, thinking of all the things he'd deprived his son of, just because he hadn't thought to do them. Up ahead, Dave had easily coasted all the way to the sand. The water was shallow, and by the time Dave reached the beach, he was just skimming the ground like he was on a giant skateboard, which he sort of was, more or less. It looked so easy. Dave was probably thirty-five, and Andrew wondered if he'd ever been married or if he had any kids. He surely would have mentioned a kid, unless it had been in some seriously bad situation and they weren't in touch, and Andrew couldn't imagine that being the case. Dave seemed like a bachelor, in a good way. Unencumbered.

A slightly bigger wave rolled out from underneath him, and Andrew pushed himself up so that he was straddling the board again, his legs dangling in the water on either side. Dave waved from the beach and shouted something that Andrew couldn't hear. He turned around to see what was coming – surfing was sort of like fishing in a lake, lots of waiting and watching, only with an increased likelihood of drowning. There was a wave coming, and Andrew decided to paddle. He flopped back on to his stomach too quickly, and it stung, but he didn't have time to think about it – he started to paddle and paddle with his head and chest up, just like in yoga class, until the wave was underneath him and the board was doing what it was supposed to – keeping him and the wave apart. For a second, Andrew was doing it – he dragged his feet to a low crouch and then pushed himself up to stand, almost. His knees were bent and his arms were out. He felt like Philippe Petit walking between the Twin Towers. Andrew wanted to look for Dave and give a thumbs-up or a wave, but he knew that if he did, he would fall. But then he started to fall anyway, and as he was falling off to the left side of the board, Andrew looked toward the beach and thought he saw Harry and Ruby standing just behind Dave, her big curly hair wound up like a ball of yarn on top of her head. But then he hit the water, and he went for a short ride in the Atlantic Ocean washing machine, and when his head popped back up, they were gone. Andrew grabbed the board and used it to kick the rest of the way to the sand.

'You totally had it,' Dave said, offering Andrew a hand. 'Next time will be even better.'

'I thought I just saw my kid,' Andrew said, looking around the beach. There were tons of young people on the sand, lying around with supermarket gossip magazines and cheap beach umbrellas, but he didn't see Harry. 'I swear, he was just standing right behind you.'

'Like a vision,' Dave said, nodding. 'Far out.'

'No, I mean, he was standing there, right there!' Andrew pointed, as if the sand would offer a map.

'I get it,' Dave said, his mouth flat, his eyes blank. So there it was – he didn't have kids, Andrew could tell. He was looking back at the water, his board sticking straight up toward the cloudless sky overhead. 'Want to try again?'

'Sure,' Andrew said. He took one last sweep of the beach, looking for Ruby's hair, but still didn't see them. She was trouble, just like her mother, and Andrew was tired of pretending not to care. 'Let's do it,' he said, and threw his board back into the water, forgetting that it was still attached to his leg, which made him stumble and fall in the low, foamy surf.

'It's cool,' Dave said. 'You're getting the hang of it already.'

Andrew was embarrassed but didn't let it show. 'Let's go again.'

Fifty-two

Elizabeth sat on the porch, sweating. She had an appointment that afternoon with a couple from Carroll Gardens who wanted a house in the neighborhood – they had a three-year-old daughter and were pregnant with another. Zoe's house was exactly what they were looking for – big enough for all the people in their family but shabby enough that they could afford it. Deirdre had a listing for a house on Ditmas Avenue, but Elizabeth knew they wanted to be closer to the park than that. A few blocks made all the difference, sometimes – it wasn't unusual to have clients who gave you exact borders that they were looking within – sometimes it had to do with school zones, but sometimes it was just personal preference. If Elizabeth ever moved, she would want an apartment on Commerce or Grove or Bedford in the West Village, a tiny little tangle of streets. Not that she wanted to move – it was just a professional hazard, seeing how other people lived their lives and measuring against your own. She also didn't really want to sell Zoe's house – it would mean that Zoe was actually leaving the neighborhood, and if they weren't neighbors, what would that mean? Would she regularly text her for a last-minute dinner date? Not that Zoe had responded positively lately – though of course they were sorting through a lot, what with the fire and everything. Sometimes excuses weren't excuses. If Zoe moved, would they sit on each other's porches and drink wine? How often would Zoe get on the subway for her? She didn't want to have to find out.

Elizabeth was sitting on the porch because Zoe was avoiding her – she wasn't responding to e-mails and texts, as if Elizabeth didn't know that she'd seen them. Sometimes she longed for the olden days, when you had no idea whether anyone had listened to your message, or that you'd called them six times in one day. Elizabeth wasn't trying to be a stalker; she actually needed to talk to her. She promised her clients that she'd ask about the likelihood of the house coming on the market, but even more than that, she wanted to know about Jane. Of course, it was all the same conversation, and one that Zoe was clearly trying to avoid. But being neighbors in addition to friends meant that Elizabeth knew when Zoe and Bingo were going to take their late-morning walk, and it wasn't breaking any kind of protocol to be sitting on her own porch at that same time, was it?

She saw Bingo first – his happy mouth open, with his leash dragging behind him on the sidewalk. Dogs were gloriously uncomplicated creatures – food and play and sleep and love, that was all they needed. People were so much worse. Zoe was a few yards behind Bingo, looking at her phone.

'Hey,' Elizabeth said, coming down her steps.

'Oh, hi, I was just about to call you back,' Zoe said, and tucked her phone into her back pocket. 'Hold up, Bing.' She bent over and picked up the end of the leash.

'Is everything okay?' Elizabeth squinted, and shaded her eyes with her hands. 'With us, I mean? Did I do something?'

'What? No! What would you have even done?' Zoe looked at the ground.

'I'm not sure,' Elizabeth said. 'That's why I'm asking.'

'No,' Zoe said. 'Really. We're fine! Things have just been hectic, with the fire, you know.'

'Of course,' Elizabeth said, dropping her hands to her sides. 'It just seemed like things were weird, and we hadn't talked about the house in a little while, and then the other day, with the pancakes, you and Jane seemed . . .'

'What? She is my wife, you remember.' Zoe sounded defensive.

'Of course! No, of course! I just thought, you know, that you guys were having some things, and we'd talked about the house, and I thought maybe there'd been some backsliding there . . .'

'Backsliding? You're saying that me and my wife are *backsliding* into our marriage, out of your greedy little hands? God, Lizzy!' Zoe shook her head. 'Maybe she was right! Is that crazy? I don't know! You honestly seem to be thinking more about your commission than our friendship, if I'm being honest.'

'No!' Elizabeth said. 'That's crazy! That's not what I meant. I promise!' Everything was coming out wrong. Elizabeth wanted to tell Zoe that she was afraid of her moving away, afraid that she would want to move, too, to the apartment next door, just to make sure that they stayed friends for the next twenty years and the twenty after that, that she was sad about the idea of Zoe and Jane getting divorced and sad about her own marriage, too, that Ruby and Harry were getting too old to be called children, and what did they call them next? But her mouth wouldn't work right, and none of it came out. 'Just, no, really,' Elizabeth said. 'I promise.'

'Can we talk about this later?' Zoe gestured to Bingo, who was relieving himself on the sidewalk.

'Sure,' Elizabeth said. 'I didn't mean anything by it, and of course, *of course* I just want you to be happy. And I'm not trying to sell your house out from under you. I just want to make sure I know what's happening. If you're telling me to pump the brakes, I will pump them, okay?'

'Okay,' Zoe said, a wistful look crossing her face. 'It's just like, everything is all fucked up right now, both good and bad, and I don't really know which end is up. I'm sorry.' She leaned over and gave Elizabeth a kiss on the cheek. 'I'll call you.'

'Great,' Elizabeth said. 'Please do.' Her clients could go live in Deirdre's listing – she didn't care about that. And she did hope that Jane and Zoe would work it out, sort of. They weren't like some of the couples she knew, who she actively thought should get divorced because they fought in public so much. They were somewhere on the middle of the scale, which is how she thought of herself and Andrew. They weren't lovebirds, like Zoe's parents, or even Deirdre and Sean, couples who rubbed each other's backs for fun, without being asked or complaining that they really needed a massage, too. Most couples she knew were in the middle, slogging it out. *Don't get divorced!* That was their shared motto. It was the only way to have a long marriage, the only way to have a truly solid family. Who needed happiness when you had stability? Wasn't that the idea behind Ferberizing babies, that a few nights of misery led to more sleep for everyone? Elizabeth looked down at her hand and realized that she was clenching her fist so tightly that her fingernails had left deep impressions in her palm.

Some people were the leavers and some were the left. Zoe was the former. Kitty's Mustache began to die when Lydia dropped out, though it didn't seem like it. Lydia had always been their weakest link, and Zoe's girlfriend at the time had a friend in the conservatory who played drums, and so that was an easy replacement. The only problem was that the new guy was a much better musician than the rest of them, which made their songs sound rinky-dink, amateurish. Nevertheless they played parties and shows all that year, even after graduation, when Zoe and Andrew were both otherwise unemployed and unoccupied. It was January when Zoe again decided that she'd had enough. She was tired of playing for freshmen clutching their first red plastic cups of beer. There was no one interesting there anymore, she said. She said that she felt old and pathetic, which was hilarious, because the whole town followed her around like she was the Pied Piper.

Maybe that was a problem – being the coolest person for miles meant that there was no one to look up to. She knew that music wasn't for her – she wasn't one of those kids who wanted her parents' life. Zoe started spending more and more time with her art professors, drinking wine at their kitchen tables and talking about New York. When winter break rolled around, she announced that she'd had enough and that they would see what happened with the band in the spring, when Elizabeth and Andrew were out of school. It was a hiatus – that's what they said to all their friends. But there was no such thing as a hiatus for a college band. Elizabeth was saddest of all, because she knew that she'd probably never be in a band again, not a real one. College was a make-believe place, where you could decide to do something and just do it, where no one was going to tell you that you weren't good enough or talented enough. Elizabeth had plenty of self-confidence, but she knew her limitations.

What was a year? When they were in school, it seemed like something. Zoe was older and wiser, which is how Elizabeth always felt – like *The Sound of Music* and she was Liesl and Zoe was Rolf, and they were dancing around that gazebo together, minus the Nazi part. It was so funny, being a parent and realizing what a year actually meant. A year was nothing! And a school year was *truly* nothing – you could be born a day apart and be in two different grades, depending on the date. It was all so arbitrary. Elizabeth wished she'd known that earlier on in life. Zoe wasn't any wiser than she was. A year wasn't a long time. She was just bored in Ohio, and that was the end of Kitty's Mustache.

There was a girl in New York, of course – Zoe was never without one for long. This one was an artist and had been known (and much admired) for walking around the Oberlin campus wearing only a pair of overalls. The girl wanted to start a new band, a duo, and Zoe was gone. It hadn't lasted very long – only as long as the romance, maybe six months, but it meant that when Elizabeth and Andrew arrived, Kitty's Mustache was a memory, not even Zoe's most recent project. It didn't matter that they'd been popular, that they'd had a record. There were so many indie labels that everyone they knew had had a record out – everyone had show posters and music videos and a box full of memorabilia. They weren't that special. It was Lydia who later made them special in hindsight, who made them a footnote in music history. And so they all moved on, and after a few years it seemed quaint, a sweet memory to tell their children about. *We were cool.* Sometimes, if Elizabeth didn't think too much about the specifics, it even seemed true.

Fifty-three

There was one more SAT class and then the test. Harry wished it would last forever – he'd move into the karate studio if he had to and take all his meals with Eliza and Thayer staring at him, chewing with their mouths open like two stoned cows. Ruby was humoring him by letting him quiz her on vocabulary flash cards. During the day, they mostly had Ruby's house to themselves, and if one of her mothers did come home, it was easy enough to wait her out. The secret truth of parenting (in houses other than Harry's own) was that parents almost always had other shit to think about, boring stuff like taxes and dermatology appointments, plus their actual jobs and whether they needed to buy milk. Ruby told him that she'd been smoking for three years – in her bedroom! – before either of her mothers noticed. Harry couldn't imagine ever not noticing anything having to do with Ruby. The day before, she'd trimmed the front half of her hair two inches, and it was the first thing he saw. She looked like an Egyptian queen, and he'd told her so. 'You make me want to shave my head,' Ruby said. 'Just to see what compliment you'd come up with.'

She was wearing one of his old T-shirts – God, she could make an ancient, stained Rugrats T-shirt look good – and a stretchy little black skirt. The air conditioner in her bedroom window was so loud that they had to turn the music way up, which made it hard to hear Ruby's answers to his flash cards, but Harry was reading her lips. They were listening to Otis Redding, and every now and then Ruby would jump off the bed and dance.

'"Showing great joy" – come on, that's an easy one. Jubilant!' Ruby rolled her eyes. 'Give me something harder.'

'You can't just do the hard ones. You need to make sure you know the easy ones, too. You can't give the easy ones away! That's how you rack up the points!'

'Harry, this is the SATs, not a video game.' Ruby clapped her hands. 'Let's go, next.'

He flipped through the cards. Temperate. Gloaming. Cloister. Ruby knew them all. She got up and turned the fan so it was pointing right at her face. She had a few tiny pimples on her right cheek, and one of her earrings had gotten infected – she'd pierced that ear herself, in the bathroom at school – and the hole was still a little bit red. Harry wished that he could videotape every second he spent with Ruby so that he could look at it in twenty years. So he could show it to her in twenty years. So they could look at it together and show their children. A boy and a girl. Twins, maybe. Was it weird that Harry was picturing twins? They'd be light-skinned, like Ruby, with chubby arms and legs, like him.

Harry had been thinking a lot about the future.

He'd be done with Whitman in less than a year – graduation was in June. That was only ten months away. He'd already told Ruby that he loved her, and he couldn't imagine that changing anytime soon. He couldn't imagine it changing, period. What were the rules for when the best person you knew was someone you'd known all your life? Were you supposed to pretend to look elsewhere, just for due diligence? Harry didn't give a fuck about who else might be out there – it seemed literally impossible that there was anyone else on the planet who he would like more. It wasn't anything as cheesy as having a soul mate – that was Lifetime-movie shit, soft focus and hokey. It was just math. Anyone else + Harry = stupid. He hoped that was one of the questions.

If he did well enough on the test, he could easily get into any of the city schools he wanted to go to, which wouldn't even be expensive. If Ruby kept working at her parents' restaurant, she'd make money. All they needed was a place to live. In eight months he'd be eighteen, and then his parents couldn't tell him not to see her. It was really just his dad, anyway, and Harry thought that there was a fairly high likelihood that he'd get over it soon.

Harry hadn't seen his friends in weeks, and he didn't care. Maybe that's what it felt like to be in love. Ruby hadn't been hanging out with her friends either – there were girls who Harry had seen her with every day for the last four years, Chloe and Paloma and Anika and Sarah Dinnerstein, but other than Sarah, he hadn't seen them all summer. That seemed weirder. He didn't really want to bring it up, because it might pop a hole in that magical, mysterious dream that they were clearly living inside, a world in which Ruby loved him back. But he wanted to know.

'Hey, what are your friends doing this summer? Chloe and them?' He chewed on his nails.

'Chloe's in Paris, Paloma's already at Dartmouth. They're on the quarter system – plus, there was some freshman camping trip beforehand. Ugh, I would rather die a slow, painful death than go on a freshman camping trip.' Ruby sighed. 'Everyone is gone but me.'

'I'm not gone. I'm here.' Harry flipped through the flash cards, quizzing himself.

'I know,' Ruby said. 'But you don't count.'

Harry looked up.

'Oh, come on, I don't mean it like that,' Ruby said. 'I just mean that of course you're here. You're not done with school yet, and plus, you're just, like, always here.'

'Uh-huh,' Harry said. 'I guess that's true. Would you rather I was somewhere else?'

'You're my love slave,' Ruby said. 'This is the only place I want you to be.' She jumped back on to the bed, stuck her legs in the air, and tugged off her skirt.

'Is that your way of apologizing?' Harry asked. He pulled his knees into his chest.

Ruby flipped over and crawled the rest of the way toward him. 'Yes.'

'I guess I could let it go with a warning. Just this once.' Harry closed his eyes and let Ruby take the flash cards out of his hand. They made a splashing sound when they hit the wood floor, and when Ruby started kissing him, Harry imagined all the words floating up in the air and making sentences about them, a miniature tornado of love poems. Maybe it didn't matter if Ruby loved him. Maybe his love was enough for both of them.

Fifty-four

Andrew was home so infrequently, it was almost like he had a nine-to-five job. Elizabeth took to staring out the window like a sailor's bride. A sailor's widow? Is that what they were called? A couple of the houses in the neighborhood had widow's walks, which didn't even make any sense – there was no view to speak of, except the roofs of other houses, and it seemed like offering burglars a runway, but there was no accounting for sense in Brooklyn real estate. Even when Andrew was at home, he treated her with a polite chilliness that usually lasted only a few hours. Now it had been several weeks, and Elizabeth was worried he might never warm back up. She missed the cat. She missed Andrew, the way he used to be, or the way she used to think he was. Sometimes at night when Elizabeth was trying to go to sleep, she would close her eyes and see Iggy, his tiny little pussycat face peeking out from under a car or behind a trash can, and then he would start to look like Andrew, and she would open her eyes and stare at the ceiling, her heart beating so fast. Iggy was lost, Andrew was lost, and so was she. Everyone except for Harry. Poor Harry! To be saddled with such parents and a missing cat, all at once. Maybe she should make an appointment for him to see someone.

Her phone rang – the house phone, the landline. No one ever used it except the office at Whitman, or sometimes some clients who were especially anxious about something that couldn't wait until morning. Elizabeth picked it up and said hello. There was a telltale pause.

'Hi there, oops, you caught me! It's Naomi!'

Elizabeth looked at the telephone. 'I didn't even realize that you had this number. Then again, you seem to have all the numbers, so I'm not really surprised. I'm much easier to reach on my cell phone, though.'

Naomi laughed. 'I'm calling for Andrew. He left me a message, and I got a little excited, you know, like, he's Mr Mistress!'

'Andrew called you?' Elizabeth pulled back the curtain again and peered out on to the street. 'To say what?'

Naomi tsked. 'You are so naughty! I guess I shouldn't be surprised.' Her voice hardened. This was Hollywood – the swift, humorless shift toward the mercenary. 'He said that he never agreed, and that as a co-writer of the song, his consent was required to use it, and that his lawyers would be delighted to talk to our lawyers about it. He also said, and I quote, "There is no amount of money that will make me change my mind." So that's interesting, don't you think?' The bubbles came back to her voice. 'Tell me he was high, Elizabeth. Tell me that it was a prank phone call.'

Elizabeth swallowed. Andrew was the one who was acting crazy – why was she the only one who noticed? Why was everything her fault?

'He is not thrilled,' Elizabeth said.

'Not thrilled with what, exactly?' Naomi said. 'Spell it out for me.'

'My husband may not have actually signed the form. Did I not mention that he was wavering?' Elizabeth knew she was being bad, couching her decision this way.

'That presents something of a problem, Elizabeth. There isn't really a huge gray area there. If he didn't sign it, he needs to. Which means we need to get him on board. You know what? I'm going to come on out. Darcey and the rest of the cast are going to be in New York next week anyway to film some things, and rather than hold up everything I'm going to make time in the schedule for a little visit. It worked for you, and I think it'll work for him.' Naomi said something to someone else in the background. 'No, it's fine,' she said, coming back to the phone. 'This will be fine. And, Elizabeth?'

'Yes?' It was like being scolded in elementary school. She wanted to curl into a ball and roll under the bed and stay there forever.

'If for some reason this doesn't work, and Andrew really does call his lawyers, I hope you've got one, too.' Naomi hung up the phone, and Elizabeth burst into tears. She heard the door unlock and footsteps on the stairs. 'Harry?' she called. 'Is that you?'

'It's me,' Andrew said, swinging open the bedroom door. 'Jesus, what happened to you?' The bridge of his nose was pink, a tiny sunburn. He hated wearing sunscreen – she practically had to hold his arms down to put it on, worse than when Harry was a toddler.

'Nothing,' Elizabeth said. She swiped at her cheeks and smiled as brightly as possible. 'I was just on my way out.' She stood up and gave herself a little shake, like a wet dog. 'Are you okay?'

'Why wouldn't I be?' Andrew said. He raised his eyebrows.

'I don't know! How would I know?' Elizabeth pushed by him and into the hall. When she got there, she realized she'd left her keys and her shoes in the bedroom, but she hated the idea of walking back in, so she went into Harry's room and started folding dirty clothes.

It was two years after they graduated from Oberlin that Lydia called about the song. She had never called Elizabeth directly in the days of Kitty's Mustache, and so when the phone rang and Lydia's voice was on the other end, Elizabeth was on high alert. The last she'd heard, Lydia had signed a record deal. There were often pictures of her in magazines and items in the gossip column in the newspaper. Everyone loved Lydia already, somehow – Elizabeth found the whole thing slightly inscrutable, but then again that was Lydia – her white-blond hair hanging in front of her eyes, her round cheeks gone narrow. She looked so different that Elizabeth bet that most people at Oberlin wouldn't even recognize her face – her first face, that is. Maybe she'd even had something done, professionally. One never knew.

'Lydia, hi,' Elizabeth had said. Andrew was out – she was in the house alone. It was when she was working as an assistant for the gallerist, and it was her day off. They were still living in Zoe's house then, in what would someday be Ruby's room. Did Ruby know that, that Elizabeth had slept in that room hundreds of times, that Elizabeth had had sex in that room eons before she was born? She felt like she was constantly swimming through time and space, her old self and her current self simultaneously, with her flat stomach and her stretch marks and the lines around her eyes. When she thought about that phone call with Lydia, which would change both their lives forever, Elizabeth wasn't sure who was talking. It was impossible that only young Elizabeth – unmarried, rootless, beer-drinker Elizabeth who was thinking about going back to school for social work or maybe early-childhood education or maybe for a fiction M.F.A. – was on the telephone, that she had somehow been the one to speak the words to Lydia.

She was calling because she needed the song. Of course! As soon as Lydia said it, Elizabeth laughed. 'I'm sorry,' she'd said. 'Go on.'

'We have lots of great songs, obviously,' Lydia had said. 'There are some fucking amazing songs. But the record company doesn't feel like they have *it* yet, you know, the single. And.'

'You want "Mistress of Myself".'

'Yeah.' Elizabeth could hear how hard it was for Lydia to say it, though it must have been her idea, because no one else knew the song. She must have sung it for them, or played them a tape. Elizabeth could picture an office full of suits, with Lydia at the center, holding up a tiny boom box, Elizabeth's voice coming out of the speakers and Lydia singing over it, drowning everything else out. People in the halls would have turned to look.

'Okay,' Elizabeth had said. 'As long as we get the publishing all squared away. I mean.'

She heard Lydia breathing.

'There is no way that I'm going to let you pretend that you wrote that song.' Even all these lifetimes later, Elizabeth was proud of herself for having said it. She could imagine Lydia's sulky mouth getting all twisted up, and she didn't care. 'You know that, right?'

'Of course,' Lydia had said. 'I'll get you the paperwork for ASCAP.'

Elizabeth had never heard of it but agreed. 'Fine.'

'Great.' Lydia had wanted to get off the phone so badly, Elizabeth could tell. Even before she knew, she knew. Lydia was a snake, slithering through the grass, and Elizabeth wanted to catch her by the tail and fling her against a tree.

'Well, good luck with the record. What's it going to be called yet, do you know?' Elizabeth knew the answer before the words were out of her mouth. Her words, Lydia's mouth. Her words, written across a photo of Lydia's face.

'We're still deciding,' Lydia said, unwilling to admit it.

'Okay, then,' Elizabeth said. 'Talk to you soon. Be good.'

And then she was gone.

Fifty-five

Dust texted HI at midnight. Ruby was on the couch watching *The Kardashians*, even though it was an episode that she'd seen before. She loved them and hated them in equal measure, and if she ever applied to college again, her plan was to write an essay about them, and how she'd always had imaginary sisters as a child, even in her house full of women. Ruby thought she probably still wouldn't get in, but at least she'd be putting her real self on paper. The first time, she knew she wasn't going to get in anywhere, and so it didn't matter. If she actually tried to get in and it didn't work, then she'd be upset. A minute later, Dust texted R U HOME? HAVE A PRESENT FOR YOU. OUTSIDE.

Ruby swiveled around and looked out the window. Sure enough, Dust was sitting on the porch. He wasn't even facing her, just sitting on the steps as if he hadn't written and invited her to join him. Ruby stuck out her tongue, paused the TV, and went out in her bare feet. Dust didn't turn around when Ruby sat down next to him, and when she looked at him, she realized why.

There was a cat cradled in Dust's arms. Not just any cat. 'Iggy Pop!' Ruby said, too loud. She covered her mouth and said it again. 'Iggy Pop!' She reached over and took the cat out of Dust's grip. Iggy was a good boy, almost boneless, with a never-ending lust for attention, and so he didn't object when Ruby began to pet him and scratch under his chin. 'Where was he? Oh, my God, Dust, they are going to be so fucking happy, you have no idea. Where did you find him?'

He shrugged. 'Around.'

'Well, I'm so glad you brought him back. Harry's mom is going to be happy. She, like, *needs* this.' Ruby snuggled Iggy against her shoulder. 'Whatta good boy.'

'He likes roast chicken,' Dust said. 'And cottage cheese.'

'How do you know? How long have you had him?' Ruby asked, even though she really wanted to ask if Dust had parents who had provided these items, or if he'd roasted a chicken himself.

'It was from the grocery store,' Dust said. 'My mom can't cook for shit.'

'Oh,' Ruby said, and immediately tried to clear her mind of all other thoughts he might be reading. How long had he had the cat? Had he found it and just taken it home, to rescue it from the streets of Brooklyn? Had he stolen it from Harry's front porch? Had he blown weed smoke in its poor little pussycat face? Ruby didn't want to know. 'Anyway, thank you.'

'It sucks about the fire,' Dust said. His hair had grown out a little over the summer – it was maybe an inch long, sticking straight out. In a few more weeks, it might start to look like normal boy hair and not a shaved head. Ruby tried to picture Dust with hair he could tuck behind his ears, like Harry.

'Um, yeah, that's an understatement. Now I think my parents are happy I didn't get into college – no tuition to pay for. When the restaurant is closed, no one is buying a thirteen-dollar hamburger, you know?' Ruby was afraid to put the cat down, even though he'd probably just run straight home. She wanted the points for bringing him back.

'Sarah was tripping balls,' Dust said. 'She thought the sparklers were fairies sending her messages. She kept trying to kneel down and get close to them. I don't think she meant to put them so close.'

'Excuse me?' Ruby scooted a few inches away. 'Did that bitch set my parents' restaurant on fire? Are you joking?'

'No,' Dust said. 'She didn't set it on fire. Not, like, on purpose. She was just putting these sparklers all around the back of Nico's house, and . . . you know, the fence behind Hyacinth is right there, and she put them all in a little line with some candles and stuff, and then I guess she came inside and forgot about them. She didn't "set it on fire." She's not psycho. She's just kind of dumb.'

Ruby had never heard Dust call anyone dumb before. That was her line – it was what she always said about him. His stupidity was the reason they weren't ever going to be serious, it was why she never gave their relationship that much thought. She'd always seen him as a cardboard cutout of a person, a type. But now she wasn't sure.

'So you think Sarah Dinnerstein accidentally set my parents' restaurant on fire?' Ruby wondered where Sarah was now, if she was at home in her family's apartment in Park Slope, in her bedroom that overlooked Prospect Park. She was probably staring into space and thinking about how she could make sure she got a private room in her dorm, just in case Dust came to visit. And who knew! Maybe Dust would go and visit her – maybe he'd take the subway to Penn Station and then a Greyhound bus, and when he got off in the bumblefuck Vermont town where her school was, Sarah would be standing there with tears in her eyes, so happy to see him, and then maybe Dust would decide to move in with her, and he'd let his hair grow, and they'd get married and have babies, and he'd teach them all how to skateboard. 'I could call the police, you realize that, right?'

'You're not going to call the police. They probably already came. I already heard, the whole thing is covered by insurance. It's not even a big deal. It could have been way worse.' Dust pulled a pack of cigarettes out of his front pocket. 'Most people's houses burn down because of cigarettes, did you know that? Cigarettes and ovens.'

'Thanks, that's great,' Ruby said. He was right – she wasn't going to call the police. What would it accomplish, except getting her in more trouble? 'Give me one of those, mine are upstairs.'

Dust plucked out another cigarette and lit it on the end of his own, the two papery embers flashing in the darkness. Ruby took it from him and plugged it into her mouth. She exhaled a string of perfect smoke rings.

'I bet your little boyfriend can't do that,' Dust said.

'Why would he need to do that?' Ruby picked a fleck of tobacco off her tongue – Dust smoked unfiltered. Sometimes he even rolled his own from a little baggie, which Ruby had always found very sexy, his fingers working so quickly.

'He's, like, a kid,' Dust said. 'Like a good little kid who always does extra credit on his homework.'

'I do my homework. Or I did.' Ruby spat. 'Your cigarettes are fucking gross. What are you, like, a cowboy?'

'Yeah,' Dust said. 'But so are you. You're more like me than you are like him, Ruby. You gonna tell his parents I gave you that cat? Or are you gonna tell them that you found it in the bushes?' Dust dropped his cigarette butt on to the sidewalk, then pushed himself up and ground it down with his shoe.

'Did you walk here?' Ruby asked. She'd never seen him without his skateboard in hand. He raised a finger and then leaned down and reached under her mum's forsythia. He pulled out his board and slid it under his feet.

'It's hard to ride with a cat,' Dust said. 'But not impossible. I'll see you, Rube.'

She watched him skate away, his willowy body shifting back and forth as he went down the middle of the street. It was dark, and there were cars, but Dust didn't care – he was immortal, just like she was, immune to common sense and traffic laws. Ruby finished the cigarette even though she wasn't enjoying it, and then took the cat down to Harry's house and knocked on the door. By the time Elizabeth came to the door, Ruby's sheepish, hopeful smile was firmly in place.

Fifty-six

Dr Amelia had both Zoe and Jane keep journals about their feelings. It was worse than the food journal Jane had kept in culinary school, a brag book that was intended to shame anyone else who happened to open it (*Lunch – seared foie gras with poached egg and frisée salad*). Jane didn't know what to write down, so she wrote down everything – when Zoe kissed her on the cheek in the morning (about half the time), when Zoe farted (often, but so did she), when Zoe said something dismissive (sometimes), when Bingo paid more attention to Zoe (always). Jane felt like it was probably stupid, but she was doing it anyway. If Zoe wanted her to do homework, she was going to do homework.

There wasn't very much to do about Hyacinth – the patio was under construction. The replacement tables and chairs were on order, as was the glass that had been broken. A special cleanup crew was working on the ceiling and the wall. Jane was on the phone with her suppliers every few days – squash blossoms, tomatoes, a new cheese, beautiful pork chops – she wanted to order it all, but they were at least a month away. During the day she took the Q to the Grand Army Plaza farmers' market, buying things for the house. She always saw other chefs there, and she'd kiss them hello. Everyone knew about the fire, everyone was sympathetic, and they all furrowed their brows before turning their attention back to the hen-of-the-woods mush-rooms or the fairy tale eggplants. Jane wandered, putting her hands on everything. She was going to grill some steaks, or maybe make some scallops, and throw some asparagus on, too, let them roll around on the fire until they were striped with beautiful grill marks, both firm and tender. Maybe a chimichurri – Zoe loved her chimichurri. Jane picked up three big handfuls of parsley. There were enormous peaches, practically already dripping, and Jane's mouth began to water. She'd make dessert, too.

When Jane got home, her shoulders weighed down by tote bags, Ruby was on the floor. She was leaning against the couch, watching television. 'Help me,' Jane said, and Ruby peeled herself up like Gumby. Together they unpacked the bags, lining everything up along the counter.

'What are we making?' Ruby asked. 'I just got so hungry.'

There was nothing Jane liked to hear more. 'Well,' she said, and immediately snapped into action. She pointed at cabinets, and Ruby took down whatever she needed – the mandoline, the immersion blender, cutting boards. It was Ruby's job to peel garlic, to be the sous. They worked silently – Jane was the captain of the ship, and she knew just what had to be done. That was what she liked most about being in kitchens – people thought cooking was about making things taste good, and it was, but it was more like being a conductor, or a choreographer – there were a thousand moving parts, and you had to be aware of them all. An allergy, a birthday, how long it took mussels to open in their buttery little bath. All the information was inside her, organized and constantly recalibrating.

'Avocado,' Jane said, and Ruby cut one open the way she'd been taught, letting the knife rest on the seed and rolling the fruit around in her hand. She handed it to her mother, and Jane made a quick mash. She tore off a hunk of bread, slathered the avocado on top just as an egg began to crack and sizzle in a pan. *Bon appétit,* she said, sliding the egg out of the pan and on to the bread, drops of olive oil polka-dotting the plate.

'Thank God,' Ruby said. 'I thought I was actually going to die.' She didn't leave the kitchen, the way she usually did, squirreling her food upstairs like someone was going to steal it from her – instead she ate standing up, hunched over the counter. Jane put the rest of the groceries away and then leaned on the counter next to Ruby and ate the other half of the avocado with a spoon. When she was a baby, Ruby would eat a whole avocado every day – she'd try to eat the peel if they let her. For a few months, it seemed like her skin might actually be permanently stained green, along with most of her clothes. Zoe had loved it – she would throw her head back and laugh, so entranced by their daughter's gusto. Jane leaned over and kissed Ruby on the cheek. 'Love you, honey,' she said.

'Jeez, Mom,' Ruby said. 'I already said thank you.' Some crumbs fell on to her shirt. Jane pinched Ruby on the nose and went upstairs to write more notes for Dr Amelia.

Fifty-seven

Harry was happy that Ruby had brought Iggy Pop home – Iggy was a good cat, and his mother was waltzing him around the house like they were in a Disney cartoon – but her story was weird. She said that she was just sitting on the stoop, and then Iggy crawled out of the bushes and on to her lap. Iggy was a lover, and he would have crawled on to her lap, sure, but if he'd gotten as far as the Kahn-Bennetts', then why wouldn't he have just come home? Cats weren't idiots. And neither was Harry. He knew that Ruby hadn't been hiding the cat – he'd been in her room a hundred times, and even with all the piles of clothing everywhere, he still would have noticed his own pet. There was only one likely candidate – otherwise Ruby's story about finding the cat would have made sense.

During the school year, it was easy to find Dust and Nico and the rest of their friends – they were always across the street from Whitman, skidding along the edge of the lowest church step on their skateboards or wrestling each other to the ground in a way that looked both playful and dangerous. That was what the girls liked about them: at Whitman, parents were everywhere – in the halls, in the audience at plays, standing along the edges of the gym during basketball games, visibly willing shots to go in – which meant that all the kids were bubble boys and girls, with no broken limbs or bruised egos. But the church-step kids had no parents. They were like kids from the 1970s, self-sufficient, with bruises and scars. Sometimes Harry was envious of them, the way their lives seemed full of empty days instead of extra-curricular activities designed to boost their chances of getting into college. But most of the time, he understood that he had it better than they did, even if they probably had more fun.

Nico's house was the first logical stop – mostly because Harry knew where it was. He waited until afternoon and then walked over, going around the block so that he didn't have to walk by Ruby's house, just on the off chance that she was looking out the window and might see which direction he was going and follow him. It was para-noid, but Harry was feeling paranoid, and so what? He got to Nico's house and rang the bell. No one answered, and he rang again. Five minutes later, he was about to leave, when he finally heard some rus-tling around on the inside. The door slipped open a crack.

'It's fucking early,' Nico said. He had a sheet wrapped around his shoulder like a marathon runner at the finish line.

'Not really,' Harry said. 'It's almost one.' They'd barely met when Harry came over for Nico's party, and he couldn't tell if Nico recog-nized him. Harry got the feeling that Nico would let anyone into his house, though, as long as the person was under thirty and looked like they might buy weed from him someday.

Nico squinted. 'Okay,' he said. 'You coming in?'

'Well, actually, I was just looking for Dust. Do you know where I could find him?' Harry peeked over Nico's shoulder and into the liv-ing room. There were other sheet-covered lumps moving around on the floor.

Nico turned around and pointed to the couch. 'Yup. I'm going back to bed now.' He propped the door open with an elbow and ges-tured for Harry to come in. Harry took a few sideways steps into the foyer, his eyes adjusting to the relative dark of the room.

Dust was prone on the couch, his face turned to the side like a sleeping baby's. He was wearing only a pair of jeans, which looked neither comfortable nor cool – the room was hot, and Dust's cheek was pink. There was a small tattoo just below his shoulder blade, a muddy-looking drawing of a lightning bolt. 'Can I help you, body-guard?'

Harry startled. 'Oh, sorry, I thought you were sleeping.'

Dust rolled over and pushed himself up. There was hair on his chest, not a lot, but more than the four that Harry had. He rubbed his face with his hands. 'Not anymore.' He opened his eyes wide and then felt around on the floor by his feet until he found a T-shirt. 'What can I do for you? You need some tips on how to make Ruby come?' He smirked.

'Actually,' Harry said, trying to maintain his composure, 'I was wondering about how exactly Ruby came to acquire my cat.'

'She told you? Man, I thought she was going to take all that glory for herself for sure. That girl loves to be the center of attention. She ever tell you how we met? She was outside school, and I was on my board, and she lay down on the sidewalk and told me that she'd only go out with me if I could jump over her. So I did.'

'No, I didn't know that,' Harry said, sorry to have learned it. 'But what about the cat? Did you have it?'

'Relax, man, I didn't steal your stupid cat. I found it on the street, I don't know. But I saw the posters. I can read. I was just trying to do the right thing.' Dust patted his jeans until he found his cigarettes. He held out the pack, and Harry shook his head. 'Oh, right,' he said.

'Ruby's with me now, you know,' Harry said. He didn't mean to sound possessive. He knew that Ruby belonged to no one but herself. And he didn't even know for sure if he *was* with her, really, or if he was just in the right place at the right time, filling a bored spell. He hadn't even meant to bring up Ruby. He'd come about Iggy. Truth be told, he hadn't thought any further than knocking on Nico's door, and the rest was a bit of a surprise.

'Is she? I hadn't heard.' Dust took a long drag and blew it out, smiling. 'I'm just fucking with you, man. You gotta relax. Ruby Tuesday needs some head space.'

'Whatever,' Harry said. 'Ruby knows what she needs. And I'd appreciate it if you wouldn't steal any more pets.'

'I'll think about it,' Dust said. 'Now I think I need to go back to sleep. Tell Ruby I say hello. And tell the cat I say meow.'

'His name is Iggy Pop.'

'Who is?'

'The cat.'

'I thought it was a girl.' Dust shrugged. 'I was calling her Whiskers.'

'I thought you didn't have her. Him.'

'Does anyone really have anything?' Dust closed his eyes, his cigarette still in his mouth. 'See you later, bodyguard.' Two of the other lumps on the floor began to stir. One of them grabbed Harry's ankle, and he let out a very small yelp before hustling out the front door.

Fifty-eight

The yoga classes required a certain flexibility that Ruby didn't possess in spades, and so she'd been spending most of her snooping time in the upstairs bedrooms. At first she assumed that the whole thing was just a cover for a whorehouse – a hippie escort-service kind of thing – but by her third visit, she reluctantly admitted that it didn't seem to be the case. Everyone at the house was earnest and open, like they'd had their senses of humor taken out and run through a car wash, which wasn't the least bit sexy. If anything illegal was happening, it certainly wasn't that. It occurred to Ruby that Andrew might just be getting into shape, the way people did when they realized they were going to die someday. It really didn't seem like a major problem. Lena was nice, though, and Ruby found that she actually liked spending time with her. It was the complete opposite of how she spent time with her friends at school, where she was never sure if they were being sarcastic or not. Lena retained eye contact for a scary long time and made Ruby tea with special little sticks and twigs that were supposed to balance her qi.

They were sitting on some pillows in the upstairs lounge, which had formerly been the attic. The ceilings weren't quite tall enough to stand under at full height, but you could sit up comfortably against the wall or just flop over on to the floor. It was kind of like being in the ball pit at a Chuck E. Cheese, only no one wore deodorant. Lena had been living at EVOLVEment for a month. She was from Rhode Island and thinking about doing her reiki training, but she wasn't sure.

'Want to practise on me?' Ruby wasn't sure how it worked, but most of the special treatments at EVOLVEment looked like napping with another person watching, more or less, which didn't seem hard.

'Sure,' Lena said.

Ruby scooted down so that her head was near Lena's lap and crossed her arms over her chest and shut her eyes tight.

'You look like a vampire,' Lena said.

'Maybe I am,' said Ruby. She opened one eye. 'You've been warned.'

'No, seriously,' Lena said. 'Lie down, arms at your sides, and try to relax. I'm just going to concentrate on your energy.'

Ruby closed her eyes again. 'Okay,' she said. 'Are you doing it yet? How do I know when it's working?'

'Be quiet,' Lena said. 'And it'll work.'

Ruby tried to settle down. 'How does this place make money? Is that a rude question?' She opened an eye again. 'I'm sorry.'

'It's okay,' Lena said. She didn't seem annoyed. 'I'll practise my acupressure instead.' She gently placed her thumbs on Ruby's wrists and pressed down. 'Dave is just that kind of guy, you know? Charismatic. People give donations. Some people give their time, like me, and some people give money. It's a really good ecosystem, actually.'

'Like, rent money?' Ruby felt a twinge in her shoulder and jerked involuntarily.

'Ooh, I hit something, let's spend some more time there,' Lena said. She moved both of her hands to Ruby's arms and poked around until she found what she wanted and dug in. 'Some people pay rent, but then there are some big investors. You know, like big money. Like to buy a house.' She moved one finger to the left, and Ruby jerked again.

'I wonder what you have to do to convince people to give you money,' Ruby said. 'I want that skill.'

Lena laughed. 'He used to be an actor. Dave. When he was a kid, like. Or a teenager, I guess. You'd recognize him if you saw him without his beard. He had a stage name – I don't remember what it was. But I think that's why. He just gets right in there with people and knows what they need to hear. It's really an amazing talent. It's like, if you love animals, Dave will tell you about how he wants to organize a retreat to the rain forest to look at frogs or whatever. And then you'll give him the money to do it, and it'll happen. Or it won't, exactly, but maybe he brings some frogs here, you know?'

'Huh,' Ruby said. She jerked again. Whatever Lena was doing was definitely going to leave a bruise. She needed way more practice than Ruby was going to give her. Ruby wondered what kind of training was actually happening at EVOLVEment, if any of them truly knew what they were doing or if they were all taking turns being the emperor with no clothes.

'It's really his most special talent. It's almost like being a therapist, you know? Or like a spiritual guide. He helps people.'

'Like, helps people part with their money.'

'No, it's not like that, it's really different,' Lena said. 'He helps people realize their potential. And if it serves EVOLVEment, even better.'

'I get it,' Ruby said. It was weird to think about other people's parents – about your boyfriend's parents – as dupes. It was like seeing them clip their toenails or have diarrhoea. Some things you just weren't supposed to see. Ruby had always thought of Andrew as the good kind of dad, the kind of dad she would have wanted, if she'd been forced to choose. He was sort of reserved, which Zoe said was because he grew up with too much money. He was masculine without being macho, and he looked good in a T-shirt, which wasn't as easy as it sounded. Andrew wasn't as bad as it came – one of her classmates' fathers had gotten caught texting dick pics to the babysitter – but Ruby felt slightly nauseous thinking about Andrew as an actual human being. A human being who was going to be really embarrassed really soon, probably.

'And you guys all know? I mean, like, who's giving lots of money for Dave's projects?'

'Well, no, not everyone,' Lena said. 'But I'm sleeping with him.'

'I see,' Ruby said.

'He's a very open guy,' Lena said. 'You should meet him.'

'I think I'm okay,' Ruby said. She rolled over to one side, squinting with pain. 'I should probably go.'

Lena held her hands in a prayer position. '*Namaste*. Call me if you change your mind.'

'I will,' Ruby said, and crawled over to the stairs on her hands and knees.

Fifty-nine

Andrew was in the kitchen, and Elizabeth was in the living room. It was the middle of the day, and he was expecting to hear from Dave about some details on the Waves. The architect had sent his drawings to the city, and they were waiting on approval, but in the meantime Andrew was having his lawyers draw up some documents. Dave had been hesitant – he said he was a handshake guy – but Andrew wanted everything to be above board. Dave had said he'd call or text as soon as he heard anything, and Andrew was lolling around in front of the open fridge like a teenager, neither hungry nor thirsty, just looking for something to do.

When the doorbell rang, both he and Elizabeth stayed put and stared at each other. 'You're closer,' Andrew said.

'I have a cat on me,' Elizabeth said back, her face hidden behind a magazine. Iggy was curled up on her stomach. This was their trump card, always, and he respected it.

'Fine,' Andrew said. He wandered over to the door and pulled it open, expecting to see one of the neighbors, maybe, not Zoe or Jane or Ruby, but one of the well-meaning half strangers, the ones who always wanted to tell you which day was alternate-side-of-the-street parking, even though their car was parked in the driveway. It could also be the UPS guy, or FedEx, but it was too early in the day – they were late on the route. There was always an outside chance it would be a fleet of Jehovah's Witnesses, the Mormons of New York City.

Instead of any of these, when Andrew opened the door, he saw Lydia.

It was her face exactly – the face he remembered most precisely. Not the bleached-out punker she became, not the fashion model she tried to be, not the junkie. It was Lydia Greenbaum in all her frizzed-out glory, angry at what she'd been given and hungry for everything else. Andrew's eyelids fluttered, and his knees softened. On the way down, he thought he saw her smile, her teeth as white as a shark's.

When he opened his eyes again, Andrew was on the couch, lying in the spot where Elizabeth and Iggy had been so smugly undisturbable. Elizabeth's face was inches from his own, her mouth hot and open.

'Oh, my God, Andrew, are you okay?' she was whispering, and looking around, as if for ghosts. Andrew wished he could ask which ghosts were present. Had he hallucinated? It hadn't felt like a vision. He should ask Dave what one of those felt like, if it was different from a regular dream.

'Wow,' Andrew said. 'I fainted? I don't know. Um, I'm not really sure what happened.'

Elizabeth smiled. 'I am.' She leaned over and helped him sit up. 'Andrew, this is Darcey. Dead ringer, huh?'

His head was sloshy and heavy, a bucket filled with wet leaves. He blinked a few times before turning in the direction Elizabeth was looking. When he did, he was sorry he had. He should have sewn his eyelids shut and stayed down, like an animal playing dead.

She didn't just resemble Lydia, this girl. Andrew got the whole thing immediately; it wasn't complicated. Someone in Los Angeles had found a girl who looked so much like Lydia that the money just flew into their hands – this was how careers were made, luck and bone structure. But what those people didn't know, what they *couldn't* know, because they hadn't known Lydia, was that this not-Lydia girl possessed the quality that was the closest to Lydia's heart – black, black, black ambition, the darkest little lump of coal right where her actual heart should have been. That was what Andrew saw when he opened the door – Pandora, just before she opened the box. Not-Lydia knew what she was going to do to him, and she was excited about it. Andrew felt sick – the movie was going to give Lydia her due after all.

'Hey,' said not-Lydia. 'Nice to meet you.'

Another woman appeared behind her, holding a glass of water. 'Oh,' she said. 'You're awake. I was going to splash this on your face. I've always wanted to do that, haven't you?'

Andrew looked to Elizabeth.

'That's Naomi, the producer,' she said.

'Well, glad I woke up, then,' Andrew said. 'Should I get my lawyer on the phone?'

Naomi walked around to the couch and sat down next to Andrew. 'I was really hoping that wouldn't be necessary.' She snapped her fingers at not-Lydia, who nodded and reached down into a large bag sitting by her feet.

'There better not be a stack of cash in there,' Andrew said.

'Right, because no one wants that,' Naomi said, rolling her eyes. Not-Lydia passed her a sheaf of papers. Elizabeth leaned forward to try to see what it was, but Andrew took the stack of pages and hunched over, as if he were a tightwad fifth-grader protecting his spelling test.

It was Lydia's handwriting. Pages and pages of it – small and neat and slanted to the right, her blocky letters. Andrew saw his name over and over again. *And when Andrew kissed me, I knew his mind was somewhere else, in the library even, or with stupid, boring*

Elizabeth. . . . Andrew came over again tonight, told me he thought girl drummers were sexy, and I slapped him, and he laughed, and then we fucked on the kitchen floor. . . .

'Who has seen these?' Andrew felt his face turn pink.

'What are they? Let me see!' Elizabeth reached for the pages, and Andrew tucked them under his legs. He looked at Naomi.

'What are you trying to do here, exactly?' he asked.

'Listen, Andrew,' Naomi said, clasping her hands together. 'I know you've been reluctant to get on board, and I just wanted to come down and try to answer some of your questions in person. Can we speak freely?' She pointed to Elizabeth.

'Let's go outside,' Andrew said, standing up slowly.

'Are you kidding me?' Elizabeth said. 'You watched me push a baby out of my vagina, and I can't listen to your conversation with *Naomi*?'

'I wasn't privy to your previous conversations, so this seems fair,' Andrew said. 'Let's go.'

Naomi shrugged. 'Hang tight, Darcey.' Darcey shrugged back – Andrew found looking at her so unnerving that he quickly turned back to Naomi, who mouthed, *Sorry,* to Elizabeth and then flashed a megawatt grin. Andrew opened the door and held it while Naomi walked through, then let it slam behind him.

'Ditmas Park is so cozy,' she said. 'It's like the suburbs, but without leaving behind any of the grime!' She ran a finger along the porch railing and then lifted it in the air. 'So authentic.'

'So, what is this?' Andrew waved the pages by his head. He was trying to breathe deeply, from his belly button, through his scapula, to his third-eye point.

'That is a very small sampling of pages from Lydia's diary.' Naomi opened her eyes wide. 'She was very detailed.'

'Yes, I can see that. My question is what you're doing here, in my house, with these pages.' He clenched his jaw.

'And I'd like to hear your reservations about seeing her story on film. We're not going to make her into Saint Lydia, if that's it. Did you see *Ray*? *Walk the Line*? Those were films about complicated people. That's what we're doing. It's going to be *Ray* meets *Sid and Nancy* minus the Sid, meets *Coal Miner's Daughter*, only the coal miner is an orthopedic surgeon from Scarsdale.'

Andrew chuckled, despite himself.

'Listen, she loved you, and you didn't love her, I get it. And then she becomes this superstar. And then she dies. That's a weird situation. And now someone is going to put it all on-screen, and you feel like an asshole.'

'That's really not the problem.' Andrew crossed his arms. There were too many problems to name just one of them. Visions of Harry watching a movie where his father slept with a dead celebrity danced in his head. Ads for *Mistress of Myself* would be on the radio and the television, with movie posters plastered all over the sides of buses. He didn't want to see Lydia's face, even if it was not-Lydia Lydia. Who would call and ask what he's done in the last twenty years? *Entertainment Tonight*? He didn't want to feel old. He didn't want to feel like a sideman in someone else's life story. He didn't want his wife to hate him. He didn't want his wife to leave him. He didn't want his wife to think that she'd fallen into a marriage by accident, by trickery. He didn't want to feel like a failure. He didn't want to feel like a rich kid who'd never had to work for anything. He didn't want to feel like he was selling out. He didn't want to feel like Elizabeth was selling out on Lydia's behalf. He didn't want to feel like he'd chosen the wrong life, chosen the wrong partner. He didn't want to sit in a dark room and watch himself make mistakes. He didn't want any of it. 'Or maybe it is, I don't know.'

'Andrew, you've got a few choices here. You can dig in your heels, and make us prove that your wife signed your name, and make a lot of things difficult for a lot of people. Or you can just sign the form, and give your consent. I know the term "life rights" sounds like agreeing to euthanasia, and trust me, we have our people working on that, too, the phrasing of it, but let me be clear: You are not giving us your whole life. You are giving permission for there to be a character in a movie who has some things in common with you. That's it. He won't have your face. He might not even have your name.'

Andrew had the brief worry that all his work at EVOLVEment was making his insides visible on the outside of his body, a giant flashing neon sign.

'So those are my options? Fight or roll over?' It was a hot day, and his upper lip was slick with sweat.

'We have very, very good lawyers. I know you have tons of money, and so you probably have a good lawyer, too, but ours are pretty much rock stars.'

Andrew twitched.

'Bad choice of words. They're the best, is what I'm saying. I'm sure that we can all come to an agreement. You just need to accept that it's going to happen. It's a movie. It'll come out, and then it'll go away. That's how it goes.'

'So you came here to tell me that I have no choice.'

Naomi rolled her neck around, producing spectacular cracking noises. 'Well, kind of. I mean, you have choices, but it's sort of like when you go to the dentist. You can choose to bite them, and to grit your teeth, but that's just going to make it take longer. I'm just here to tell you to open up and say ahhhh. You might even enjoy it.'

'The dentist?'

'The movie. In my experience, people often enjoy seeing versions of their lives on-screen. It doesn't happen to everyone, you know.'

All of a sudden, Andrew heard 'Mistress of Myself' begin to play, a tinny, canned version.

'Oh, that's my phone,' Naomi said, and reached into her back pocket.

'You're kidding,' Andrew said.

'Hang on,' Naomi said, answering and then skipping down the porch steps to the sidewalk. In Andrew's head the song kept playing, a shitty karaoke version of his life. He closed his eyes and imagined an ocean wave crashing over him and pulling him out to sea.

Sixty

Darcey was smiling politely, but Elizabeth could tell that she was doing something else – research, maybe. She was wearing a black tank top and cutoff shorts. She was thinner than Lydia had been at Oberlin, but that was the magic of the movies, the removal of cellulite and blemishes. Elizabeth leaned back and looked out the window. She missed actual Lydia's sturdiness, the prickly hair on her legs.

'What was that?' Naomi was facing the street, and Elizabeth couldn't see her face. Andrew looked pissed off, but then he laughed. She wasn't sure.

'Oh,' Darcey said. She reached back into the bag at her feet. 'Copies of this.' She pulled out a marbled notebook and handed it to Elizabeth. 'You should really meet my friend Georgia, the one who plays you. You really look like you could be her mom – it's, like, perfect. She's so uptight, and I'm always the one who's, like, let's go run around naked! It's hilarious.' Darcey wiggled back and forth. 'Hilarious.'

'Thank you,' Elizabeth said. She opened the notebook gently. Lydia's handwriting was distinctive – the product of a carefully crafted personality. That was probably under 'traits of narcissists' in the *DSM*. 'I feel guilty, but I probably shouldn't, right?'

Darcey nodded. 'That's just what Georgia would say. As you, I mean. Classic victim stuff.'

'Excuse me?' Elizabeth said, but then she began to read, and she understood.

She'd never been a jealous girlfriend. That was for other people, insecure people. Elizabeth had always felt as solid as a tree trunk. When she was heavily pregnant with Harry, at her last ob-gyn visit, her doctor had pronounced the baby enormous, but then when Elizabeth had slid ungracefully off the paper-lined table, he had looked at her hips and said, Oh, you'll be fine. She hadn't been wounded. Zoe would have cried. Lydia would have burned the place to the ground. But Elizabeth had thought, *Yes, I will*. She wasn't a saint, of course – Elizabeth had always been jealous of Zoe, and other girls too, high-school friends, or other young mothers she'd had tea dates with when Harry was small. But she'd never been a jealous girl-friend. It was a psychological math problem: twenty years later, was she angry? She thought about the restaurant, about Lydia's snuggling against Andrew's chest, the way Lydia had always looked at her with crocodile eyes. Yes, she was angry.

'Excuse me,' Elizabeth said. She stood up and straightened out her skirt. Darcey pulled out her phone and started texting, probably writing to Georgia to describe whatever she felt had just occurred. Elizabeth herself wasn't sure. She walked slowly to the door and opened it. Andrew was sitting on the porch with his eyes closed. Naomi was halfway down the block, laughing loudly into her cell phone.

'Andrew?' Elizabeth said.

He opened his eyes and looked at the notebook in her hand. 'Fuck,' he said.

'Yes,' Elizabeth said. 'That seems to be the problem.'

'What did you read?' Andrew shoved his fingers into his mouth and began to chew.

'Does it really matter? She's not making it up, right? You were sleeping together?' Elizabeth heard her own voice getting louder at a somewhat alarming rate, like a fire-engine siren. The neighbors would hear. She couldn't help it. In her whole childhood, she had never heard her parents speak loudly to each other, and during Harry's entire childhood, she had only yelled when he was about to jump off something he shouldn't, or lick an electrical outlet. She didn't shout. And yet her voice was getting so loud that her ears began to ring.

'It only happened a few times. Half a dozen, maybe. Lizzy, it was a lifetime ago.' Andrew started to walk toward her, but Elizabeth put her palms up, a traffic light. A few aggressive bees circled Andrew's head, and he swatted them away. Elizabeth wished they would all sting him simultaneously.

'You were never going to tell me, obviously.' Elizabeth kept her hands out.

Andrew shook his head. 'I didn't think it mattered. I mean, at the time. We weren't even married yet. Doesn't that make a difference?'

'Oh, yes, I think it does. I think it does make a difference that I married you without knowing that you'd been cheating on me. Don't you think that might have affected my decision to do so? I'm not saying I expected you to be a virgin, but come on, Andrew.' Elizabeth heard something inside and turned toward the window – Darcey was leaning against the window, her ear to the glass. She waved. 'Jesus!' Elizabeth said. 'She's everywhere!'

'I was going to tell you.' Andrew crossed his arms over his chest.

'You just said that you weren't!' Elizabeth's voice went up several octaves – if she'd known that her voice could do that, Kitty's Mustache would have been a better band. Across the street one of their nosiest neighbors, a tall woman with a German shepherd, turned to look and gave a half wave. *Good luck ever selling* her *house,* Elizabeth thought.

'Back then I wasn't. But with the movie and all this.' He gestured toward Darcey, still a little goblin in the window. 'I was pretty sure I would have to. Can't say I was looking forward to it, but I will say I did not imagine it going quite this badly.'

Elizabeth felt like she had a hair ball stuck in her throat, and hacked up a cough. 'I'm so sorry for your experience.'

'Come on, Lizzy,' Andrew said, but even he didn't sound convinced.

'You know what, honey?' Elizabeth tried to speak in her mother's voice – even and cool – 'Why don't you go on over to your yoga teacher's house tonight? They have beds over there, don't they?' She laughed. 'Of course they do, what am I saying! With girls in them! Go and sleep over there tonight, will you? Because I don't want to look at your face.' The coolness had evaporated quickly, leaving behind red cheeks and eyes filled with tears. She spun around and knocked on the window, startling Darcey. 'And you!' Elizabeth said, through the glass. 'Out!'

Darcey put a demure hand to her chest: *Moi?* Elizabeth yowled, and then Darcey quickly scrambled to the door. 'Can I have the diary back?' she asked on her way out. Elizabeth gave her a look. 'It's really important to my process.'

'Have Naomi come get it later,' Elizabeth said. 'Now, out, all of you.' She swiped some hair off her forehead, where it had begun to stick in stringy bits, and tucked it behind her ear. 'I'm going to take a shower. When I'm done, I want all of you gone.' She could still hear Naomi's throaty laugh echoing down the sidewalk. 'Her, too,' Elizabeth said. She went inside and slammed the door, nearly catching Iggy's tail. She wanted to call someone, but couldn't think of who to call, and so she went straight upstairs and into the bathroom. The bathtub was a mess – it looked as if Harry had used every towel on the rack and then strewn them everywhere, as if he were trying to mop up blood at a crime scene, but Elizabeth didn't care. She climbed over the damp mountain of towels, turned on the cold water, and then got in with her clothes on.

Sixty-one

Having sex again was better than going to Barneys and trying on expensive dresses. It was better than getting a facial by her favorite Eastern European sadist. It was better than fresh ricotta on toast. Zoe felt like she was twenty-five. Maybe thirty-five. Either way, she felt young and flushed with blood. Sweaty Brooklyn August didn't bother her the way it usually did, but on a whim, she booked two nights at an Airbnb in Montauk. She left forty bucks on the kitchen counter for Ruby to order dinner. It was a Wednesday. The restaurant had weeks more work, at least, and she and Jane had been there every day, supervising. A little break sounded good. Zoe tucked a few vibrators in the bottom of her bag, and then they were driving down the LIE, holding hands.

The rental was a shacky little house just off Ditch Plains, where the cute surfers and their admirers hung out. All the kids had bare feet and sandy blond highlights in their hair, and Zoe wanted to swallow them whole. She'd loved growing up near the beach, and always felt sad that even though New York was on the coast, it just wasn't the same. Ruby and her friends never cut school to go surfing or have bonfires on the sand. Zoe held Jane's hand, and they walked up and down the beach, stooping over to pick up pretty little shells, tossing them back into the ocean when they were cracked.

'How's your homework going?' Zoe asked. She hadn't been keeping the diary for Dr Amelia, not on paper. It seemed antithetical to their kind of marriage, which had always been about passion and taste. Zoe had never liked busywork, and that's what this felt like – in reality, all she and Jane had to do was resolve their shit. Yes or no! In or out! How on earth was a shopping list of their problems supposed to help answer that question?

'I kind of like it,' Jane said. Sweet Jane. Before Zoe knew for sure that she was a lesbian, when she was still just a kid fumbling around with other kids' bodies in their teenage bedrooms, several of the boys she'd romanced had looked more or less like Jane – tall, with fair hair and skin tan from the sunshine. Indoors, at night, their sweet little fish bellies would bump together in the dark. It had been such a relief when she slept with her first girl and suddenly all those little bumps were moving in the right direction. It wasn't that way for everyone, of course – Zoe knew lots of women who were truly bi, but she just wasn't. She loved bodies, and beauty, but just because she thought Brad Pitt had a lovely face, that didn't mean she wanted to sit on it.

Zoe's phone began to trill. 'Hang on,' she said, and pulled it out of her pocket. Elizabeth. She pushed IGNORE and put it back in her pocket, but the phone began to ring again immediately. 'She probably hit it again by mistake,' Zoe said, but the phone rang again, and Jane shrugged, so Zoe answered. 'What's up?' she said, plugging her finger in her other ear to block out the sound of the waves. 'Whoa, whoa, whoa, what's going on? Are you okay? Slow down, I can barely hear you.' Jane waved her up the beach, where she could hear better, and then turned and walked down to the edge of the water. She slipped off her shoes and let the tiny waves slosh over her feet.

'Start again, I can hear better,' Zoe said.

On the other end, Elizabeth took a big gulp of air and then launched into Darcey and Naomi and Lydia and Andrew and fake Lydia peeking through the window at her while she yelled at her husband. Elizabeth sobbed through it, taking little breaks to blow her nose. Zoe wanted to say, *I KNEW IT*. Just in general, as a rule, she had known that something was happening between Andrew and Lydia and also that Andrew was kind of an asshole, but that wouldn't have helped. 'Oh, honey,' she said instead. It had been a long time since Elizabeth had called her like this, in a panic that had nothing to do with a weird rash on Harry's butt or how to register for summer camp. Then again, it had been a long time since anything had seemed so urgent at all. Urgency was for younger people, for teenagers and dramatic twenty-somethings, for young hypochondriac parents. When you got older, urgency was for hearing that your parents had fallen ill, and you needed to book a flight as quickly as possible without maxing out your credit card. In between, things were sort of calm, running on autopilot. The kids were in school. The marriage was what it was. Everything was more or less fine.

Jane was facing the water. Her body bowed out slightly over the tops of her pants, as if in a sigh. Exercise was not something Jane had ever been interested in – no running, no team sports, no yoga. It all bored her. She'd probably have a heart attack when she was sixty, but Zoe could imagine even that as something of a joke, the two of them in a hospital room, and Jane telling Zoe all about which nurses were in love with her. They'd hold hands under the starched sheets and the paper gowns and look out the window at the city.

Elizabeth was still talking. Her voice was herky-jerky, and it sounded like she was banging around in her kitchen – there was the noise of doors opening and closing. At one point Zoe heard the toilet flush.

'Are you okay? Where is Andrew now?' Zoe waved to Jane, snapping her fingers to try to get her attention. The wind carried the tiny sound away.

It wasn't clear if Elizabeth was slurring her words, or if it was just all the snot.

'Are you drinking?' It was just past noon. The sobs turned into whimpers, which Zoe took as a yes. It was like trying to have a telephone conversation with a Chihuahua. 'Listen,' she said, 'Jane is probably going to kill me for saying this, but why don't you come out here? Just get on the train, we'll pick you up at the station. You'll be here by dinner. We'll eat mussels and talk about what the fuck we're going to do to your husband, okay? Come out. I'll text you the info, okay? Okay?' Elizabeth agreed quietly, and after she hung up the phone, Zoe looked up to see that Jane had walked several yards farther down the beach. She didn't have her shoes, or a wallet, or keys – everything was in Zoe's purse. Marriage was about trust, and kindness. She and Jane were in a funny spot, or maybe they were just coming out of one, and wounds were still tender, but Elizabeth's voice had made clear that things were worse next door. People didn't take turns having difficult moments; they came all together, like rainstorms and puddles. Zoe could invite Elizabeth – could explain this all to Jane – because she knew that the sky over their heads was clearing up, and the clouds were still heavy and dark over her friend.

Sixty-two

Andrew didn't like being told what to do, but he knew enough to get out of Elizabeth's way when she was breathing fire. In their entire marriage, it had happened only a handful of times: when her younger brother had crashed his car into a tree, stone drunk, and walked away with a scratch; when Andrew had accidentally bought lobster rolls for a friend of Harry's who was allergic to seafood. (The boy was fine. Covered in welts, but fine.) He walked over to EVOLVEment with his shoulders slumped forward, willing everyone in the neighborhood to leave him alone, and they did – the wrinkled old ladies sitting in front of the library, the people walking their dogs – everyone Andrew normally would have greeted with a wave and a smile, they all got nothing.

There was a yoga class in session when he walked into EVOLVEment, and so he entered the house as quietly as possible, slipping his shoes off just inside the front door. Salome winked at him from her spot by the altar and then pointed upstairs. Andrew climbed over people's backs – there were new people all the time, the classes were full – and tiptoed up the stairs.

Dave usually used the bedroom at the far end of the second floor, an almost empty room with a few cinder-block shelves holding up his sacred texts – the *Bhagavad Gita*, some Pema Chödrön, some Sharon Salzberg, *The Artist's Way*, several books about medicinal plants, plus *Meditation for Dummies*, which Andrew thought showed that Dave had a sense of humor, probably rare in a guru. Humble, even. Being in the house made him begin to calm down a little bit, and he thought about how he would describe his fight with Elizabeth to Dave. *You know,* he'd say, *it's kind of a funny story.* And he'd tell him about Lydia and about being young, and Dave would nod along, maybe stroke his beard, understanding everything perfectly. Andrew started to laugh to himself, just thinking about it. It wasn't that big of a deal, what had happened with him and Lydia. The ice block of the secret had already started to melt. Elizabeth would probably get over it soon – it was ancient news that had no bearing on their future. Andrew rolled his shoulders around as he walked down the hall. He cleared his throat and knocked on Dave's bedroom door.

'Just a minute,' Dave said. Andrew drummed his thumbs together. The door opened, and two young women came out, their otherwise naked bodies wrapped in sheets. Through the doorway, Andrew could see Dave's bare butt. He was standing up, facing the window. It overlooked the back of the house, which meant that no one walking by would be able to see him, but there were no curtains, and this was still Brooklyn, so the odds of someone in a neighboring house seeing his junk were extremely high. When Dave turned around to face Andrew, he was still erect, and his penis swung toward Andrew as if it, too, were saying hello.

'Oh, sorry, man,' Andrew said, closing his eyes before turning away. 'I can come back.' Then he felt like he was being too prudish, and swiveled his body back toward Dave.

Dave put his hands on his hips and looked down at himself lovingly. 'No reason to cover up. It's pretty as a picture!' He laughed and bent over to scoop up a pair of shorts off the floor.

Andrew was about to open his mouth and begin his rehearsed tale of marital woe, but Dave started talking before he could get out the first word.

'Listen, man, I'm glad you're here. Got some news this morning. From the city. It's a no go.' Dave stretched his arms overhead and leaned to his left, his thick body a taut rubber band.

'What's a no go?' Andrew crossed his arms.

'The city denied the rezoning. No hotel, at least not there. It's cool – I was starting to get some pretty dark vibes from the neighbors, so I think somebody probably ratted on us, you know? People can be so negative.' Dave stretched the other way.

'Okay, well, that sucks.' Andrew heard his stomach churn and bubble. He put a hand flat against his belly. 'What happens now?'

'We look for a new location. The plans will roll over – we'll have to get new drawings, of course, but the vision remains the same. We just need to find a new slice of property. These things happen.' Dave straightened up and clapped Andrew on the biceps. 'It's all a part of the process. Worst-case scenario, we have to raise a little more money, maybe start looking more on Long Island or up in the Hudson Valley. There's a lot of land out there, you know? Just waiting.'

'But wasn't part of the idea to revitalize the Rockaways? To bring in business? I have the papers from my lawyers, too,' Andrew said, and then he suddenly felt a jab in his lower intestine. 'I'll be right back.' He walked quickly to the bathroom in the hall, where there were two young women dawdling outside, not the ones wrapped in sheets – there was an endless supply of twenty-three-year-olds at EVOLVE-ment, and the fact of their youth shoved Andrew in the gut even harder. 'Excuse me,' he said, and locked the door behind himself, just barely making it to the toilet before his insides commenced their immediate evacuation. He heard the women outside giggle and hurry away, and he let his head fall into his hands.

Andrew's phone buzzed, and he dug it out of his pocket, baggy by his thighs. A text from Elizabeth: GOING TO STAY WITH ZOE AND JANE IN MONTAUK FOR THE NIGHT. YOU MAY GO HOME IF YOU LIKE. FEED HARRY. A bubble appeared with three dots – she was typing more – but then disappeared. He gave it a few more minutes, but clearly she was done. It wasn't like Elizabeth to drop out like that – that had always been his final move, the melodramatic walkout. Andrew flushed twice and washed his hands. He wanted to deserve his wife. He wanted to deserve his beautiful boy. He wanted to trust that their marriage was strong enough to vanquish old dragons. Didn't everyone secretly think that, that their tiny rowboat was somehow sturdy enough to sail the entire ocean?

When he opened the door to the bathroom, one of the sheeted young women who had ducked out of Dave's bed was standing across the hallway, leaning against the wall. She had gotten dressed, barely, and Andrew felt like a lech for even noticing.

'I'm Lena. You're Andrew?' She stuck out her hand, and Andrew offered an awkward fist bump in return.

'My hands are wet,' he said.

'It's okay,' Lena said. She had curly hair and a mole on her cheek. 'You know Ruby, right?'

'Ruby Kahn-Bennett?' Andrew had a brief panic that this Lena girl went to Whitman with Harry.

'I thought so. She's been here some, and she was asking some questions. I think she's worried about you.'

'Worried about me? Ruby?' Andrew ran his hands through his hair. 'That doesn't make any sense.'

Dave appeared in the doorway, still half naked. 'You two met! I love it. Andrew, Lena does the best reiki in the house. You should try her – magic hands, seriously. You want to head downstairs and grab a kombucha and we'll talk?'

Lena looked at Andrew with tight eyes, and he thought he saw her shake her head, just the tiniest fraction of a movement, before turning toward Dave and smiling with all her teeth.

'You know, I was just stopping by to say hi,' Andrew said. 'I'll come back later, cool?'

'Cool, cool,' Dave said. He flashed a peace sign. 'Lena, can you come work on my neck?' He winked at Andrew and went back into his room. Lena followed quickly without another word.

Sixty-three

Harry liked the idea of a grand gesture. It had worked so far. Since the fire, he and Ruby had been together almost every night. All four of their parents were on Mars. Zoe and Jane were locked in their room, or cuddled up on the couch, or laughing in the kitchen, and they didn't seem to notice or mind that Harry darted up the stairs every night. His dad was acting the same way he'd acted the summer that Harry was nine, when he'd gone upstate to 'wander around in the woods,' as his mother put it. He'd come home with a shaved head and a tan and a small tattoo on his calf of the number 8, which he said was for infinity and also because Harry's birthday was on the eighth of October. Elizabeth was the worst of all – it seemed like she'd mostly stopped going to work and also washing her hair. When Harry tried to talk to her about it, she got this look on her face like she was trying to look cheerful when really she just looked like an axe murderer. Harry wanted to help, but he also just wanted to spend as much time as possible with Ruby, Ruby, Ruby.

She was the one who'd mentioned a ring. It wasn't exactly in context – they were watching *The Bachelor*, and the bachelor in question was picking out rings for his two potential brides, a dental hygienist named Kimberly and a medical assistant named Kenderly, and all the rings on display were so gigantic they could be seen from space.

They didn't look like diamonds, they looked like small drinking glasses turned upside down. Ruby had stuck out her tongue and blown a raspberry. 'Barf,' she'd said. 'I want the opposite of that. A black diamond. A tiny black diamond. Like a poppy seed. Something that no one else could see unless I stuck it right in their eyeball. Who is that even for? How do you live your life with something like that on your finger? Do they wash dishes? Do they wake up with weird scratch marks all over their body? It just seems *dangerous*, you know? Not to mention a giant waste of money that young couples have been tricked into spending by the patriarchy of advertising.'

So Harry was looking for a poppy seed. There was one sort of crafty place in Park Slope that sold jewelry. His mother had dragged him there a few times after school, when she needed to buy a present for someone, and that was the only place Harry could think of. It didn't seem exactly like Ruby's taste, but he'd spent a few hours scrolling through rings on Etsy, and that seemed even worse. How could he describe how big he thought her fingers were? He couldn't. So he took the train to the Slope and walked down Fifth Avenue until he found the place. Something buzzed when he walked in the door, which made him immediately start to turn around, but the young woman behind the counter was already smiling and waving, and so he was stuck.

'Can I help you find anything?' The woman had dark hair and heavy bangs and an extra-large stud in her nose.

'I'm looking for a ring. For my friend. She wants something little and black. Do you have anything like that? Her finger is sort of medium-sized, I think. Kind of long and bigger than mine by a little.' He held up his hand. 'But I don't know which finger I'm supposed to be talking about, really, so I guess it depends.'

The woman sucked in her lips and nodded. 'I think I have a few things that you might like. What's your price range?'

Harry hadn't thought about the money. He had his parents' credit card, which is what he planned to use. It wasn't exactly kosher, but both his mother and father had forgotten all about him all summer long, and so he didn't think they'd notice one small charge on their card, especially since it was a place he knew his mother liked. He wasn't at Tiffany's. He wasn't in the city, somewhere fancy. 'A hundred?' Harry said. 'I'm not really sure.'

The woman reached down and slid open a case. She plucked out a few rings and set them on a square velvet pillow on the counter. One had a little green stone, one had a pink stone, and one was dark red, like a tiny drop of blood.

'You don't have anything black?'

'We have one,' the woman said, 'but I think it might be on the expensive side.' She cocked her head to one side and gave him a look. 'Is this for your girlfriend?'

Harry coughed into his hand, trying to hide his proud blush. 'Yeah.'

She held up a finger and walked over to another counter. She came back with the ring slung loosely around her pinkie and held it up in front of Harry's face before she let it slide on to the pillow.

The ring was perfect – a thin gold band that looked like a woodpecker had hammered it, with a million little holes and notches, and a small black pebble on top. It was bigger than a poppy seed but smaller than a watermelon seed, and perfectly flat. 'It's two hundred and ninety-five dollars,' the woman said. 'I guess it depends how serious you are.'

Harry picked up the ring and put it on his middle finger. It slid down to the knuckle. If that was a challenge, she didn't know who she was messing with.

'I'll take it,' he said, and slapped his mother's credit card on the counter.

Sixty-four

It was officially the most horrible time of the summer, when everyone was starting to come back, unpack, do laundry, repack, and go to school, all while noisily updating social media with pictures of everybody hugging each other and their stupid siblings and their stupid dogs. Ruby had been dreading the end of August ever since graduation. When her entire class was off in the Hamptons or the Berkshires, it was gloriously easy to pretend that her life was still perfectly on track, and that nothing had gone disastrously wrong. But soon it would be September, the first September in twelve years (fifteen, counting preschool) that Ruby hadn't gone back to school, and she wasn't exactly feeling great about it.

That morning, she had woken up from a sex dream. In it, she and Harry had been at the beach, their beach, only it was completely abandoned, and it was only after Ruby realized that her body was covered in goose bumps that she noticed it was winter and there were huge mounds of snow all around them. She and Harry were kissing, and then they were doing it, and then he was on top of her, but instead of Harry, it was Dust. Harry/Dust opened his mouth and said, in a perfect Harry/Dust voice, 'It's just you and me next year.' And that was so horrifying that Ruby sat up in bed and was awake for good at seven a.m., which was practically a crime in and of itself on a summer morning.

Her phone had been blowing up all night – she almost didn't want to look at it, but she had to, because she was a glutton for punishment. There were six texts from six different friends, plus group texts – Chloe was inviting her to Bridgehampton for one last slumber party, Anika wanted to go do karaoke in Chinatown, Sully was going vintage shopping on Saturday, and did she want to come? All summer, they'd been off having adventures, and they wanted to squeeze as much of high school as possible into their last five minutes in the city. Ruby didn't want to get squeezed.

A new text came in – Sarah Dinnerstein: MEET ME IN THE PARK? HAVE A JOINT. Ruby imagined the whole scene: she'd meet Sarah, they'd smoke the joint, and then Ruby would punch her in the face. For Hyacinth. For her moms. It sounded like a pretty good way to spend the afternoon. They made plans to meet by the dog beach and then walk together to the hidden spot behind the natural playground, which was always empty except for sometimes when old men with radios would sit and listen to baseball games.

The walk to the park was sticky – Ruby was wearing as little as possible, but by the end of the summer in New York, you could be naked and still feel overdressed. She should have put on sunscreen; she should have worn a hat. By the time Ruby got to the dog beach, Sarah was waiting, in one of her countless hippie-dippie dresses that showed off her boobs, which weren't even that impressive.

'Hey,' Ruby said.

'Hey-o,' Sarah said, opening her arms wide for a hug. Ruby could smell the patchouli before they were even five feet apart.

'You know,' she said, stopping just before Sarah's arms could reach her, 'I'm not sure I'm ready for that.'

'Is this about Dust? I'm so glad we're talking about it. Because he told me that you knew, but then I thought he was bullshitting, and I really didn't want to leave for school with, like, unfinished business between us, you know?' Sarah put on her concerned face, which looked like the love child of a Gremlin and a pug, squashed nostrils pointing in the wrong direction.

'Fine, whatever, let's walk,' Ruby said, turning on her heel and walking down the hill into the woods. *If* she were going to college, *if* she were leaving New York, Prospect Park would be the thing she'd miss the most. Unlike Central Park, where you could always see identifiable buildings and therefore know exactly where you were in space, Prospect Park felt like the wilderness, filled with dark paths and secret corners. Whenever she came to the park with her moms when she was little, Ruby loved to scare them by running away and hiding behind trees, just off the path but tucked out of sight. Bingo would always find her first, but for a few minutes Ruby could pretend that she lived in a magical forest and that her mothers were witches or fairies and that she alone could save the world.

'I never come here,' Sarah said. 'There are too many crackheads. And yuppies. Both.' Ruby didn't even respond. Sarah lit the joint, and they walked a little bit more slowly, curving by a small waterfall and then turning deeper into the wilderness. 'I heard that there's a really big cruising spot right here. For gay sex.' Ruby raised an eyebrow. 'Not that there's anything wrong with that, obviously, I'm just saying, that's what I heard.'

'I'm not the gay police,' Ruby said, taking the joint out of Sarah's hand. ·

They got to the main road, and Ruby tucked the joint into her hand. The coast was clear, and they walked through the playground, which was empty. The hidden spot was empty, too, except for an old guy in a tank top doing half push-ups on a bench, but he wouldn't bother them. That was another thing Ruby would miss about New York, if she were leaving: she'd miss how much space people gave you.

You could have a fucking sobbing fit on the subway and no one would mess with you. You could barf in a garbage can on the street corner and no one would mess with you. If you were giving off invisible vibes, people respected that. People thought New Yorkers were rude, but really they were just leaving you to your own stuff. It was respectful! In a city with so many people, a New Yorker would always pretend not to see you when you didn't want to be seen.

'So, he told you?' Sarah said, once they were sitting on a bench in the shade.

'He didn't have to tell me. It's pretty obvious that you guys are together.' Ruby passed the roach back to Sarah and pulled a cigarette out of her bag.

'Oh,' Sarah said. 'No, I mean, we are, but I meant about your parents' place.' She clipped the roach and held it still until it had cooled down, and then tucked it into her little crocheted weed necklace. 'About the fire.'

'He told me that you did it by accident, basically on purpose. That's what he told me.' Ruby stared at Sarah, whose eyes were streaked with red, like little peppermints.

Sarah giggled. 'Are you serious? Then why would you come and meet me? Jeez, Ruby! Are you going to kick my ass?'

'I was thinking about it,' Ruby said. She crossed her arms, but then she couldn't smoke, so she uncrossed them again and just cracked her knuckles instead.

'Oh, my God, Ruby, no!' Sarah waved her hands like they were stuck on a deserted island and she was trying to signal a passing airplane. 'It was Dust! That's what I was trying to talk to you about! Dust totally set the fire! I was right there. We were in the little alley, you know, behind Nico's house, and behind Hyacinth, and Dust was all, "Let's go down here and see if we can get into the kitchen, I want some of that cheese" – what's that cheese you guys have?'

'Mozzarella?'

'No, the fancy kind, on the sandwich with the eggs and the cucumbers? It's like cream cheese, only sort of sour? Anyway, he was like, "Let's see if we can sneak in there after Ruby closes," which, I grant you, would have been a fucked-up thing to do anyway, but it probably wouldn't even have happened. Anyway, so we get to the fence, and we could see the people leaving, and you and the other guys cleaning up, and then I look at Dust, and he's got this little wad of newspaper and his lighter, and he's trying to light the fence. I was like, "What the fuck?" and he was like, "Sarah, this doesn't concern you," and I was like, "Hell yes it does, if you go to jail for setting something on fire, because obviously I'm the one who's going to have to hire a lawyer, you know?" And so I went back into Nico's house, and then a little while later Dust came back in, and then we all heard the sirens, and I was like, "Shit."'

'He told me that you set it by accident, with some candles.' Ruby couldn't tell if the fogginess in her head was the weed or what Sarah was telling her. 'But you're saying that Dust did it? Actually on purpose?'

Sarah giggled again. 'I know it's not funny, but seriously, Ruby, you are way, way weirder than I thought. How many times do I need to say it? Dust set the fire. On purpose.'

'And he's your boyfriend.' Ruby knew she sounded like a moron, but her brain wouldn't make better sentences. She felt like she was trying to talk with her mouth full of cotton candy.

'It's pretty serious,' Sarah said, happy to switch topics of conversation. 'We've been talking about moving in together, up at school. He could get a job, maybe audit some classes. Dust wants to be an architect, did you know that? He's got all these models at his house, little things he's built. He's really good.'

'You've been to his house?' This was the twilight zone. It must be the weed. Sarah was probably saying something completely different. Maybe Ruby was still asleep! That must be it.

Sarah looked offended. 'Of course I've been to his house. I'm his *girlfriend*.' She narrowed her already beady eyes at Ruby. 'You never went to his house?'

'What makes you think that I'm not going to call the police?' Ruby was flushed, and sweating. She piled her hair up on top of her head and stuck it there with a big plastic clip. The old guy was peeling off his tank top and laying it over the back of the bench. He dropped to his knees and started doing crunches, squeezing his wrinkled brown belly together over and over again.

'I would, if I were you.' Sarah shrugged. 'I mean, obviously, I don't think you should, because I don't want him to get into trouble, but I think that if I were you, I totally would. It's up to you. We'll be gone soon, you know? Like, who would it help? He's not going to set your house on fire. He's not even going to be here.'

'Even Dust isn't going to be here,' Ruby said, more to herself than to Sarah. She took a long drag of her cigarette and then let it drop to the ground. 'Fuck it,' she said. 'Fuck it all.' Ruby stood up and walked away without saying good-bye. Behind her, she heard Sarah start to sing some Bob Marley, and so Ruby jogged until she was out of earshot and out of breath.

Sixty-five

Elizabeth arrived at the Montauk station with nothing but a prickly straw hat, a bottle of wine she'd plucked out of the fridge, a toothbrush, a bathing suit, and a clean pair of underwear, all of which were jammed into a tote bag on her shoulder. The hat had been scratching her arm since the Atlantic Terminal station, but the train was crowded, and there was nothing to be done. Add one more wound to the pile. The train car was full of frat boys and other summertime revelers at full tilt, and so Elizabeth decided to stay seated until they'd all stumbled off. She wasn't in a rush. The invitation had barely been real – she knew that. But she also knew that she needed to get out of the city, and that Zoe was her friend, and if Jane didn't like it, well, tough. She'd had two glasses of wine at home and another two on the train, which was way more than she ever drank, especially during the day. Even though the train had stopped moving, it still seemed to be swaying slightly, and when the rest of the car was empty, Elizabeth clutched the back of her seat and stood up, knocking her forehead on the baggage rack overhead.

The Kahn-Bennett Subaru was waiting, just as Zoe had promised. Elizabeth waved and squinted, trying to make out who was inside, and hurried as quickly as she could, though her flip-flops kept sliding off, and then she'd have to chase them a bit. When she finally made it to the car, it was only Zoe.

'You okay?' Zoe asked. She looked great – summer was her season. Her skin was clear and glowing like bronze, and her hair was pushed off her face with a colorful scarf. Bingo poked his head out of the backseat, and Elizabeth leaned over and let him lick her on the nose.

'I'm pretty much not great,' Elizabeth said. She pulled the bottle of wine out of her bag and handed it to Zoe.

'Let's go back to the house before we open this, okay? I don't think a DUI is going to help any of us.'

Elizabeth puffed out her lower lip and turned toward the window. 'It's just been a weird summer. And there was no toilet paper on the train.'

Zoe murmured her disappointment with LIRR and then didn't say anything for the rest of the ride, but held out her hand for Elizabeth to hold in the center well, above the cup holders.

The rental house was small but cute. An easy sell. It had one bedroom and a pullout sofa, which either Zoe or Jane had already pulled out, and a small kitchen/dining room. It smelled like salt, and there was sand underfoot. Jane was grilling something outside on the deck when they walked in, and Zoe slipped the tote bag off Elizabeth's shoulder and set it down on the floor.

'We're back!' Zoe called, even though the sliding door to the deck was open and there was no way that Jane could have missed their entrance. 'She'll be fine,' Zoe said, and patted Elizabeth on the arm.

'Is something wrong?' Elizabeth asked, steadying herself on the kitchen counter. The wine sloshed in her stomach. She should have eaten lunch. She shouldn't have had so much to drink. She should have stayed home.

It was so pretty out at the very end of the island – Elizabeth always forgot that. It was an occupational hazard, sizing up real estate. Montauk was a decade behind the Hamptons, but ahead of the North Fork. The houses were small, and most of them were a short drive away from the main street, which, after all, didn't have that much. But who was Elizabeth kidding? She didn't care about selling beach houses to the party animals she'd been on the train with, or to their calmer older brothers with wives and toddlers. Brooklyn was bad enough. She didn't need to deal with people who had so much disposable income that they were buying a second house.

'I think I need to sit down,' she said, and then collapsed on to the pullout sofa, leaning against the foam backrest with her legs extended in front of her.

'Me too,' Zoe said. 'But hang on.' She walked around the sofa bed and out on to the deck. Elizabeth watched as Zoe put her arm on Jane's back and then rested her head on Jane's shoulder. They were facing away, pointed toward the wild grass and, somewhere in the distance, the ocean. It was impossible to tell if they were talking, but they didn't move for a few minutes, except when Jane picked up her tongs and flipped something over on the grill.

It was a pretty night – there was a steady breeze, and the sky was washed with pink. Elizabeth wished that she and Andrew had a place like this, a modest hut somewhere in the country – why hadn't they ever done that? All their vacation time had always seemed so precious, especially after Harry was born – his day camps and art classes, his creative-movement classes in Prospect Park, where the children just rolled around in the grass at a coordinated time every week for two hundred dollars. In theory they were free to go wherever they liked, and they had traveled some – a trip to Mexico when Harry was eight that horrified Andrew's parents, a drive up the California coast wherein they learned that Harry got carsick when there were lots of turns, and so they drove on the highway instead, getting to San Francisco four days earlier than planned. One trip to Italy. It was scatter-shot, random. Elizabeth had gone to the same girls' summer camp every summer of her life, then Cape Cod for August, and she'd wanted to give Harry more adventures. But instead they'd just stayed home, with views of Argyle Road and the Q train rumbling in the distance.

Zoe kissed Jane on the cheek, and then Jane turned around to wave at Elizabeth. It was all going to be fine. Elizabeth raised an invisible glass their direction. 'Clink,' she said.

They ate at a small round table outside. There were ants, but nobody cared. Jane opened the wine that Elizabeth brought, and they drank it all, though Elizabeth had to squint a bit to make sure she had one glass and not two. Grilled fish, an avocado salad, little mussels that popped open over the flames. A peach tart made upside down, so the little peaches looked like they were mooning you. Fresh whipped cream. Elizabeth wouldn't divorce Jane either.

'So, what's this place he's been going to, Lizzy?' Jane asked, forking a flaky piece of fish into her mouth. 'It's Buddhist? Or something?'

'Or something,' Elizabeth said. 'I don't really know. I think they do yoga, and maybe have orgies. They sell juice. Kombucha? Is that different from juice? It seems like a nightmare, but what do I know? I'm a square.' She poked the bowl of whipped cream with a finger and then licked it off. She was truly drunk now, and feeling loose.

'You're not a square,' Zoe said.

'You're a little bit of a square,' Jane said, and Zoe pinched her on the arm. 'What? There are worse things to be. Also, kombucha is totally different than juice. It's fermented. Like beer. Do they make it themselves? That seems a little bit dodgy. And they sell it? Are they licensed to do that? I would look into that, if I were you. Or if I were trying to get them in trouble.'

Elizabeth lowered her head to the table and then bolted back up.

The room spun. 'You know, I've been thinking a lot about trouble lately. Did Zoe tell you what Andrew did? Before the yoga, I mean?' In her head everything was a straight line, and it was all pointing backward. 'He slept with Lydia. When we were kids. Not just once. If it was just once, eh.' She waved her hand in the air like she was signaling a waiter for the bill. 'If it was just once, that would be one thing. But this was over and over and over again, when we were together. And so when I signed his name on the form, he's just picturing his bare ass, you know? And I'm thinking it's about him being a snobby cinephile or something. Ha!' Zoe and Jane both looked confused, but Elizabeth forged ahead. 'I mean, I wouldn't want my naked butt in a movie either, even if it is some eighteen-year-old's adorable butt. It's still my butt, you know? So that's why I'm mad. Because it's not like I never thought about it. I'm not a saint! But if I had, I would have told him before we got married, or at some point in the last seven hundred years.' Elizabeth swiveled her head toward Jane, pointing a finger. 'Speaking of, did Zo ever tell you about the night we *al*most got together?'

'No,' Jane said, amused now. 'She didn't. Do go on.'

Elizabeth put her hands up next to her face, forming a little wall blocking Zoe from view. 'This is totally different, of course, because nothing happened. But at Oberlin, we were at her apartment one night, watching *Bonnie and Clyde*, and she put the moves on me.'

'I don't think I've ever seen *Bonnie and Clyde*,' Zoe said. 'Who's in it, again?'

'That's your response?' Jane looked tickled, and leaned forward. 'Tell me more, Lizzy.'

'Nothing happened,' Elizabeth said, waving her hands in front of her face and accidentally flinging a fork into the bushes. 'But it could have.'

'Wait, are you being serious?' Zoe put her hand on Elizabeth's arm to steady it in the air, narrowly avoiding being clonked on the head.

Elizabeth dissolved into giggles. 'Is this for her benefit?' she said, talking as low as she could. She looked at Zoe, beautiful Zoe. She was wearing a loose white button-down shirt, and it looked like something in a store window, with a breeze from an unseen fan blowing the hem just so. Sometimes Elizabeth thought that if she'd met Zoe a little bit earlier, or a little bit later, her whole life could have been different. Not that she and Zoe would have ended up together, but that every domino started a new chain. Maybe it wouldn't have been Andrew – maybe it would have been the redheaded boy in her English class or the spazzy drummer they got to replace Lydia, who she'd once seen getting out of the shower and thought, *Oh*.

Timing was everything – that was more and more obvious the older you got, when you finally understood that the universe wasn't held together in any way that made sense. There was no order, there was no plan. It was all about what you'd had for breakfast, and what kind of mood you were in when you walked down a certain hallway, and whether the person who tried to kiss you had good breath or bad. There was no fate. Life was just happenstance and luck, bound together by the desire for order. Elizabeth understood why so many people believed in God – it was for precisely this reason, so they'd never have to close their eyes and think, *What the fuck did I do to my life?* She had a storm-cloud headache brewing, the kind you could see coming six miles away. Cumulous clumps of regret were already low on the horizon line, but she couldn't stop herself. It wasn't funny; none of this was funny. 'I don't think she'll be jealous, Zo.' Elizabeth tried her best to smile, and then she tried her best to keep her eyes open. It had been such a long day. Sleep sounded good, especially since she was half sure that she was already dreaming. She gripped the lip of the table with both hands and set her forehead down between them.

A glass of water appeared in front of her, and Elizabeth drank it. Both Jane and Zoe were helping her up, and then pulling down the sheets on the fold-out sofa. She rolled over and said good night, but the words didn't come out.

The sun was bright, and it took Elizabeth several minutes to remember where she was. The windows were in the wrong place; so was the door. Slowly, the previous evening came back to her.

'Oh, God,' she said, and yanked the sheet up to her chin.

'Hi.' Zoe was sitting at the table outside with a cup of coffee and her laptop. 'Jane's a late sleeper.'

'Good morning,' Elizabeth said, scooting up so that her back was against the cheap foam back of the couch. She rubbed her eyes. Her mouth felt like sandpaper. 'I don't usually drink that much.'

'I know,' Zoe said. 'Come out here.'

Elizabeth rolled off the sofa bed. The floor was cool. She grabbed the knit blanket that she'd kicked to the floor at some point during the night and wrapped it around her shoulders. It was early – before seven, probably, and the only sounds they could hear were seagulls and waves. Elizabeth settled into the chair next to Zoe. 'That hurt,' she said. 'My whole body hurts. I'm too old for this.'

'Tell me again what you were saying last night,' Zoe said.

Elizabeth hid her face. 'Oh, come on,' she said. 'I was drunk.'

'Yes, you were. But I want to know what you were talking about.' Zoe leaned forward, her face serious but soft. 'Tell me. Not the part about Andrew. The part about us.'

Elizabeth wasn't sure what was more embarrassing – the fact that she'd kept the secret for so many years, or the fact that she remembered it at all. There were layers of shame, ending with the moment that she was sitting in, with the salt air and the smell of Zoe's coffee, which smelled both completely delicious and like it might make her throw up. 'Okay,' Elizabeth said, and she started at the beginning. When she was done – TJ, the hallway, the two of them on the stairs – Zoe was smiling.

'I do remember that,' she said. 'I definitely was hitting on you. Pretty hard, too. If someone did that to Ruby, I would call it sexual assault. It's appalling! You should have called campus security and gotten a ride home.'

'But you don't remember *Bonnie and Clyde*?'

'Not a second of it. That's how beautiful you were, Lizzy.' Zoe reached over and squeezed Elizabeth's cheek. 'So, were you interested?'

'I was interested. I mean, I loved you! I love you! You were like a goddess to me! But I didn't know about, you know, all that. I was too scared. And plus, there was Andrew.'

'Who was having sex with Lydia.'

'Who was having sex with Lydia! God!' Elizabeth let out a huge gulping laugh. 'The irony.'

Zoe took a slurp of her coffee. 'Isn't it so funny, to think about whatever we were doing a hundred years ago, as if it actually mattered? I had so many girlfriends who I thought I was going to be with forever, you know, go on old-lady bird-watching cruises with when we were eighty, or whatever, and then we'd break up in six months. I can't even picture their faces. And when I met Jane, I thought we'd be together for six months! And here we are. So. I don't know.'

'I guess that's the question,' Elizabeth said. 'Does it matter at all, what happened a million years ago? Is it relevant? In some ways, I think of course not, it's all ancient history, but then again, I don't know. It matters to me that Andrew slept with Lydia, but mostly because of the way he's acting now. And that night with you on the couch, it does mean something to me – otherwise I would have mentioned it a hundred times, whenever I wanted to tease you, you know? It's hard to explain.' Elizabeth reached one hand out of her blanket and pinched the air, reaching for Zoe's coffee cup. 'You actually wanted to kiss me?'

'I sure did, babe,' Zoe said, and handed her the cup. She picked up her chair and scooted it closer to Elizabeth's. She leaned over, giving Elizabeth a sweet, small kiss on the mouth. It wasn't romance; it wasn't sex. Elizabeth had given Harry the same kiss a thousand times, and her own mother, and Andrew, even stupid Andrew. It was just love.

'You're my best friend,' Elizabeth said.

'Ditto,' Zoe said, and leaned back in her chair, smiling at the sun.

Sixty-six

No one was anywhere. Ruby called her mom's cell, her mum's, the restaurant. They were still in Montauk, she assumed, but usually they checked in to make sure she hadn't had a party or set anything on fire. They'd already had the fire, maybe, so why worry? In two weeks, Harry had to show up for senior orientation at Whitman, which was when the college counsellors split everyone into groups and talked about the process – where eventually, as Ruby had discovered last year, you found yourself sitting in a semicircle with your friends, talking about the three schools you already knew you wanted to apply to. Harry would be fine – he'd be with the dorks, talking about how Providence really was a cool town, they'd all heard. He'd apply early. He'd get in. Ruby could already see the text message popping up on her phone, maybe a sheepish emoji face. He'd be happy.

But for now Harry was still asleep in her bed.

His hair had gotten longer in the last few months, which was starting to pull the curls down. There was a little spot of saliva on the pillow just below his lips, which Ruby thought was cute. Being with Harry was kind of like doing Teach for America or being a Big Sister or something – really making a difference in someone's life by giving him or her some attention they might not get otherwise. A sex mentoring program. Not that she didn't like Harry – she did, a lot. But

Ruby was sanguine about the affair. It was a practice run. Everyone did it, whether anybody admitted it or not – almost all teenage love was a performance, with real emotions and real heartbreak. But it was a performance just the same. How else would you ever tell someone that you loved them and mean it, if you'd never said it before? When Ruby thought about Harry, she liked that they'd know each other forever. He wasn't going to vanish like Dust, or any of her friends from Whitman, people who could just choose to go to college and completely change their personality overnight. Harry was always going to be Harry, and his parents were always going to live up the block, and they would always be in each other's lives, and some year, twenty years or more in the future, they would all be together for Thanksgiving, and Harry would be married with kids who looked just like him, and she'd be really fucking glamorous and exciting, and they'd kiss each other on the cheek and think about this summer, and they'd go to bed with tummies full of turkey and memories of each other's bodies.

Lena had texted her about seeing Andrew at EVOLVEment. Elizabeth was right – the whole thing seemed super shady, not to mention sad. Lena said that she'd seen Andrew and Dave talking, and Andrew seemed kind of weird. OH, she said, I REMEMBERED HIS ACTOR NAME – DAVE WOLFE. LOOK HIM UP – YOU'LL TOTALLY RECOGNIZE HIM. Ruby opened her laptop and typed the name into IMDb.

The photo in the corner looked like an ad for body spray – Dave was shirtless, with a chunky beaded necklace at his clavicle. Instead of showing off his full, dark beard, his cheeks were freshly shaved, leaving only a small triangle of hair beneath his lower lip. 'Not a *soul* patch,' Ruby said, groaning. 'That is the worst.'

'What's going on?' Harry said. He rolled and stretched and reached for her. Ruby picked up her laptop and climbed back into bed.

'This is your dad's yoga guy,' Ruby said.

'Oh, God,' Harry said. 'Really?'

'Really.'

'Wait a minute – isn't he from that movie, you know, the one where the juvenile delinquents get sent to prison? From the eighties? And they lead a revolt?' Harry rubbed his eyes. 'I swear that's him.'

Ruby clicked on his filmography. '*Bunk 6*? That was him all right.'

'And he teaches yoga?'

'And makes juice?' Ruby chewed on a fingernail.

'Huh,' Harry said.

'Do I have something in my teeth?' Ruby said. She leaned over him, her hair falling in his face. Harry pushed it aside and looked.

'No,' he said. 'But that reminds me. I got you something.'

'Is it a bacon, egg and cheese? I really hope so.' Ruby flopped over on to her back. 'What do you want to eat? There's a shitload of pesto in the fridge, I think Jane is preparing for the apocalypse. Want some pasta? It's sort of lunchtime.'

Harry was digging around in his pants pocket, his body half on and half off the bed. 'Here,' he said, wiggling backward until he was sitting cross-legged in front of her.

All jewelry boxes looked scary. This one was a small, white rectangle, which was better than a black velvet square, but still, Ruby recoiled.

'What is that?' She pointed at it.

'It's just a present, Ruby.' Harry lifted the lid of the box with his other hand.

Sitting inside, on a bed of cotton fluff, was a tiny, perfect ring. No one except her mum and grandma, maybe Chloe or Paloma, had ever given Ruby jewelry before, and those were usually made out of string or little vintage things her mum found at a flea market. Nothing from a boy. Nothing from a boyfriend.

'What is it?' she asked.

'It's a ring.' Harry's cheeks were pink, but he was smiling. It wasn't nerves; it was excitement. 'Go on, look at it. It's like a poppy seed, like you said.'

Ruby reached in with her thumb and pointer finger and plucked it out. A thread of cotton stuck to it, and Harry pulled it off. It did look like a poppy seed, sort of. Had she said that out loud?

'I think he's a total fraud, and that he's trying to steal your dad's money,' Ruby said, holding the ring in front of her face. She slipped it on her middle finger, where it slid easily down to the knuckle and then, with a little nudge, down the rest of the way.

'Why do you think that? Also, I was thinking maybe about that finger,' Harry said. He touched her ring finger.

'What are you talking about?' Ruby scrunched up her forehead.

'Marry me?' Harry was kneeling now, on the bed, his bare legs sinking into her comforter. Harry, who had never had a job. Harry, whom she'd bathed with as a child. Ruby imagined Thanksgiving again, this time with herself as Harry's wife, wearing pearls and a twinset and a puffy headband. It was like the last scene of *The Wizard of Oz*, where Dorothy looks around and realizes that her friends are still her friends, no matter if they're people or lions or made out of tin. It was supposed to be comforting, like, oh, yes, they've been there all along, but Ruby thought it made the whole world look tiny and claustrophobic, like you could go to a whole other dimension and just see the same people you've seen your whole life, and she wanted more faces than that.

'I'm going to sail a boat to Mexico,' Ruby said, and just like that, she was.

Sixty-seven

It was almost noon, and Elizabeth still wasn't back. Andrew wasn't sure what to do with himself. He'd cleaned the entire house, and cooked a lasagna, even though it was too hot to eat it. It was something to have in the fridge, a bona fide meal that Harry could pick at whenever he wanted. There was a yoga class at EVOLVEment, but Andrew felt weird about going back. He sat on the couch for a few minutes, bouncing on his heels, and finally decided to just go. The lawyer was expecting him to return the signed contracts, the pieces of paper that said how much money Andrew had given Dave, and why, and for now Andrew had no idea if any of his money would ever reappear again. But he wasn't sure what else to do, and so he walked the three blocks and unrolled his yoga mat in the only available spot, right next to the door, so that anyone else who came in would have to climb over him.

Dave was teaching. It was Thursday, which meant that the class was a mix of dharma talk and asana, with a focus on maintaining energy. Other studios focused on different things – Bikram was all about sweat, and Iyengar was all about precision, or that's what Dave said – but Dave was all about energy. He was shirtless, as usual, and bowed to Andrew when they finally made eye contact. The class was full of people Andrew had never seen before – young, flexible bodies.

Andrew was doing better than he had been at the beginning of the summer, though, and he could keep up. Every now and then, he felt someone looking at him, and he'd swivel around just in time to see one of Dave's minions turning away.

'Draw your breath in through your rib cage,' Dave said, 'and then exhale through your toes.'

All around him people were doing what Dave said. Andrew was trying, but every time he tried to breathe through his ribs, he felt like something was in the way – his liver? his heart? You couldn't breathe through your ribs, you just couldn't. And you definitely couldn't breathe through your toes. Andrew opened his eyes.

From his spot by the door, Andrew could see through the foyer and on to the porch, where there were two uniformed policemen peering through the glass. They knocked, but Dave never answered the door during class. Andrew stood up and walked to the door.

'May I help you?' he asked.

'Yes, sir, we've had some reports that we'd like to follow up on, some illegal activity. Is this your place of business? Do you live here?' Andrew recognized one of the policemen from when he and Elizabeth had gone to fetch their delinquent son.

'Well, yes and no,' Andrew said. 'I don't live here.'

'May we come in?' A walkie-talkie on the cop's hip blared out something indecipherable.

Andrew turned back to face the room. In the hall leading to the kitchen, several of the EVOLVErs were scurrying around, several holding large buckets.

'Um,' Andrew said, and the cops pushed past him into the house.

Everyone was in downward dog, their bottoms poking into the air. Most people were peeking through their legs, watching the action unfold upside down, but some had decided it was going to be worth seeing right side up and had come out of the pose to sit and watch. The two policemen stood on the side of the room, as if they were about to play a game of Frogger and hop across the yogis to the other side but didn't know how to start.

'May I help you, Officers? We're in the middle of a class.' Dave was as cool as a lake in Maine, with nary a ripple of anxiety.

'Are you in charge here? We've had reports of some illegal activity. Some illicit substance being sold without the proper licenses. We're here to seize' – here the officer paused to look at a note on his sheet of paper – 'some kambacha. Some illegal kambacha. May we see your kitchen, please?'

Dave rose slowly, his bare feet sticking to the wood floor with a little *thuck-thuck* sound. 'Everyone, please continue your own practice as needed. Salome?' She was lurking in the hall, and shook her head vigorously. 'Annaliese?' A girl Andrew hadn't seen before quickly popped up from a mat in the third row and made her way to Dave's mat, where she began to move through some sun salutations. Several people rolled up their mats and hung around for a few minutes before leaving, but other, more dedicated yogis stayed and moved from upward-facing dog to plank and back again.

Andrew watched Dave lead the officers into the kitchen, and then up and down the stairs, on a full tour of the house. There was weed everywhere – Andrew had never noticed it before, not really, but now the house stank of it, and of the vats of kombucha in the basement, and the unpasteurized juices, and the herbal supplements that Salome put together herself for teas. Of course there were no licenses. Where were all the signs like they had at Hyacinth, EMPLOYEES MUST WASH HANDS, or the one with the cartoonish description of the Heimlich maneuver? EVOLVEment had no signs. He'd been so eager to find something to devote himself to that he hadn't noticed he was spending all of his time in a glorified flophouse.

Several of the bearded young EVOLVErs were pacing the front

room or talking in small, hushed huddles. Andrew tried to listen in, but they'd just shuffle a little farther away, until they were standing in the far corner of the room, leaving Andrew alone at the center.

After about ten minutes, the cops came back through. One of them, the young man that Andrew recognized, was gripping Dave tightly on his elbow.

'Wait a minute,' Andrew said. 'This is my partner – where are you taking him? What is going on?'

The officer stopped. Dave exhaled loudly, emitting a low om. 'Will you stop doing that?' the cop said. 'It's freaking me out. What do you mean, "partner"? Do you know this guy?' the cop asked Dave, who was staring straight ahead, at some unseen drishti.

Dave's eyelids fluttered. He stared at Andrew, and then slowly shook his head. 'This man is one of our yoga students, but I've never spoken to him before. Peace for your good thoughts, friend.'

The officer shrugged. 'Whatever, man. Excuse us,' he said to Andrew, and led Dave by the elbow out to their waiting squad car. Trailing behind, the other cop carried two barrels full of liquid that smelled like beer, one under each arm.

'I see,' Andrew said to no one. 'I see.' He walked outside the house and watched the cops maneuver Dave into the back of the police car. Dave stared straight ahead. A woman walking her fluffy white dog down the street stopped in the middle of the sidewalk, waited for the cop car to drive off, and then shook her head.

'It's always the good-looking ones,' she said. 'Criminals.'

If it hadn't been for the money, Andrew would have taken this as a sign: he was free. The correct choice had been butchery, or maybe rooftop beekeeping. He hadn't built anything in two months. He wasn't becoming a hotelier, at least not with Dave. He was just a patsy standing in front of a yoga studio. In his pocket, his phone started to ring. When he slid it out, Elizabeth's face filled up the whole screen, and he was so happy to see her that he nearly burst into tears.

'Honey,' he said, talking before she had the chance. 'I am so, so sorry.'

Sixty-eight

And on the other end, on the train platform in Montauk, Elizabeth pulled her straw hat over her face and listened to her husband talk. In some ways, it was both better and worse than she imagined. Andrew hadn't slept with any of the mostly nude young women at the juice emporium. He hadn't slept with the guy with the beard, which had crossed her mind briefly, and which had bothered her somewhat less, as an idea, than the nude young women. Andrew told her about the money, which stung, though she certainly didn't think of it as *her* money, or even *their* money, and so she was willing to chalk even that up to Andrew's stupidity and/or open-mindedness, one of which she felt pretty good about, in general.

In a funny way, everything that Andrew was saying made Elizabeth think that a long marriage truly was possible, in part because it only ever *seemed* like they'd told you all their secrets. There were always more.

'Who did I marry?' Elizabeth asked, out loud, amazed. The train was scheduled to arrive in five minutes. Zoe and Jane had dropped her off at the station together. They'd gone swimming that morning, and the tips of Elizabeth's hair were still damp on her shoulders, slightly crunchy with salt and sand. Her headache hadn't gone away, but it was getting better. They were all getting better, at least some of the time.

'Listen,' Elizabeth said. 'The train is about to come. I'll be home in a few hours. Be there, okay? I want to really talk to you.'

'Of course,' Andrew said.

'When we were kids, I almost kissed Zoe once. And we just talked about it for the first time.' She wanted him to know that he wasn't the only one who hadn't opened all his doors.

'When?' Andrew asked.

'At school. When we were young. When we were children. Just like you. I mean, almost. I didn't actually do anything. But I know, Andrew, I know that we were children then. We were Harry's age, more or less. Can you imagine?' What Elizabeth couldn't imagine, not really, was that all the years in between had actually happened to her, and to Andrew, and to all their friends. That they had passed through those years unscathed, escaping with their lives and one another. It seemed mathematically unreasonable, to think that they were all still standing. Except for Lydia. Lydia was doing something else entirely – not standing, maybe, but simulated, reproduced. In certain ways, Lydia would outlive them all.

There was a little fluttering in her stomach, exactly the feeling that she'd had when she and Andrew decided to get married. Nerves, or excitement. The unknown. The train was pulling in to the station, and a new crop of drunken louts poured out. Elizabeth tucked herself as much out of the way as she could without getting swept along. Life swept you along enough – she planted her feet and sharpened her elbows.

'I'll see you soon,' she said. 'I miss you. I hate you and I miss you.' Elizabeth was talking to the angry boy who'd ordered her the scrambled eggs from the diner near his parents' house. He still didn't know better. She could help, or not. It was all up to her. Elizabeth took off her hat and fanned it in front of her face. 'I will be calm calm calm,' she sang, at full volume. The kids looked at her like she was crazy, and she said louder, 'I will be calm calm calm!' When it was time to board the train, Elizabeth took a window seat and held her notebook in her lap and didn't stop writing until she was home.

Sixty-nine

Jane came back from Gosman's Dock with their evening's lobsters, either Minnie and Mickey, or Fred and Ginger, Jane couldn't decide. She found Zoe on the porch, hunched over a notebook.

'Are you working on your diary for Dr Amelia?'

'Sort of. Come here.' Zoe patted the chair next to her, and after Jane put the lobsters in the fridge to chill them before the ritual murder, she sat down and looked at what Zoe had been working on.

Zoe flattened her hands over her notebook. 'Listen,' she said, her voice low and even. 'Here's what I think. Hyacinth will be back up and running soon, which is great, but I think it's time for something new. I think we need a change.'

'Shit,' Jane said. 'Shit! I really thought that things were getting so much better, Zo! How do you not see it? I know my temper isn't great, and I know that I'm moody, and that I haven't been to the gym in ten years, but come on! How do you not see that we are good?' Jane could feel her heart rate skyrocketing. 'I love you. Don't leave me. I will do anything.'

Zoe smiled and moved her hands. Hidden underneath them was a drawing of a storefront. There were windows all along the street, like at Hyacinth, but with small round tables facing out. Above the door, the sign read HOT + SWEET, with a drawing of a pretzel. 'It doesn't have to be a pretzel,' Zoe said. 'I just like the shape. It could be a croissant. Or a muffin, maybe. No, I don't like the way muffins look. But it could be a croissant.'

'What is this?' Jane turned the page and saw that there was more. More drawings, more notes. 'Ditmas Park's First Gourmet Bakery.' A list of their suppliers, some menus.

'We make everything. You make everything. I already know what light fixtures we should have. This kid out in L.A. makes these lamps that look like mod octopuses. . . .' She was still talking when Jane stopped her with a kiss. Zoe was laughing, and they were kissing, and then Jane was laughing, too.

'You scared me,' Jane said. She shook her head. 'Don't scare me like that.'

Zoe took her wife's face in her hands. 'Never again. Now, tell me, what do you think?'

'Hot and Sweet,' Jane said. 'I love it.'

'Good,' Zoe said. 'Because Elizabeth thinks she has a place. You know where the hair salon is, with the yellow awning? Before that, like maybe ten years ago, it was a tiny little Dominican coffee shop? Right across from the fire station?'

Jane closed her eyes. 'With the patio. We could have outdoor seating on the side.'

'Exactly.' Zoe reached over and slid her arms around Jane's waist, folding herself on to Jane's lap. 'A new project. A new baby.'

'A new baby made out of butter.'

'Best kind,' Zoe said, nuzzling in as close as she could, and then even closer.

Seventy

The office was just as Zoe had described – nicely messy, with stacks of books on the floor beside the bookshelves. Elizabeth and Andrew shuffled in awkwardly and sat down next to each other on a well-worn tufted couch.

'So,' Dr Amelia said, 'what brings you here? Elizabeth, we spoke on the phone briefly, but I always like to start out couples that way, so that we can all be on the same page. In the same boat. On the same team.' She nodded at both of them, her lips pursed with anticipation. The appointment had been a gift – Jane and Zoe were skipping their session and sent Elizabeth and Andrew instead. It wasn't a present you could give to everyone, but there you were.

'Well, I, um,' Andrew began. 'I think I've been feeling a bit lost, professionally, for, um, for some time.' He paused. 'I think that's where this started.'

'Really?' Elizabeth said, her head rearing back. 'I think this started when we were about nineteen years old, don't you?' Ever since leaving Montauk, Elizabeth had slowly been feeling layers of her anxiety flake off, like a snake's old skin. Bits and pieces dropped off all the time – Harry having sex, Harry having sex in public, her first gray hair, the fact that her boss sometimes still called her Emily, the way Lydia looked at her a million years ago, the way fake Lydia looked at her now, the way she'd always been worried about how Andrew was feeling. Dr Amelia and Andrew were both looking at her with wide eyes, and Elizabeth realized she was talking.

'And then I also think we should talk about how you basically just joined a cult by accident because you need friends, and a job, and a vocation, which I know isn't easy to come by – I mean, I'm a real-estate agent, which isn't exactly something children dream about becoming, you know?' She was panting slightly, but it felt good, like she'd just run around the block. Elizabeth wanted to run. On the train home, she'd written three songs, and she was pretty sure that at least two of them were as good as 'Mistress of Myself.' She wanted to play them for Andrew, but she also wanted to make a demo and send them to Merge and Sub Pop and Touch & Go and say, *Hey! Here I am! I've been here all the while!* She knew some of the right people, at least to start. She just needed to figure out which direction to go. It was exciting, almost, like having a fever so high that you thought you were on another planet. 'I think I need a break, maybe. Like a few months. I think I need to travel by myself for a little bit.' Elizabeth rubbed her hands on her thighs. 'Maybe rent a house somewhere, record some music, just take some time.'

'Okayyy,' Dr Amelia said. 'Let's start there. Andrew? Jump on in here, the water's fine.'

'The water is definitely *not* fine,' Elizabeth said. She threw her head back and laughed. 'The water is not fine.'

'Come on, Lizzy,' Andrew said. 'We were totally cool a few minutes ago, weren't we?'

Elizabeth looked at her husband. There were so many pieces of advice she'd heard over the years: not to marry someone she wouldn't want to be divorced from, not to marry someone she wouldn't want to be, not to marry someone who didn't treat her as an equal if not a superior being, not to marry someone for sex, to marry for sex, to marry for friendship, not to marry for companionship. They'd been together for so long that Elizabeth didn't know which of those rules she'd followed – she certainly hadn't known when they got married. Those guidelines were all for people like Ruby and Harry, city kids who probably wouldn't get married until they were thirty and wouldn't have kids until they were thirty-five. Somehow, though they hadn't meant to, she and Andrew had behaved like they lived in the 1950s, rushing into adulthood with no sense of themselves as individuals.

Dr Amelia stuck the tip of her pen into the hollow of her cheek, leaving a small blue polka dot. 'What do you think about that, Elizabeth? Are you cool?'

The air-conditioning clicked on, sending a sudden blast of freezing cold air on to Elizabeth's right side. Andrew gave an involuntary shake, and she saw a path of goose bumps pop up on his bare forearms.

'I don't think we know the answer to that yet, Dr Amelia,' she said. She tugged a pillow from behind her back and laid it on her lap. 'I think we're really just getting started here.'

Andrew had the strangest look on his face – partly a grimace, and partly a grin, like he couldn't tell his lips what to do and so they were making their own suggestions.

'You know what, though?' Elizabeth said. 'This just occurred to me. I actually don't think it's all your fault what's happening here.'

'That's good, sharing the responsibility,' Dr Amelia said.

'Yes,' Elizabeth said. '*Yes*. It's also clearly my fault for not losing my mind ten years ago,' she said. 'Or twenty. If I'd been more wild, more willing to experiment and crash and burn and fail, then I don't think we'd be here right now. We might not be here at all.'

'What do you mean? That we'd be dead?' Andrew, the poor dear, looked so confused that Elizabeth wanted to sit him in the corner with a dunce cap.

'No, not dead. Just not married. I'm not saying that I want that. Maybe I want that, I'm not sure yet. But I do think that we're both so static – and that's why we're sitting here.'

'This is such a good session already,' Dr Amelia said. 'I'm really impressed.'

Elizabeth beamed. 'Thank you,' she said. 'No one's complimented me for what feels like a really long time.' She turned to Andrew, whose face had turned pale. 'You can start there, if you like.'

Andrew swallowed. 'I will.'

'Now would be a great time, Andrew,' Dr Amelia said. 'Why don't you tell your wife what you think she's great at? It can be something big or small, doesn't matter.'

Andrew looked down at his hands and knocked his thumbs together. The room was silent. 'You're a great songwriter,' he said. 'Truly great.'

'Thank you,' Elizabeth said.

'And you're an incredible mother. Harry adores you.'

'Thank you,' Elizabeth said.

'That's a great start,' Dr Amelia said. 'Elizabeth?'

'Hmm?' She looked up.

'Anything you'd like to compliment Andrew for?'

'Maybe in a little while, but I'd really like Andrew to keep going, for now, if that's all right.' She crossed her arms and waited.

Seventy-one

Once Ruby decided she was going, the plans came together fast. She would fly into San Diego on the last day of August, and fly out of Loreto, Mexico, three months later. The program was for people over seventeen, offered college credit and provided all the equipment. After Mexico, she was considering doing a program in South America, but it was mostly hiking, and she wasn't sure. Harry was helping her pack. Ruby's flight was in two days.

The proposal hadn't gone precisely the way he'd hoped – Ruby had slipped the ring on to her middle finger and said 'No,' clear as day, but he understood. They were too young. He still had a year of high school left. No one got engaged in high school, not really. He was glad she'd kept the ring.

It was late in the afternoon. Ruby's mothers and his mom were at the new space – they couldn't stop talking about it, the three of them, cackling like witches about doughnuts and jam. It was cool, Harry thought. They were making something out of nothing.

Ruby was standing in front of her closet. She wasn't supposed to bring any clothes like the ones she wore – there was a list, and everything was made of out bathing-suit material. She was going to be sitting in a kayak for three months, but still, for now, Ruby was trying on dresses, maybe to say good-bye. She was pulling on hangers over her head, so that she looked like Frankenstein's monster, with metal bolts jutting out of her shoulders.

'That's the one you wore to graduation,' Harry said. The white tassels swung by her bare thighs. She was wearing only underwear. Harry wanted to take pictures of every part of Ruby's body, but knew that was no way to keep her.

'When you were my hero,' Ruby said.

'You were always my hero,' Harry said. 'Let's be clear about that.' He got up and walked over behind her. 'I want to hug you, but I don't want to impale myself.'

Ruby laughed and pulled the hangers off. 'You may hug,' she said.

Harry wrapped his arms around her and looked at the two of them in the mirror. 'Hey, you know what? You were supposed to bleach my hair, but you never did.'

'Want to do it now?'

'Are you still my girlfriend?' Harry wasn't sure why it mattered, but it did.

'I think I'm your girlfriend until I get on the airplane,' Ruby said. 'How does that sound?'

'I can live with that. Let's do it.'

She clapped her hands and pointed to the bathroom. 'Step into my salon!' Harry sat on the lip of the bathtub while Ruby opened and closed all the cabinets. 'Aha!' she said, and started performing a chemistry demonstration in a plastic bowl in the sink.

Ruby started painting his hair with some cold, white goop. After a few seconds, Harry's scalp begin to itch and then sizzle. 'Is this normal?' he asked, and Ruby rolled her eyes.

'Guys are such wusses,' she said. 'Yes, it's normal.' She worked her way around his head, section by section. When she was done, she pulled a giant plastic shower cap over the whole thing.

'Will you play some music?' Harry asked. He needed something to take his mind off the fact that his head felt like it was on fire. Ruby pulled out her phone and scrolled through until she found what she was looking for, hit the button, and then set the phone on the lid of the toilet.

It was a slow song, one Harry didn't know. A guy sang 'Love and happiness,' and then a guitar did a little wail behind him, and the rest of the band kicked in.

'It's Al Green,' Ruby said. She started to dance. Harry put his hands on her thighs and closed his eyes, trying to memorize everything he could. They listened to the song three more times before she hit a button and played the rest of the album. 'Okay, let's check your hair.' She pulled back the shower cap and peeked. 'Oh, shit,' she said. 'It's kind of orange.'

Harry pulled the cap off the rest of the way and stood up. It looked like he had bright orange dreadlocks. 'Well, let's wash it out, maybe it's not as bad as it seems.' He shoved his head under the faucet, and Ruby rinsed, her fingers separating the bigger clumps. She washed it twice before she let him get up and dry off with a towel.

They stood next to each other, shoulder to shoulder. Instead of blond, Harry's hair was the color of bright new rust, or a very dirty traffic cone. He touched a curl and then put his hand on his chin. It was terrible, so terrible that Ruby couldn't even argue otherwise for show. They grimaced in unison.

'Do you have clippers, by any chance?'

'I think my mom does. Hang on.' Ruby scampered up the stairs to her parents' bedroom and came back wielding a pair, the cord dangling behind her. Harry plugged them into the wall and switched them on. 'Have you done this before?' she asked him.

'Nope,' he said. 'But there's a first time for everything.' He started at the front – you had to start somewhere – and dragged the clippers back along his scalp. A long strip of hair fell first to his shoulders and then to the floor.

'Wow,' Ruby said. 'Keep going.'

He did the right side first, leaving the hair about an inch long, maybe less, with no trace of the bleach. He stopped long enough for Ruby to take a picture, one half orange, one half gone. She put a towel on the floor to catch all the falling locks.

It only took a few minutes. 'I guess I wasted your bleach,' Harry said, swiveling from side to side to look at himself.

'Here,' Ruby said, and handed him a mirror. 'Look at the whole thing.' She held it up in his hands like he was in a barbershop, and spun him around so that he could see the reflection of the back of his head in the mirror.

'I look like my dad,' Harry said.

'Kind of,' Ruby said. 'I think you look more like you.'

He knew what she meant. Harry looked like a different person – older. Tougher, even. He ran his hand over his head, which was both prickly and still itchy from the bleach. He didn't look like a kid anymore, and he didn't feel like one, either.

'I should go home,' Harry said. 'Just for now. I'll come back tonight.'

Ruby nodded. 'I love you, Harry Marx.' She kissed him on the cheek, both of them covered in strands of his hair. There were so many ways that he wanted to remember Ruby, images of her that he wanted to freeze forever, but this was what Harry wanted to freeze for himself – however he was, right at this second, when those words came out of her mouth, and he was still standing, still able to walk out the door. There would be no better summer, as long as he lived. Harry kissed her back and then closed her bedroom door behind him.

He went down the stairs slowly, petting Bingo's head on the way out. The day had started to fade. Harry wanted to walk past someone he knew, someone from school, just to see if they'd recognize him, but Argyle Road was empty. He was at his own driveway, and the garage door was half open. Through the four feet of open air, he could see his mother's legs, and her amp. She was playing something quiet, and Harry walked a little bit up the driveway to listen. It was pretty – something new. There were fireflies starting to flicker, and Harry turned around to watch one float up into the tree. The garage door opened a few more feet, and his mom ducked underneath, poking her head out. 'Harry, is that you?' The air smelled like fall, and Harry watched the firefly go all the way under the canopy of leaves before turning back around.

PART FOUR

Ephemera

NEW YORK POST

Cops Bust Brooklyn Yogis for Extra Funk

This week, the 67th Precinct got more than they bargained for when following up an anonymous tip that EVOLVEment, a hipster yoga establishment in Ditmas Park, Brooklyn, was illegally manufacturing and selling highly potent kombucha, a fermented alcoholic beverage. In addition to the kombucha, the police also found several marijuana plants, some psychedelic drugs, as well as a large number of unidentified natural products such as twigs and leaves that EVOLVEment used to make teas and other ingestible beverages.

EVOLVEment received a misdemeanor citation for selling the kombucha without a license, as well as several other misdemeanor citations for the additional illegal drugs found on the premises. 'We aren't selling drugs,' EVOLVEment leader David Goldsmith told reporters. 'We are a holistic community, and are deeply invested in the spiritual and physical health of our members and of the human race. It saddens me that the NYPD doesn't understand what we're doing here, but in time they will.'

No arrests were made, but the EVOLVEment website says that all yoga classes and services (including, presumably, kombucha fermentation) are suspended while the center is under further investigation.

- Dave speaks fluent Sanskrit.
- As a teenager, Dave won second and fourth places in two celebrity surfing contests, competing against David Charvet and Eddie Cibrian.
- Dave's facial hair grows so quickly that it's listed as a 'special talent' on his résumé.

NEW YORK TIMES ARTS SECTION

Review: *'Mistress of Myself'* Goes to the Origin of an Icon

NYT CRITICS' PICK

Lydia Greenbaum sang like her house was on fire. With no vocal training, and pitch that could generously be described as 'approximate,' Lydia (who dropped the Greenbaum during her brief tenure at Oberlin College) became a star in the early 1990s, bolting from obscurity to ubiquity in a matter of months. This softly lit and romantic biopic concentrates on the period just before Lydia's stardom, when the soon-to-be star spent most of her time eating Tater Tots in her college cafeteria.

It's a humanizing choice. The film avoids the standard arc of so many musical biopics, perhaps because Lydia's arc was less a curve than an arrow. Instead of focusing on her later drug abuse and sudden death, the film chooses to exist in a somewhat fuzzy pre-fame time period, where the viewer is encouraged to imagine a different end for Lydia (played in the film by Darcey Lemon, a look-alike with capable acting skills suited to the dreamy mood of the film, and a surprisingly sharp voice).

The strongest section of the film, and the filmmaker's best decision after casting Darcey Lemon, is the time spent on Kitty's Mustache, Lydia's college band, to which (the film implies) she contributed very little. The love story between Lydia and her bandmate Andrew Marx (played by a brooding young Samson Tapper) is the linchpin of the plot, and when the romance ends, so does the band and, shortly after, so does Lydia's college career. It's a reminder that it wasn't so long ago that celebrities were allowed some privacy and also of Lydia's own power of reinvention, which allowed none of her soft, lovesick past into her onstage persona.

'Mistress of Myself' doesn't save Lydia from the fate to which we know she is doomed, but the film does deepen our understanding of a complicated artist. Lydia joins Jim Morrison and Kurt Cobain as one of the members of the 27 Club whose brief, impactful lives now exist on film as well as in memory, and it feels like a gift to have been granted access to a prickly performer's tender beginnings.

GRUB STREET

Openings

Hyacinth Team Brings the Butter to Ditmas Park

Five months after the fire that shut down the kitchen at their Brooklyn locavore pioneer Hyacinth, Zoe and Jane Kahn-Bennett are open for business at their cozy new bakery, Hot + Sweet. Located two blocks away from Hyacinth, on Ditmas Park's miniature restaurant row, Hot + Sweet is now open seven days a week for breakfast and lunch.

There are no cronuts, no macarons, no cake pops – Hot + Sweet's menu is strictly old-fashioned, and that's just how the Kahn-Bennetts want it. 'Why mess with perfection?' chef Jane Kahn-Bennett asked us. 'I would rather have a perfect apple turnover or croissant than some trendy thing any day of the week, and I know the neighborhood agrees, because they've been asking us for ten years when we were going to expand.'

There are also chocolate cream pies, cinnamon rolls, and enormous chocolate chip cookies.

FROM THE *PITCHFORK REVIEW*

Top Ten Moments from All Tomorrow's Parties Festival, New York City

3. Best Reunion of a Band No One Ever Listened To

Kitty's Mustache is famous for being Lydia's college band, but in the two months since the release of the *Mistress of Myself* biopic, the college band has garnered some pretty big invitations, including ATP. I showed up not knowing what to expect with Lydia's absence, but the band – Zoe Kahn-Bennett, Elizabeth Marx, Andrew Marx and *Mistress of Myself* actress Darcey Lemon stepping in for the chorus of the title song, none of whom addressed the crowd except for singer Elizabeth Marx – was tight and sounded as angry and vital as they must have on cassette, with wobbly guitars and short skirts. A girl next to me said, 'She's an icon!' about Marx, and her friend replied, 'And I read on BuzzFeed that she's a real-estate agent!' which tells you pretty much everything you need to know about surviving on the paycheck of modern music.

Weddings

Sarah Annabelle Dinnerstein, daughter of Hannah and Eugene Dinnerstein of Park Slope, Brooklyn, was married Saturday to Anthony Dustinsky, the son of Elena Rodriguez, of Greenwood Heights, Brooklyn, and the late Leopold Dustinsky, of Ridgewood, Queens. The Rev. Elliott Beall, a Unitarian minister, performed the ceremony at the Boathouse in Prospect Park.

The bride, 24, who is keeping her name, works in the public-relations department for Jah Juice, a Rastafarian juice company based in Brooklyn. The groom, 26, is an architecture student at Columbia University.

CONDÉ NAST TRAVELER

Brooklyn Food Royalty Goes Native

Ruby Kahn-Bennett has lived in Mexico for five years – first on the Baja California peninsula, where she landed after a sailing course following her high-school graduation, then a short spell in Mexico City, and finally on the east coast, in beachy Tulum – but the native New Yorker says that it took her until now to feel like she was at home. 'I couldn't drive until I was twenty,' she told us, laughing. 'And I moved to Mexico when I was nineteen. That was a rough year. Lots of buses.'

Kahn-Bennett seems to have figured some things out, though, and has set down roots of her own, at the intersection of tourism and comfort food from home in Brooklyn. Her pizza shop, Brooklyn's Finest, is close enough to hotels to service traveling Americans but has earned a loyal local following as well, due to Kahn-Bennett's embrace of local flavors. 'Mexico has the best peppers in the world, so we do lots of different combinations. My current favorite is a white pizza with queso Oaxaca and poblano peppers.'

Kahn-Bennett's mothers, Jane and Zoe Kahn-Bennett, are still in Brooklyn, dividing their time between Brooklyn favorite Hyacinth and their new bakery, Hot + Sweet, but Ruby says that her family comes to Tulum at least once a year. 'My moms love it,' she says. 'They keep threatening to open a Mexican place back home.' As for Kahn-Bennett, Brooklyn's Finest keeps her busy, though she does return to New York every summer, when she forces her mothers to cook her a proper Thanksgiving dinner. 'I would come home for it,' she says, 'but it's our high season! Someone has to make the pizza!' And so Thanksgiving in July will have to do for now.

PROSPECT PARK YMCA MONTHLY
NEWSLETTER

Big Brothers Basketball Game
Has All Winners

This month, our Big Brothers program capped off its summer season with the annual basketball tournament. Big Brother mentor and volunteer coach Andrew Marx said just after the game, 'It was one of our best tourneys yet – the kids all played their hearts out, and everyone had a really good time. It was the highlight of the year for us, for sure.' *(Pictured in photo: Big Brother participants and Andrew Marx, at center.)*

HARRY MARX

BROWN UNIVERSITY

English Department Honors Committee

Thesis Proposal

Proposed Title: *Friends and Neighbors*

The novel will be inspired by the tropes of classic love stories such as *Romeo and Juliet* and *Tristan and Isolde*, set in modern-day Ditmas Park, Brooklyn, with two neighboring families falling in and out of love simultaneously. My plan is to write a novel that both celebrates the youthful embrace of reckless love and the way that older people struggle with those same feelings some decades down the line. I plan to incorporate ideas from Jacques Derrida and Michel Foucault as well as to draw inspiration from hypertext-based Internet platforms, which I think will provide an interesting juxtaposition with the somewhat old-fashioned and straightforward form of the novel.

Thank you for your consideration.

TIME OUT NEW YORK

Listings

Elizabeth Marx, Bowery Ballroom

In the year since the release of 'Mistress of Myself,' former Kitty's Mustache singer Elizabeth Marx has had a stunning resurgence, though 'discovery' is probably even more apt, as few people ever heard any Kitty's Mustache material aside from the song made famous by Marx's former bandmate, who needn't be mentioned here. Marx is promoting a new record, *Modern Lovers*, out this fall from Merge Records.

Acknowledgments

Enormous thanks to my glamorous agent, Claudia Ballard, as well as Laura Bonner and Tracy Fisher at WME, and to the whole team at Riverhead Books, especially Sarah McGrath, Claire McGinnis, Geoff Kloske, Lydia Hirt, Danya Kukafka, Jynne Martin, and Kate Stark. Thanks to Riverheaders emeritus Megan Lynch and Ali Cardia for their continued love and support. Thanks to my UK squad, Jessica Leeke and Cathryn Summerhayes. Thanks to the friends who loaned me their rich and varied expertise for this book: Rob Newton, Kerry Diamond, Bill Sheppard, Jo Anne Kennedy, Stephin Merritt, Meg Wolitzer, Lorrie Moore, the staff of Rookie, Ry Russo Young, Christina Rentz and Isabel Parkey.

Special thanks to my family: the Straubs, the Royals, and my handsome husband, Michael Fusco-Straub, without whom I would be forever lost. Astonished thanks and total devotion to my two beautiful children, one of whom is still inside my body as I write this, but who is expected to make his entrance into the world before too long.

Thanks as always to my beloved independent bookstores, and their brilliant proprietors and booksellers, especially Mary Gannett and Henry Zook of BookCourt, Stephanie Valdez and Ezra Goldstein of Community, my sugarplum Christine Onorati of WORD, Jessica

Bagnulo and Rebecca Fitting of Greenlight, and Parnassus' Mary Laura Philpott, Niki Coffman and Ann Patchett. I would also like to thank Ann Patchett for being Ann Patchett.

And lastly, thanks and love to the old friends I've kept, and also to the friends I haven't, with kisses unkissed flying toward them across time, space and circumstance.

Reading Group Questions

1. *Modern Lovers* explores the concept of aging. How do you think these characters feel about their own journeys into adulthood? How does the adults' description of youth compare with the teenagers' experience or description of youth? What about their different perspectives on adulthood? Which of them – the adults' or the teenagers' – is more accurate? Is one perspective more true than the other?

2. Lydia soared on to become a star, leaving the rest of Kitty's Mustache behind. How does Lydia's success – and subsequent death – affect the current actions of these characters? Specifically, Elizabeth, Zoe, and Andrew – do they see themselves in opposition to Lydia? What if she hadn't died?

3. Do you think Andrew was right in lying to Elizabeth about his relationship with Lydia? How might things have been different if he had told her the truth from the start?

4. Should Elizabeth have gone through with the Kitty's Mustache documentary, even without Andrew's approval? Considering the

events that are set in motion, do you think this decision helps their marriage or hinders it in the end?

5. Does the fire at Hyacinth, though devastating at the time, actually lead to a happier marriage for Zoe and Jane? Why or why not?

6. Are Ruby and Harry a good romantic fit? Are they too young to know whether they are?

7. Self-image plays an important role in *Modern Lovers*. All of these characters have specific ideas about themselves, and often the realities don't quite match. Discuss how the characters want to be seen, in comparison with who they actually are.

8. Discuss how the characters' friendships change over the years – from college to early parenthood to middle age. How are their relationships with one another and their perceptions of themselves linked? How does one affect the other?